SHIELD of
TERRA

BOOK FIVE
OF THE DUCHY OF TERRA

SHIELD OF TERRA

BOOK FIVE
OF THE DUCHY OF TERRA

GLYNN STEWART

FAOLAN'S PEN
PUBLISHING
faolanspen.com

This edition published in 2019 by:

Faolan's Pen Publishing Inc.

22 King St. S, Suite 300

Waterloo, Ontario

N2J 1N8 Canada

ISBN-13: 978-1-988035-88-8 (print)

A record of this book is available from Library and Archives Canada.

Printed in the United States of America

1 2 3 4 5 6 7 8 9 10

First edition

First printing: March 2019

Illustration © 2019 Tom Edwards

TomEdwardsDesign.com

Faolan's Pen Publishing logo is a trademark of Faolan's Pen Publishing Inc.

Read more books from Glynn Stewart at faolanspen.com

CHAPTER ONE

"Hyperspace emergence in ten minutes. All hands to battle stations. All hands to battle stations."

Tinashe Mamutse's voice echoed through the corridors of the Duchy of Terra cruiser *Tornado*, ordering his crew to report before they reached their destination.

Annette Bond, Duchess of Terra and Captain Mamutse's ultimate boss, wasn't paying that much attention to the announcement—primarily because she was already on *Tornado*'s flag deck, watching the continually updating status reports on the Ducal cruiser.

And the sixteen Imperial super-battleships escorting her. Twenty-one years earlier, the A!Tol Imperium had conquered Earth. Annette Bond had taken this ship into exile to try and stop them.

She'd failed, but she'd also realized that the A!Tol were better than the alternatives available. Surrendering and returning to Earth had seen her appointed the planet's ruler in the name of their alien conquerors.

Now she was heading to Arjzi, the homeworld of the "alternative" to the A!Tol: the Kanzi. Blue-furred religious slavers, the Kanzi were now faced with the return of some exiles of their own and desperate to make an alliance with the Imperium.

For her sins, Annette Bond was the Imperium's ambassador today. Once, she'd commanded a single ship turned privateer as she tried to steal enough technology from the A!Tol for Earth to break free.

Today, she was responsible for the fates of fifty entire species—the Imperium's member races and the Kanzi's slave races alike.

"Dan!Annette Bond," a voice interrupted her thoughts, and she turned to study the screen next to her. The Dan!—the ! was a beak snap for the A!Tol or a guttural stop for humans—was the formal version of her title.

Its use by the A!Tol on her screen was a sign of deep respect, but Fleet Lord !Olarski had spent three weeks dealing with her. The multi-limbed squid-like alien was surprisingly comfortable with the fact that her Empress had sent a non-A!Tol to negotiate for the Imperium.

"Yes, Fleet Lord?" Annette replied.

"The squadron and our escorts are at battle stations as well," !Olarski told her. "I would hope it remains unnecessary, but it counters the tides for us to trust the Kanzi."

The A!Tol literally wore their emotions on their skin, and !Olarski was currently the purplish-blue of stressed uncertainty.

A tiny device in Annette's ear was translating the A!Tol's speech for her, drawing on *Tornado*'s computer for an in-depth language database. The device could only hold three or four languages on its own.

"How many people, Fleet Lord?" Annette asked. "We were promised the liberation of every slave of an Imperial subject race. How many people do you figure that is?"

A flash of orange anger crossed !Olarski's skin and she shook herself, manipulator and motive tentacles shivering.

"Millions," she said flatly. "It's worth the risk. It just runs counter to the tides."

Against the grain would be the equivalent English metaphor, the curvaceous blonde Duchess reflected.

At well past seventy, she was grateful for the Imperium's medical treatments—and honest enough about herself to admit that she could have gone gray and been hobbling with a cane and she'd still be here.

"We'll bring them home, !Olarski," she promised. "And we'll make sure both the Theocracy *and* the Imperium benefit from this." She shook her head. "Our enemy may be born of the Kanzi, but I don't get the impression they know the Taljzi any better than we do."

"Enough better to be more afraid," the Fleet Lord replied. "Which is to our advantage...even if they are correct to be afraid."

HYPERSPACE WAS A GRAY VOID, featureless even to most sensors beyond roughly a light-second. Hyperspatial anomaly scanners could see farther than that, but all they could really pick out was stars, most planets and spaceships.

The Arjzi System was very clear on those scanners, not least from the fact that Bond and her escorts were only a tiny fraction of the traffic converging on the star system. She'd seen A!To itself, though, and the beating heart of the Imperium easily rivaled the nearly unimaginable busyness of the Kanzi home system.

A hole tore in the void of hyperspace in front of her ships, !Olarski's super-battleships taking the point. *Tornado* was in the center of the formation, the two-million-ton heavy cruiser less than an eighth of the size of any of her escorts.

They flashed into the star system, and Annette watched as the version of the system stored in the records updated to the current status.

Arjzi—the Heart of God—was an immense blue-white star, turning its inner four worlds into cinders of ash and heat. Two more worlds past that were too hot for anyone to inhabit, but the seventh world, Kanarj, was solidly in the liquid water zone and the home of the Kanzi race.

The eighth world was on the edge of the liquid water zone and wouldn't have been habitable on its own. When Annette looked at Kanjel, she saw the blue-green colors of a habitable planet. A pair of massive stations hung in carefully balanced orbits over the planet, still showing the signs of their initial purpose as solar reflectors.

"Face of Heart and Face of Light," she murmured the translations aloud. The homeworlds of the Kanzi, the one where they'd evolved and the one they'd terraformed before they'd cracked the secrets of hyperspace.

Kanjel's terraforming had been finishing up around when William the Conqueror had crossed the Channel to invade England, long before Europeans had ever set foot in Annette's native midwestern United States.

"The slavers do have poetic names, don't they?" Mamutse said grimly. *Tornado's* current captain was an absolutely immense black man from central Africa. His opinion of slavers was...expressive. And involved curse words that no one had ever programmed into the translators.

"I think you can credit the planet names to the Kanzi's more religious side," Annette pointed out as she traced the system's orbits farther out. A massive asteroid belt orbited outside Kanjel, providing the fuel for the Kanzi's industry, and a ninth rocky world orbited outside that.

That world looked almost sadly alone against the five gas giants that orbited outside it. Arjzi was a *massive* star system by almost any standard, with a mind-boggling amount of resources and real estate.

Here, looking at everything the Kanzi had done over the millennia, something finally struck home for Annette that hadn't truly before: the A!Tol had been traveling the stars while humanity was fighting with armored knights.

The *Kanzi* had been traveling the stars while the A!Tol had been inventing the steamship. The A!Tol seemed old and powerful to humanity, but the Kanzi were older...and were losing the race of technological advancement and power over time.

———

"ARJZI SYSTEM CONTROL has given us a vector into the system," Mamutse reported a few minutes later. "We are to rendezvous with the convoy in Kanjel orbit." He paused and audibly scoffed.

"They have requested that we stand down from battle stations before entering the planet's orbit," he noted.

"Inhabited planet with a population of just over eleven billion," Annette pointed out. "Asking us to power down our weapons is more than reasonable."

"And suicidal!" Mamutse retorted.

"Leave the Sword turrets online and the shields up," Annette ordered. "But power down the offensive weapons." She glanced over at her link to !Olarski. "That goes for your ships as well, Fleet Lord."

"Of course," the A!Tol confirmed. "Orders are already passed. We are prepared to defend ourselves." She paused. "It will take us several minutes to bring most of our main weapons back online."

Annette nodded silently. She didn't really need to say anything. *Tornado*'s sensors were still counting the warships and weapons platforms in the system. Kanjel's defense constellation might lack the hyperspace missiles and hyperfold cannons the Imperium and the Duchy of Terra Militia had used with such effect against the Taljzi, the Kanzi's genocidal exiles, but it was definitely worthy of the population it defended.

The immobile defenses alone would probably suffice to stand off !Olarski's entire squadron, and two ten-ship super-battleship squadrons stood escort over the world as well.

"Do we have a read on the convoy yet?" she finally asked. There was no point saying anything more about their status. She was in charge of the mission, but she was *not* in command of the fleet. She was a politician and an ambassador now, not a naval officer.

"Looks like they're hanging out next to the southern polar squadron," Mamutse told her. "I'm reading..." He half-whistled. "I'm reading one hundred and seventy-six ships, large personnel transports of various types."

"How many people are we looking at?" Annette said.

"We don't have all of the ship types in our files," !Olarski admitted. "We only really have details on the Kanzi's military ships—our interaction with their civilian economy is limited at the best of times."

"And?"

"The ones we can identify should be able to carry between fifteen and twenty thousand people in reasonable comfort."

Annette did the math. Three million people, give or take. After several centuries of war and border raiding, she wasn't sure she believed that was *all* the slaves from the Imperium's twenty-nine member species.

"We'll have to press, make sure they realize *we* know this isn't everyone," she said aloud. The terms of the Empress's deal had been very straightforward: the Kanzi liberated every slave they had of the A!Tol Imperium's species, or the Imperium wouldn't even talk to them about peace treaties or alliances.

"Yes, your grace," Mamutse agreed. "Slavers will *always* try to get away with less."

Annette managed not to wince at the comment. Despite twenty years of effort on the part of the Imperium and the Duchy, central Africa was still one of the worst-off regions of the planet. Better off, perhaps, than anywhere on Earth had been twenty years before, but still lagging behind everywhere else.

The reason was partially that they had been so far behind and partially...well, exactly what Mamutse said. The countries who'd wrecked Africa repeatedly were only so willing to take responsibility for their ancestors' actions.

And the responsibility for *fixing* that was Annette's.

She sighed.

"I presume I'm not meeting with the High Priestess on Kanjel?" she asked aloud.

"From what Control said, we are rendezvousing with the convoy to allow us to validate that they've made the promised effort," Mamutse replied. "From there, we'll be heading to Kanarj and the Golden Palace."

"Well, then. Let's get to it."

CHAPTER TWO

Annette and !Olarski's shuttles touched down less than two minutes apart on the launch deck of the "flagship" of the convoy, a massive transport more regularly used for landing interplanetary invasion forces.

To Annette's surprise as she exited her shuttle, power-armored Ducal Guards in tow, there wasn't a single Kanzi to be seen in the waiting party. All of the crew that they could see were of a species she wasn't familiar with, a tall humanoid species with skin ranging from dark blue to dark green—all of them wearing a distinctive gold-colored collar around their neck.

Like most Kanzi slave races, they fit into the same basic bipedal form as humans. That was part of humanity's biggest issue with the Kanzi—their religion said that their four-foot-tall, blue-fur-covered shape was the perfect form of God. And that all other bipeds were a poor imitation, put into the galaxy to serve them.

These strangers towered over Annette, and as one in a solid gold harness approached her, she realized that they all had what looked like *plant* growths on their shoulders, small bushes of loosely waving tendrils.

"Greetings," the gold-harnessed creature said to her and !Olarski with a deep bow that almost put their nose on the floor. "I am Oathbound Ship Master Steeva."

"'Oathbound'," !Olarski echoed, her skin turning a deep, angry red. "You mean you are a slave."

Steeva's left shoulder-tendrils spasmed violently in what Annette guessed to be an emotional response.

"That is...not inaccurate but incomplete," they said carefully. "I am an Oathbound Keeper. I am owned, as you would say, by the Great Church. As an Oathbound Ship Master, I command this vessel in the service of Her Holiness."

"Let it be, Fleet Lord," Annette told !Olarski. Her A!Tol companion was roughly as enthused with slavers as her African Captain. This was going to be an interesting trip.

"You have the promised freed slaves?" she demanded.

"The commitment Her Holiness made was to release all Oathbound Keepers, Servants, and Workers of the twenty-nine species recognized as subject races of the A!Tol Imperium," Steeva stated precisely.

"This task was delegated to a working group of senior Oathbound," they continued. "We have consulted the records of the House of Ownership and identified all members of these races that are in our files.

"We have begun purchase and transfer arrangements to bring all identifiable candidates to Arjzi for transport to the Imperium. Those arrangements are not yet complete," Steeva admitted calmly. "The convoy I command carries three million, five hundred and sixty-eight thousand, two hundred and eighty-three candidates."

"And the rest?" Annette asked slowly.

"As I said, the arrangements for their transfer to the Great Church and hence to the Imperium are being made," they replied. "We also have research teams attempting to identify any Workers who were never properly registered."

Both shoulder-bushes trembled.

"It is an unfortunate truth that captives taken by Clan raiding parties may never have been registered at all," Steeva explained. "We will do all within our power to find them, but I would be failing in the duty Her Holiness charged me with if I did not confess that we may not find them all."

!Olarski's skin was getting redder, and Annette wanted to join the A!Tol in anger. This fussy alien was telling her that they might never get everyone who'd been taken back...and yet they were *also* telling her that they were doing their best.

"We will need to carry out our own audit of those records," she finally said. "To make certain that you truly are committing a good-faith effort."

"Anything less would defy the orders of Her Holiness," Steeva said, his shoulder-bushes pulling back, away from Annette. "But I see no reason not to permit said audit. For now, may I offer refreshment?"

STEEVA LED them to a side room, large enough to allow the assorted bodyguards in, and produced drinks and food suitable for humans and A!Tol.

"I assume you will be escorting the convoy back to Imperial space?" they said as Annette carefully sipped her drink.

It was a blue fruit juice of some kind, completely unfamiliar to her but surprisingly pleasant. The current mostly-closed border didn't allow for much in terms of trade, so it wasn't like the people making it could sell it on Earth...but she could tell it would be popular there.

"Half of my force, under Echelon Lord Traskall, will accompany your convoy to A!To," !Olarski told them. "Part of their task will be to make certain that there are no unexpected detours or losses."

The shoulder-bushes shivered again.

"I understand your concern," Steeva allowed. "We are not spies. We are Oathbound Keepers of the Great Church, tasked to fulfill the orders of our High Priestess. You demanded that these candidates be returned, and Her Holiness has ordered that we fulfill that request."

Annette leaned forward.

"Your crews are entirely Oathbound?" she asked. "No Kanzi?"

"We have some Kanzi security detachments aboard," the alien allowed. "Oathbound are forbidden lethal arms, which can cause issues when attempting to suppress violence. Other than those soldiers, the crews are Oathbound, yes. It was judged that we would be less likely to...be a provocation in Imperial territory."

"All your people?" !Olarski said.

Steeva's shoulder-bushes shivered in confusion.

"Oh, you mean Satarda?" they asked. "No. Satarda are likely a slight majority, but only because we make up many of the Great Church's starship-trained Oathbound. Many species will be represented among the Oathbound serving the Church aboard these ships."

Annette nodded her understanding, managing not to openly shake her head.

There was no polite term in her head that equated to these "Oathbound." *Favored slaves* was probably as good as she could get. They had some similarities to the Janissaries of Earth's old Ottoman Empire, she supposed, but it was hard to tell how much power they really wielded.

She certainly hadn't expected to be having *any* meetings with someone who wasn't Kanzi.

"Your convoy is ready to leave immediately?" she asked. "My orders are that I cannot meet with the High Priestess until Echelon Lord Traskall and his charges have left the Arjzi System."

"We are ready to leave," Steeva confirmed. "If we were to wait a few day-cycles, a few thousand more candidates would arrive, but we have most of what we will have soon aboard already."

"Then we'll put you in contact with Echelon Lord Traskall to organize the convoy's movements," Annette said firmly, finishing her glass and rising. She probably hadn't even needed to be there, though it had definitely been educational.

It was easy to forget from the outside, after all, that any long-term slave system had to have found some way to co-opt at least a portion of the enslaved.

CHAPTER THREE

THE GOLDEN PALACE WAS SOMETHING OF A MISNOMER, Annette realized as her shuttle dropped through the clouds above the High Priestess's center of government. Kanarj's capital city occupied most of an Australia-sized continent on the planet's equator, and the Golden Palace occupied most of a mesa plateau on the northern shore of that continent.

The mesa itself was probably twenty or thirty kilometers across and had been built up so thoroughly over the millennia that it was basically one structure. It had been a site for religious pilgrimage before it had become the heart of an immense empire and then a world government. Despite the massive development inevitable in being the heart of an interstellar empire, an effort had been made to keep the mesa beautiful.

"Landing site is there," her pilot told her, haloing a landing pad on the side of the tallest part of the palace. The woman shook her head. "I'm having flashbacks to bad twenty-first-century science fiction, ma'am."

"Any particular one?" Annette asked. "I don't think there are many centuries without lots of bad science fiction."

"I don't remember the name, but it was something where all of Earth had been turned into a giant cathedral to a god-emperor." The pilot gestured at the kilometer-and-a-half-tall multi-spired central structure of the Golden Palace.

"I think the artists may have seen this place in a fever nightmare or something."

"So long as we can land safely, I think we'll refrain from the esthetic critique," Annette told the pilot. "Though I question the economics of finding *quite* so much gold leaf."

At least they'd only coated the central cathedral in gold. The rest of the Golden Palace appeared to be merely built from yellow rock.

There'd been a moment during the descent when Annette hadn't been sure.

THE LANDING PAD *looked* well supported, but it was still eerie to leave the shuttle on a platform suspended at least seven or eight hundred meters in the air.

Annette's own government used a landing pad at roughly the same height, but it was on *top* of a building, not hanging out in the air. She had to assume the Kanzi had a good idea of its safety, though, and it *was* attached to their capital building.

A double file of the first actual Kanzi she'd seen in the system were waiting for her as she left the shuttle, lining each side of a deep purple carpet that had been quickly rolled out to the shuttle ramp.

Kanzi were no more uniform in height than humans, which meant that the exactly matching heights of the thirty-two soldiers was intentional. They wore identical golden armor and carried plasma carbines covered with gold inlay.

The golden armor, however, was top-grade commando power armor, and the plasma carbines looked perfectly functional. These troops might be a decorative welcoming party, but they were also entirely practical.

Annette's own party of guards—four power-armored human Ducal Guards, four power-armored A!Tol Imperial Marines—were more functional than decorative. They'd cleaned up and polished their power armor, but the Duchess of Terra was still an American at heart.

Ceremony was not her strong point.

She strode forward through the Kanzi guards, her escort following behind, until she reached the end of the column and found a single unarmored Kanzi waiting for her.

Annette had enough experience with the blue-furred aliens to recognize that this Kanzi was old. His blue fur was edged with white across his disturbingly human-like face, and he was clearly using a ceremonial staff of office as a walking aid.

Given Kanzi medical technology, that was either a choice or a sign of extreme injury. Nonetheless, he drew himself up to his full hundred-and-thirty-centimeter height, allowing heavy white robes to drift in the chill winds of their altitude as he faced Annette.

"I am Sai Iril," he introduced himself. "First Chamberlain to Her Holiness Reesi Karal, High Priestess of the Great Church, the Divine Chosen, Guardian of the Theocracy, Princess of Kanarj and Kanjel and Mistress of a Hundred Worlds."

That was a mouthful—and the heavily abbreviated version of the High Priestess's titles.

"You know who I am," Annette told the Kanzi. "Take me to Karal."

"That is impossible!" Iril exclaimed. "There are rituals and ceremonies to go through first. You cannot stand before Her Holiness unclean and unprepared!"

Annette smiled thinly.

"You can make it possible," she suggested. "I am the ambassador of the Empress of the A!Tol. The Duchess of Terra. I am no supplicant, Chamberlain. I will not be dictated to."

Despite the blue fur and the diminutive height, Kanzi looked a *lot* like humans and had very similar facial expressions. She could *tell* that Iril was utterly horrified and unsure how to balance his duties with his intransigent guest.

He finally coughed.

"Her Holiness is not yet available," he told her. "Her schedule was based on your taking appropriate preparations before meeting with her."

"Then show us to our quarters and inform the High Priestess that she can visit me there at her leisure," Annette replied. She knew perfectly well *that* wasn't going to happen—she wouldn't have permitted it on Earth, so there was no way the religious dictator of a hundred worlds was going to.

Iril clearly drew the same conclusion, but he bowed stiffly.

"I will see you to appropriate quarters where you can refresh yourself," he said slowly. "I will then arrange for a minimum of ceremony before you meet Her Holiness. Understand, 'ambassador,' that she and I are bound by law and tradition and will not ignore our duty."

His smile was equally thin.

"You may not be a supplicant, but neither is Her Holiness. Be careful what battles you choose."

"That will be acceptable, for now," Annette replied. "And trust me, Chamberlain Iril, I am very aware of what battles I choose."

THE "MINIMUM CEREMONY" was still enough to make Annette chafe. She was led through a darkened room filled with aromatic smoke, while a chorus of robed and hooded chanters recited some liturgy in a language her translator earbud didn't know.

She'd been vaguely aware that the Kanzi used a six-point compass compared to humanity's four-point one, and now she'd had that confirmed. She'd been guided around the darkened, presumably circular room to six shrines, one at each of their cardinal points, where she stood still as bundles of burning herbs were waved all over her.

The priests—or what she assumed were priests, anyway—were taken aback by her armored Guards at the first shrine. By the third shrine, someone had brought out a set of some kind of ceremonial oils, and a tall robed figure—she *thought* it was a Satarda Oathbound, but she couldn't be sure—dabbed oils at the joints and foreheads of the armored troopers.

Power armor wasn't great at transmitting body language, but Annette had two decades of experience at reading armored bodyguards. The discomfort of her guards at the ceremonial anointing amused her.

It would have been less amusing, she supposed, if she wasn't entirely certain the guards had scanned the oils to be sure they were harmless first. Even if her Guards had forgotten, the Imperial Marines wouldn't have.

After six shrines, six batches of different-smelling herbs and four batches of anointing oil on her guards, they were led through a doorway in a garden atrium. There was only one path through the atrium visible to Annette, across a bridge that was over an artificial brook and was being constantly sprayed with water by the gentle waterfall a couple of meters away.

The hooded monk who'd led her silently through the ritual chamber disappeared behind them as Sai Iril appeared from a concealed entrance, and bowed to her.

"Duchess Bond."

"Chamberlain Iril. Is this sufficient for you?" she asked.

"It is very abbreviated, but there are protocols for that," he told her. "I must ask your guards to leave their weapons here. Ancient tradition allows them to wear their armor, but they cannot enter Her Holy Presence armed."

The power armor was probably more dangerous in closed quarters than the plasma carbines her people were carrying, and from Iril's tone, he knew that. And even if they *were* fully armed, Annette would have been stunned if the High Priestess's security was light enough that they could manage to achieve anything.

"Very well," she conceded. There were battles to fight and battles to concede. She would not come before the High Priestess of the Kanzi entirely according to the Kanzi's terms, but this *was* their territory.

"Thank you," Iril said as the guards laid aside their weapons. "You have the sacred promise of Her Holiness that your arms will be returned to you."

He gestured toward the bridge with its continual shower.

"I walk into the purification of the waters of the Heart of God," he said formally. "Will you walk with me?"

WITH FOUR CLEANSING rituals behind her, Annette was finally escorted into the main receiving chamber. The room was *huge*, at least thirty meters wide and twice that in length. The sides were lined with gorgeously worked seats rising up in five rows on each side.

Every seat was full, and she had to wonder how much of the ritual cleaning the court attendants and general hangers-on had gone through. Despite the appearance of an ancient religious court, however, she could also recognize that at least most of the audience was basically a press pool.

Cameras and microphones with varying levels of concealment filled the massive chamber, focusing on Annette as she followed Iril along the literal golden path down the center of the room toward the throne at the far end.

Said throne was a monstrosity of gold and a deep yellow stone with the texture of marble, placed on a raised stage of the same stone that was at least two meters above the main floor.

All of this was a grand display to raise the High Priestess above any supplicant, but to Annette, it had a very different result.

Reesi Karal was a small woman even by Kanzi standards, topping *maybe* a hundred and ten centimeters. With the slim build of her species, she looked like nothing so much as a child in blue face paint playing in a movie set.

Karal wore a simple robe of a plain white fabric and a circlet that seemed to have been carved from a single ruby. She waited on her throne in silence as Annette approached her.

"Bow," Iril hissed as they reached some unmarked line, and the Chamberlain prostrated himself.

Annette did no such thing and the High Priestess stared down at her.

"I see the ambassadors of the Imperium still have yet to learn respect," Karal declared. Her voice was a soft purring sound, readily translated by Annette's earbud. "What do you have to say for yourself?"

"I kneel to no one," Annette replied. "And if I do not kneel to *my* Empress, why would I kneel to you?"

"Because I am the Divine Chosen of God, the voice of the holy in this universe," the High Priestess said calmly. "And because I can have you killed where you stand for your disrespect."

In theory, that was true. It would also be one of the worst ideas Annette had ever heard. If the Kanzi wanted their peace treaty and the alliance with the A!Tol that they needed in the face of their prodigal enemy, well...

"How many wars does the Divine Chosen wish to fight at once?" she asked.

The room was silent, the court of the High Priestess stunned to silence.

Then Karal giggled. This tiny creature, who *did* have the power to have Annette killed right there, had a giggle like a mischievous schoolgirl.

"I am honored to greet the representative of my sister, the Empress A!Shall," she stated, nailing the click perfectly. "Approach, Dan!Annette Bond. We have much to discuss."

IT DIDN'T LOOK like there were going to be chairs or anything similar offered. Annette was clearly expected to stand in front of Karal for the entire conversation, which hopefully suggested that this wasn't going to be the main negotiating session.

"My papers," Annette said calmly, offering a folded leather pouch to Iril to bring to his monarch. "I am charged by Empress A!Shall to negotiate a treaty of peace and nonaggression with the Kanzi Theocracy, to allow us both to focus our attentions on the Taljzi threat. I am also authorized to negotiate terms for a temporary treaty of military alliance and mutual defense against the threat of the Taljzi.

"Our two nations have not had regular economic or diplomatic communication for some years," she continued. "It is my Empress's desire to change this, and I have staff qualified to negotiate trade terms with your chosen experts."

The *reason* there had been no such communication for two hundred A!Tol long-cycles—a bit more than a Terran century—was that the A!Tol Imperium had refused to even talk to the Kanzi unless the slaves taken in the various border raids were returned.

Since that demand had now been met, A!Shall wanted Annette to see what they could extract in terms of peaceful cooperation.

"We are more than pleased to agree to an end to the long-standing conflict between our nations," Karal said loudly. "And to agree that our forces will not attack the Imperium, barring provocation."

She gestured, and a female Kanzi emerged from around the stage. This one was dressed in the same fashion as the High Priestess, but her circlet was merely gold and her robes were a deep blue.

"I charge Grand Priestess Shalla Amane with the details of the treaties to assure such," Karal told Annette. "If there are to be closer relations between our empires, then it shall fall to Grand Priestess Amane to speak with you on those details."

Translation: Amane was the designated negotiator and Annette was probably going to get to know the blue-furred woman far better than she wanted to know a Kanzi.

"As for alliance..." A Kanzi shrug was identical to the human gesture. "I will not see my glorious fleets used as blade-fodder by the Imperium, spent as living shields to cover your ships. I will not see my warriors treated as peasant levies, dying to allow their supposed betters to live."

Annette wasn't even entirely sure what Karal was going on about for several seconds, then it hit.

Far more Kanzi ships had died in the clash with the First Return than Imperial. It wasn't that there had been more Kanzi ships there or that the Kanzi ships had fought harder. It was that the Imperium had an entirely new generation of military technology based off systems begged, bought and stolen from the Core Powers.

It was unevenly implemented, but it had been enough to make the A!Tol ships both tougher and deadlier than their Kanzi equivalents.

"If there is to be a military alliance between the Great Church and the A!Tol Imperium, then the Imperium must provide the *full* technical specifications of their new weapon systems...what I believe you call the 'Gold Dragon' upgrades."

Karal exposed brilliantly white teeth in what might have charitably been called a smile.

"This will not be negotiable."

There were few limits on the authority Annette had been given, but a major technological transfer was definitely *not* within her authority—and she already knew what A!Shall would say if she asked.

The negotiations might be even harder than she was expecting.

CHAPTER FOUR

"I COULD DEFINITELY LIVE WITH NEVER HAVING COME BACK here again."

Captain Ngai Vong's voice was wry as the Chinese Captain watched black hole DLK-5539 in the center of the screen. The accretion disk around the black hole looked almost unchanged from their last visit, several months before.

Commander Morgan Casimir, tactical officer of the Duchy of Terra Militia battleship *Bellerophon*, could only agree with her Captain. The blonde officer was young for her role, the result of a promotion for merit in the face of the enemy.

Of course, the actions involved in that promotion had resulted in *Bellerophon* taking weeks to be put back together after the Battle of Asimov. They'd done a number on her engineering spaces to get a task force to the system in time to stop the First Return of the Taljzi.

That Return, however, had come through this system.

"Why are we here again?" Victoria Antonova asked. The battleship's communications officer shared Morgan's blonde hair, but was a tall and willowy Russian woman to Morgan's curvaceous American.

"I thought the Navy had sent a squadron to scout this place?" Antonova finished.

"They did," Morgan agreed, her hands running across her panel. The last time they'd been in DLK-5539's orbit, they'd fought a vicious close-range battle with a Taljzi super-battleship and won. On the other hand, the last time they'd been there, Commander Masters had been *Bellerophon*'s tactical officer.

Masters was now the *executive* officer of the *Bellerophon*-class ship *Rama*, a well-earned transfer that had left Morgan as the head of *Bellerophon*'s tactical department. If she didn't feel ready for that command, well, that wasn't a confession an officer was allowed to make.

"The Navy didn't find anything, but DragonWorks still had some sensor gear they hadn't put into active deployment," she continued. "They shoved it into a *Thunderstorm*-D coming off the assembly line, stuck a crew on her and sent her our way.

"So, here we are."

The *Thunderstorm*-D in question, *Squall*, hung slightly off the center of their formation. *Squall* was supposed to be in the center, but the voyage out from Asimov had proven one thing already to the other crews of the scouting flotilla: *Squall* was a solid ship with a solid crew...and that crew had been aboard her for less than two weeks.

They didn't have half a damn clue what they were doing.

"Us and our little scouting flotilla," Vong agreed with a snort, glancing at the icons of the pair of super-battleships that formed the heavy core of the "little flotilla."

Rear Admiral Octavius Sun was aboard the *Duchess of Terra*-class super-battleship *Chancellor Merkel*, in command of the entire flotilla. The two super-battleships were accompanied by *Bellerophon* and *Rama*, two of the most modern warships in the A!Tol Imperium, plus sixteen *Thunderstorm*-Ds like *Squall*.

Another sixteen-ship squadron of destroyers filled out Rear Admiral Sun's force, providing more sensor platforms as they swept around a ruined desert in space that they'd already picked over a dozen times.

"This is as far back as we've traced the Taljzi Return," Vong reminded them all. "If there's a clue as to where the tattooed smurfs came from, it'll be here."

———

"TACHYON SCANNERS ARE DRAWING AS MUCH of a blank as everything else did when the Navy came through," Morgan reported half an hour later. There'd been Militia ships with the Navy when they'd surveyed the system, solely because the *Thunderstorm*-Ds hadn't entered Imperial service yet and the Militia ships had tachyon scanners.

Bellerophon was enough bigger than the *Thunderstorm*s that her sensors were more sensitive, so Morgan had figured it was worth a shot.

"Found the planetoid they were using as a gravitational anchor," she continued. "But we already went over that as cleanly as we went over the transport we captured."

"I know," Vong agreed. "But I have to agree with Admiral Kurzman-Wellesley. We have no other leads. Our only hope is that the gravimetric scanners *Squall* is carrying see something the rest of us didn't."

Morgan nodded, checking the icon for the cruiser with the upgraded sensors.

"I'm hoping they're better at sensor sweeps than they are at formation-keeping," she noted. "They're off position again."

The Captain looked and then sighed.

"Not our problem," he pointed out. "She's an HSM-equipped warship with scanners I don't pretend to understand. I'll be quiet about the flaws in rushing her into service so quickly."

Hyperspace missiles were the newest and greatest toy the Duchy had. *Bellerophon* carried two separate versions of the weapon: the dual-portal weapons that were launched externally and entered and left hyperspace on their own; and the single-portal weapons that were fired through a portal contained inside *Bellerophon*'s hull.

The latter were apparently unique in the galaxy—though they were *still* bigger and less effective than the dual-portal version used by the Mesharom, the galaxy's eldest race.

"Orders from the Flag," Antonova reported. "Admiral Sun is asking us to fall into escort position on *Squall*. She's going to do a circuit of the outer perimeter of the accretion disk at point five *c*."

Morgan looked at the scan of the system and concealed a wince. The accretion disk was two light-days across. That meant the perimeter was over six light-days, which meant that at point five *c* the sweep was going to take almost two weeks.

"Understood," Vong said calmly. "Get us into position, Commander Hume. Let *Squall* take the lead...and keep enough of a safety margin that we can dodge if somebody slips on her bridge."

Bellerophon and *Squall* both had a regular top speed of point six *c* with another point-zero-five-*c* "sprint" they could sustain for a few minutes. At over fifty percent of lightspeed, an error at the controls could put the ship a *long* way out of position before it was caught.

Squall's crew hadn't shown that kind of incompetence yet, but Morgan was watching them. Time should shake them out...but she couldn't help but feel like time should have already *done* that.

"Once we're on course, stand down the alpha shift," Vong ordered. "We'll step down to standard readiness and shifts. We're waiting to see if *Squall* finds something. No point in sitting at battle stations, I don't think."

———

"SIR? WE THINK WE FOUND SOMETHING."

One thing Morgan's new role had brought with it that she was less than enthused about was paperwork. Even while in active service, in the field and hunting the enemy, there was always paperwork to fill out and reports to review or file.

The interruption of her new junior tactical officer's voice was more than welcome. Lieutenant Augusta Ruskin was junior for her role, but she was what HerCom—the Duchy's Human Resources Command—had been able to find in the rush to staff the new ships and restaff the old ones.

"Define 'something,' Lieutenant," Morgan suggested.

"No one's sure yet," Ruskin admitted. "*Squall* thinks they have a trail, but it leads into the accretion disk."

"A gravity trail?" she asked. That was...possible. One of the things they suspected about the Taljzi warships was that they used gravitic singularities as a power source. They knew the Mesharom did, as had the half-mythical Precursors.

And since they knew the Taljzi had access to at least one semi-functional Precursor facility...

"That's what they said, sir," Ruskin said. "I don't know enough about these new scanners to make sense of their data, but they're trying to refine a course."

"Into the disk?" Morgan repeated, to be sure.

"Yes, sir."

"There was a second depot," the Commander realized aloud. The depot they'd found had been empty by the time it had been raided, cleaned out to fuel the Return's attack on Imperial and Kanzi space.

A two-light-day-diameter accretion disk, however, made a fantastic landmark and had a lot of hiding places. A second storage depot would make sense—and it might be more intact, with more useful information, than the one they'd hit before.

"I'll be on the bridge in five," Morgan told Ruskin. "Is the XO there?"

"Yes, sir. Commander Abbasi is contacting the Captain as I'm talking to you."

Morgan chuckled. If Commander Fox Abbasi was on the bridge,

that explained why her junior was contacting her first. Let the XO talk to the Captain; Ruskin could deal with the tactical officer.

"Then I imagine I will meet him on the bridge. Keep me informed, Lieutenant."

"WELL, GUNS?" Vong asked Morgan when he entered the bridge, several minutes after she did.

"*Squall*'s sensor team was right, unsurprisingly," she replied. "It's a trail, all right. Looks like seven microsingularities traveling at about point four *c*...three months ago."

"Am I right in guessing that makes it hard to tell where they went?" he asked.

"Bingo," she confirmed. "*Squall*'s sensor team is good; I probably wouldn't have picked the trail out of the background."

It was a relief to know that at least some aspect of that seemingly cursed ship was achieving what it needed to.

"What does it tell us?"

Morgan studied the vague line on her screens and sighed.

"That they went into the accretion disk. No surprise there, really," she admitted. "One of the thicker parts, too." She paused and traced a line on her screen with a finger.

"Commander?" her Captain said slowly.

"Once we're into the accretion disk, there's too much background noise in the gravity data for us to follow that old a signature," Morgan pointed out. "But...we *can* backtrack orbits of the actual *objects* out there and look for a common disruption vector."

"And if that disruption happens to be roughly three months ago, that will give us the gravity trail again, if in a much more brute-force fashion," Vong agreed. "Can we do it?"

Morgan was already waving Ruskin over. The redheaded Scotswoman was almost as good a programmer as she was, and a better sensor data analyst. They might not be able to match *Squall*'s gravity scanners, but they could certainly scan debris fields for disruption patterns.

"I think so," she said carefully. "If we coordinate with *Squall*'s sensor suite, we can get two angles on our patterns and nail down the course."

"We have nothing but time right now, Commander Casimir," her Captain pointed out. "Right up until the Taljzi come back—and if we don't find them, we don't know when that will be."

"So, no pressure, right," Morgan said with a forced chuckle. "All right, Lieutenant Ruskin. Let's get *Squall*'s tactical and sensor teams on the line and see if we can get some drones into space.

"The more angles we have on the debris field, the more data we get, the faster we should find the pattern."

"Keep in the back of your mind, Commander, that we're going to have to follow that path into the debris field," Vong reminded her. "A plan for that won't hurt."

CHAPTER FIVE

"TAKE US IN, COMMANDER HUME."

Vong's order echoed in the quiet bridge as *Bellerophon* prepared to dare the accretion disk again. *Squall* hung back, waiting to follow down the trail the larger ship cleared.

"Holding our speed at five percent of light," the Indian navigator replied, edging the ship into the debris field.

Icons flickered across Morgan's display and she shook her head slightly.

"No significant impacts," she reported. "Shields are holding."

"I trust your judgment on the bigger objects, Commander," Vong told her. "You are authorized to use the hyperfold cannons to clear our path."

"Thank you, sir," Morgan replied. "Ruskin. Protocol Seventeen-Kay-Dee-Six."

"Yes, sir."

17KD6 was pretty basic. It put the ship's weapon systems in a semi-manual mode linked to the missile defense sensors. New data-codes attached themselves to the icons in Morgan's display, marking the objects that were large enough and fast enough to pose even a slight threat to the ship.

"Ruskin, can we confirm our path forward?" Morgan asked quietly.

"Path has been identified for two full light-minutes," the junior officer replied. "Commander Hume?"

"Loaded in," Hume confirmed. "What happens at that point?"

"We keep scanning the debris field for patterns," Morgan said. "I just want to make sure we can start plowing the road without hurting our ability to follow it."

Captain Vong made a small "go ahead" gesture when Morgan glanced back at him, and she tapped a command.

Bellerophon's Charlie and Delta batteries totalled forty-eight hyperfold cannons, long-ranged faster-than-light energy weapons. Their range was nowhere near long enough to threaten the identified path, so Morgan simply tagged every potential threat inside their range and fired.

For six seconds, icons flickered across her panels as the cannons fired, then her screens calmed again.

"Path is clear of threats for ten light-seconds," she reported. "We should be safe to move faster."

"It's your call, Commander Hume," Vong told the navigator. "Please don't break my battleship, but everyone will be happier the sooner we find whatever the Taljzi came here looking for."

Hume chuckled.

"Bringing us up to point two *c*," she reported. "We'll reach the end of our identified path in just over ten minutes. What then?"

"We're already reviewing the data we're picking up as we go," Morgan replied. "We know what we're looking for and where the wake ends. Even from inside the disk, we should be able to track the wake at least forty light-seconds ahead of us."

Twelve million kilometers was more than enough to make sure they kept both *Bellerophon* and *Squall* safe.

"What if the Taljzi left behind surprises, sir?" Ruskin asked softly. "If I wasn't expecting to be coming back this way, I'd wire whatever I left behind to explode...and that's assuming I didn't have mines of any kind."

Morgan mentally kicked herself.

"That's a good thought," she told her junior. It *was* a good thought. One that Morgan should have had herself.

"Bring the Sword systems fully online," she continued. They were using the antimissile turrets' sensors, but the lasers themselves weren't online. "You handle the plowing; I'll start tracking for radiation signatures."

An even *more* horrifying thought hit her and she swallowed.

"And I'll get *Squall* tracking for unusual gravity signs," she concluded. "If they have microsingularity power cores, who knows what *other* uses for the things they have?"

THANKFULLY, black hole mines weren't a thing—so far, at least.

Straight-up antimatter mines with multi-gigaton warheads, on the other hand, definitely *were*.

"We've got antimatter signatures ahead," Morgan reported as they passed their original two light-minute mark. "Big ones. I'd say we're looking at a minefield, sir."

"Bring us to a halt, Commander Hume," Vong ordered. "Good catch, Tactical. Recommendations?"

Morgan looked over the data she had. The Taljzi had only really mined their trail, but even that was a huge volume in space. The mines presumably had some kind of terminal attack mode that gave them an effective radius, but there were still at least a thousand of them out there.

"If we blast our way through, we'll lose the trail," she told her Captain. "The explosions will make it impossible for us to tell where the Taljzi went from here. I think we need to try and go around."

"Should be easy enough," Hume noted. "No worse than the rest of this trip, anyway. Presuming you can give us a safe distance to keep away from them."

That was the catch from Morgan's perspective. The A!Tol Imperium didn't have antimatter mines in their inventory—every naval force that she'd studied in her Militia officer training used automated missile launchers and proton-beam platforms in that role.

"The mines are positioned roughly fifty thousand kilometers apart," she said. "I think if we keep a million-kilometer safety radius from the minefield, we should be safe from more than maybe a couple of leakers."

Unspoken was that *Bellerophon*'s defenses could handle said leakers. The battleship could probably handle going straight through the center of the minefield and letting her automated antimissile defenses and shields handle it.

But that would cost them their trail.

"Ruskin, start plowing us a clear trail around the minefield," Morgan ordered. "Hume, can you get us a preferred course? We'll keep our eyes on the trail and make sure you know where we're going."

"Carry on, Commanders," Vong said cheerfully. "I'll let Captain Ortez know that we're adjusting course to avoid a minefield. We don't want *Squall* to lose our trail."

It was, Morgan suspected, a dangerous sign for Captain Ortez's future career prospects that Vong was willing to join in even gentle mockery of *Squall*'s inexperienced crew.

BELLEROPHON HAD COMPLETED HER LONG, curving sweep around the minefield and they were dropping back onto the trail of the Taljzi ships when the missiles fired.

"Vampire!" Ruskin snapped, but Morgan was already on it.

"Bucklers deploying," she reported. "Sword turrets online; slaving hyperfold cannons to the antimissile system."

Lasers and hyperfold beams spoke as missiles began to swarm out of the debris field. First, there were a hundred. Then two hundred. Then four hundred.

And they just kept coming.

"Do we have a source for them?" Vong asked.

"Negative, they were left floating in space," Morgan replied. Her focus was on the Buckler deployment, leaving the incoming fire to her subordinate. *Bellerophon* had as many Buckler antimissile drones as she had Sword turrets, so getting the drones out doubled their chances of surviving this.

"*Squall* is firing her hyperfold cannons in support," Ruskin noted. "Her Bucklers are deploying as well." The junior officer paused, and there was an audible smile in her voice as she continued.

"Deployment time twenty-two seconds," she concluded. "Ours was twenty."

Morgan swallowed a chuckle. Perennially cursed *Squall* might seem, but her crew appeared to actually have it where it counted. The standard the Militia trained to was a twenty-five-second cycle from target detection to Buckler deployment.

Both *Squall* and *Bellerophon* carried the latest generation of the drones, as well. These ones had light hyperfold cannons included amongst their lasers.

Combined with their motherships' tachyon scanners, they had real-time detection and engagement across a ten-light-second range. Morgan was grimly certain they were going to need every scrap of that distance, as even *more* missiles poured out of the debris field.

The first salvo collided with the Terran ships' missile defense and vanished, but the second salvo was bigger—and after that, the unending stream of missiles wasn't really dividable into individual salvoes.

"I have in excess of ten thousand missiles on my screens," Morgan said. "What's controlling them? Ruskin—there's got to be a sensor platform out there. *Find it!*"

Leaving that task to her junior, Morgan threw herself into making sure her ship survived the firestorm crashing down on them.

The Buckler drones headed out toward the incoming missiles, cutting the distance between their weapons and their targets. More hyperfold cannon and laser fire cut past them, smashing vast holes in the incoming salvo.

"Missiles are moving at point seven *c*," she noted aloud. That was slow—especially for Taljzi missiles. "Some are starting to come in faster, but it looks like they may be damaged."

She wasn't getting a lot of time to react. They'd spread the scanners out and had a few extra seconds of warning of the missiles' drives coming online, but they were launching from barely thirty light-seconds away.

Inevitably, some were going to make it through, and the reports on *Bellerophon*'s shield showing on Morgan's screen flashed warning icons as the first weapons struck home. Thousands of missiles were being destroyed, but dozens were making it through.

Bellerophon's shields could take this for a bit, but not forever.

"There has to be an *end* to them," she muttered.

"If they dumped out an entire logistics depot's missile supply, it might not be soon," Vong noted. "Anything useful, Commander?"

"They're activating in batches of a thousand, roughly one batch per second," Morgan said aloud, her fingers dancing across her console as she launched a new wave of Buckler drones. "We're stopping almost all of them, but..."

"*Got it!*"

An icon flashed across Morgan's screen, informing her that one of the internal hyper-portals for their hyperspace missile launchers was live. She hadn't authorized any such thing—but it was the right call and six missiles flashed into the portal.

A quarter-second later, a new icon appeared in the midst of the missile storm—for about half a second before the HSMs hit. Antimatter explosions tore through the debris field, vaporizing the automated control platform.

The incoming missiles didn't slow, but *new* missiles stopped appearing. For ten more eternal seconds, missiles continued to hammer against *Bellerophon*'s shields.

Then silence.

Morgan swallowed as she studied her screens.

"Shields are in rough shape," she reported. "No breaches, but I don't know if that would have lasted much longer."

"Well done," Vong noted calmly. "Do we still have the trail?"

The trail. They'd just set off six twenty-gigaton antimatter warheads. That...wasn't a good sign.

Morgan pulled her scanner data up and then slowly shook her head.

"No, sir," she admitted. "We have the vector it was following; we can go after it. But we'd need to stand down on clearing a path and let the shields take some hits." She paused. "I'm not sure the shields can take those hits."

"We'll hold here, make repairs and retrieve the Bucklers," Vong ordered with a sigh. "Then we'll see what we find if we follow the line. They were being nice and straightforward up to this point. They might have kept going."

Morgan nodded silently, not saying what came to mind.

If the Taljzi had set a trap, they'd expected someone to follow them...which meant they had probably been going in a straight line to lure people into that trap.

CHAPTER SIX

THE BAD NEWS WAS THAT THE TALJZI HAD TURNED SOMETIME after laying their trap. The *good* news was that they'd underestimated the sensors available to their pursuers.

"Unless I'm severely mistaken, that *was* a singularity power core," Captain Ortez said grimly over the shared conference channel as he indicated a series of lines drawn on a chart of the accretion disk. "It was here for a long time, too, from the gravimetric signature."

"*Was* implies that it isn't anymore," Vong replied.

"It's gone," Ortez confirmed, the dark-skinned Spanish officer looking tired. "We can't tell if it was destroyed or simply shut down."

"We can trace the old orbit of the core, see where its container should be," Morgan pointed out. "Should get us within a few dozen light-seconds—hopefully within tachyon-scanner range, at least."

Vong shook his head and sighed.

"Make it so, Commander. I am very much ready to get out of this rock grinder."

The conference wrapped up reasonably quickly after that, but Morgan was already working on one screen while keeping an eye and ear open to make sure she wasn't needed.

There were a lot of tiny factors at play in the orbit of something in the accretion disk, but they all paled in comparison to the monster at the heart of the area. The black hole defined the entire "system" with its presence.

The irony was that Morgan could detect the rest of the flotilla from there. Their hyperspatial interface momentum engines—interface drives—showed up on her anomaly scanners like tiny suns. If anything in the disk was under power, she'd have been able to detect it instantly.

The interface drive didn't leave that much of a trail, though, not after three months. The strange singularity-fed matter conversion power cores the Taljzi were using left one that the gravity scanners aboard *Squall* could pick up, but if they hadn't had those scanners... they'd have found nothing.

Instead...

"I'm launching drones on our three highest-probability vectors," she announced. "We should be able to retrieve them, and it'll save us investigating all of them ourselves."

"Good call," Vong told her. "I don't want to take *Bellerophon* back into the debris field without a destination."

The accretion disk wasn't *that* bad, really, but it was almost as bad as a science fiction movie's "asteroid belt." It was a lot denser than the battleship was designed to fly through.

Morgan's drones flashed away, robotic craft traveling at sixty-five percent of lightspeed. They didn't have tachyon scanners, but they could cut through the accretion disk at full speed without worrying.

In the worst-case scenario, after all, they were merely expensive. If she lost a drone, the only people who were going to be upset were accountants.

And if she lost it keeping people safe, *Militia* accountants were likely to regard it as a worthwhile investment.

"AND THERE YOU ARE," Morgan half-whispered almost an hour later. "Sir!" she said more loudly. "Take a look at the feed from drone two."

She waited a moment for Vong to bring it up on his screen, and then haloed what she was looking at.

"Spectrographics say that chunk of debris isn't a rock," she told him. "In fact, they're showing it as a titanium-steel alloy. It's rough around the edges, but it's smooth enough to be some kind of depot platform, especially if you figure that this and this"—she haloed two specific parts of the object—"were holding spars for cargo containers. The cargo containers were removed and the holding spars got snapped off, probably around the same time they killed the power.

"Infrared shows that there's residual heat, as well," she continued, dropping a second layer onto the feed. "Not much on the surface, but you wouldn't expect there to be. But there's about what you'd expect for leftover heat at the core that's slowly leaking out.

"I'd put it at about ninety percent we're looking at some kind of logistics depot that got stripped and abandoned when the survivors from the First Return came through here."

Vong waited out her summation in silence, then took control of the feed himself, running through several other layers of data almost faster than Morgan could follow.

"I agree," he told her. "Well done, Commander Casimir. Despite everything our enemies tried to keep us from finding their holdout, you found it anyway."

He leaned back in his chair and smiled.

"Commander Hume, get the coordinates from Casimir and set a course. Major Phelps!"

Presumably, the Captain had opened a channel to the battleship's senior Ducal Guard.

"Get your Guards ready," he ordered. "It looks like we finally found ourselves somewhere for you to land."

ONCE *BELLEROPHON* and *Squall* had taken up position around the abandoned platform, there was no question as to what it was. Like many things built by the Taljzi, the design was Kanzi to its core. Most Taljzi ships were built with technology the Kanzi didn't have, but they were the same species and the Taljzi were a derived culture.

They designed their space stations and ships along the same logic. In this case, it resembled nothing so much as a child's spinning top with bits missing where ships would dock.

Close up, it wasn't quite as small as it had felt at a distance, either. The station was larger than *Bellerophon* herself, almost two kilometers across and twelve hundred meters high at its largest dimensions.

And, despite the slowly radiating heat, it was dead as the grave.

"No lights. No power. No sensors," Morgan reeled off. "On the positive side, no weapons. It looks like they had ten missile launchers and five proton beams mounted on the exterior of the platform, but they're all dead."

"And I imagine their ammunition is back in that lovely mine-field," Vong agreed. "Do you have an approach vector for the Guards?"

"If they're going to trap us anywhere, it's going to be the exterior airlocks," she pointed out. "On the other hand, at this range, I have to reiterate my guess as to what happened to their cargo spars."

She haloed the broken structure.

"There may be an airlock in there, but that's a giant gaping hole to space right now, sir," she concluded. "We can fly a shuttle *into* what's left of the spar, which should give the Guards a solid starting place."

"It's a two-kilometer station," Alexander Phelps pointed out on the com channel. "A solid starting place is going to help us stay sane, but we're going to be searching this place for *days*."

"Maybe, Major," Vong agreed. "But that's what we're here for. Are your teams ready?"

"Born ready, sir," Phelps confirmed. "Let's go grave-robbing."

CHAPTER SEVEN

THE VIDEO FEEDS OF THE TALJZI STATION WERE AMONG THE creepiest things Morgan had ever seen. They'd boarded Taljzi ships before, but those had been pocked with plasma fire and strewn with corpses—the Taljzi crewed their ships with indoctrinated clones. They fought to the death or committed suicide.

The Taljzi station was intact but empty. Corridor upon corridor of bare metal, tying together dark control rooms and empty storage spaces.

"Wait, what's that?" someone said. Morgan checked to be sure it wasn't anyone on the bridge.

"Guards?" she queried.

"Hold on," Phelps replied. "I'll show you."

The camera feed marked as showing the Major's viewpoint trembled as Phelps shuffled into a larger room and tossed a light into the air. Without magnets like the ones holding the Guards' feet to the floor, the light drifted across the surprisingly huge space, shining on the statuary and friezes that filled it.

Statues of six Kanzi, three male and three female, were arranged facing each other across what Morgan guessed was a temple of some kind. All six were painted the same blue as Kanzi fur, without any of the patterns of white or darker blue most Kanzi had...and without the brands and tattoos all of the Taljzi bodies the Imperium had seen so far had carried.

The statues each had a place in the plaster sculptures that lined the room, a path leading toward a raised stage with a lectern. There were no seats, but the cushions that had covered the floor had been scattered around the room when the air had been evacuated.

"That's quite the chapel for a logistics depot," Vong said. "Take as much footage as you can and we'll send it back to the Imperium via the relay network. The xenoculturalists are going to have a field day with this."

Thanks to the hyperfold communicators, *Bellerophon* and her sisters had a solid faster-than-light connection back to the Imperium so long as they were out of hyperspace. Inside hyperspace, the old starcoms could still reach them.

The hyperfold coms had a strictly limited range and did have a transmission delay. Starcoms had neither but were extraordinarily finicky devices that took years to construct and could never be moved. Hyperfold coms worked much better for small colonies and starships.

"Fascinating as this is, it doesn't tell us much," Morgan pointed out. "Unless you can see a map in that mess?"

"Actually..." Phelps's voice was amused. "Take a look at this."

It wasn't a map. It *was* a stylized image of an alien sky, with constellations picked out in bright blue. For all of the effort that had been put into this chapel, it was still all cheap plaster and paint.

Morgan had to wonder if the Taljzi mass-produced these chapels, mechanically cloning their faith even as they biologically cloned their populace.

"Assuming this is remotely accurate, we should be able to back-calculate *something*," Morgan said. "But that's a hell of an assumption, and it requires that we be able to ID the stars."

"Well, there's another one over here," one of the Guards pointed out. The second map was at the beginning of the chapel, above the woman on the left of the entrance.

The astronomy program Morgan was bringing up recognized *that* one instantly.

"That's from the northern hemisphere of Kanarj," she told them. "My program says it's probably from the Golden Palace itself. Are there more?"

There were.

There were, in fact, seven. The one above the main podium at the end of the room and then one above the right shoulder of each statue. Morgan fed them all into her astronomy program and looked at the immediate results.

"So, we're going to need to do some crunching on most of these," she told Vong and Phelps after they'd loaded them. "But the first three? Our system knows them. First one is Kanarj, in Arjzi. Second one is in a system called Syah." She shook her head. "I feel like I should know that one."

"That's because it doesn't exist anymore," Vong told her. "It's the system the A!Tol used a starkiller on back when the Kanzi and Taljzi were originally having their civil war."

Morgan swallowed hard. Right. Now she remembered the name. Since the Ducal Guard didn't *have* starkiller weapons, she tended to happily forget they existed.

And, even more so, to forget that the government that ruled humanity was one of the few interstellar polities to ever actually *use* one.

"That...makes sense, then, for those being their starting point," she admitted. "Their race's homeworld and the dead world where their faith was born and they went into exile from."

"You said we IDed one more?"

"Yeah." Morgan tapped it. "It's in the Imperial files, not Kanzi. Way out on the edge of our surveyed frontier, a system we only have a number for.

"I'll need to dig into our files to see what we know, potentially even request more data from the Imperium," she continued. "But...it gives us a vector that the Taljzi fled into exile along. One that lines up with them coming *back* through DLK-5539."

"Well done, Major Phelps, Commander Casimir," Vong told them. "Major, finish your sweep of the station. Antonova—send everything we have on that chapel back to Rear Admiral Sun's staff.

"That one extra system gives us three points to draw a line with, people, and *that* gives us a vector to hunt for our enemy along."

He smiled.

"They're going to regret that."

CHAPTER EIGHT

"Are we ready?"

Jean Villeneuve felt old today. He felt old most days, and the irony of the fact that Imperial medical technology meant he had longer to live now than before the A!Tol had arrived twenty years ago wasn't lost on him.

The Councilor for the Militia was, however, almost a full century old. His hair had gone white before the Imperium had arrived, and while he wasn't bald, it was getting thinner with each passing year.

He'd managed to avoid the stooped build of many humans of his age, and the French ex-Admiral still stood tall and gaunt as he studied Hong Kong from the window of the Ducal Council's main meeting chamber, on the top floor of Wuxing Tower.

"*Ready* is a strong word," Ducal Consort Elon Casimir pointed out. Age had muted the brown-haired industrial magnate and tech trillionaire's chubbiness slightly, but other than a few wrinkles, the last twenty years hadn't changed the short man much. Of course, he wasn't quite sixty yet, over a decade younger than his wife.

"Fleet Lord Tan!Shallegh is bringing the entire Grand Fleet," Casimir continued. "That's a *thousand warships*, Jean. Twenty squadrons of capital ships alone. We don't have the yards or the slips to refit them at once, but we've been tasked with refitting all of them with the Gold Dragon technology."

Elon Casimir was still the majority shareholder of Nova Industries, even if his place in the government meant those shares had been held in a blind trust for almost twenty years now. Nova was Earth's biggest shipbuilder and space industrial firm still, though its competitors had closed much of the difference since the time when Nova had built every warship the United Earth Space Force had fielded against the A!Tol.

"And the Imperium and the Duchy alike are spending money like water to expand those yards," the Councilor for the Treasury pointed out. Li Chin Zhao was a massively obese Chinese man, the former Chairman of the China Party that had run the Republic until the A!Tol arrived. Despite being barely older than Casimir, Zhao looked older than Jean.

The treasurer's health had never been good and it was failing faster now. From what Jean had been told, his weight was helping stave off the rapidly increasing seizures by absorbing toxins away from the brain.

Not that Jean pretended to understand Zhao's condition. There were few things that Imperial medical science couldn't cure, and Zhao's near-unique form of epilepsy was sadly one of them.

"Do you really want to look at me and tell me I've spent *a trillion Imperial marks* and we're not ready?" Zhao demanded.

"We are closer than we were," Casimir replied. "We have expanded the Raging Waters of Friendship Yard as far as reasonably possible. We'll be refitting two full squadrons of capital ships there, thirty-two super-battleships.

"Our own Militia construction yards are tied up with the new *Bellerophon*-B design, but we've begun assembling a new refit facility at the second Earth-Sol Lagrange point. That won't be online when Tan!Shallegh arrives, but it will be in roughly two weeks."

"When is the Fleet Lord due, anyway?" Pierre Larue, the Councilor for European Affairs and the other Frenchman on the Council, asked.

"Hyperspace isn't neatly predictable," Jean said quietly. "And the Grand Fleet was coming a long way." He shrugged. "The earliest they could have arrived was yesterday. The latest is almost ten days away. Most likely, he'll be here in about five days."

"At which point we might actually start feeling safe," Larue noted. "Do we know anything more about these 'Taljzi'?"

"They're a rogue sect of Kanzi that the Theocracy tried to exterminate a few centuries ago," Casimir told him. "We know that. We know they're manning their ships with clones. That's...about it."

"Rear Admiral Sun's scouting group has learned some more cultural background, we think," Jean pointed out. "I'm leaving that to the xenoculturalists to sort out. Sun is out looking for them. Once the Grand Fleet is ready, we'll need a target."

"If they're Kanzi, aren't they the Kanzi's problem?" Larue asked.

"I'd agree...except that they've killed way too many of our people as well," Jean told him. "And the Empress is on the same page as I am. No, Pierre. Once we're ready, the Imperium is going after the bastards.

"No more worlds are going to get burned while the Empress can stop it."

Jean smiled out the window at Hong Kong.

"And I have to admit, I find that attitude on the part of our supreme overlord *quite* reassuring."

LIKE THE REST of the Councilors, Jean had an office in Wuxing Tower. He even used it, which he hadn't done when he was the commanding officer of the Duchy of Terra Militia.

That role now fell to Admiral Patrick Kurzman-Wellesley, whose husband, General James Wellesley-Kurzman, commanded the Ducal

Guard. The husband-and-husband pair were both supremely competent and loyal to Annette Bond.

Both had been on her privateer cruise twenty years before. There were few left from that mission who remained in the Duchy's service —they'd had to put someone who *hadn't* served on it in command of *Tornado* for the first time a year before.

There was a knock on his door, and Jean tapped a command to open it. Few people would have been allowed past the ex-Guard who acted as his secretary and aide. He wasn't entirely surprised to see General Wellesley-Kurzman stepping through the door.

The younger brother of the current Duke of Wellington, James Arthur Valerian Wellesley-Kurzman was just as tall as Jean himself. The Guard carried a lot more muscle on that frame than Jean did and his hair was still *mostly* black, but age was starting to take its toll on Bond's core companions.

"James. What do you need?" Jean asked.

The General snorted and dropped an old-fashioned brown paper bag on the Councilor's desk.

"Cognac," he explained. "Best I could find on short notice."

Opening the bag, Jean wasn't entirely surprised to discover that it was his preferred brand...and a specially aged vintage version of that brand that was almost impossible to find.

"By which you mean the best a dedicated staff could find on a day or two's notice with a near-infinite budget," Jean concluded. "Now that we're bribing me, what's going on?"

Wellesley chuckled, produced two glasses from the sideboard in Jean's office and poured.

"To old soldiers," he toasted.

Jean clinked his glass with the General and took a sip of the brandy.

"To old soldiers," he finally conceded. "Which ones are you concerned about today?"

"Tan!Shallegh," Wellesley admitted. "Earth's conqueror and savior, hero and villain...and soon-to-be guardian.

"If I'm reading the numbers from Nova right, he's going to be in Sol for weeks. Months, even, as we refit his fleet. If there's anybody left in the shadows with a grudge against the Imperium, he's target number one."

"He's been here before," Jean pointed out. "No one tried to kill him then."

"Things were still settling out then," Wellesley replied. "Now we know where we are, who we are, what we do. There are people out there with private grudges who have built resources under the new regime that they didn't have last time he was here."

"You think the Fleet Lord is in danger?"

"I don't know," the General admitted. "But I want you to make sure you're keeping your eyes and ears open, as well as us."

Jean sighed and turned to study the artwork on the wall behind him. Every capital ship of the Duchy of Terra Militia was represented there. Some of those ships were gone now, lost in the bloody fighting over Asimov.

Four squadrons. Sixty-four ships. The holes would be filled by the *Bellerophons'* commissioning, even as they refitted their own older ships with the new technology. One of the most powerful Ducal Militias in the Imperium, one the Duchy's economy *barely* supported.

But their position on the frontier with the Kanzi had required it. It wouldn't be enough to stop the Taljzi, though, not if someone did something *stupid*.

"I'll pass the word," Jean replied. "I assume your husband already knows?"

"He's been briefed," Wellesley-Kurzman confirmed. "So were you, in general at least. It wasn't a big deal until Tan!Shallegh was on his way...and we found some more links recently that I don't like."

"Wonderful. Because what we need while staring down the barrel of a fleet of genocidal fanatics is a schism with the *Imperium*."

CHAPTER NINE

THE IMPERIAL EMBASSY ON KANARJ WAS BOTH MORE AND LESS than Annette had been expecting.

More, in that it existed at all. The Imperium and the Theocracy had been in a state of cold war for longer than Annette had been alive, and Kanzi fleets had fought Imperial fleets since she'd become Duchess of Terra.

In at least one case, in the Sol System!

For being an embassy, though, it was surprisingly unimpressive. Her Satarda Oathbound Keeper guide—and her skin was still crawling at having slaves assigned to "assist in her needs"—led her to the office suite in a run-down-looking part of the Golden Palace in near-silence.

She had a moment of wanting to ask the tall blue alien if they were playing games with her. They were in a mixed office-and-residential structure on the edge of the plateau, about as far from the core cathedral spire as you could get and still be on the plateau.

Of course, everything on the plateau was linked together at the base, with multiple layers of skyways, tunnels and ground-floor structures. The Golden Palace had no streets.

Her bodyguards would probably take the suggestion that the Keeper had misled them poorly, she reflected, so she stepped forward to check the small nametag next to the door.

The script was A!Tol, which was a positive sign. Given the translation tools available to her, reading A!Tol script was still difficult for her, but she could puzzle through a few words faster than she could pull out her communicator.

"This is the embassy?" the senior Ducal Guard hovering at her shoulder asked.

"That's what the sign says," she confirmed. "Well, all the sign says is that the suite belongs to the A!Tol Imperium, but I'm guessing we don't own a lot of suites in the Golden Palace."

With a sigh, she pressed the buzzer next to the nondescript door.

"Scanner above the door just turned on," the Guard murmured. "We're being watched."

The door slid open without further question, though, and Annette strode into the embassy.

The front hall looked like the receptionist area of any cheap office on any planet. There was a desk, an assortment of cheap seating furniture for different biology, and random art.

Glancing around, though, Annette realized the art was far from random. It was warships, officers, star systems...all of which had been key in various defeats the Theocracy had suffered. Random it might appear, but the art was making a point.

A threat, in fact.

Reinforcing that threat were the statue-still forms of two Rekiki Imperial Marines standing at the back corners of the room. Annette was familiar with the crocodile-like centauroid aliens—several still served in her Ducal Guard, descendants of a group she'd dragged out of piracy along with her.

If she hadn't been, she might have mistaken the armored figures for statues. They wore light power armor, enough to completely encase their bodies, and had set the color to match the stone of the several statues that *were* present.

The third occupant of the room was a single A!Tol sitting behind the desk. From her sheer size, the A!Tol could only be female. Her skin was a flickering mix of red and blue—pleasure and curiosity.

"Dan!Annette Bond," she greeted Annette. "I am Shelah. How may I assist you today?"

"I need to meet with Ambassador Rejalla," Annette replied. "I'm looking for some background information, and I hope she knows more about the politics here than I do."

Rejalla was an Anbrai, a massive race that was not generally thought of as deceptive or subtle. In Annette's experience, that was a failing of imagination on the people who knew them. They were also relatively long-lived and slow-breeding, even by the standards of spacefaring civilizations. Their numbers were small, and few had ever met them.

If Rejalla was the Imperium's representative to the Kanzi, she'd almost certainly earned that spot the hard way.

Or been exiled there to keep her out of trouble. It could go either way, and the file Annette had been given on her was slim.

"Rejalla is currently occupied," Shelah admitted, her skin flashing an embarrassed purple. "She'll definitely be free in a twenti-eth-cycle, and I'll check in and see if her meeting can be cut short."

A twentieth-cycle was roughly seventy minutes, but...truth be told, Annette didn't have anywhere else to be today.

Being the plenipotentiary representative of an interstellar empire was proving surprisingly slow on a day-to-day basis.

"Let her know I'm here," she ordered. "I'll wait."

ANNETTE ONLY ENDED up having to wait about ten minutes before Shelah got a message and her skin flashed bright red in pleasure.

"Dan!Annette Bond? Rejalla is free now." The A!Tol paused. "Your guide will have to stay out here."

The Satarda, who had never given Annette a name even when asked, simply bowed.

"I will await."

Annette found the slaves present throughout the Golden Palace off-putting. They were all Oathbound Keepers, apparently a higher tier of slave than most. They also all seemed perfectly happy with their lot in life, entirely accommodating. Even happy.

But they were still slaves and, so far as she could tell, couldn't do anything outside their assigned tasks without permission—and, without a specific task requiring it, they could not leave the Golden Palace.

She was still shaking her head as Shelah led her past the armored Marines and deeper into the embassy.

It was very clearly a somewhat informal affair. From the moment she was past reception, Annette realized that the embassy staff also lived in the suite. One corridor led toward the offices, the other toward a set of what looked to be relatively small apartments.

Her trained, if unpracticed, eye picked out the security systems as Shelah led her toward the offices. There were almost certainly more Marines in there somewhere, but probably not many.

If the entire suite held twenty people, Annette would have been surprised. There were concealed automated weapons and such too, but if the Kanzi wanted to wipe out the Imperium's embassy, it wouldn't take them very long.

On the other hand, Rejalla had been here when Kanzi fleets had attacked Sol. There seemed to be *some* degree of restraint on the Kanzi side.

The A!Tol gestured for Annette to continue through a door, and the Duchess of Terra stepped in to find herself face to face with Rejalla.

Rejalla was on the small side for an Anbrai. She was "merely" a bit over two meters tall standing on four legs with a barrel-like torso and a pair of massive arms. She was covered in light brown fur and, in this enclosed space, managed to be even more intimidating than she probably wanted to be.

"Duchess Bond," Rejalla rumbled, Annette's earpiece translating the Anbrai's speech to English for her. "Welcome to the Imperium's foothold on Kanarj, such as it is. How may I assist you?"

"I didn't realize until I started looking at my files that we even had an embassy here," Annette admitted. "I was hoping you could give me some background on the politics here. The High Priestess lobbed a good-sized bomb at me on our first meeting."

"I heard." Rejalla shook her entire torso. "Take a seat, Dan!Annette."

The ambassador did so herself, looming noticeably less from a chair.

"I've been here for fifty long-cycles," Rejalla said calmly. Roughly twenty-five years by human calendars. "I had Shelah's job when I first arrived: ambassador's aide and general extra hands. We prefer not to have an A!Tol as the ambassador, though my military commander is also one."

A!Tol had a hard time lying, so that made sense.

"I get along relatively well with the Kanzi's governing structure, so I've been stuck here for longer than you've been part of the Imperium," the Anbrai told Annette. "Sadly, your role is clearly temporary. It appears I'm not being replaced just yet."

"Stressful?" Annette asked.

"Like high noon on a desert mountainside," Rejalla confirmed. "Most of the time, they're reasonable enough. And then, occasionally, you can just *feel* yourself being measured for a collar."

She shook herself again.

"And then there's the mix between the times the Clans are acting up and causing border trouble...and the times the Navy is doing it and blaming the Clans," she concluded. "My job is to find the truth behind that wild beast shit."

The massive alien rolled her shoulders.

"And then to deliver Her Majesty's threats in the most...effective way possible."

Annette couldn't help chuckling at that. She'd met few more intimidating creatures in her life than aggravated Anbrai.

"But you wanted background," Rejalla continued. "I'm guessing you want to know if the High Priestess is serious about her 'all tech shared' line, right?"

"There aren't a lot of limits on what I can offer here," Annette admitted. "But *that* is off the table."

"And trust me, Duchess Bond, Reesi Karal *knows* that," the ambassador told her. "Don't be fooled by her size or the swarms of slaves and advisors around her. Reesi Karal did not become the unquestioned dictator of half a trillion souls because she's stupid.

"She knows that you can't offer her the Gold Dragon technology. She has intentionally put forward an impossible requirement."

"Much like we did with the requirement that they surrender the slaves of the Imperium's subject races," Annette said slowly. "Eventually, they met that."

"Because that wasn't impossible, merely very difficult," Rejalla said. "It is possible that we might become desperate enough to provide the Kanzi with tachyon scanners and hyperspace missiles, but Karal is hoping we don't."

"I was under the impression they needed this alliance."

"They do," the Anbrai agreed. "Or at the very least, they need the peace and nonaggression agreement. You'll note that Karal basically agreed to those on the spot, without argument or even conditions. But an alliance, sunstorms, even an open trade border, is a critical threat to the Theocracy."

"More critical than a Taljzi invasion?" Annette asked.

"Potentially. You've met the Oathbound," Rejalla told her. "There are almost as many Oathbound Keepers on most Theocracy worlds as there are Kanzi. They are the administrative bureaucracy of the Kanzi, and they are what every lower-tier slave aspires to be."

"I don't follow," Annette admitted.

"To you and me, the Kanzi society is anathema. Morally, economically and factually wrong," the Anbrai told her. "It requires a careful balancing of hope versus fear. They have slaves running complex industrial equipment, Dan!Annette Bond. Their entire industrial economy is slaves, with a handful of Kanzi overseers. The supervisors of their slaves are simply slaves with nicer housing and more privileges."

The big alien shivered.

"The only part of their society that doesn't have slaves in it somewhere is their military," she concluded. "Without slavery, their entire economy—their entire *culture* collapses.

"Now, personally, my reaction is that the sun can burn that crop and no one will care," Rejalla concluded. "But Reesi Karal is sworn to protect and preserve that society. To keep the people that make it up from harm.

"An alliance with us would see military officers fighting side by side with our people. It would see their slave-based logistics organization colliding with ours. Their slaves would see a free society, and their slave-*owners* would learn of a set of morals that calls their very existence evil."

"I'm not seeing that as a bad thing," Annette told Rejalla.

"No. I don't think so either, personally. But Karal does."

"And she'll risk losing the alliance to avoid it?" Annette asked.

"Possibly. There's been no more Taljzi seen since the Battle of Asimov. Much of the leadership of the Theocracy believes that it will be years or decades before they will return, if they ever do. They don't see the purpose in risking the society they protect—and the society that has made them rich and powerful!—to stave off a danger they don't truly believe in."

Annette sighed.

"So, is it Karal driving this...or her court?"

"It's Karal...but she's doing it to keep a part of her court under control," Rejalla said. "She knows perfectly well that many of her own reform-minded people see this alliance as a chance to undermine their society, to break down the strictures of the Theocracy and find a new way for their people."

"A new way that would not see Karal as unquestioned dictator of half a trillion souls," Annette pointed out.

"Exactly. Reesi Karal is caught between a rock and a hard place. She needs peace. She quite possibly needs an alliance...but the closer she lets her people get with the Imperium, the more she risks destroying the society she's sworn to protect."

Annette snorted.

"I'd sympathize more if we weren't talking about the largest slave-holding hierarchy *ever*."

"I don't sympathize," Rejalla told her. "But you and I...we do need to understand."

CHAPTER TEN

HYPERSPACE WAS BORING. IT WAS ALSO DISCONCERTING AND somewhat painful for the human brain, at least, to keep watching for an extended period.

Morgan checked the time as she switched from the visual of the gray void around them to a computer representation of their position. They weren't making a long-enough jump to call for a lot of variability, but...

"Commander Antonova," she said softly, calling the communications officer over. Antonova had been promoted shortly after Morgan, and this was Morgan's watch either way. The older woman was there double-checking the very calculations Morgan was looking at, a training exercise mostly to keep up her certification if she wanted to switch branches.

"Casimir," Antonova replied. "Looking for a refresher on interstellar navigation?"

Morgan chuckled.

"Not while I'm on duty, at least," she said. "Just noting that we were adjusting our course here. What happened?"

"We don't have charts out here," Antonova reminded her. "Our scanners have picked up a current over there, but without knowing more about where it's going or how strong it is, we don't want to take the flotilla into it."

A current was usually faster than traveling through "calm" hyperspace. Both had a degree of randomness to them, and both got denser as you traveled closer to the core. Without a map of the currents, though, avoiding one made more sense.

"We'll keep our scanners on it as we go," Antonova continued. "We might be able to use it to come back."

"May make a difference, may not," Morgan concluded. "I make our ETA to target one just over six hours?"

"Same," the other officer confirmed. "Alpha shift, right?"

"We're both back on duty, yeah," the shorter blonde said with a chuckle. "All hands on deck, ready for action."

Morgan shook her head.

"We have no idea what's in this system," she continued. "It's the first one on the line we drew that's outside our maps."

They'd visited another system already that had, at least, been surveyed before. There'd been no surprises there.

This system could *only* have surprises. They knew nothing.

"First humans to set eyes on a new system," Antonova agreed. "That would be a nicer feeling if we weren't expecting a fight."

"First *Imperials*, even," Morgan said. "No one from the Imperium's made it out this far. We're blazing a trail the Navy will probably follow. Will hopefully follow, if we find what we're after."

"Yeah."

The two women watched the projection in companionable silence for a few minutes. There were other people on the bridge, but they were the only officers, and no one was paying them too much attention.

"You know," Antonova finally ventured. "This would be a good mission to make sure we're all up to date on navigation and mapping. If you *did* want a refresher tutorial on interstellar navigation, I could make some off-duty time free for you."

Morgan didn't say anything initially. The offer *sounded* aboveboard and proper, entirely within appropriate lines for on-duty conversation...but Antonova's hesitancy in making it added another layer.

One that wasn't entirely a surprise...or unwelcome.

She chuckled.

"Let's compare schedules after emergence," she told the other woman. "I'm sure we can line up a window we're both free."

She couldn't see Antonova's face, but she suspected the other woman was trying to conceal a blush.

"I'd like that," Victoria Antonova said softly.

THE SUPER-BATTLESHIPS LED the way again, the two *Duchess of Terra*–class ships swanning out into the unknown system with every sensor and weapon bristling.

The two *Bellerophon*s followed, and the cruisers and destroyers filed in behind them.

"No energy signatures other than us," Morgan reported as she reviewed her scanners. "Six planets, no large asteroid collections." She shook her head.

"Not much of use to anybody," she admitted. "Planets aren't habitable; the only gas giant is tiny."

This system was looking like a pretty epic bust. Ships were spreading out in a scouting pattern, but Morgan had a pretty solid feeling about what they were going to find.

"I don't think there's anything here, skipper," she told Captain Vong.

"I would tend to agree," he said. "But we'll sweep the system anyway, I'm sure. The last thing we want is to miss a sensor platform or a similar warning system. We'd rather the Taljzi not know we're coming."

Morgan nodded, checking the tactical network for instructions.

"We have a request from the Flag to contribute drones to a system-wide search," she reported. "Deploying now."

This time, there was no question over whether they'd get the robotic spacecraft back. The worst she could see happening to them would be running into a rock somewhere, and the drones were smart enough to avoid that on their own.

Vong studied the deployment pattern and leaned back in his command chair.

"Commander Casimir, run me a post-processing scan for stealth ships," he ordered. "Everyone else, stand down to normal third-shift watches." He smiled. "I have the conn."

"Yes, sir."

As crew, including Antonova, began to troop out, Morgan started the data-processing run. It was a logical precaution, one she should have thought of on her own.

"Casimir?" Vong asked softly.

"Yes, sir?"

"Stop kicking yourself."

"Sir?" She hadn't thought she'd been *that* obvious.

"Your shoulders get *visibly* tight when someone suggests something you feel you should have thought of," Captain Vong told her gently. "You're young for your rank and new at this role. You are *expected* to be learning. Don't make the same mistake more than twice, and you're doing just fine. Stop beating yourself up. Am I clear?"

"Yes, sir," Morgan said carefully. She wasn't entirely sure she agreed with that logic...but when the Captain gave an order, the tactical officer fell in line!

CHAPTER ELEVEN

"SO, THIS SYSTEM WAS A BUST," MORGAN TOLD ANTONOVA THE following evening. "Constellations don't line up and there's nothing here. The gas giant isn't even the right proportions for us to skim for reaction mass."

The *Bellerophon*s operated primarily on matter-converter units, based on a design stolen from a Core Power, and could be fueled by anything. The rest of the flotilla, however, ran on a mix of fusion and antimatter cores. While they carried their antimatter stocks, they needed to be relatively regularly refueled with fuel for the fusion cores—and for the matter part of the matter-antimatter reaction.

The cores could run on several different varieties of hydrogen and helium, but only one at a time. The antimatter cores were designed to use the same gases, for ease of fuel storage. There was a wide variety of proportions the flotilla could use for fuel...and the gas giant in this system was none of them.

"Dead-end system at the edge of nowhere," Antonova said. The communications officer had doffed most of her uniform, down to the single-piece black bodysuit that formed both its base and its emergency vacuum protection.

"We didn't have to stop here," she continued. "But without clues, we don't know which systems along this vector are important."

"Hence the tutoring on navigation," Morgan replied. She was currently being *very* aware of just how formfitting the bodysuit layer of Victoria Antonova's uniform was. She had her suspicions as to why the other woman had offered to tutor her, but she wasn't going to presume her assumptions were solid enough to act on.

"Exactly," Antonova replied with a grin. She rose from the couch in her quarters and tapped on the wall. The haptic feedback field recognized her command and turned the wall into a screen, showing *Bellerophon*'s course.

"Hyperspace is hardly an even thing," she told Morgan. "It gets denser as you get closer to the Core and sparser as you get out towards the Rim. We're already moving about five percent slower versus normal space as we would be at Sol."

"So, we look for currents and such," Morgan agreed. "We have the scanners for that now."

"Except we can't tell where the currents are going," the other woman replied. "We could use our scanners to project a few hours' flight ahead of ourselves, which should be enough, but it's a risk. One that Admiral Sun has chosen not to take because we can't afford for this mission to go astray."

Morgan chuckled, studying the screen.

"So, that's about all of the refresher *I* need," she pointed out. "I'm hardly going to be calculating courses; I just need to understand them."

She wasn't getting up to leave, though. There was a reason, after all, that Morgan was also only wearing the underlayer of the uniform, and it *wasn't* because this was an informal meeting.

"You could, um...stay for a drink?" Antonova suggested after a moment, flushing slightly as Morgan grinned at her.

"Commander Antonova!" she said in mock outrage. "Are you implying that your intentions here may not be entirely aboveboard and correct?"

To her surprise, that managed to reduce the other woman to flustered silence.

"I'll stay for a drink," she assured Antonova after a few seconds of this. "I *do* like women, if that's your concern."

Sexuality was a far less-judged topic in the Duchy than it had been at many points in the past, but it was still easier to find relationships inside the usual paradigm—out of sheer odds, if nothing else.

Still flustered, the other woman produced a bottle of wine and a pair of glasses. Morgan took one with a smile and shook her head.

"I'm sorry, Victoria," she said gently. "I didn't mean to upset you."

"It's fine," Victoria replied with a small smile. "You just took me by surprise. I know you turned down that Guard Major a few months ago..."

"Yes," Morgan confirmed. "Because four months ago, I was maybe six weeks from being dumped for being a bad girlfriend." She sipped the wine and gave Victoria a warning look. "And I'll warn you before this goes any further: I am a *terrible* girlfriend, regardless of whether I'm dating men, women or whatever.

"Remember that my most recent ex broke up with me because I gave her all of two hours' warning that I was shipping out on *Bellerophon* and didn't make time for even a video call inside the sixteen or so hours I had." Morgan shook her head. "I can try to do better, but I can't promise success."

"You're putting the cart ahead of the horse here," Victoria told her...but she'd joined Morgan on the couch and the two of them were sitting mere centimeters apart.

Morgan shifted on the couch so that they were touching, her leg pressing against Victoria's, and smiled.

"Perhaps," she conceded. "Am I reading too much into this, though?"

"I *could* just be after a quick roll in the hay, you know," the other officer told her.

"We're outside each other's chain of commands and we're the same rank," Morgan observed. "There's no *regs* against anything, but we both know a quick roll in the hay would cause complications out of all proportion to any benefit."

"That's true."

The bodysuits did a surprisingly good job of transmitting body heat where they were touching each other, and Morgan twisted slightly to be able to see Victoria's face.

"And?" she murmured.

"Oh, screw it."

Victoria kissed her. Morgan kissed back.

Things went *very* positively from there.

THE "YOUR SHIFT is in one hour" alarm on Morgan's communicator woke her from a light doze to an extraordinarily pleasant situation. Victoria Antonova was draped, naked, across her chest.

Victoria was slowly blinking awake as Morgan regretfully extricated herself to turn off the alarm.

"That's the sound of duty calling," she told Victoria. "I need to get back to my quarters and grab a fresh uniform."

The bodysuit was designed to be worn for days on end if needed, but everyone was happier if they could toss their uniform in a cleaner and shower before going on duty.

"I'm on duty a few hours after you," her new lover told her. She paused. "We both know this has to end at the door to our quarters, right?"

"Right," Morgan confirmed. "Regs are fine with this so long as we continue to be responsible officers...but if we're not responsible officers, Captain Vong will come down on us like a ton of bricks."

Victoria chuckled softly and kissed Morgan.

"Good. I figured we were both smart enough to figure that out, but avoiding complications is always a good i—"

"*Battle stations. All hands to battle stations. This is not a drill. All hands to battle stations!*"

The klaxon tore through Victoria's quarters, and the two women met each other's gaze in shocked silence for a moment—and then dove for their uniforms.

Morgan's desire to get cleaned up fell a *long* way down the list from needing to be on duty.

CHAPTER TWELVE

"What have we got, Chief?" Morgan asked as she dropped into her seat on the bridge. In the back of her mind, she was aware that she and Antonova had arrived together, which was certain to raise eyebrows if it happened more than once, but it also wasn't important right now.

Chief Petty Officer Yewande Afolabi had been the senior NCO holding down the tactical section on the XO's watch. As the full crew swarmed in, the pitch-black woman was the one who was going to have to brief her officers.

"Hyper portal near the gas giant," Afolabi reported. "Rear Admiral Sun has ordered the flotilla to intercept."

"If they're friendly, we'll know before we open fire," Morgan agreed. "If they aren't, we can't let them escape."

"That was my reading as well, Commander." The NCO abandoned the main tactical officer's seat for Morgan, taking a position on a support console. "We don't have a lot of details yet, but we're definitely looking at multiple ships."

Morgan pulled up the sensor data herself, confirming that before she passed it on to the Captain.

"Casimir, what's our status?" Vong demanded as he dropped into his chair behind her. If the Captain was later than Morgan and Antonova, he must have actually been asleep when the alarm hit.

Poor bastard.

"Flotilla has gone to battle stations and we are maneuvering to intercept potential hostiles who emerged from a hyper portal at five light-minutes ten minutes ago," she reported.

Lightspeed delays and the range limits of the tachyon scanners meant that they'd only *seen* the hyper portal five minutes before. They were too far away for decent scans of the ships, as well. They had blips of interface drives; that was all.

"Do we have any probes nearby?" Vong asked.

"*Chancellor Merkel* had three probes near the gas giant, scanning the moons," Morgan replied. She knew that off the top of her head, but she was checking to see their status. "They were on their way back, but they're already heading back to the portal."

New data started flowing into her screens as the fleet tactical network caught up with its orders.

"The probes' hyperfold coms are online. We're now down to a sixty-second time delay on the tactical network."

And from a light-minute away, the probes' sensors were at least sensitive enough to identify individual ships and engines.

"I make it five ships, varying from two to six million tons," Morgan reported. "Velocity point four *c*."

Those were odd numbers. Few warships were that slow, and while there were warships belonging to both the Kanzi and the A!Tol in that mass range, they tended to be rare, specialist ships.

Kanzi heavy attack cruisers and A!Tol fast battleships fell in that range, for example, but to have five ships in that range at that speed...

"Sir, they're *freighters*," she concluded aloud, and more data started coming in. "Freighters that know we see them. Fleet's getting Imperial shipping codes."

"Okay," Captain Vong said slowly. "That's very odd. Orders from the Flag?"

They weren't in range of the flotilla's arsenal yet...but the *Bellerophon*s and *Thunderstorm*-Ds would be in range for their hyperspace missiles before the freighters could escape.

"Hold fire," Antonova reported from her station. "Admiral Sun is attempting to make contact. They're a long way from home."

Ships this far out were unlikely to be doing everything aboveboard. This was unexplored space, after all, though not *ridiculously* out of Imperial territory...if, for example, you were trying to go around the fortified Kanzi-A!Tol border to smuggle goods.

"The admiral's message will arrive in three minutes...wait, they're running," Morgan reported. "At a guess, they finally IDed us beyond 'Imperial warships.' They're headed back to their hyper portal zone at point four five lightspeed."

They'd found some extra speed somewhere. That was pretty common for ships that were spooked.

"Can we intercept?" Vong asked.

"I can put hyperspace missiles into them," Morgan replied. "That's all."

"Figured." The Captain leaned back in his chair. "It's the Admiral's decision, but I doubt we'll do anything. We'll let the Imperium know, but they're almost certainly smugglers—and we have much higher priorities."

Morgan had to agree, even if went against the grain to watch probable criminals escape to safety.

They couldn't even justify using a hyperspace missile as a warning shot, and the hyperfold drones just let them watch the smugglers vanish into a hyper portal from closer in.

"I don't suppose the beacons we got were useful for identification?" Vong asked.

"No, sir," Morgan told him. "Generic shipping beacons. Detailed IFFs are normally attached but were disabled this time."

He grunted.

"Thought so." He shook his head. "Senior officers meeting in an hour," he told them. "I'll confer with the Admiral, see what our plan is."

Vong sighed.

"We're almost certainly going to continue along this course and hope we find ourselves some sign of the Taljzi."

CHAPTER THIRTEEN

"Well, I don't suppose we can hope for the entertainment of smugglers this time?" Captain Vong asked as *Bellerophon* plunged back into normal space for the third time in a week.

Smugglers had been the most interesting thing they'd seen in two star systems. The second system had been a complete bust, its only value in Morgan's mind was that it had been quiet enough to allow her to sneak Commander Antonova away for the closest thing a warship had to R&R time.

In this case, that had mostly involved the two women in Morgan's quarters with a bottle of wine. There really weren't that many amenities on a warship.

They shared a taste in bad old 2-D movies, it turned out, even if the movies hadn't actually been *watched* that much.

"I wouldn't count on much, skipper," Morgan told her boss, shaking the pleasant memories from her head. "I'm reading exactly *one* planet, a super-Jovian so big, it's almost a binary component."

The data kept pouring in.

"A lot of asteroids, as I would expect from that kind of mess," she continued. "The star isn't really warm enough to support life, and the super-Jovian hasn't *quite* ignited and... Wait."

There was a telltale spectrography signature in the orbit of the super-Jovian.

"The *combination*, however, of one not-quite-warm-enough star and one not-quite-ignited gas giant seems to have provided a small miracle," Morgan explained after a few seconds' analysis. "I'm picking up liquid water and potentially oxygen on the largest moon."

She kept going over the data and smiled.

"Of course, said 'moon' is fifteen percent larger than Earth," she noted. "Hard to estimate gravity at this distance, but I'm guessing at least one point one, maybe a tad more. Big rock."

"Now, that *is* interesting," Vong said. "Is the Flag sending out probes?"

"We're tagged for three drones of a Very Large Array and two close-in probes," Morgan confirmed, checking her console. "Deployment underway."

"Orders are for *Bellerophon* and *Rama* to move in deeper with *Squall* and the destroyers," Antonova read off a few moments later. "*Chancellor Merkel* and the rest of the flotilla will hang back in case something gets tricky."

"Makes sense," Vong confirmed. "Commander Hume? Take us in."

New icons flared on Morgan's display as the two battleships slipped out of the main formation, the updated cruiser and the older destroyers falling in around them.

"That gas giant should be useful for refueling, and there's water in them there hills," the Captain said cheerfully. "Let's go see if anyone lives there."

NO ONE HAD EXPECTED to actually find anyone or anything on the planet, Morgan was reasonably sure. If they had, they would have been harshly disappointed.

The planet had liquid water, yes. And oxygen, too. It had too much of both, a glittering ball of liquid water with almost no surface visible to the eye—and an average surface temperature of almost seventy degrees Celsius.

"So, the pole on the far side from the gas giant would be roughly equivalent to living in a hot spring twenty-four/seven," Morgan concluded as she went over the data. "The planet is tidally locked, so the range *there* is between a mere thirty-five degrees Celsius and fifty-ish."

"It's a beautiful planet," Vong said. "But I don't see anyone living there, you're right."

He shook his head.

"I was hoping for something useful—or at least interesting."

Morgan was about to comment on that when a program she'd initiated finished and she swallowed hard.

"I think we may have just checked your boxes, skipper," she told him. "According to my program, this is one of our mystery planets from the Taljzi chapel."

Vong sat straight up.

"What?"

"Backtracking constellations from here, we're damn close to the design of the second middle constellation in the chapel," she told him. "Assuming they were here between two hundred and eighty and three hundred years ago."

"Which is around when they were driven from Kanzi space," the Captain agreed. "So, they stopped here to refuel and, what, decided to immortalize it forever?"

"Something happened here that they thought was important," Morgan said. "It's not like we have whatever revisions the Taljzi have made to their religious texts in their exile."

The planet rotated on her screen and she haloed a location.

"But I don't see anything to suggest that the planet has changed much in the last three centuries, and *this* is the only landmass anywhere near either pole. It would still be disgustingly hot but potentially at least livable for Kanzi—or humans."

"Do we have a probe close enough to take a look?" Vong asked.

"Already vectoring," Morgan replied. "Sixty seconds, sir."

The probes she was currently using couldn't enter atmosphere. She *had* probes that could do that, but they weren't deep-space vehicles that traveled at over sixty percent of lightspeed. These could get into a low orbit and get her images of the surface.

Those images answered at least part of her question. The landmass was a large island, the caldera of some immense underwater volcano. A circular wall rose out of the planetwide ocean, forming a natural dike that kept a rough ten-kilometer circle dry.

Inside that circle was a ruined city. Well, colony, anyway. Several ships had been landed and refurbished to act as homes. The local stone had been worked to provide more structures.

Heat and moisture had wrecked most of the stone structures, but ship hulls could withstand several centuries even of this planet's weather.

"I'm not an architectural expert, sir," Morgan said slowly, "but those look like Kanzi buildings to me."

"To me, too," Vong agreed. "And now I wish we had an archeologist aboard." He shrugged. "We'll see what Major Phelps's Guards can work out."

"Permission to accompany the landing party, sir?" Morgan asked. "I'm not an archeologist, but I'm probably the closest thing we have to a xenoculturalist."

The Captain hesitated, then nodded slowly.

"You go armed, Commander," he instructed sharply. "And Major Phelps is in command, understood?"

"Yes, sir."

"Then go find yourself a suit and a sidearm, Casimir. I'm pretty sure this rock is as safe as any morgue, but we want to be careful."

CHAPTER FOURTEEN

MORGAN WASN'T THE TALLEST WOMAN TO BEGIN WITH, BUT THE Guards around her made her feel positively minuscule. Most of them were larger to begin with, but they were also now wrapped in the several centimeters of advanced alloys that protected their power armor.

"Commander Casimir," one of the anonymous suits greeted her in a familiar voice.

"Major Phelps," she replied gratefully. The Guard officer had asked her out once, but he didn't seem to have taken being turned down too badly. They were still friendly enough.

"I hear we're taking you to see the sights," Phelps said. "Anything in particular you're looking for?"

"Well, let's start with the basics. Can any of you read Kanzi?" Morgan asked brightly.

There was a long pause.

"We have translator software for that, but no, none of my Guards can," he admitted. "You can?"

"Yes. And I've spent part of this trip brushing up on what the dialect and text would have looked like when the Taljzi went into their exile," she told him. "So, we're looking for text. Even street signs and door nameplates might be useful."

"Any idea what happened here?" the Guard Major asked as their shuttle slipped away from *Bellerophon*. "Seems like a pretty big settlement to just...empty out like this."

"No idea at all yet," Morgan replied. "My first guess is that it wasn't big enough for all of the Taljzi and was damn uncomfortable for them, so once they found somewhere they *could* all live, they picked up and moved out."

"And just left everything behind?"

She shrugged.

"From what data we have on the Taljzi, their runaway fleet had a lot of civilian shipping they could convert into living space, but not that many actual *people*. Maybe a hundred, hundred and fifty thousand Kanzi—and they wouldn't have brought slaves with them."

"Scans show the colony probably could have held most of that... but not all," Phelps agreed. "Not comfortably, anyway."

"And this planet isn't really set up for anything we'd call real industry," Morgan continued. "They could operate in space, but even with artificial gravity, long-term occupation of space isn't entirely healthy. This was the only piece of habitable real estate in the star system."

"And it's terrible," Phelps agreed, bringing up a hologram of the volcanic caldera between them. "Not to mention the constant wondering just how dormant the volcano actually is."

"Yeah." She shook her head as she looked at the image of the colony. "I'm not surprised they left, Major. I'm just hoping they forgot something useful."

She tapped the largest structure, which appeared to have started as a mid-sized bulk freighter. "Let's start here. Most of the ships they landed got chopped up pretty thoroughly, but this guy is still mostly intact. Not intact enough to lift off, but intact enough that they were clearly using it for something."

"Makes sense to me." Phelps paused. "Are we expecting

trouble?"

"It's possible they left automatic defenses behind," Morgan admitted. "I don't know how well those would still work, but they might be there. I'll...be hiding behind the power armor, if no one minds."

———

IT WAS one thing to look at the temperature and humidity numbers for the "habitable" portion of the moon and recognize that it was going to be miserable.

It was an entirely different thing to step out of the shuttle, wearing an environmental protection suit, and *still* be hit with an almost physical wall of heat and humidity.

"I make it forty-eight degrees Celsius and a hundred percent humidity," she said after a moment. "How's the armor holding up?"

"Your environmental suit is actually slightly better for this than our armor," Phelps said grimly. "My people are checking their system settings. Make sure yours are properly set, too. At least one of my Guards nearly got instant heat stroke since their gear wasn't set right."

Morgan checked. Her gear was set to an automatic health-preservation mode that would keep her heat within a safe range.

"Safe" did not necessarily equate to "comfortable." She used the computer on the suit's arm to reset the temperature down to the usual shipboard temperature of twenty degrees Celsius and breathed a sigh of relief as her skin noticeably cooled.

And then winced as her suit told her that it only had the power and other supplies to keep that up for an hour. Sighing, she turned it up to twenty-five degrees and was informed that she had five hours' supplies for that.

"Operating down here is going to suck," she said calmly. "But so long as no one tries to wander around without environment protection of some kind..."

"Sensors say the air is breathable," Phelps told her. "High oxygen levels. Might even be good for us." He chuckled half-under his breath. "Also might drown us. The Kanzi have *fur*, right?"

"Yes," she agreed. "However miserable this place would make us, the Taljzi must have hated it even more."

Humanity had evolved from savannah pursuit predators that moved in family and tribal groups. Kanzi had evolved from tundra ambush predators that moved in packs and families. Both could survive in this environment with difficulty and shelter.

Humans would find it uncomfortable at best and deadly at worst. Kanzi would find it *hell*.

Looking around, Morgan could see that the structures had clearly once had supports for awnings and cloth covers everywhere. The city's streets had probably been completely shaded from the light and heat of the gas giant the moon orbited.

It would have bought them a few precious degrees' worth of cover.

She crossed to one of the half-ruined stone buildings and checked it over. Age and heat had wrecked the building, but there were still some intact stones. They were perfectly sized and shaped to slot into each other, like children's toys.

"Laser-carved stonework," she said aloud. "They didn't necessarily have modern conveniences, but they had a lot of tech to work with. Probably running off fusion cores from the ships they broke up to start the place."

"Those would be dead now, right? Without maintenance, they couldn't be pulling enough fuel in to keep them operating."

"They could have a system to pull heavy water out of the ocean around them, but unless the main ocean is unusually non-salty for a major planetary water body...that system would have been wrecked ten years after they left."

She poked at the stones again, taking a sample of one of the broken ones for analysis back aboard *Bellerophon*.

"And while I won't know the exact date until we're back in space,

I can tell you it's been more than ten years."

AT SOME POINT after they'd landed, the Taljzi had replaced the main airlock of the big ship with a massive set of double doors. Presumably, they'd been powered originally, but at this point, they were frozen shut, their tracks clogged with sediment from the water in the air and the doors even sealed shut with a layer of salt.

"Major?" Morgan indicated the big doors. "Think we can deal with this?"

Phelps continued to study them for a couple of seconds.

"Without knowing what's behind them, I'm guessing blasting is a bad idea," he finally concluded. "Who knows; the answer to all of our questions could be on a mural on the inside of the door!"

"Unlikely but possible," Morgan agreed. "I'll take blasting over not getting into the ship, though."

Phelps laughed.

"We're good," he promised. "Kay, Peller. Tear it open, if you please."

Those two worthies turned out to be the Guards standing closest to the doors. They approached the doors, studied them for a few seconds themselves, and then rammed armored fingers through the original gap.

Salted shut or not, the doors weren't resisting power armor. The two Guards calmly pulled away from each other, the door screeching as exoskeletal muscles exerted force no mere human could match.

It still took a good thirty seconds to get the doors open, but they did so with minimal damage.

"Shall we?" Phelps gestured.

Morgan activated the light on her suit and stepped forward. She made it all of halfway to the door before there were Guards ahead of her and she remembered she was supposed to be *behind* the suits of power armor.

"Whoa."

She wasn't sure who had spoken, but the exhaled exclamation of awe was fitting. The Taljzi had gutted the portion of the ship around her—probably a cargo segment or even living quarters; she couldn't say at this point—to create a massive open lobby.

The lobby split the old ship in two, stretching to the outer hull on all sides. Murals covered the walls. There were no statues, but she thought she recognized several of the Kanzi in the murals from the statues aboard the station in DLK-5539.

"I only see four constellations here," Phelps said after a moment. "And my suit computer makes them Kanzi, the Taljzi system, their outbound stop...and here."

"So, this is the earlier version of that chapel," Morgan concluded. "The religious gathering place of their colony. Makes sense."

Of course, with only half of DLK-5539's constellations, there was no further evidence there as to where the Kanzi had gone. She was looking for something else—and found a set of directions carved into the wall by the door that she studied for a moment.

"Okay, according to this, there are four different sections to this building," she said aloud. "First, what translates roughly as the 'Grand Chapel of the Survivors.' I'm guessing that's where we are.

"Second is the 'Convocation of the Host of the Minds of God,'" she continued. "The last bit is the Taljzi, so I'm guessing that's their administration center. The forward half of the ship, where the bridge and her administration offices would have been to begin with.

"Third is the 'Sinews of the Power of the Survivors,' which I'm presuming to be their power plant." She pointed. "That's the back half of the ship, where the power cores would have been. I'm guessing they were running this building as their main church, administration center and power plant."

"What was the fourth part?"

Morgan looked over the text. It was even more archaic and fanciful than the rest, and it took her a minute to translate.

"I'm not sure," she finally admitted. "The 'Heart of Ancients' or something like that? It's apparently...beneath us." Morgan paused. "Now, the administration center is what I *was* looking for, but now I'm wondering.

"And it says the stairs down are that way."

THE CHAPEL HAD AT LEAST HAD some light coming in through the open doors. Once they found the stairs, behind a badly rotted but still-present heavy curtain, they ran out of light very quickly.

Morgan's suit had a light on her helmet and another on her wrist that she could point at things. The power-armor suits had much the same arrangement, plus night-vision gear built into the helmets.

It was enough for them to carefully pick their way down the stairs. They passed from the old ship onto carved stone almost immediately, and then hit a security checkpoint roughly a story deep into the rock.

"How deep can this go before there's water?" Morgan wondered aloud as the Guards carefully dismantled the barricade—built from starship-hull alloys—and security equipment.

"Well, assuming that the volcano goes all the way to the ocean floor...all the way?" Phelps suggested. "There were mounted plasma guns here, Commander Casimir," he added. "One's *still* here, though it's corroded to hell."

The Guards still carefully dismantled the once-automated weapon before they let Morgan approach.

"What were they guarding?" she wondered aloud. "If they'd dug the colony underground for temperature control, they wouldn't have had the surface structures at all."

"Maybe a strategic command center?" Phelps said. "They might have planned for being found and bombarded. They *did* have their home system blown to hell by the A!Tol, after all."

Morgan shivered at that thought. Insilja had been home to four *billion* people, one of the Kanzi's most heavily industrialized and populated colonies, when the civil war had started. They'd been the industrial core of the entire Taljzi war effort...and then all of that, all of those billions of people, had died in a single moment of scientific terror.

"In that case, if there's an answer to where they went, it's going to be down here," she said. "Let's keep going."

At the second security point, another two stories down, Morgan started getting worried. The Guards dismantled all four defunct automated plasma guns before she got near them, but the security checkpoint had clearly been left running when the Taljzi left.

"We're twelve meters below the surface," she reported. They still had radio contact with *Bellerophon*, thankfully. "The stairs keep going. I think we're most likely to find answers down here, sir."

"It's your ground party, Commander Casimir," Captain Vong told her. "If you lose radio contact, make sure to check in within an hour. Otherwise, we're flooding that hole in the ground with more Guards, clear?"

"Clear, sir."

Dropping the channel, she turned over to Phelps.

"We're going deeper," she told the Guard Major.

"I presumed," he said. "I want to drop a radio relay here with a pair of Guards. Make sure we keep contact."

"Good call," she agreed. "Something's down here, Major. Something important."

They kept going. Another story. Another.

A third security checkpoint at twenty-four meters underground. It had been left fully active and corroded into uselessness, like the second one.

They were *fifty* meters down into the volcano before they reached the end of the stairs.

"Air is getting damp," Phelps warned her. "We're getting close to water of some kind—and the air isn't much better than water!"

Morgan checked.

"Enough air pressure to keep it dry-ish despite it being below general sea level," she agreed. "This is weird."

Weird didn't cover what came next. The corridor they were following ended at a clearly modern door—made of some kind of mechanically reprocessed stone.

"That doesn't look like anything else in the colony," she said aloud, stepping closer to study it. It slid aside easily at her touch, balanced with a precision she'd rarely seen.

Beyond, the raw stone gave way to a smooth, almost polished surface. It was still the native stone, but something had been done to it. Something familiar.

"Nano-reconstructed stone," Phelps said slowly. "We use it for rapid fabrication of landing sites. That's quick and dirty, though. We can just turn a circular area into harder rock. We don't have enough flexibility in our nanobots to build a structure...let alone an underground structure."

Morgan turned up the power on her wrist-lamp and lit the entire space. It was a circular promenade of some kind, an entryway above what was presumably a deeper facility.

It was hard to say, as water had filled up to the level of the balcony around the access. She could make out what she thought were stairs leading deeper.

"There's no script on the walls here," she said slowly. "Some basic Kanzi markings, but they're almost graffiti...added later."

She stepped over to the pool of water and shone her light down into the depths. There was a structure down there, an old building of some kind.

Very old. She recognized the style.

"'Heart of the Ancients,'" she repeated. "They didn't just land here because it was the only habitable real estate in the system—they had the ships to move on. They were looking for something.

"This wasn't a colony, except in that it was a handy place to stash people while they explored further.

"This was a *dig site*."

CHAPTER FIFTEEN

"Admiral Villeneuve."

The officer welcoming Jean aboard the *Manticore*-class battleship *Chipmunk* saluted crisply as the Councilor for the Militia stepped off his shuttle.

"*Non, non, s'il vous plaît,*" he insisted. "I am no longer an Admiral."

"*Vous serez toujours notre amiral,*" the young Militia Commander told him gently. "We know our own, sir. You may be retired, but you're still the founding Admiral of the Militia!"

The old man took a moment to identify the young-seeming woman as Commander Lucette Clément—which meant that "young" was entirely in his head, as *Chipmunk*'s executive officer was closer to fifty than to forty.

Which meant it would be at most six months before she had a command of her own. She was as old for her rank in the Militia as *Chipmunk* was young for a capital ship in the A!Tol Imperium.

"Captain Lawrence sends their regrets," Clément continued. "They're tied up in a series of briefings on the new weapons systems that was *supposed* to be concluded an hour ago."

"I helped write the briefings, Commander," Jean pointed out. "I could have warned them that they would run over."

Chipmunk already carried a small arsenal of the hyperfold cannons, but she wasn't yet equipped with hyperspace missiles. A rough refit planned in the near future would attach a single six-launcher battery of single-portal weapons to the warship, but it would be months or years before she could be fully refitted.

The reason for that was why Villeneuve was aboard her today.

"What's the ETA on our hyperspace signatures?" he asked.

"Just over two hours. *Sphinx*, *Nymph* and *Chipmunk* are deploying forward as an honor guard," Clément told him. "And a cautionary measure if they *aren't* the Grand Fleet."

Jean managed not to shake his head at the younger officer.

If the immense hyperspace anomaly they'd picked up six hours' flight out of Sol *wasn't* Fleet Lord Tan!Shallegh and the Grand Fleet, the Duchy of Terra was screwed.

"And Admiral Kurzman-Wellesley?" he asked.

"He left a message for you," Clément told him. "My understanding is that he and Vice Admiral Tidikat will be standing by at one light-minute with First Squadron."

Vice Admiral Tidikat was the Duchy of Terra Militia's senior Laian officer and the commander of First Squadron—which consisted of sixteen *Vindication*-class super-battleships. Refitted with hyperfold cannons and external hyperspace missiles, those were currently the most powerful super-battleships in the Imperium.

If their visitors weren't Tan!Shallegh, they might not be able to do *much*. They'd try anyway, though.

They were Terrans, after all. Regardless of their individual species.

"WELCOME ABOARD *CHIPMUNK*, ADMIRAL VILLENEUVE," Captain Lawrence told Jean when he arrived on the battleship's bridge.

The Captain, an androgynous Middle Eastern officer wearing a black turban, had apparently arrived immediately before Jean.

"Do I need to tell everyone I'm not an Admiral anymore?" Jean asked.

"Retired Admirals still get the title out of respect, do they not?" Lawrence asked. "Or is that not a French thing?"

"I don't recall including that in the Militia's regulations," the Councilor replied. "I'm rarely surprised by things the Militia does."

Lawrence shrugged and gestured Jean to an observer's seat by the Captain's chair.

"We're on our way out to meet our new guests," they told Jean. "Most recent count makes it between eleven and thirteen hundred hyperspace anomalies."

Jean shook his head.

"We must hope that it is Fleet Lord Tan!Shallegh," he noted. "If it is not..."

"Earth's fucked," Lawrence said bluntly. "We can't stop a thousand warships. Maybe half that, depending on tech and classes."

"That is why the Imperium is sending us the Grand Fleet," Jean confirmed. "Do we have a new ETA with that count?"

"Sixty-three minutes, assuming they're coming out at a standard distance," the Captain replied. "We're meeting them with three battleships, with sixteen supers and escorts hanging back at support range."

"It should not be needed," Jean said precisely. "But I must confess I am glad to have them. Commander Clément said there was a message for me from Kurzman-Wellesley?"

"It's waiting in the queue on the observer station," Lawrence told him. "We both know what it's going to say. You can call him and yell at him from there, too."

Jean snorted and carefully folded his old bones into the chair, activating a privacy bubble so he could review Kurzman's message.

The stocky form of the former football player appeared in front of him. Age had been somewhat unkind to Patrick Kurzman-Wellesley, with weight and time dragging down on his once heavily muscled broad build. His hair was mostly gray now, for all that Imperial technology would hold off the worst of the effects of aging for a while yet.

"Councilor Villeneuve," Kurzman greeted him. "I know we discussed having both of us meet Tan!Shallegh, but on consideration, I think it's better we keep the interaction between the Duchy and the Imperial Fleet, without pulling the Militia in.

"There are enough people in the Fleet who think the Terran Militia is too big for our seats. Keeping it a *political* discussion protects us all, I think. And means *I* don't have to sit in on a meeting with multiple A!Tol."

Jean sighed. Just because Earth's politicians and military officers were *used* to the A!Tol didn't mean they *liked* being around the giant squids.

"We'll stand guard as the Fleet Lord moves his ships into refit, but with that many Imperial warships around, we're not going to pretend that the Militia has primary responsibility for Sol's security."

A smirk turned grim.

"Of course, if they *aren't* A!Tol, it's going to take all of First Squadron to extract you and your escort," Kurzman said flatly. "We think we know who's coming, but we've learned that lesson."

***

"HYPER PORTAL OPENING!"

There was less urgency to the report than Jean had heard in the past. If nothing else, the Duchy of Terra had laid a series of scanner beacons in hyperspace around the star system. They had *hours* of warning of incoming hyperspace ships now.

Jean, like everyone else on *Chipmunk*'s bridge, could read the icons on the screens without assistance. There were few more formal reports as the first wave of super-battleships roared into the Sol System. Then the second. Third. Fourth.

"Confirmed," *Chimpunk*'s tactical officer finally reported. "Lead squadron are *Vindication*-class ships. We built them. They're Imperial."

Further data tags added themselves to the capital ships that continued to stream into the system in a calm procession.

Ten squadrons of super-battleships, a hundred and sixty ships.

Ten squadrons of battleships, another hundred and sixty ships, and four of "fast battleships," sixty-four of the smaller capital ships humanity tended to call battlecruisers.

Twenty squadrons of cruisers, three hundred and twenty starships.

Thirty squadrons of destroyers, another four hundred and eighty ships all on their own.

Almost twelve hundred starships of the Imperial Navy, easily a third of the A!Tol Imperium's military strength, streamed into Jean's system in a seemingly unending line of metal and interface drives.

"Admiral Villeneuve," the communications officer reported. "I have Fleet Lord Tan!Shallegh on the com for you."

"Put him through," Jean ordered.

The familiar form of the A!Tol officer appeared on the screen. A male, Tan!Shallegh topped out at slightly under two meters, significantly smaller than females of his species. The parasitical natural life cycle of the A!Tol had left their females large and with powerful regenerative capabilities.

Only the fact that reproduction *killed* female A!Tol had allowed anything resembling gender equality for most of their history, and a male Fleet Lord was *still* a rarity.

"Greetings, Admiral Villeneuve," Tan!Shallegh said loudly, and Jean swallowed a sigh.

"Fleet Lord Tan!Shallegh. Welcome to Sol once more. It's been a long time."

"It has," Tan!Shallegh agreed. "I wish we'd met again in warmer waters, Admiral. Are the Duchy's yards prepared to receive the Grand Fleet?"

"Not all at once," Jean said with a chuckle. "We have cleared most of the slips for your vessels, though, and we had design schematics for the refits. My understanding is that the shipwrights are confident in their designs for the *Vindication*-class ships and other vessels built here but would like to consult with your Fleet's engineers before they finalize the other work."

"Then we'll get the *Vindication*s in immediately," Tan!Shallegh replied, "and my engineers will place themselves at your shipwrights' disposal. The quiet of our enemy's waters makes me nervous. Still waters are rarely safe, Admiral."

"And you never know what they hide," Jean agreed, picking up what he could of the A!Tol's metaphor. "We will be working as swiftly as we can."

"I know your people, Admiral Villeneuve," Tan!Shallegh told him. "Neither I nor my Empress have any concerns about that."

CHAPTER SIXTEEN

THE ENTIRE FLOTILLA CROWDED THE SPACE AROUND THE habitable moon, battleships and super-battleships alike trying to maintain a rough orbit above the polar island as Morgan faced a holographic assembly of the starship captains.

"We've got divers on site, trying to get deeper into the facility to see if we can sort out what the Taljzi found," she told them. "We've found the remains of several pumping sections, so it looks like the Taljzi drained the place of water to get into it as best as they could."

"But what is it?" Rear Admiral Sun asked. "If the Taljzi drained it, I'm guessing it wasn't theirs?"

"We're still working out what exactly it was supposed to be," Morgan admitted, "but we know whose facility. It's a Precursor base, people, belonging to the same aliens who built the scout ship we found in Alpha Centauri fifteen years ago.

"Hence, no signage, no labels, not much we'd even recognize as doors once you're past the main entrance," she explained. "They used a cybernetic implant based on technology we can't replicate and had everything linked to a permanent distributed internet."

"That sounds...useful but problematic," one of the captains observed.

"We're not entirely sure what happened to the Precursors, but we know their implants all stopped working at one point," Morgan told them. "And killed them. All of them."

That brought the room to silence.

"We haven't found any bodies in the facility yet, so I suspect the Taljzi removed them all. What we have seen tells me that the facility was here during the last active period of the volcano."

"You mean it was buried by the volcano?" Vong asked.

"Exactly," she confirmed. "Whatever access the facility originally had was covered by magma. I'm guessing the door we found was originally on the surface, but then the volcano erupted and the whole thing was buried.

"That's why I think the Taljzi had to know it was here. They came to this system looking for it and settled here, at least partially, for a while. Then they found whatever they were looking for in that base and left."

"So, we're following in the path of a three-century-old treasure hunt?" Sun asked.

"It's possible," Morgan admitted. "It seems likely, given DLK-5539's alignment with the vector of this system, that the line we've been following will continue towards the Taljzi's new home base.

"It also might not. I believe that the Taljzi came here looking for the location of something *else*. They found it and that's where they went from here. There may be an answer in the administrative office of the colony or the answer may be inside that flooded base."

"Or the Taljzi may have destroyed any records of their destination before they left," Sun pointed out. "This is better than a wild goose chase, Commander, but not by much. We need to find these bastards, and a three-century-old archeological dig is not the best source of answers."

"Yes, sir," Morgan agreed. "It may be the only source we have, though."

"Agreed. We'll spend five days here, people, and if we haven't found anything by then, we'll proceed on our previous course." He shook his head. "We'll probably leave a team and a ship behind either way. There's too much potential information here for us to pass up, but we can only spare so much time."

THE WALLS of Morgan's office were lit up with a dozen different sub-screens. Several were live feeds from the divers, others were still images taken from the video of the administrative section of the old ship.

Other teams were exploring the rest of the Taljzi settlement, but Morgan didn't think they were going to find much of use. This had been a medium-term stopover and she now doubted that anyone had stayed here more than twenty years.

A lot of the people there had just been waiting for the researchers to finish their task and the explorers to find their next destination. They'd been the ones to build new stone buildings and cover the streets with canopies.

It had still been a miserable hell for the Taljzi. It was miserable for the humans on the ground right now, and they weren't going to have to live there for years. There was only so much adaptation you could do, after all.

She'd hoped that the Taljzi's difficulty adapting meant they'd rushed cleaning up when they'd abandoned the settlement, but it didn't look like it. The administrative offices had been cleaned out. No computers, no paper, nothing.

If they'd left paper behind, it had rotted. There were some larger murals and such on the walls, and Morgan was studying them when someone knocked on her door.

"Come in," she instructed, turning away from the images on the walls.

Victoria Antonova slipped through the door with a smile, closing it behind her and taking a seat without asking.

"You *are* off duty, you know," Morgan's girlfriend pointed out gently. "And I've buzzed your com three times in the last hour."

"Really?" Morgan asked, then glanced at where she'd abandoned the scroll-like device on her desk. "Shit. Sorry."

"I guess I was warned," Victoria said drily. "And I'm not even surprised, to be honest. Don't feel too bad."

Morgan flushed. She hadn't quite planned on neglecting her lover *entirely* while she was face-deep in a problem, but it appeared that had been where she was headed.

"No, it's fine," Victoria repeated. "This needs to get done. I don't suppose you've had any sparks of inspiration?"

Shaking her head, Morgan stepped away from the screens to embrace Victoria and kiss her. Unexpectedly, but quite pleasantly, she found herself in Victoria's lap, leaning against the taller woman's shoulder as she looked back at the diagrams.

"Furry buggers did a good job of cleaning out their own offices," she admitted. "Nothing in what's left to give us a clue. If there's anything useful, it's going to be in the Precursor base...but I don't even know where to tell the divers to *look*. Every time I think we've found the end of it, someone turns a corner and finds another massive chunk of it."

"It would help if we could read the signs, huh?" Victoria asked, embracing Morgan gently as she spoke.

"The signs are basically RFID tags in the walls, and they ran out of power a couple thousand years ago at least," Morgan explained. "I'm not even sure what the damn place *is*." She tapped a command on the communicator she could reach from Victoria's lap, pulling a number of the screens back to show the full known extent of the base.

Victoria was silent for several long seconds...and it wasn't the silence of ignorance.

"Victoria?"

"That's because nobody ever builds them on planets," she said, very, very slowly. "Morgan...that's a starcom."

Morgan rose from her comfortable seating arrangement to look at the design of the base on her screen. Mentally stripping away the rock, she shook her head and fiddled with her communicator again.

A new image appeared next to the facility on the screens: the rough schematic of the Sol Starcom Station.

"Take away the bits necessary to be a space station, add the mother of all geothermal plants..." she said quietly. "You're right. It's about half the size of one of our space stations, but we knew the Precursors were more advanced than anyone we know."

Victoria came over to stand next to her.

"And if it's a starcom, the transmission chamber is here," she said, pointing at a specific set of chambers. "And if the Precursors think anything like the current generation of races, they'll have kept their administration center near the transmission chambers...and somewhere in there, they'll have a map of at least their nearby starcoms."

"You're brilliant," Morgan said, staring at the map and following Victoria's line of thought. She stepped over and haloed the area with the haptics over the screen. "Let me send a note to Major Phelps," she continued. "Then, I promise you, I will *actually* take some off-duty time."

CHAPTER SEVENTEEN

THE VIDEO FEED FROM THE TEAM OF DIVERS WAS ALMOST nausea-inducing. Even with the auto-stabilizing, the swimmers' cameras were following their eyes and it didn't travel the way the brain expected.

"There it is," Major Phelps concluded as he led his team into the transmission core. "I recognize this stuff. Doesn't look quite right, but I agree with Commander Antonova. This is a starcom, all right."

Most of *Bellerophon*'s senior officers were gathered in the Captain's day room as they watched the feed. Morgan had actually managed to get some rest the previous night—once Antonova was through with her, at least—and was feeling better about this whole situation than she had before.

"Do we think they stuck to tags and computers in here?" Captain Vong asked. "Are we likely to find *anything* useful?"

"If there's anything useful, anything the Taljzi would have used to find a new destination, it's probably here," Morgan pointed out. "And the area is deep enough that it might have taken them years to get down here. We just have to deal with water. They had to deal with convincing the Precursors' bloody clever doors that pretend to be walls to open."

The Precursors built their bases, ships and doors out of a material very similar to the mobile microbot layer that supported modern Imperial starship armor. The doors looked like walls until given power and a command, at which point they opened.

All of those doors that the human teams had encountered were already open.

"We know the Taljzi found something worth packing up the entire colony and moving for," Antonova added. "So, there had to be something."

"Having spent three days on this planet, I can tell you that I'd pack up the entire colony and move for the location of a Snickers bar," Phelps told them. "For an ice cream shop, I'd do it in *seconds*."

"You're under half a kilometer of water, Major," Captain Vong said. "You can't be *that* hot."

"We're also inside a volcano, sir. The water is seventy-five degrees Celsi—"

"Major?" Vong asked. "Do we still have a link?"

"We do," Phelps replied, the banter of a moment before completely gone. "I just lost the link to one of my forward Guards. Moving to investigate. Stand by."

"Good luck, Major," the Captain replied, then hit a command that muted the microphone in his day room.

"I think we can wait until the Major has found his missing trooper before we continue backseat driving this mission, don't you?" he said mildly.

THE NEXT FEW minutes were fraught with tension as the group of officers, over thirty thousand kilometers away, watched several video feeds as the Guards traveled deeper into the watery depths of the Precursor communication facility.

And then those feeds cut off. One by one. First Phelps, then his Guards.

"Sergeant, report," Vong finally ordered gently as he opened a link to the senior remaining NCO.

"I'm not sure, Captain," the Guard admitted. "We're holding position, trying to get a visual. The drone we sent after the Major went dead as well. No sign of violence."

"We've got to be looking at jamming or something similar," Antonova said. "If they're all going quiet at the same point..."

"Can you flag the border, Commander?" Vong asked—but Morgan and Antonova were already on it.

Red dots started appearing on the map, marking the turns in several corridors deeper from the starcoms central transmission chambers.

"There's your line," Antonova said grimly. "Looks like a straight cut about five meters below the transmission chamber. Anyone who goes deeper, we lose."

"*Testing, testing. Can you hear me?*" a voice came in—and Major Phelps's video feed returned simultaneously.

"We hear you, Major. What the hell happened?" Vong asked.

"I don't have a clue, sir," Phelps admitted. "We lost coms at one point, but I kept going to try and find my people...and then we lost all electronics. The suits are tough on their own, but it's hard to move without the powered muscles."

"You still have people in that zone?" the Captain demanded.

"We're setting up a reel and line now, and then I'm going back in to grab them," Phelps replied. "The oxygen systems will work for a bit without power, but right now my priority is getting my people out."

"Agreed. I'll touch base with the other ground teams and have help and medics on the way," Vong told the Guard. "Our people come first, Major."

IT TOOK over half an hour to get the Guards pulled back out to where their suits were working and everyone had communications. No one appeared to have been significantly injured, but there was some clear concern about trying to go deeper.

"It appears we're looking at some kind of Precursor defense system," Morgan concluded. "Power-dampening field of some kind." She shook her head. "I have no idea how that would work, but that's par for the course for Precursor tech.

"I'm guessing the Taljzi made it through somehow."

"You could do it," Phelps confirmed. "They pumped out a lot more of the water than we did, but you could also do it with chemical lights and extended oxygen lines. Images would be harder."

"There's something down there," the Guard who'd gone silent first interjected when she got her breath back. "Looked like some kind of galaxy model. Stars, nebula... Was hard to see in the dark, though."

"That, it seems, is what we're looking for," Vong said. "All right, Major. Pull your people back out of the water for now. We'll go over the flotilla's resources.

"I know we can pull together oxygen lines and chemical lights, but I have to wonder if we have *anything* resembling a non-electronic camera aboard our starships."

Morgan had to swallow a chuckle. An old-fashioned chemical-exposure camera was the answer, the Captain was right...but he was also right that it was extraordinarily unlikely that they had a water-proof exposure camera on a fleet of super-modern interstellar warships.

CHAPTER EIGHTEEN

Grand Priestess Shalla Amane impressed Annette—though hardly in a positive way. She'd never known anyone who was so able to spin practically nothing into days upon days of meetings.

They'd sorted out the peace treaty and nonaggression pact in less than two days, maybe four hours of meetings, once Amane had actually deigned to meet with Annette.

It had taken five more days to sort out a second series of meetings, which had proven pointless. Annette had now been on Kanarj for almost a month with nothing to show for it.

Thankfully, she had a solid link back to the Imperium through a series of covert hyperfold relays. That relay link was also serving the Imperium's intelligence efforts, she was certain, but it kept her informed on what was going on as well.

The Taljzi had not rematerialized. Tan!Shallegh was at Sol with the Grand Fleet. The Militia scouting force had found an early Taljzi exile colony and was digging for answers.

They had time. So far. Annette was starting to be grimly certain that these negotiations weren't going to go anywhere until and unless the Taljzi returned and started blowing up planets again.

"Grand Priestess Amane has arrived for your meeting," her aide, Maria Robin-Antionette, told her. The blonde woman was one half of the married pair of women who kept Annette's life and media presence running in a sane fashion.

Her wife was back on Earth with their children, however, continuing in her job of Director of Public Relations for the Duchy of Terra. Unlike Jess, though, Maria Robin-Antionette went where her Duchess did.

She was far more than a secretary, and more than one political career in the Duchy had come to a screaming halt due to treating her as one.

"Let her wait," Annette decided, looking at her half-finished mug of coffee. "I'm going to need this caffeine to put up with her, and I think she needs a reminder of which one of us is responsible for the genocidal maniacs at everybody's door."

She took a long sip of the coffee.

"Of course, our Grace," Robin-Antionette responded, and Annette sighed.

"You only call me that when I'm wrong," she pointed out. "Am I being petty?"

"Yes," her aide replied crisply. "I don't blame you...but the Grand Priestess is just as powerful and influential a figure in the Theocracy as you are in the Imperium. We taunt her at our peril."

Annette sighed and finished her coffee in one large gulp.

"As usual, you're right," she conceded. "Make sure someone delivers more coffee to the meeting room. I get the feeling I'm going to need it."

GRAND PRIESTESS AMANE WAS ACCOMPANIED, as always, by a pair of Oathbound slaves. Annette wasn't familiar with the species, a stocky bipedal race slightly taller than the Kanzi with reptilian scales in iridescent colors.

They were entirely unclothed and their scales had been polished, resulting in a glittering rainbow effect that even Annette had to admit was gorgeous. She was more than a little disturbed by the use of sentient beings as mobile decoration, though.

One of the slaves was pouring Amane a glass of water as Annette entered the room, and the Priestess was eyeing the pot of coffee waiting by the Duchess's spot.

Annette took her seat wordlessly and poured herself a cup of coffee. *Her* two companions were bodyguards, unarmed but commando-power-armored Ducal Guards. She could pour her own drinks.

"*Must* you insist on taking stimulants before every one of these meetings?" Amane asked disdainfully.

"It's a warm, delicious alternative to giving up on this whole affair," Annette replied in a forced sweet tone.

The Grand Priestess sniffed derisively. The similarities between human and Kanzi body language were downright eerie at times.

"You have been advised of our High Priestess's requirements," she told Annette. "We can continue to argue around the details if you wish, Duchess, but you have yet to answer whether the Imperium will provide the technology the Divine Chosen has requested."

"We both know I don't have the authority to agree to that," Annette demurred. "It's being debated on A!To, though I must admit the odds are low. As your 'Divine Chosen' knew when she made that demand."

"And just what are you implying, Duchess Bond?"

"I am not implying anything," she replied, putting down her coffee cup and glaring at the Kanzi. "I am *stating* that you are not negotiating in good faith. You don't appear to want this alliance. There are powerful factions in the Imperium that would leave you to face the Taljzi alone. They are, after all, a monster of your creation."

"We did not destroy a star to defeat them," Amane replied. "That was *your* people."

Annette smiled.

"And if it becomes necessary, we shall do so again," she told the Kanzi. "I am not concerned about the Imperium's ability to defend ourselves against your prodigal genocides. We have defeated them already and we will stop them again.

"Can you say the same, Grand Priestess?"

"We are the Great Church of the Faces of God," Amane said sharply. "Our sword does not bend; our fleet does not yield. We do not fear the Taljzi."

"Then why are the two of us even here?" Annette asked. "If the Imperium doesn't really care about this alliance and the Kanzi don't want it...perhaps I should just pack up and go home."

She started to rise, but Amane remained seated, studying her.

"Sit down, Duchess Bond," the Grand Priestess requested. "Please."

That was the first time Annette had heard anything even resembling *please* from a Kanzi.

"Why?" she asked gently.

"Because we do need this alliance. Both of us," Amane told her. "Because if the Taljzi have the power to move against us, they will. If they have the strength to bring the fire and the sword against either or both of us, they will.

"As we believe we are charged by the Greatest God to protect and guide Her lesser images, the Taljzi believed they are charged to *destroy* them. The A!Tol would not be targets in their own right, but your own race? The Yin? The Indiri?

"The Taljzi would put all of these to the sword...and they would shatter the Great Church and warp the survivors into that sword."

Amane shook her head.

"There are limits and conditions on what either of our empires can accept, but we must find a compromise or my wayward kin will kill us all."

Annette slowly sank back into her seat.

"All right," she conceded. "Then what *can* we compromise on, Grand Priestess?"

She wasn't sure this meeting was going to be any more successful than most of the others, but it was starting to sound like it might at least be more productive.

CHAPTER NINETEEN

"Oceans of sun and shadow."

Tan!Shallegh's curse came through the translator in an almost prayerful tone, and Jean couldn't help but smile.

He'd had much the same reaction the first time he'd taken a ship *through* Jupiter's atmosphere to the bubble of open vacuum maintained by massive shield generators. Five hundred kilometers beneath the surface of the immense gas giant, this was DragonWorks.

If you looked closely enough at the massive space station that was the heart of the facility, you could still find the ring station that Elon Casimir had converted into his secret BugWorks research facility forty years earlier.

That station, hidden in the asteroid belt, had spawned humanity's version of the interface drive, among other technologies. After the standoff between the Core Powers in Alpha Centauri, the same concept had been applied here: a station was a hidden research base where the A!Tol Imperium's best scientists worked around the clock to reverse-engineer technology begged, borrowed and stolen from the Core Powers.

DragonWorks contained the only samples of Precursor technology outside Mesharom territory, too.

Jean wasn't sure how long that would last. The Mesharom were, from what Annette had said, *furious* that humanity had recreated Precursor tech on their own.

"How many ships are here?" Tan!Shallegh asked, the squid-like alien focusing on what had to be the key item to him.

"Elon?" Jean turned to Casimir, the Ducal Consort standing with him and the Fleet Lord as they surveyed the Consort's baby.

"DragonWorks currently has eight *Bellerophon*-B class ships under construction and two *Galileo*-class ships," Casimir reeled off. "The *Galileo*s are new, super-battleships built on the same design schema as the *Bellerophon*s."

"Are they being adjusted for the same changes as the B-type ships?" Tan!Shallegh asked instantly.

"Yes," Casimir confirmed. "All the lessons we learned from the *Bellerophon*s going to war have been incorporated into the *Galileo* design. And the refit designs we're implementing on your fleet."

"In my experience, there is a vast gap, Consort Casimir, between a refitted ship and a ship designed from the ground up with that technology," Tan!Shallegh pointed out. "Our *Duchess of Terra*–class ships are powerful and capable units, but they pale in comparison to the *Vindication*s. I suspected our refitted *Vindication*s will see similar comparisons to the *Galileo*s.

"When will they swim our waters?"

"Not soon," Casimir admitted. "*Bellerophon*-Bs will be six months, just under a long-cycle. *Galileo* and *Socrates* will be ten. Three hundred–odd cycles."

Most humans could translate between Terran and A!Tol calendars in their head at this point. Especially the Duchy's leadership.

"The tides can be moved by no creature's will," Tan!Shallegh conceded. "Do we have any new systems coming across the ocean for us?"

"A few. Nothing as dramatic as the hyperspace missiles," Casimir confirmed. "Jean?"

"We have a tour scheduled," Jean told the alien fleet commander. "Casimir is more familiar with the science side of it than I am. I just sign the checks these days."

Jean wasn't as familiar with A!Tol skin colors as he was with their fleets and politics...but he was quite certain that the repeated flicker of red across Tan!Shallegh's skin was the equivalent to a chuckle.

"IS THAT...WHAT I think it is?" Tan!Shallegh asked slowly some time later. They hadn't yet made it aboard any of the under-construction warships. Instead, Casimir had taken them to an isolated research station, well away from the rest of the facility.

"If you think it's a crude microsingularity power core, you're right," Casimir told him.

"I thought ours weren't working yet?" Jean asked. The basic concept behind the singularity core was relatively straightforward: contain a black hole with the mass of a few planets and feed it piece by piece into a matter converter.

A planetary-mass black hole didn't radiate much, but it was still a *very* dense source of material for the mass-to-energy conversion process. If you had it controlled...

"Is it *safe* to have this here?"

"This version survived crash testing in deep interstellar space before we ever brought it home," the Ducal Consort replied. "As did the previous two."

"And how many before that didn't?" Jean asked.

"Seventeen. We've been *careful*, Jean. We haven't lost a single person along the way." Casimir shook his head. "We've lost twenty test platforms and a frankly ridiculous number of sensor drones, but no one has died."

"An expensive proposition," Tan!Shallegh noted. "Has it been successful?"

Casimir gestured through the window. Compressed-matter struts held a containment chamber in the center of a spherical empty space. The gravity and electromagnetic fields active in the space were actually *visible* in the ripples they caused in the air.

"We're still working on proper containment," he admitted. "That containment chamber you see is almost eighty times the size of the one in the Precursor ship—and the rest of that reactor chamber is still unsafe.

"And our power production is half of what we think the Mesharom are getting in a quarter of the space, let alone what the Precursors got."

"And?" Jean queried.

"We've sorted out the interface drive field interactions, thanks to our Mesharom friend giving *Bellerophon* the calculations necessary to get close to DLK-5539. Once we get the containment fields sorted —and we're close, gentlemen—we'll have something we can produce.

"It won't be anything resembling mass production. The singularities themselves are *hell* to manufacture, but we'll start around one singularity power plant every thirty cycles. We'll scale from there."

"How much power?" Tan!Shallegh asked. "That's a significant investment in time just for the production, even ignoring the research investment."

Casimir grinned and quoted a number.

Jean blinked.

"That's four times the production of one of the matter-conversion plants," he said in a stunned voice.

"And a matter-conversion plant needs to be refueled," Casimir agreed. "A singularity core has a *hundred-year* life expectancy." He shrugged. "Of course, at that point, you need to replace the entire core and toss the remains of the old one into the plant that's making new singularities.

"As we saw on Centauri, the core will continue to produce *some* power for a very, *very* long time. But useful levels are sustained for about a century. Two hundred long-cycles, give or take."

"One of these would replace the entire power requirements of a *Bellerophon*," Tan!Shallegh pointed out.

"Our designs call for using two for redundancy, with a pair of matter converters for backup," Casimir said. "The extra power should allow us to upgun both the plasma lance and the hyperfold cannons."

"And the Mesharom version is better?" Jean asked.

"Best guess is twice the power in a quarter the space," the engineer confirmed. "What we have on the Taljzi suggests something comparable, if not superior. I'd give a lot for an intact Taljzi warship."

"We captured a transport, did we not?" Jean said.

"By destroying its power plants," Casimir said. "Which was the only way to stop the crew destroying the ship with everyone aboard, so I don't expect to get my hands on a Taljzi power plant anytime soon."

"We shall have to see waters we can swim in the future," Tan!Shallegh replied. "If we can capture enemy vessels, we shall, but I do not expect our foes to be so cooperative."

"So, we're looking at new power-generation options," Jean continued after a moment. "Anything else we should be showing the Fleet Lord?"

Casimir shrugged.

"We're working on a better interface-drive missile and extending the range of the hyperfold cannons, but none of that's ready for deployment," he admitted. "We should be able to get our missiles up to the point eight five *c* we think is the theoretical maximum within a long-cycle or two. Most other things are still in the air.

"There's a lot of experiments and testing going on here in DragonWorks," he concluded. "A lot of it goes nowhere. Some of it is game-changing. I don't think we're going to get anything as dramatic as the Gold Dragon suite for a while yet, though."

"I will be content with arming my fleet with hyperspace

missiles," Tan!Shallegh said. "Those alone will finally bring the A!Tol Imperium into the same weight class as the Core Powers."

"Speaking of which...do we know if there's been any luck in the attempts to convince the Core Powers to get involved with the Taljzi?" Casimir asked.

Jean looked uncomfortable and gestured for Tan!Shallegh to answer.

"The Mesharom see the Taljzi's use of Precursor tech as their problem, so they have ships coming," the Fleet Lord replied. "They have a long way to go, though. We'll start seeing their Frontier Fleet battlecruisers soon, but their true warships are still a long-cycle away.

"As for the other Core Powers..." He fluttered his manipulator tentacles in a shrug. "The Laian Republic has agreed to make sure none of the other Core Powers interfere. Given that the Reshmiri are eventually going to realize we stole their matter converters, that's not without value, but it's not war-dreadnoughts in the front line, either."

"So, it's down to us," Jean told Casimir. "Us, the Mesharom, and the Kanzi if the Duchess succeeds. And right now, we're swinging in the dark until Rear Admiral Sun finds something."

"That should have been an Imperial mission," Tan!Shallegh said calmly, the alien studying the prototype singularity core as yellow and purple anger and disappointment rippled over his skin.

"We had the ship with the gravity scanners and we had the ships to spare for the scouting flotilla," Jean replied. "The mission couldn't wait, Fleet Lord. We needed to act."

"Those waters are clear enough," the Fleet Lord allowed. "But your people's impetuousness is going to get you in trouble eventually."

CHAPTER TWENTY

"And I think today's lesson is never to underestimate a ship's engineering Chiefs," Antonova murmured.

This time, the video feed was coming to the bridge. Morgan and Antonova were on duty and watching the Guard make their second attempt to penetrate the strange "dark zone" inside the Precursor communications base.

One of *Squall's* senior engineering Chief Petty Officers had turned out to be a serious aficionado of pre-digital camera work. With full access to the machine shops of the flotilla and the know-how of the *rest* of the engineering CPOs aboard the ships, she'd not only managed to produce waterproof cameras but an entirely mechanical and chemical waterproof *video* camera.

Morgan didn't even pretend to understand how that worked—something to do with reels of tiny cellulose frames being fed through the exposure light by a manual crank—but the Guards were now carrying the fruits of the flotilla's machine shops into the murky depths.

"Camera team has crossed the blackout line," Phelps reported.

"Oxygen lines are flowing steadily and the chemical lights just came up."

Whoever had designed the emergency chemical lights the Ducal Militia had acquired had made them extremely multipurpose. In their default state, they provided bright waterproof light for about five hours. With an additional additive, conveniently packaged with the tubes, they also put off a significant amount of heat and could be used for both emergency heat and cooking.

"How deep are we going?" Morgan asked on the coms channel.

"We've got a kilometer of oxygen tubing here for each of them," Phelps reported. "And the same for an emergency team to go after them if needed." He paused. "Thankfully, we managed to dig up some waterproof guns. I wouldn't want to use them against anyone with real armor...but no one is going down this hole in real armor."

Real guns, as Morgan understood it. The old-fashioned chemical burners that had been on the edge of obsolescence for almost two centuries before the Imperium showed up. It said everything about the accuracy of most of those claims of obsolescence that the Ducal Guard and the Imperial Marines, who used nerve stunners and plasma guns as their primary arms, still kept chemical firearms in their armories.

Minutes ticked by in silence as the oxygen tubing continued to coil out. Morgan managed to keep herself from checking the time more than once every five minutes or so, watching the video feed from the backup team with one eye as she continued her work.

"There's the signal," Phelps suddenly reported. "Three tugs on the tubing. We're starting to rewind the coil and they are coming back up."

"Think they found something, Major?" Morgan asked.

"They had two hours of film and they were only down there for fifty-five minutes," he replied. "I think we found something."

ALL OF THE senior officers of the flotilla were linked into the video-conference as the analysts finished turning the pictures and video footage into a three-dimensional model of what the Guard divers had found.

"It looks like a regional map," Morgan explained to them. She'd been pigeonholed as the flotilla's xenocultural expert for now, which was fine. They had entire university departments available at a few hours' transmission lag. When they moved out of what she was comfortable with, they could send it on.

They were sending it all on anyway. She was a tactical officer with a minor and a hobby. The PhDs were going to make so much more out of this.

Interpreting the data as a regional map, though, was pretty easy. The small models had once hung from the ceiling on stiff wires. The water had preserved them handily, though she suspected not all of the positions were quite right anymore.

"Unfortunately, there's no legend in the room," she pointed out. "I suspect the Taljzi already had a working knowledge of Precursor iconography. We don't."

With a swipe of her hand, she cleared away the water and the wires and the room the model had been in. A three-dimensional projection of the Precursor map now hung in front of everyone on the conference call.

"This is our current location." She haloed the central star, marked in bronze. "Commander Hume has confirmed that the stars line up with the local region...once we account for the expected sixty thousand years of stellar drift."

The Mesharom, the galaxy's current elder race and a tentative ally of the Imperium, had crawled their way *back* into space about forty thousand years ago. They'd once been a subject race of the Precursors and had been knocked back into the Stone Age by whatever hellstorm had destroyed their masters and the other subject races.

"Most of the stars are done in plain steel," she continued. "With over a thousand stars represented on this map, I think we have to assume that means those systems didn't have a Precursor presence."

"This system's Precursor presence makes no sense to me," Captain Vong admitted. "Why have a starcom and nothing else?"

"They almost certainly didn't, Captain," Rear Admiral Sun said grimly. "While your crew has focused on the moon, the rest of the flotilla has been examining the rest of the star system. My current guess is that this was an anchorage of some kind, a refueling base with R&R facilities on the surface. They used the geothermal energy from the volcano to power their planetside systems, including the starcom, but most of their presence was in space.

"After sixty thousand years, the orbits are all decayed. There's enough debris left for us to reasonably project the presence of multiple significant structures, but they're now either in the star or the gas giant. No use to us."

"And anything that was left, the Taljzi probably took with them," Vong said with a sigh. "That makes sense, at least. My apologies, Commander Casimir. If those stars are unmarked, I'm guessing some *are* marked?"

"Yes, sir," she confirmed. Seventeen stars on the map lit up.

"There are ten stars marked in copper," she noted. "One of those is relatively close, but they're scattered across a region of space almost a hundred and fifty light-years in diameter." The closest copper star haloed more brightly.

"There are also five stars marked in gold"—those flashed—"and two marked in silver. There are specific images present on all seventeen different stars, but we don't have a lexicon of the Precursor language or iconography."

"So, there were seventeen systems in this area that the Precursors had an interest in," Sun concluded. "Some were probably colonies. Some were probably military bases. Some were research facilities. One of them is where the Taljzi have settled, likely one with a Precursor cloning facility.

"Any suggestions on what we check out first?" he asked Morgan.

She swallowed. She'd half-expected that, but it was still terrifying to basically be asked to pick the next destination of the flotilla.

The copper icon closest to them flashed again as she tapped a command.

"We designated this system PC-One—Precursor Copper One," she noted. "It's just over eleven light-years from here and is the closest of the seventeen flagged systems. Without any basis to decide between the three types of system we're seeing, I think distance is our best filter."

It was also on the vector they'd originally been following, though Morgan was reasonably sure that was pure coincidence now.

"I agree," Sun said after a moment. "We've spent a lot of time here, people. More than I really wanted to, but it looks like it was worth it." He looked around. "We're going to leave *Stormcloud* here to continue the review. I've requested that Admiral Rolfson send a team, either under his wife or recommended by her, to complete a full xenoarchaeological workup on this colony."

Admiral Harold Rolfson was now the second-ranking officer of the Duchy of Terra Militia, charged with the security of the Asimov System after the battle there. Most importantly for Sun's comment, though, his wife was humanity's premier xenoarcheologist, Dr. Ramona Wolastoq.

"The rest of us will move out at oh eight hundred GMT tomorrow," he ordered crisply. "PC-One is our next stop. I'm not expecting it to be the final answer, people, but I think Commander Casimir is right: it's the best target for now."

And after that, Morgan knew, they had sixteen more targets.

The Taljzi, after all, had packed up an entire colony and left after finding this map. They'd been able to read it and that meant that one of those seventeen systems had been important enough for them to move their entire fleet.

CHAPTER TWENTY-ONE

"DUCHESS BOND!"

Annette looked up as Robin-Antionette barged into the suite the Kanzi had oh-so-genteelly provided her. Since she'd refused to have slaves taking care of her, her aide was acting as her effective butler, managing the staff of three people that Annette had brought down to Kanarj with her.

"Yes, Maria?" she asked calmly. She wasn't exactly dressed, currently clad in a loosely tied warm dressing gown, but Robin-Antionette had seen worse. She'd once rushed in on Annette and Elon while the latter was tied to a four-poster bed with silk ropes.

"Captain Mamutse is reporting in from orbit," Robin-Antionette told her. "They've been watching local traffic from *Tornado,* and there was just a huge arrival: almost two dozen super-battleships, plus escorts."

That *was* a huge arrival. It increased the forces present in the Arjzi system by almost twenty-five percent.

"What are they doing here?" Annette asked.

"He said he was going to make contact with the local Navy presence and try and work that out," her aide replied. "He should know by the time you're dressed and able to call him."

Annette chuckled and wagged a finger at her assistant.

"Just for that, I'm tempted to call him like this," she told her.

"You are, of course, the Duchess of Terra, your grace," Robin-Antionette replied brightly.

Laughing, Annette rose to get dressed. There was still a chill running down the back of her neck as she did so, though.

There was no way more than two squadrons of Kanzi super-battleships had arrived in Arjzi unexpectedly, but the Kanzi hadn't bothered to warn her or her people. There were eight *Imperial* super-battleships in orbit. While neither Annette or her subordinates were inclined to start an incident, those capital ships could cause a lot of damage if they were threatened.

She would have warned her if the positions had been reversed, but it seemed the Kanzi were still going to play games.

CAPTAIN TINASHE MAMUTSE looked like the unexpected arrival of twenty-plus potentially hostile super-battleships was the most exciting thing that had happened to him in weeks.

It probably was.

"Well, Captain? Did our hosts decide to illuminate us on who arrived?" Annette asked.

"Eventually," Mamutse confirmed. "After Fleet Lord !Olarski offered to help protect Kanarj against the potentially hostile ships. I think they decided they'd rather tell us what was going on than watch us shoot at their current hero."

"*Hero*, is it?" Annette murmured. "Cawl?"

Fleet Master Shairon Cawl had been in command of the Kanzi forces in the region when the Taljzi had arrived. Unlike his Imperial and Terran counterparts, the old Kanzi warrior hadn't had direct lines of communication to his superiors. He'd decided to make an alliance with the Imperium to stand against the Taljzi entirely on his own authority.

He'd saved untold millions of lives on both sides of the border by doing so—but tens of millions of Kanzi and their slaves had died in his area of operations before the Taljzi had been stopped.

"Shairon Cawl, yes, your grace," Mamutse confirmed. "He's apparently arriving with a portion of his fleet to meet with the High Priestess and receive a medal for his actions against the Taljzi. I've sent a request back along the hyperfold relay for our information on the whole thing."

"It wouldn't be entirely out of the question for High Priestess Karal to hang an award around his neck for saving the day and then order him executed for the people who died, would it?" Annette asked.

"Not from my understanding of Kanzi politics," Mamutse agreed. "The ambassador might be a better one to talk to there."

"That's true. Thank you for the update, Captain," Annette said briskly. "I think I need to call the ambassador."

If nothing else, Ambassador Rejalla should be able to get Annette into the damn room while Reesi Karal was deciding Shairon Cawl's fate...and somehow, Annette felt that she should be there for that.

Cawl had, after all, saved tens of millions of *human* lives at Asimov.

⸻

"CAWL IS *HERE*?" Rejalla asked, the translator picking up her incredulity.

"Headed into orbit aboard a super-battleship," Annette confirmed. "I take it the 'Great Church' didn't tell you either, huh?"

"They don't tell the Imperial embassy anything, your grace," Rejalla admitted. "The Kanzi government only talks to us when they need to." The Anbrai shivered in a full-body equivalent to a headshake.

"Can you get me into his audience with the High Priestess?" Annette asked. "Assuming that he has one?"

"They didn't recall the Fleet Master who just fought one of the biggest battles in the last three hundred long-cycles to Kanarj for him to quietly retire to a sunny field," the ambassador replied. "He's either here to be commended or executed."

"Potentially both?"

"Potentially both," Rejalla agreed. "While there's an understanding that I'm not actually allowed to use it *often*, I have an open pass for two individuals to attend the Divine Court. *Technically*, we have to go through the full purification rituals along the way, but the reality is that most of the people with a pass go through a much-abbreviated version."

"I think I saw that one," Annette said. "It was still bloody long."

"Then you're probably thinking of the right one," the ambassador admitted. "I can get us in. Any particular reason, your grace?"

"If possible, I want to talk to Cawl," she replied. "And I want to know where the old warlord stands with his people when I do so. Best way I can think of to make sure of both is to be there when he meets the High Priestess."

"Makes as much sense as anything else on this mount of rotten stone," Rejalla said. "I'll get us in, and I'll see what I can arrange for you meeting Cawl afterwards. I can't promise anything, though. My contacts are political. He's a soldier."

"He fought shoulder to shoulder with our people," Annette said. "So long as we can get the message to him, I'm sure he'll meet with me."

"Likely." The big Anbrai shook herself again. "Be careful, though. Cawl is a known reformist. Meeting with him may not look good for either of you."

"I am the Empress's personal representative," Annette noted quietly. "If the Kanzi want to cause me trouble, *let them try*."

ONCE AGAIN, Annette found herself led through the six shrines, with the six sets of burning herbs and the six sets of anointing oils. The path then led her through what she *thought* was a different garden atrium with the same type of waterfall-washed path and into the glorified bleachers of the throne room.

"The least they could do would be provide blow-dryers," Rejalla grumped, the ambassador's dark brown fur still clearly damp from the waterfall. "There's more reasons than one that I don't attend court in this mountain-shadowed place."

Annette kept her peace as she and the ambassador headed to the seats set aside for them. Her status had gone far enough to get their bodyguards into the court, but not far enough to get those bodyguards *seats*.

The pair of power-armored Ducal Guards settled in behind her and Rejalla with grace, however. From her own experience, she knew the suits could lock in place and keep them relatively comfortable while they were standing.

Potentially more comfortable than they would have been on the stone seats designed for a species that averaged a good forty centimeters shorter than Annette. Even here, in the section set aside for ambassadors, the Kanzi had made no effort to design seats to accommodate anyone else.

Rejalla took one look at the seat and settled herself onto the floor like an immense cat. There was no way the Anbrai was folding herself into the stone chairs.

They were *slightly* more comfortable than the floor for Annette. Probably. Her legs were awkwardly positioned, but she was at least sitting as she looked out over Reesi Karal's throne room.

There was a more martial tone to the room today than there had been when Annette had had her audience. Banners of military regiments hung along what had been a bare roof before, and display cabinets of war trophies had been added to the floor. Several of those trophies—an entire case's worth—were of A!Tol power armor, guns and other military paraphernalia.

High-pitched trumpet-like instruments announced the arrival of the guest of honor, Kanzi Marines in ceremonial armor stepping through the main doors in perfect synchronicity.

Annette eyed the soldiers carefully. They carried swords instead of modern weapons, but something in the way they carried themselves suggested that these were real troops, not parade-ground decorations.

A simple cart rolled forward behind the blue-furred soldiers, guarded by another group of soldiers. The cart held the broken components of several sets of Taljzi power armor and a half-melted golden symbol Annette guessed to be the equivalent of a commissioning seal for one of the Taljzi warships.

Shairon Cawl followed the cart. The old Kanzi Fleet Master was resplendent in a glorious white leather uniform unlike anything Annette had ever seen on a Kanzi before. The cane Cawl required to walk was a length of pure white metal, glittering with bright yellow gemstones along its length.

The Kanzi had some of the darkest fur Annette had ever seen on one of his race, a blue so deep as to be almost purple. Streaks of a grayer blue crisscrossed his visible fur, and a white splash covered a scar that crossed his entire face and covered his right eye. The eye had been regrown, but the scar remained.

His formal uniform was cut to conceal the powered brace Annette knew he wore around his right leg, but he'd made no attempt to hide the cane. He slowly and smoothly approached the High Priestess behind the cart of trophies and carefully bowed to his mistress.

"Your grace, Divine Chosen of God, I present to you the trophies of war from our new enemy," he declared loudly. "Arms and armor taken from the wreckage of the ships of our rogue cousins. The defining symbol of one of their warships. Proof of our victories in the field."

"Your trophies are noted," Karal replied. "First Chamberlain Iril, have them sorted and cataloged to add to the collection."

Sai Iril appeared from behind his mistress's throne with a group of robed slaves. They swiftly removed the cart of trophies from the court as Cawl advanced, slowly, up to the middle of his escort and slowly sank to one knee.

"I am summoned before your grace, Divine Chosen," he said loudly. "What would you have of me?"

The court was silent, hanging on Karal's words.

"Many of our children are dead," the High Priestess told him. "A Fleet Master, killed in battle. Worlds burned clean of life. All in the territory you were charged to defend. What tale have you to tell of this, Fleet Master Cawl?"

Cawl remained kneeling in front of Karal.

"The enemy attacked us with unexpected force and no warning," he said calmly. "We all believed the Taljzi to be no more. My watch was upon the A!Tol, not the Taljzi, and I failed to recognize the new threat in time to save many of the people I was charged to defend."

It wasn't, Annette noted with interest, an excuse. Simply a statement of fact.

"I do not hear a defense, Fleet Master. No justification for your failure."

"There is no justification," Cawl admitted. "I was charged with the security of thirty stars. I failed. That I *avenged* our dead does not bring them back to life. I will accept whatever punishment the Divine Chosen would lay upon me."

To Annette's surprise, Karal did not immediately reply. Instead, the Kanzi High Priestess stepped down from her throne and crossed the stone floor of her court to where Cawl kneeled.

"I *am* the Divine Chosen," she said fiercely as she stood over him. "And in being Chosen, I am given sight beyond others. Even *I* did not foresee the return of the Taljzi, Fleet Master Cawl. Even *I* did not warn you that a horde of murderers was about to descend upon us.

"You may have misjudged your enemy, but none of us believed that she even existed."

Reesi Karal reached down and helped Cawl back to his feet.

"And you avenged our dead. You wisely made peace with the A!Tol to stand together against an enemy that threatened us both. Your wisdom and bravery outweigh an error shared by us all."

She carefully and formally kissed the old Kanzi's forehead.

From the shocked inhalations around the court, Annette guessed that was something meaningful.

Karal's simple white robe didn't look like it had pockets, but she produced a length of chain from somewhere. Even from this distance, Annette could tell that each link in the chain was carved from a single gemstone, bright yellow to match the stone on Cawl's cane.

Presumably the stones were reinforced somehow; otherwise, that chain wouldn't hold up to heavy wear for long.

The High Priestess of the Kanzi laid the golden stone chain around Cawl's neck.

"We proclaim you a Guardian of the Great Church," she said firmly. "A Companion of the Divine Chosen and a worthy warrior of our people. You have faced an enemy we never saw coming and did so with courage and skill.

"We would fail in our duty if we did not recognize this...and your honesty in admitting your own failures, Fleet Master Cawl. Guardian. Companion. *Kanzi.*"

THAT SEEMED to conclude the formalities of this part of the day. Kanzi body language was close enough to human that Annette was reasonably sure that Cawl was completely shocked, but he was still paying attention.

As he bowed stiffly and withdrew, he clearly spotted her in the gathered court. It couldn't have been too difficult—there were less than a dozen non-Kanzi in the audience, and Rejalla was the single largest individual present.

He met Annette's gaze and gave her a slight bow of the head, easily interpreted.

I know you're here. We'll talk later.

There weren't many species that could manage cross-cultural nonverbal communication. For all that the Kanzi and humans had effectively been in a state of cold war for as long as they'd known the other existed, they were among those few.

"Okay," Annette breathed out. "Care to explain all that to the poor woman who just has to deal with it?"

The last of Cawl's guards had withdrawn and Karal had returned to her throne like she'd never left it. A new set of petitioners was being announced—and, unfortunately, the passes they'd used meant they were trapped there for at least another two hours.

"Companion of the Divine Chosen was what the kiss was about," Rejalla said first. "At one point in the past, the Companions were the Divine Chosen's lovers. She kept a stable of warriors and warlords who were expected to service the needs of her flesh at her whim.

"Since they were the lovers of the High Priestess, they were untouchable," the ambassador noted. "That got formalized into something similar to diplomatic immunity, even as the other aspects of it faded. Cawl being...five times Karal's age, I doubt she wants him to service her."

Annette wasn't sure how close Kanzi were to humans on that scale, but she could certainly see reasons why a *human* in Karal's place might take Cawl to her bed. Not all of them were reasons of state, either, though having a reformist fleet commander emotionally attached to her would probably serve the High Priestess's whims.

"The kiss is all that's left of that," Rejalla continued. "But being declared a Companion means Cawl is above all question and prosecution. No one except Karal can judge him now...though Karal can still order him executed without reason."

Annette shivered at the *still* in that sentence. The Duchy of Terra functioned as a constitutional monarchy, as did the A!Tol Imperium. She was used to people with noble titles and vast power— she *was* one of them—but those people also had strict limits on what they could do with that power.

Reesi Karal did not.

"And I'm guessing Guardian is an award for valor and courage?" Annette asked. Equivalent to an old English knighthood, if she was reading the subtext correctly.

"Exactly. Like the Companion title, it used to mean something else, but the High Priestess is guarded by an entire army now, not a small team of elite warriors—and the Guardians always tended to serve more as generals than bodyguards."

"So, she's showing as much approval for his actions as is practically possible," the Duchess concluded. "Given that Cawl pushed for the alliance I'm supposed to negotiate, I can't help thinking that's a good thing."

"Cawl's a reformist, if a quiet one," Rejalla replied. "The more influence he gets, the better. The faster we can undermine the Kanzi institution of slavery, the more comfortable I am with this alliance."

Annette nodded but sighed.

"And that attitude is exactly what Karal is afraid of, isn't it?" she asked.

"I understand where she comes from," the ambassador replied. "I still have no sympathy for the system she defends."

Neither did Annette, when it came down to it.

CHAPTER TWENTY-TWO

"Fleet Master Cawl's people reached out to us while you were trapped in court," Robin-Antionette told Annette as the Duchess returned to their suite. "He's extending an invitation to you and Ambassador Rejalla to join him for a private dinner in his penthouse in the city."

Annette closed her eyes with a sigh. Only Maria Robin-Antionette was around, which meant she could *do* things like that. Self-control was an ironclad rule for her in most places, but it was even more important on a functionally hostile planet.

"Which city?" she asked.

"I'm sorry, let me clarify," Robin-Antionette said drily. "The City."

The capital letter was clear this time and Annette chuckled.

"I'm guessing the one around the plateau the Golden Palace is built on?" she asked. "The Kanzi do seem to go in for declaratives for this area."

"Exactly. The Fleet Master keeps a penthouse here for when he's on planet, managed by his daughters while he's away."

"They must love it when he comes home," Annette considered

aloud. If his daughters had access to a Fleet Master's penthouse in the capital, she suspected it saw a *lot* of use when Cawl wasn't around.

"From what Rejalla's files say, the three daughters are wealthy and successful in their own right—but not enough so to own a penthouse in the City," Robin-Antionette agreed. "They make full use of it in his absence, but given that a senior priestess, the equivalent of a corporate CEO and a Kanzi Army Guard Keeper all canceled every plan they had to spend time with him while he was on planet..."

"Cawl's daughters are at least moderately fond of him," Annette concluded. An Army Guard Keeper was equivalent to one of her Ducal Guard Colonels, commanding a force of around five thousand Kanzi. The Fleet Master's daughters had done quite well for themselves.

"Are they going to be at the dinner?" she asked.

"Cawl's aide didn't specify, but the invitation was for tonight and I can't see him taking his first evening on Kanarj entirely away from his daughters," Robin-Antionette pointed out.

"I wouldn't," Annette agreed. She wouldn't even have scheduled anything resembling a working dinner on her first evening back on planet. On the other hand, other than Morgan, her oldest children were still only teenagers. Adults would probably understand better.

"So, how long do I have?" she finally asked.

"Three hours or so. Cawl is assigned several drivers and vehicles while he's on the surface, so he'll send a vehicle for us then."

"All right. I'm going to take a nap and a shower," Annette replied. "I'm guessing uniform for the dinner?"

"That's my read as well," her aide replied. "We'll have it laid out for you."

Annette shook her head with a smile.

"I don't deserve you lot," she told the other woman. "I really don't."

"Keep keeping our planet intact, and I'd say you do," Maria

Robin-Antionette replied. "Now go rest. We have everything under control."

THE "VEHICLE" Cawl sent for them turned out to be an aerial gunship. It was a vectored thrust aircraft with a passenger compartment and an array of modular weapons systems.

Unlike what Annette presumed to be its normal battlefield complement, all of those weapons systems today were purely defensive. She identified a large ECM jammer and what looked like an antimissile laser suite.

She also suspected the passenger compartment wasn't normally filled with comfortably upholstered recliners and a small but staffed wet bar.

Annette and her guards, clad in commando armor instead of all-up power armor for a "social" event, declined alcohol. The Kanzi bartender seemed unsurprised and served up glasses of the blue fruit juice she was starting to get used to.

It was a surprise to her that the bartender was Kanzi, though. She'd seen nine species in that role at various locations since arriving on Kanarj and none of them had been Kanzi. All had been collared slaves, though mostly Oathbound with functionally decorative collars.

"Is the bartender Kanzi because it's a military aircraft?" she murmured to her aide.

"No idea," Robin-Antionette replied. "It would make sense, I suppose. They really don't like having slaves involved in military operations."

"Interesting either way," Annette admitted. "Keep your eyes and ears open, Maria. I've got an odd feeling about this dinner."

"You too, huh?" The perfectly coiffed blonde woman shook her head. "Everything looks aboveboard. Even the rush could be because he has to get back out into space soon, but..."

"But it feels like there's something else going on," Annette agreed. "I wish I could justify us being armed."

Even the Ducal Guards escorting them were only carrying stunners. Annette and Robin-Antionette were both qualified on a number of easily concealed firearms, but she'd chosen to err on the side of trusting Cawl.

"Cawl is on our side, I think," Annette continued. "In many ways, though...I think that might actually be a danger to us."

A KANZI WOMAN in black robes that almost blended with her dark blue fur met them at the landing pad. The familial resemblance to Fleet Master Cawl was striking, and Annette gave the priestess a firm nod.

"I am Duchess Dan!Annette Bond," she introduced herself. "This is my aide, Maria Robin-Antionette."

Ambassador Rejalla was due to arrive shortly after them. A different vehicle had been sent for the Anbrai diplomat.

"Welcome to my father's home," the Kanzi woman greeted them. "I am Priestess Asiri Cawlstar, daughter of Fleet Master Shairon Cawl. If you will follow me, please?"

It seemed the priestess was their hostess tonight, so Annette fell in behind her with practiced grace. Greenery festooned the roof of the apartment building, an entire garden carefully shielded from a landing pad designed to handle everything from their aircraft to a surface-to-orbit shuttle.

The garden appeared a chaotic mess, but from the ease with which Cawlstar guided them through it, Annette presumed there was some order to it. The "chaotic mess" was contained in specifically placed beds of earth, too, so someone had planned it.

She wouldn't have been surprised to discover that the chaos hid at least one security post with armed guards. Fleet Master Cawl was probably the building's most important occupant, but the tower was too close to the Golden Palace itself to be occupied by many nobodies.

Instead of the elevator Annette was expecting, Cawlstar led them to a flight of stairs and down into a glass-walled lobby. The lobby did have a pair of elevators in the middle, but it had two sets of doors leading off to the penthouses.

The lobby split the building in two and was filled with more greenery, glass walls easily carrying the brilliant light of Arjzi through the space.

Security here was more obvious than it had been on the roof. A pair of fully-armored Kanzi soldiers stood outside one of the sets of doors, plasma rifles at port arms as the priestess and her guests approached.

One of the soldiers stepped forward, clearly scanning them. He went over Annette, her aide and her first bodyguard without pausing, then stopped at her second bodyguard.

He held out an armored hand.

"The armor-piercer, please," a translated voice emerged from the suit.

Annette turned an eye on the guard.

"Sergeant?" she asked.

Commando armor only covered the head when fully activated, so the Guard's sheepish look was clearly visible on her face as she extracted a single-shot armor-piercing weapon from under her chest plate. The one-shot was exactly what the name implied...but it would take down a power-armored attacker.

"I am sworn to defend the Duchess," the Sergeant said simply as the Kanzi took the weapon.

"As I am sworn to defend the Fleet Master," the guard said genially. "We will return it when you leave."

The guard took Annette's bodyguard being more armed than promised entirely in stride. Once he'd put away the one-shot, he opened the door for them and gestured them through.

"Come," Priestess Cawlstar instructed. "My father and his other guests are waiting."

Other guests.

As Annette had suspected, this was no social dinner.

IT WAS obvious that no one regularly lived in the penthouse. Annette had a similar residence on Earth, and even after a cleaning staff swarmed over it, it never quite got over the fact that it was occupied by two teenagers, a preteen and a not-quite-toddler.

Cawl's apartment was *pristine*. It was what humanity called "open plan," with almost the entire core area consisting of a single room. If that room had regular sitting areas or anything of the sort, their furniture had been tucked away somewhere.

Instead, four tables had been set up in a large square, enough for at least twenty people. The perimeter of the penthouse was lined with statues of armored Kanzi, ranging from a figure carrying an axe and wearing crude chain mail to a statue of a power-armored Kanzi Marine so realistic, it took Annette a moment to realize it *was* a statue.

Rejalla wasn't there yet but it looked like Annette was otherwise the last to arrive. Shairon Cawl was leaning against the slightly larger table at the far end of the square, next to the windows that looked out over the City. He'd traded the white leather dress uniform for a dark green tunic-style garment that didn't hide the leg brace at all.

And that was telling on its own to Annette. Cawl was a soldier and a politician. If he was showing enough weakness to leave the brace fully visible and to lean against a table, he knew every one of the twenty or so Kanzi in the room—and trusted them completely.

As Asiri Cawlstar led the Duchess and Robin-Antionette over to Cawl himself, Annette was assessing the people as she passed. There were three distinct groups in the room, she noted, each anchored around one of Cawl's daughters.

One group, the one that Cawlstar passed most comfortably through, wore the same long robes as she did. Of the six other robed Kanzi priestesses, three wore the black of senior priestesses like Cawlstar herself, two wore a green color Annette hadn't seen before —and one wore the dark blue of a Grand Priestess, one of the High Priestess's right-hand women.

The second group, effectively holding court around a Kanzi woman in a skintight black dress that wouldn't have looked out of place at a cocktail party on Earth, looked like businesspeople. They had the look of executives and engineers and were the single largest group, with eight of them present.

The last, smallest group—with only five of them there including Cawl's daughter—were soldiers. They were in formal civilian tunics like Cawl himself, but there was no hiding the way they carried themselves. Using the woman who looked like Cawl as a metric, Annette quickly established that they were wearing informal insignia, too.

Cawl's daughter wore a brooch of a sword crossed with a rifle on her shoulder, as did two of her fellow officers. The last two military officers had a similar brooch of a stylized rocket. Navy officers.

Cawlstar led Annette through the crowd to her father and embraced him.

"The guest of honor, esteemed patriarch," she told Cawl.

Tone didn't always carry through the translator, but Annette suspected that the affectionate irony her software was suggesting was bang on. The old Kanzi's daughter was *very* fond of him.

"Duchess Bond," Cawl greeted her. "You've met my eldest daughter." He waved the other two over to him. "Be known as well to Kisan Cawldana and Guard Keeper Streya Cawlan." He indicated the businesswoman and the soldier in turn.

It was hard for Annette to judge Kanzi ages, but she guessed that the three daughters were within a few years of each other.

"It's a pleasure," she told them. "I'll admit, this was more...extensive than I was expecting."

"I apologize," Cawl told her. "I have only a little time on Kanarj before I must return to my fleet. The Divine Chosen wished to honor me in person, but I must serve my duty regardless."

"I know how that goes," she admitted. "I've been here too long, I think."

"And the Great Church's games will keep you longer, I'm afraid," he conceded. There was no response to that, which was interesting. With seven priestesses of the Great Church standing around, Annette would have expected more objection to that kind of comment.

"Come, sit with me," he continued. "Your ambassador will be here shortly, and my chef is looking forward to the challenge of feeding an Anbrai!"

PROBABLY THE BIGGEST surprise was that Cawl's staff had managed to find a seat that was sized and cut for the massive barrel-like torso of the Anbrai ambassador. It was set at Annette's right hand, and Annette was at Cawl's right hand, the place of honor in Kanzi culture as well as many human ones.

If Rejalla towered over Annette, she outright *loomed* over the Kanzi. Annette had between twenty and sixty centimeters on any of the blue-furred humanoids in the room. The ambassador had at least a meter on them all.

Some of the other guests seemed intimidated by that, but Cawl was unbothered.

"My chef has spent all afternoon researching what he can feed you," he told Rejalla. "I hope he comes at least passably close." He smiled. "He was with me at Asimov, so he has experience feeding humans and adapting, so I have hope!"

Rejalla chuckled.

"You might be the first Kanzi not to offer me a platter of

Universal Protein," she pointed out. "I'll give your chef a fair chance before I toss the meal off a mountain."

Universal Protein was a keystone of interstellar trade, shipping and nutrition. Any proteins of any orientation or chemical makeup went into the machine, and a completely harmless base came out. The process wasn't simple, but it produced a food that any species could eat.

That food was basically flavorless gray putty, of course, but that was what spices and species-specific nutrition powders were for.

"I appreciate you giving us the chance," Cawl said with a chuckle. Annette suspected he was talking about more than the food.

That food arrived as he was speaking and Annette had to control her surprise. There were no slaves serving there. There were three servants running around the penthouse, and all of them were Kanzi.

Unlike the bartender on the shuttle, this didn't have the excuse of being a military craft. This was a conscious choice on Cawl's part— and even if he'd only done it for tonight to make a point to the Imperials, it was still a message.

As the first course was cleared away a few minutes later, Annette looked around the room, studying each of the groups. Religious powerbrokers—government, really, here. Corporate CEOs and leaders. Military officers.

"I feel like I should point out, quickly and strongly, that under no circumstances am I permitted to support a coup against the Kanzi Theocracy," she told Cawl.

The room was silent for several long seconds, and then Guard Keeper Cawlan broke into laughter.

"I see my esteemed patriarch is hardly as subtle as he wishes," she said loudly. "No, Duchess Bond, we are not contemplating a coup."

One of the priestesses coughed.

"*Anymore*," she growled.

Cawlan threw up her hands and chuckled again.

"We've had that debate," she admitted. "Even if the A!Tol were prepared to support us, I'd be hesitant to reopen it—and Duchess Bond has made her Imperium's refusal clear."

"Then what is this meeting about?" Annette asked.

"The future," Cawl told her, the old Fleet Master looking tired. "Some of this, Duchess, is about a religious argument of textual interpretation."

Annette paused and raised a hand.

"Okay, that lost me," she admitted.

"Asiri?" Cawl gestured to his priestess daughter.

"There is no real argument in the followers of the Great Church that the Kanzi are the only true and right image of God," Cawlstar told Annette. "I'll concede that is not an opinion that the rest of the galaxy shares, but it is what our scripture tells us, and no variant of the Church has ever argued that point.

"What has been argued, as you well know, is what that status means," she continued. "The Taljzi believed they better knew the mind of our shared God than the rest of our race, hence the name they took for their heresy.

"They believed that all 'imperfect images' of God should be destroyed. This takes a...rather complex and twisted reading of the scripture," the Priestess said carefully. "Indeed, it is entirely unsupported by any version of the documents I have read, leading me to wonder just what text they were referencing."

She shrugged.

"It is quite possible that the Divine Chosen of the time ordered the translation or version of the text they used destroyed. It would be within her authority."

Annette realized she'd apparently volunteered for a history lesson. It was fascinating to see the scholarly side of the Kanzi religion she'd normally only encountered as a justification for conquest and slavery.

"There are several key interpretations of the texts now, followed by various factions and groups inside the Great Church," Cawlstar told her. "The dominant sect for a very long time has been the one you are most familiar with: the one that the Clans use to justify their not-quite-disobedience of the Church's authority and the one that calls for the Kanzi to treat all the lesser children as servants who have not learned their place."

Hopefully, Annette's clenched fists were hidden under the table. That "dominant sect" had tried to kidnap and rape her crew at Tortuga and *had* kidnapped thousands of humans to sell as slaves on the Kanzi homeworld.

She could only be so calm when discussing them.

"There is another major sect, Duchess Bond," Cawlstar said quietly. "Every Kanzi you see in this room is a follower of it. We and the High Priestess and her followers agree on the translation but not on the emphasis."

"I may be lost again," Annette told her hosts.

"*You are called to guard and keep and hold the lesser children, that they may find the true path to God,*" Asiri Cawlstar quoted, the words level and firm.

"We believe, as have others before us, that our God meant for us to stand as guardians of the other peoples, much as the A!Tol do," she told Annette. "We believe that the slavery our people have practiced for so long is a crime in the eyes of our own God, a violation of the charge laid upon us to guard and keep them."

"Reformers," Annette said quietly. "I'm sitting in a room with a bunch of Kanzi reformers."

"Basically," Cawl told her. "We have some political and economic influence. More, I think, than the mainstream church realizes. We have worked to improve the lot of the lesser children in the Theocracy for centuries.

"The alliance with your Imperium is our greatest chance yet. The greatest hope to turn the balance of this argument and truly change the course of our people."

"The government of the Theocracy believes that they have time," Cawlan told Annette. "They are wrong. We are not ready to fight the Taljzi. If they come again, we cannot stop them without the A!Tol."

"Our military leadership realizes this," Cawl finished for his daughter. "But they serve the High Priestess. They follow her orders, and her own faction requires this game. What is most dangerous, however, are those who do what they think Karal *wants* instead of what Karal has *ordered*."

The second course arrived, cutting off Cawl's words as they dug into the admittedly excellent food. Annette was processing everything that had been said and still wasn't sure what the blue-furred aliens wanted from her.

"What do these officers think Karal wants?" she finally asked as she laid her utensils down.

One of the other military officers swallowed hard and laid her hands on the table.

"I am Oath Master Liri Neysallan," she introduced herself. "Commanding officer of the super-battleship *Signs of Glory*. I have been involved in conversations I wish I had never heard, but I cannot keep secret what I have heard, either."

"Tell her, Neysallan," Cawl ordered. "It should be the last time, I think."

"The commanders of the Divine Fleet are all loyalists," Neysallan said quietly. "Fanatics, even for us. They understand that we cannot defeat the Taljzi, but the Taljzi are not their focus. They look at the weapons and ships your Imperium has mustered, and they believe we can't trust you.

"They expect you to break the truce, perhaps even the alliance if it is forged, and invade. With your new fleets, that war would last weeks at most."

Annette was silent. The Imperium didn't want to fight the Kanzi, but they also couldn't allow Kanzi slavery to continue forever. If the Taljzi waited long enough and the Imperium finished refitting their fleet, that kind of invasion was possible. Not *likely*, the Imperium didn't want a war...but possible.

"They see only one area where we remain the equal of the A!Tol Imperium," the starship captain continued. "Our fleet of starkillers."

There was a chill silence to the room now, not just Annette's attempt to conceal a moment of guilt. Given the hesitancy of any sane power to actually *use* the things, it was easy to forget that every Core Power and most of the Arm Powers possessed an arsenal of weapons that could induce artificial supernovas.

Even the Core Powers' version was a big, bulky thing. Annette had once been in possession of a smaller version of the weapon, and she had no idea how it came to be. No one had duplicated those starkillers before or since...and she'd destroyed both the weapons and the people who'd created them.

"Starkillers," she finally said. "And...what are they planning on doing with them?"

"The only way they think that they can guarantee the safety of the Theocracy is to threaten the very existence of the Imperium," Neysallan told her. "They are secretly moving starkillers into Imperial space, pre-positioning them to strike if the Imperium acts against us. Or if they are ordered to."

"That's a violation of the treaty we already signed," Annette pointed out. "Even if they're unescorted and they argue that no *warships* have violated the border, that's still insane."

"It is insane," Cawl agreed. "We have proof. Not enough to take to the High Priestess, but enough that you should be able to find them."

"Find them?" Annette asked.

"In many ways, Duchess Bond, I would prefer your Imperium conceded to Karal's demands," he told her. "I would rather be allies with the A!Tol as equals than as the junior partner—but I understand that the A!Tol trust us even less than we trust them.

"I will not expect or ask you to negotiate with a sword at your throat," he continued. "Nor will I condone the use of starkillers. If we destroy your stars, you will destroy ours. I know there are secret fleet bases with hidden starkillers that we will never find.

"These fools would start a war we couldn't win even without the Taljzi looming at our border, Duchess Bond. You must find them.

You must stop them. And you must present your evidence to the High Priestess, because this betrayal cannot be permitted to stand."

Cawl grimaced.

"They have broken *her* sacred oath, her promise of peace and nonaggression," he told Annette. "That should be enough for you to get your alliance, Duchess Bond. And we need that alliance.

"The Taljzi are coming. I will not see the madmen of my own fleet destroy our only hope of survival."

CHAPTER TWENTY-THREE

"Starkillers," Fleet Lord Tan!Shallegh said grimly. "Those are weapons I would be glad to see left in the darkest waters and forgotten."

Jean Villeneuve could only agree with the A!Tol officer. The very idea of a weapon that could destroy an entire star system made his skin crawl. None had ever been present in the Sol System, thankfully, but he knew that Bond had held a number of them at one point.

Destroying them had been what had earned humanity their modicum of autonomy.

"What do we know?" General Wellesley-Kurzman asked. "If there's one near Sol, we are in serious trouble."

"There is one near Sol," Zhao said bluntly. The sickly treasurer also ran the Duchy's intelligence service. Anyone who underestimated China's former ruler due to his obesity and ill health soon learned their error.

"The information the Duchess has managed to send us is far from complete, but it doesn't appear that any of the reformists who met with her were involved in this scheme," he continued. "Which was, I suppose, wise of the madmen behind this."

"So, there is a weapon capable of destroying this entire star system just...out there? Somewhere?" Admiral Kurzman-Wellesley demanded. Like Tan!Shallegh, the broad-shouldered Militia officer was aboard his flagship in orbit.

"The likelihood that they could manage to deliver a starkiller through your Militia and the Grand Fleet is low," Tan!Shallegh pointed out. "There are enough tachyon scanners in this system that there are few waves shadowed enough for them to sneak in."

"I have to agree," Jean said. "But Sol is unusual in that, people. We're the source of those systems and currently host to the largest A!Tol Imperial fleet presence in existence. Anywhere else they're threatening can only be more vulnerable."

"And we don't have enough details to locate those ships," Zhao admitted. "I don't even have enough to find the one positioned to threaten us. I only know that it's near us."

"If we send out patrols to search, they'll realize and hide," Kurzman-Wellesley admitted. "If I know where they are, I can catch them. But I don't think we can hunt them, not and have proof."

"We need proof," Zhao told them. "We need evidence Her Grace can take into the High Priestess's court and hand to Karal. Only the High Priestess can order those ships back. We won't even be able to find them all."

"We can find the one near Sol," Jean said quietly.

"The Militia can't. Neither can the Navy," Kurzman-Wellesley said. "Not without them getting away."

"And the Navy should deal with them," Tan!Shallegh noted. "Your security is our concern."

"If the Navy deals with them, we have an active battle between elements of the Imperial and Theocracy Navies," Jean pointed out sharply. "You *cannot* solve this problem, Fleet Lord. It must be the Militia.

"And I have ways to find them," he continued. "Old friends with strange assets—but not ones that can meet with Lord Tan!Shallegh."

The Fleet Lord flashed bright blue, the equivalent to a human nod. He knew who Jean meant.

"If that...old friend is willing to help, I will take it," Tan!Shallegh agreed. "You are right. We must find this weapon and we must catch them at it...and it must be the Militia that does so."

The big squid did *not* look happy. Jean had enough experience with A!Tol in general and Tan!Shallegh specifically to get that from the vibration of his tentacles.

"I will talk to her," he promised. "I don't see another solution."

A MILITIA SHUTTLE met Jean Villeneuve on the roof of Wuxing Tower, the main governmental structure of the Duchy of Terra. He wasn't entirely surprised when General Wellesley-Kurzman appeared as he was boarding it.

The old French admiral stopped and took a long look out over Hong Kong as the Guard commander crossed the rooftop to him. Wellesley was, if nothing else, still in *far* better shape than the Councilor for the Militia.

"James," he greeted the younger man. "I take it you're coming along for the ride?"

"That is my intent, yes," Wellesley-Kurzman confirmed. "Unless you believe you can order my people to remove me from the shuttle?"

Jean chuckled. Time and age had worn away some of the precise accent the Duke of Wellington's younger brother had brought into space with him, but nothing could undermine the eternal confidence of the descendants of the man who'd defeated Napoleon Bonaparte.

"Hardly, *mon ami*," he told Wellesley. "Do you know where we're going?"

"To see Ki!Tana," the Guard officer replied. "She's currently living in a secure facility on the moon, along with several other alien VIPs that like us better than our lords and masters. A facility, I'll note, secured by *my* people."

Jean gestured Wellesley ahead of him.

"That's fair. I'll admit, to you at least, that I don't know if Ki!Tana has a ship," he told the other officer as they took their seats. The door closed behind them and the shuttle smoothly lifted off.

He'd given the pilots instructions before Wellesley had shown up.

"I'd be shocked and appalled to discover that Ki!Tana was relying entirely on our security," Wellesley replied. "The old pirate likes us, but I'm not sure she trusts us."

When Annette Bond had gone into exile as a privateer, the A!Tol Ki!Tana had ended up serving aboard *Tornado*, acting as the Duchess's native guide to the strange and terrifying world humanity had ended up in.

Ever since, she'd had a habit of showing up whenever Earth was in dire straits. Unfortunately, Ki!Tana was what was called a Ki!Tol— she'd passed through the birthing madness where most female A!Tol committed suicide rather than give in to their bodies' demand that they breed—and die painfully doing so.

While she'd found a form of sanity on the other side of that madness, she still couldn't be around males of her species. There was too much risk to everyone involved.

There were enough A!Tol on Earth these days that she couldn't even spend time on humanity's homeworld. Moonbase Delta, however, had only humans and their special guests in it.

Everyone needed some degree of privacy, after all.

"I'm assuming she has one, yes," Jean admitted. "I'm *hoping* it's that old Mesharom scout ship she used to have. A stealth-fielded ship is the perfect tool for this task, and I trust Ki!Tana's judgment over most of our human officers."

The moon was growing rapidly in their screens. An interface-drive shuttle could make the trip to Moonbase Delta in minutes, a far cry from even the hyper-efficient rockets of Jean's youth.

"We'll see what she has to say," Wellesley-Kurzman agreed. "She isn't our only hope, but she's damn useful."

"AH, Admiral Villeneuve, General Wellesley, it's a pleasure to see you two again," Ki!Tana greeted them as they were ushered into her section of the moonbase.

Unless Jean was mistaken, she'd grown even more since the last time he'd seen her. A!Tol females were big. They didn't stop growing or healing until they died. Ki!Tol...didn't die, so...

Ki!Tana was well over three meters tall at her full height, an immense creature that made his hind brain gibber about monsters that ate fishing boats.

"Ki!Tana. Are your quarters to your liking?" Jean asked. "I apologize for not having time to come visit."

"My rooms are acceptable," the A!Tol told him. "Annette's girls visit and video-chat, so it's not like I am completely ignored."

She raised a tentacle with a flush of red amusement as Jean started to try and find an apology.

"You are at war, Admiral Villeneuve," she said. "I understand. It's nice to relax somewhere truly safe, I must admit. It's been a long time."

"I'm glad," he said. "We need your help, if you're able to offer it."

The A!Tol flashed a questioning blue and gestured them to seats.

"That depends on which waters you would have me swim," she noted.

"A rogue faction of Kanzi are deploying starkillers in Imperial territory as a countermeasure to our new technology advantage," Jean said bluntly. "The High Priestess has promised peace and nonaggression but is dragging her feet on the actual alliance we're trying to negotiate."

"She fears what it will do to her power and her people," Ki!Tana replied. "Starkillers?"

"We don't have an exact location, but we know that one was sent to watch over Sol."

"Darkest waters," the old alien spat. "Do those fools *want* my nightmares?"

Jean winced. He'd been *told* that Ki!Tana had once been the A!Tol Empress who'd ordered the starkiller used on the Taljzi, but it had been second-hand. He'd forgotten.

"We want to stop them," he told her quietly. "If we can catch their starkiller and assemble definitive proof that the Kanzi have broken the nonaggression treaty, then Annette may be able to use that as a hammer to break the impasse at the negotiations.

"But none of our ships can find them in stealth."

"And you're hoping I still have a stealth ship floating around?" the A!Tol asked.

"It would be consistent with your past actions," Jean admitted.

"And you would be correct," she replied. "I did leave that ship here. Unfortunately, Interpreter-Shepherd Adamase was rather upset with me for keeping the secret of your Gold Dragon research programs, and I've been locked out."

"*Merde.*" Jean shook his head. "I hadn't even considered that."

Interpreter-Shepherd Adamase was the Mesharom responsible for their Frontier Fleet operations in this region of space. They'd once worked with humanity in exchange for a Precursor ship...which humanity had kept samples from.

Now only the oncoming Taljzi threat had bought humanity clemency from a furious friend.

"They are not your waters to swim," Ki!Tana pointed out. "They are mine. I made my choice long ago. Adamase understands. They're just angry. Those waters will pass." She shivered. "For now, however, I cannot access that scout ship."

"So, what do we do?" Wellesley asked.

"We find someone who can," the A!Tol told them. "I am scheduled to have dinner with Interpreter-Lieutenant Coraniss. Let me speak with them—alone, of course. They may be able to access the ship even if I cannot."

Mesharom didn't like crowds. Or aliens. Or...each other, really.

They were incredibly antisocial creatures, though spaceship crews were less so. The officers who served as Interpreters were almost capable of dealing with aliens regularly.

Almost.

Coraniss was very young—but if they had the key to find the starkiller before it destroyed Jean's star system, he'd do whatever they needed.

CHAPTER TWENTY-FOUR

"Emergence."

The single word hung in the still air of *Bellerophon*'s bridge as the scouting flotilla dropped out of hyperspace. PC-One was, one way or another, going to be the answer to several of the Militia force's questions.

"Scanners live," Morgan reported. Her systems were drinking in the electromagnetic energy of the star system and a dozen more esoteric types of particles...and they were finding things.

"Flagging Target Alpha," she continued sharply. "I have an active space station in the outer system, orbiting a gas giant. Emissions are Taljzi. Repeat, emissions are *Taljzi*."

"Understood. Deploy a Buckler array and stand by for orders from the Flag," Captain Vong ordered. "You are authorized to engage any vessels that attempt to flee with HSMs. We can't afford messengers getting away."

They didn't know whether the Taljzi had hyperfold coms or not, but it was unlikely there was a starcom there. Most likely, the only way their enemy had to get a message home was by sending ships.

Morgan was running through more data as it came in. Eight

planets in the star system, one in the liquid-water zone. Two gas giants outside an asteroid belt that was confusing her scans of the inner system.

There was no question on the station, though. Her sensors were breaking down details as she ran the data through the computers. Multiple platforms, though it didn't *look* like there were any starships there.

"Rear Admiral Sun is ordering the flotilla to move against the space station immediately," Antonova reported. "We're to neutralize any and all defenders and deploy Ducal Guard boarding parties."

"Makes sense. Hume, set a course," Vong ordered. "Major Phelps, prep your people for boarding operations coordinated with the rest of the flotilla. We're going to want as much data as possible from that base."

The core station looked like a cloudscoop to Morgan, a series of flimsy tubes descending into the gas giant's upper atmosphere. There were definitely fuel tanks, storage containers...

"It's a logistics depot," she concluded aloud. "A refueling station, potentially set up for the attack on us."

"Well, then, taking it out is definitely going to be to our advantage," Vong replied. "ETA to range, Commander?"

"We'll be in hyperspace missile range in just under two minutes," Morgan told him. "Regular missile range in ten. Hyperfold cannons, plasma lance and proton beam range around twelve."

Bellerophon had a lot of different weapon systems. That would need to be simplified in the next few generations of warships, but for now, Morgan was responsible for six different types of weapons.

And the sensors, which pinged at her as she began to focus on the Taljzi base. She brought up the alert and stared at it in shock for several long minutes.

"Captain, I'm seeing evidence of civilization around the third planet," she reported. "Not intensive enough to be the Taljzi home-world, and emissions seem low for even what I am seeing...but there's definitely artificial objects in orbit."

"I'm guessing that, Commander, is what the Precursors flagged this system for," Vong said quietly. "Right now, however, our priority is that fleet base.

"We can worry about archeology once we've dealt with the enemy."

MORGAN WASN'T ENTIRELY surprised when the flotilla entered hyperspace missile range of the Taljzi base without opening fire. Every starship under Rear Admiral Sun's command could take multiple hits from conventional interface-drive missiles before their shields went down and their armor was needed.

They could afford the risk of closing into regular missile range with even an unknown defensive constellation. More so, at least, than they could afford to fire off any of their limited supply of hyperspace missiles. Given asteroids, of which this system had plenty, the Ducal warships could replenish their interface-drive missiles.

They couldn't do the same with their hyperspace missiles. The weapons in their magazines were all they had.

"Station is definitely active," she reported as they continued to close. "We are being pulsed with targeting scanners, and I'm detecting what looks like a constellation of automated missile and energy-weapon satellites."

"Commander Hume, please make *damn* certain we stay out of range of their disruptors," Vong ordered calmly.

The Taljzi had a highly effective counter for the Imperium's— and hence the Duchy's—primary energy weapon, the proton beam. They didn't even carry the beams themselves. They carried a shorter-range weapon that induced atomic fission at range.

Thankfully, it was a relatively limited range weapon by space-combat standards, but the Taljzi's disrupters were terrifying regardless.

"No further orders from the Flag," Antonova reported. "Standing by to relay additional instructions."

"Understood." Vong studied his own screens. "Commander Casimir—in the absence of orders to the contrary from the Flag, you are to target any identified weapons and sensor platforms as soon as we enter regular missile range.

"Commander Hume, you will bring us to a halt relative to the base at two point five million kilometers," he continued. That was outside proton-beam range but inside range for both the hyperfold cannons and the plasma lance.

"Additional updates from the Flag," the com officer said a moment later, then she looked up at Vong and grinned. "Target identified platforms once we're in missile range, halt the fleet at two point five million kilometers."

Sometimes, it was *very* obvious that the Duchy of Terra Militia had a small group of senior officers who'd trained together their entire lives.

"Engage as specified, people," Vong confirmed. "Let's see what the Taljzi kept around their base."

THE ANSWER, easily resolved as they approached the light-minute mark, turned out to be missiles. Lots and lots and *lots* of missiles. The Terran flotilla's conventional missiles were outranged by the Taljzi's weapons, which was why they'd deployed the Buckler anti-missile drones.

"I make it at least a hundred individual platforms," Lieutenant Ruskin said calmly. "Roughly five hundred launchers across those."

"And four forts," Morgan noted. "Each of them with fifty launchers. Nothing we can't handle. Ruskin, handle the defense. I'm releasing the Bucklers and the hyperfold cannons to you."

"Yes, sir."

She tapped a sequence of commands that gave the same instruction to the ship's computers. Her junior officer now had control of *Bellerophon*'s massive defensive batteries—and it fell to Morgan to neutralize the same platforms launching at them.

There was a tactical network flowing between all thirty-plus ships of the flotilla, target assignments being passed down from the Flag. There was discretion within those assignments, but not much.

The cruisers and destroyers were going to handle the automated platforms. The forts, their likely control centers, were down to the capital ships.

"Target Alpha-12 is first on the chopping block," she said aloud as her fingers flew over her console. Two super-battleships and two super-modern battleships focused their scanners on the fort Rear Admiral Sun had designated, and Morgan took a moment to absorb all of their data.

The first was identical to the Kanzi designs she'd studied in training. A hexagonal disk, four hundred meters across and fifty meters thick. All of its weapons and armor were on the "upper" side, the side facing the base it was defending noticeably less warlike.

In theory, she could loop her missiles around. In practice, the platform's shields were equally spread around the hexagon and could only be brought down by concentrated fire. At a full light-minute of range, they couldn't make certain all of their missiles hit the same spot...but they could make sure they all hit the same side of the station.

In the absence of a brilliant idea on her part, her missiles were slaved to *Chancellor Merkel,* and all four capital ships fired in the same instant.

"First salvo away, ninety seconds to impact," she reported aloud. "Enemy fire at thirty seconds and closing."

Only tachyon scanners made that assessment possible. Without the faster-than-light scanners, *Bellerophon*'s defenses would have seen the missiles, traveling at eighty-five percent of the speed of light, only fourteen seconds before they arrived.

That was the environment their defenses had been designed for. With the extra warning the tachyon scanners gave, well...

There was a reason Morgan had handed the defense of her ship off to her junior while she dug for vulnerabilities in their enemy.

Not every ship in the flotilla had hyperfold cannons, but all of the capital ships and cruisers had both the faster-than-light guns and the faster-than-light sensors to aim them. The incoming fire entered the range envelope of those guns and started to disappear.

"Second salvo away," Morgan reported as *Bellerophon* shivered beneath them again. There were a lot of missiles in space already, but the Flag was continuing to focus on the first target. They knew the Taljzi had compressed-matter armor superior to their own, which meant the fort was going to take a *lot* of killing.

"First enemy salvo neutralized," Ruskin reported. "Retasking to target the second salvo."

Roughly half of the flotilla's Bucklers had been upgraded with a secondary set of light hyperfold cannons. In hyperspace, the weapons would be useless. In regular space like this, however, they added a massive advantage.

The regular antimissile lasers hadn't even fired yet. The hyperfold cannon alone were annihilating the incoming fire.

"Forts are maneuvering," Morgan said aloud as she spotted it in the sensors. "Won't help them much, but it will protect them from debris hits."

Debris hits, however, really required active defenses of some kind, and the forts were completely lacking in those. Like the First Return that had assaulted Asimov, they relied on shields and compressed-matter armor to absorb incoming fire.

"Their shields are tough," she reported as their first salvo struck home. "Target Alpha-12's shields are still up after a full salvo."

"Time to lance range?" Vong asked. The Captain seemed as perfectly calm as ever. Morgan could only hope to one day match his cool.

"Thirty seconds."

"Hold the hyperfold cannon for missile defense, hold the lance for the Flag," Vong ordered. "In the absence of orders, engage your—"

"Receiving lance and hyperfold targeting orders from the Flag, sir," Morgan interrupted. "Stand by."

The interface drive didn't accelerate or decelerate as such. It took a modern drive just under four seconds to go from half of light-speed to a relative halt. The flotilla started slowing as they passed the ten-light-second mark and hit the designated range seconds later.

"Firing the lance."

Even *Bellerophon*'s mighty missile batteries only caused the ship to tremble. Her plasma lance, however, concentrated the fusing hydrogen from four fusion power cores into a single projectile and accelerated it to nearly the speed of light.

The entire ship lurched with the recoil as the massive weapon fired, a projected magnetic tube lashing out into space and latching on to target Alpha-13. Twenty lances from the cruisers and capital ships struck as one, and the fortress didn't have shields that powerful or armor that heavy.

Alpha-13 vaporized, even as Alpha-12's shields and armor finally gave way under the continual pounding of the capital ship's missiles. The escorts had gutted the defense constellation, leaving only the two fortresses as a threat—and they were well out of range of their own energy weapons.

"Flag is retasking hyperfold cannons," Morgan said calmly, even as she reassigned her own systems. "We're targeting Alpha-11 and...firing."

Both remaining fortresses vanished in simultaneous balls of fire. There were small cheers from the rest of the bridge, but Morgan was watching the timing.

"That wasn't us," she reported. "That was—"

"*Singularity alert!*" Ruskin snapped. "They've ejected singularity cores at us. Estimated one point two Earth masses per core; I'm reading at least three."

"Get us out of here!" Vong ordered. "Evasive maneuvers, maximum velocity!"

The Flag was slow in seeing what *Bellerophon*'s crew had seen. Half the ships scattered on their own before orders came down—but the orders were in time.

Almost.

CHAPTER TWENTY-FIVE

"THE GOOD NEWS IS THAT THAT ISN'T GOING TO BE SOMETHING they can do very often," Morgan said quietly several hours later. "It looks like there were eight singularity cores in the fortress and the core logistics facility, and they blew up every other power core to try and hit us with them."

She shivered.

"Best guess is they killed about ten thousand of their own people to launch that attack," she continued. She wasn't the only tactical officer in the flotilla giving this briefing. The same conversation was going on aboard every remaining ship.

"One of the cores in the main station imploded in place. That captured another one and threw three more into the gas giant, where they're no threat to us."

Four or five extra planetary masses weren't going to cause much damage to a gas giant that massed twice what Sol's Jupiter did—not in a time frame that the flotilla would care about, anyway. What the three singularities had done to the Terran flotilla, however...

"Captain Singh is continuing the survey, but all evidence suggests *Jean Chrétien* is a complete write-off," Morgan said with a sigh. *Chancellor Merkel* and both *Bellerophon*s had evaded the attack. The other *Duchess of Terra*–class battleship, Captain Singh's ship, had taken a singularity right down the center. Shields and compressed-matter armor paled in the face of that kind of strike.

Two of the *Thunderstorm*-Ds had been hit as well, but they hadn't had the mass to survive at all. Those cruisers were simply gone.

"Our scans suggest the remaining stations are uninhabited," Morgan concluded. "They destroyed every facility with a live power source and suicided the entire base crew. We'll want to survey what's here before we leave, but I doubt there's much left of value."

"Damn." Commander Anja Tanzi was the battleship's Italian-born executive officer, a dark-skinned woman who spent most of her time either buried in paperwork or buried in personnel crisis.

Morgan's department had so far avoided the latter, so she hadn't spent much time with the woman.

"They killed themselves to avoid capture?" Tanzi asked after her curse had hung in the air for a few seconds.

"It's consistent," Vong agreed. "Sacrificing ten thousand lives to try and take out our fleet makes a certain cold-blooded sense, in any case. The capital ships alone have twenty thousand people aboard."

Jean Chrétien's crew had been lucky. About half of the six thousand people aboard the super-battleship had survived. They'd now reinforce the crews of the rest of the flotilla.

"We'll stand by for further orders from the Flag," Vong continued. "*Chancellor Merkel* got caught up in the edge of the singularity that crippled *Jean Chrétien*, so Admiral Sun is distracted still.

"Casimir—I want you and Major Phelps to work up two plans. One for a search and survey of the wreckage of the Taljzi base, one for a search and survey of the infrastructure you detected in the inner system.

"Sadly, I don't think we're going to find any smoking guns anywhere, but any data we can find will help."

The battleship's captain shook his head.

"Or it better, at least," he admitted. "This mission is starting to feel like throwing darts blindfolded."

———————

MAJOR ALEXANDER PHELPS joined Morgan in her office shortly afterward, the Guard officer looking as dashingly turned out as ever. She'd seen him in power armor, but otherwise, she'd mostly seen him in a shipboard uniform that cleanly showed off his muscular form.

She was monogamous, after all, not *blind*.

"How are we doing, Commander?" he asked as he took a seat. "Captain said we were looking at searching debris either way, right?"

"Exactly," she confirmed, bringing up a hologram of the system. "Possible targets are here, at Target Alpha, or over here at Target Bravo."

Target Bravo was the orbital debris around the third planet.

"We have pretty detailed scans at Target Alpha; the biggest problem is going to be deciding what's actually worth landing troops on," she told him. "We're not even entirely sure what Target Bravo is."

"A colony of some sort?" he asked, studying it. "Looks like orbital infrastructure."

"I'd agree, except it's all too cold," Morgan told him. "Look at the temp and EM readings. They look like space stations, but if they are... they're dead. And they've been dead a long time."

Phelps shivered.

"So, probably not a Taljzi outpost, then," he agreed. "But the planet's habitable? Why would they ignore it?"

"I'm not sure yet," she admitted. "The asteroid belt is pretty rough, so I don't have clear data. I can tell it's in the habitable zone and I'm picking up oxygen and liquid water in the atmosphere, but I can't say for sure until we get someone inside the belt."

"Probes?"

"We focused them on the Taljzi base," Morgan replied. "I've got a set queued up and ready to go, but we're waiting for orders from the Flag. We need to be sure everything here is safe and handled, but we also need to take a trip in-system and see what's there."

"If all of the orbitals are cold, I'm pretty sure I know," Phelps told her. "Would it be in character for the Precursors to have flagged a system for sentient life?"

"That's what Captain Vong thinks and I agree," she said. "Most likely, they flagged it for a Bronze Age or even Stone Age civilization. When the Taljzi showed up, I'd guess they were late pre-FTL."

The Guard Major was silent for several seconds.

"We're not expecting to find anyone alive in there, are we?" he finally asked.

"I wouldn't be able to pick up nuclear winter with the interference," Morgan said very quietly. "So, no. I'm not expecting to find anyone alive. But given our mission, we need to find out one way or the other, don't we?"

Phelps exhaled.

"Yeah," he agreed. "Well, let's pull our shuttle numbers and see what we can match up against our own drives and your probes. Whichever way the Flag sends us."

MORGAN WAS BACK on the bridge when the call finally came in.

"*Chancellor Merkel* and *Rama* are going to remain here with the cruisers to cover the evacuation of *Jean Chrétien* and the survey of Target Alpha," Antonova reeled off as the orders came in. "We're ordered to take half the destroyers and survey the inner system, with a focus on Target Bravo. Specifically, Admiral Sun wants us to locate any Taljzi elements in the inner system and make contact with any local non-Taljzi sentients."

She paused, then swallowed and looked back at the Captain.

"You are authorized to use whatever means necessary to protect the flotilla's ships and crew, sir," she told Captain Vong in a small voice. "He specifically includes orbital bombardment of hostile planetside facilities."

"Hopefully, the Taljzi won't have dug in quite that hard," Vong said brightly. "All right, Antonova. Get Commanders Casimir and Hume a network with the destroyers.

"Hume, plot a course to get us and the destroyers into orbit of Target Bravo. Casimir, I presume you have a drone spread set up to survey the inner system?"

"Yes, sir," she confirmed.

"Launch at your discretion," he told her. "If you need extra eyes, lean on the destroyers."

There was no question that a battleship captain was senior to a destroyer captain. Unless Commodore Huber decided to accompany half of her ships in-system, Vong was in command of this sub-expedition—and that was clearly Admiral Sun's expectation.

"I should have enough," Morgan replied. The program had been waiting in her system since about ten minutes after the shooting had stopped. A single command sent the battleship's systems into motion, deploying her intelligent and not-quite-suicidal robotic minions into space.

She might be all but certain she knew what they'd find in general, but the specifics were important as well.

The Taljzi had almost certainly burned a civilization to ash. Hopefully they'd left something useful behind when they had.

CHAPTER TWENTY-SIX

THE PLANET WAS DECEPTIVELY INTACT FROM ORBIT, A BLUE AND brown marble glittering in the light from the nearby star.

Morgan's probes and scanners told the truth, though. As did the brown color of most of the landmasses. The planet was emerging from the end of a decades-long "nuclear" winter triggered by massive deployments of kinetic weapons.

Her scans suggested that the biosphere had survived and was beginning to flourish again, but they also showed her the craters that had been cities. Towns. Farms, even.

It looked like the worlds the Taljzi had visited during the First Return, only more so. Those worlds, even the heavily populated Kanzi ones, had been colonies. Millions of people at most.

This had been the homeworld of a species with late pre-FTL-era technology. They'd had enough infrastructure in orbit that building a starship had probably been within their grasp, even if they'd never managed it.

From the gaping holes in the debris ring, the Taljzi had deorbited some of the larger stations to start their bombardment, then moved in with lighter ships to hit every power source they could detect with kinetic rounds.

And then they'd dropped a midsized asteroid in the largest ocean. Just to be sure they'd killed everything.

"There are no power signatures on the surface," she finally told the rest of the bridge crew as everyone stared at the dead world. "There are a handful of active surveillance platforms in orbit, but nothing significant. We could take them out with our beam weapons without a major investment of time."

"Do it," Vong ordered.

There was no real *point* to destroying the surveillance satellites. They were only able to transmit to the now-gone logistics base, and they were scanning for a return of intelligent life that Morgan didn't expect them to ever find.

And yet...she followed Vong's orders without hesitating. Proton beams capable of splitting battleships hammered into surveillance satellites the size of her work console.

The Taljzi had left twelve robotic spies in orbit of the dead world, and Morgan wiped them all out in a matter of seconds. It felt good, even if it was pointless.

"I've flagged the largest remaining stations," she reported. "Passing them on to Major Phelps.

"They haven't had power in a long time—the Taljzi took out their reactors with long-range beam fire—but we're more likely to find something intact in orbit than...down there."

She gestured vaguely at the planet.

"I'm not detecting even any significant ruins," she told the Captain. "They bombarded anything they could detect even before they intentionally triggered a blackout."

"How long ago?" Vong asked.

"I can't be certain," Morgan warned. "I'd guess sixty to a hundred years. They didn't come here directly from the Precursor starcom. They came here on their way back."

"Which brings us, once again, to the theory that they knew exactly what they were looking for on that map," the Captain said. "We now know what the copper tags are for. We'll want to sweep those systems later on, I'm sure, in case the Taljzi didn't...but I think we need to move on to the other tags."

"We'll want to see what we find here," she suggested. "We don't know what these people may have known, after all. It's not impossible they tried to preserve something."

"COMMANDER CASIMIR, can you take a look at this?" Ruskin asked. "We're getting a feed from one of the destroyers and I'm not sure what they've found."

"Put it on my screen," Morgan instructed. She'd been watching the camera feed from Phelps's Guards as they swept through the wreckage of what had once been a massive transshipment station for people and goods leaving the planet.

Vacuum was an extraordinarily good preserver. Morgan now knew exactly what the pale-skinned and tall humanoids that had lived on this planet had looked like. She wasn't sure if the near-translucence of their skin was natural or a side effect of the mummification process.

All she knew was that the space station was full of the dead and not much of use. Any distraction was worth her time right now.

The image that appeared on her screen was a different space station. Like everything else she'd seen, this one had a hole blown through its power plant. Unlike the ones from the planet's orbit, this one looked like it had been taken out by a missile.

The sheer speed of the impact had actually minimized the damage, the Taljzi weapon punching through the station rather than obliterating it in the crash. Bits of a massive dome shape remained, strangely familiar to Morgan's gaze.

"Where is this?" she asked.

"Solitary orbit halfway out to the asteroid belt," Ruskin replied. "*Pangaea* picked it up on one of their probes and moved in to take a closer look. It's almost a loose station, but I swear I should know what it is."

"It's a radio telescope, I think," Morgan said as she studied the station. That was the "dome"—the massive dish of a large-scale radio telescope. A telescope floating in the middle of nowhere in deep space...that sounded familiar.

"Sir?"

Morgan was already plugging a search parameter into her console.

"It was something my father worked on," she told her subordinate. "Something about radio telescopes in deep space..."

"Dark Eye," Vong said over her shoulder, just as the search returned.

"Yes," she confirmed. "A deep-space surveillance program, forty-two radio telescopes in the ecliptic plane of the Solar System, looking for signs of intelligence."

"And we found it," Vong agreed, the Captain looking at the summary on Morgan's screen. "That's how your dad knew anything was coming. I studied it in my own academy days," he told Morgan when she looked back at him.

Vong had been part of the first generation of Militia officers who'd never served in the UESF, recruited out of college eighteen years ago. Dark Eye pre-dated him.

"Ruskin, let's scan through everything we've got and look for more of these," she told her subordinate. "If they were trying to build the same kind of system, it almost certainly wasn't just one platform. Might not have been forty, but there was definitely more than one."

"You're thinking the Taljzi might have missed one?" Vong asked.

"Maybe," Morgan agreed. "Or even just done less damage than they did to this one. If there's anything in this star system that will tell us where the Taljzi *came* from, it's the computers on those telescope stations."

———————

"THIS ONE IS DEFINITELY our best shot," Phelps said calmly over the channel as his shuttle dove towards the wreckage. "Fourteen stations and this is the most intact?"

"Don't be picky, Major," Morgan told him. She was watching through his camera feed again. "There might be more, but we only have so much time."

"Is this thing safe?" the Guard asked.

Morgan could understand where he was coming from. The station he was heading toward was the most intact of the telescope platforms they'd found. Of course, that meant that the missile that had killed it had hit on one side of the station instead of going right through the middle.

Half of the station was gone. Half was still there—and that half included the base of the radio telescope, where the core receivers and computers should be.

"If it was safe, would you even want to go?" Morgan asked back. "I thought the Ducal Guard didn't go in for easy."

She pretended not to hear Antonova's muffled chuckle. Her lover knew that reputation as well as she did.

"Fair enough," Phelps replied. "So, no oxygen. No gravity. No power. What are we looking for?"

"Magnetic hard drives, optical disks, any physical data storage media," Morgan instructed. "Anything that would survive the loss of power and looks like it was shielded against stellar radiation."

Anything they found was going to be badly degraded, but if they got *enough* of the station's computers and backups...

"I've been given less specific directions," the Major said. "All right. We're jumping clear. Watch through the feed; tell me if you see anything that looks useful."

The camera feed shifted as the shuttle hatch popped open and the power-armored Guards jumped out. Their suits had a limited thrust capability, but it was enough to cross the hundred or so meters the shuttle had left.

"You know, keeping the shuttle that far out doesn't reassure me on the safety of this stunt," Phelps pointed out as he drifted through space.

"I'm more concerned about wiping any data storage that's still intact and vulnerable," Morgan told him. "Plus, that's a spiky wreck of a space station. Be careful."

"I didn't think you cared," he grumped, but from the vector analysis the feed was showing her, he was following instructions.

Of course, he was paying more attention to the vectors of the other Guards with him.

"That should be the main link to the telescopes," Morgan told him, haloing the target. "If what we need isn't there, we should be able to follow the links back to it from there."

"Who's this 'we'?" she heard Phelps mutter under his breath, but she let it go. He had a point.

"Wait, is that..." He focused his light. "Is that my jackpot, Commander Casimir?"

"It's at least a backup," Morgan confirmed as she looked over the computer hardware he was scanning. "Grab it, but see what else you can find. The more data we have, the more likely we are to find something useful."

"Got it."

The Guard started packing up the hardware, and another Guard followed the data cables to a door. Popping it open earned them all a shock as another tall and pale corpse broke free and "fell" toward them.

"Fuck me," the Guard cursed. "Okay...bad news, corpse in my face. Good news, I think we found the data center."

A new camera feed lit up on Morgan's screen as the Guard shone her light into the space. Arrays of servers, almost recognizable from her classes on the history of computing, hung in the core of the old space station.

"Good news indeed," she confirmed. "Pull it all, Major. Then we get to see if the software and hardware our Imperial friends gave us is as good at translation as they think it is."

CHAPTER TWENTY-SEVEN

THE BRIEFING ROOM NEXT TO *BELLEROPHON*'S BRIDGE SEEMED very quiet as Morgan faced the gathered officers of the battleship—and the officers of the rest of the flotilla through virtual conferencing.

Bellerophon's Guards had extracted the datacores, and Morgan's team had translated the data and extrapolated the scenario.

Which left Morgan telling the officers of the flotilla how a species had died.

"We have bits and pieces of data from the four most intact telescope platforms," she explained slowly. "Everything we extracted was fragmentary and damaged—we're accessing backups and cold storage systems in the main, and these systems have been without power for fifty-three years."

She grimaced.

"We can now confirm that time frame," she noted. "Comparing the stars in our reconstructed scenario with the space around here, we can nail down the year, if not the exact date, of the Taljzi's arrival.

"This coincides closely enough with our estimate of the impact winter on the planet to be considered confirmed."

A hologram of the system appeared in front of her, relayed to every ship in the Militia flotilla.

"Our A!Tol translation software was more than up to the task of breaking open the software and databases we retrieved," she told them. "Consolidating the fragmented data into a single reconstruction of the fate of this system took longer.

"The locals called themselves Sedetch," Morgan explained, bringing up an image of the tall and translucent-skinned bipeds. "The surveillance platforms weren't targeted at aliens. They apparently had colonized a nearby system with slower-than-light colony ships well before the Taljzi arrived.

"They were in a state of cold war with their colony system, with the surveillance platforms intended to detect incoming interstellar bombardment missiles."

The concept of trying to engage in even a *cold* war across three and a half light-years without hyperspace travel hurt Morgan's head. From the scale of the construction the Sedetch had engaged in, though, it looked like at least the bombardment missile threat had been quite real.

"With a real, if somewhat long-term, threat to face them, the Sedetch had devoted a larger portion of their resources to a spaceborne military than Earth had before the Annexation," she continued. "Most of their ships were extraordinarily small by our current standards, fusion-torch ships with massive power-to-weight ratios intended to intercept missiles coming in at half the speed of light or more."

An image of a Sedetch interceptor appeared on the hologram, replacing the image of a Sedetch next to the map. Icons sprinkled across the entire system, marking where the locals had positioned their defenders.

"Lacking in interface-drive ships or missiles, they were even less able to resist the Taljzi attack than Earth could stand against the A!Tol," she said quietly, hitting PLAY.

"The Taljzi arrived with a force of ten of their super-battleships and escorts. We don't have copies of any communications between the Sedetch and the Taljzi, but we do know that the Sedetch at least tried to communicate."

The Taljzi strike force appeared on her map, zooming toward the planet at half the speed of light.

"The Taljzi did not respond and the Sedetch attempted to intercept them."

Morgan shrugged as the battle played out on the hologram, trying to steel herself against the imagery she'd already seen.

"They were capable of shooting down Taljzi missiles, but that was all. The Taljzi didn't lose a single ship and obliterated the interceptors before carrying out their bombardment."

The accelerated time frame didn't really help. The events taking place in her hologram could easily have been Earth's fate if the A!Tol had been genocidal instead of colonizers who desperately needed humanity's people.

High-tech civilizations had population growth problems. The A!Tol solved that by uplifting and integrating new sentient races. The Kanzi solved it by enslaving other races.

The Taljzi cloned themselves and killed everyone they encountered.

"Once the bombardment was complete..." she said, then swallowed against a suddenly dry throat. She took a long drink of water, then resumed.

"Once the bombardment was complete, they left a squadron of destroyers to sweep the system for stations and colonies they'd missed. The telescope platforms were among the first destroyed in that sweep, so we have no further information on this system.

"We do know that the super-battleships set out for their colony system," she said quietly, then took another sip of water. "We can presume that despite having colonized a second star system, the Sedetch have been exterminated."

"We know where they went," Sun said grimly. "That doesn't really help us."

"I know," Morgan conceded. "What does help us is that two of the telescope platforms had rudimentary hyperspace anomaly scanners. The Sedetch completely disregarded the data from them, which leads me to conclude they were experimental at best."

"If they had anomaly scanners..." Sun raised an eyebrow at her questioningly.

"We know what vector they arrived on, sir," Morgan told him. "There is a star along that route, about fifteen light-years away. It's one of the systems the Precursors had marked in gold—PG-Three."

"It appears that the copper stars were local sentient races," Sun concluded. "It seems time to find out what they meant by gold. Well done, Commander Casimir."

The Admiral looked around at everyone else.

"Set your courses, people," he told them. "Unless someone needs more time, we leave for PG-Three in twelve hours."

CHAPTER TWENTY-EIGHT

"UNKNOWN HYPER PORTAL!"

As Councilor for the Militia, Jean Villeneuve really had no place on the bridge of Orbit One. This was the primary command center for the defense of the entire Sol System, with hundreds of officers and NCOs in the main space, and a dozen subordinate spaces like it.

Of course, no one in the Duchy of Terra Militia would have dreamed of telling Jean that, so he'd happily traded on his old rank to get into the command center as he waited for word from Ki!Tana.

"How can we have an *unknown* hyper portal?" Rear Admiral Malina Gabrielli demanded. The black Italian woman currently holding down the center seat did *not* look pleased to have that announcement made while Jean was on the bridge.

"We're supposed to have anomaly scanners in hyperspace to see things coming from ten light-years away," she continued sharply. "Are they unscheduled? Unidentified? Tell me what we know!"

"Um. Nothing, sir," the Commander running the sensor team admitted. "There was no ship on the other side, according to our sensor stations. There's...nothing on *this* side, sir. Just a hyper portal."

"That's impossible, Commander Vasylyk," Gabrielli pointed out.

"Start an immediate processing run for the anomalies of a stealth screen." She turned away and gestured for a communications officer to approach her.

"Get Commodore Jardine on the line," she ordered. "She's the closest cruiser force to the emergence locus. Get them moving to investigate the portal *ASAP*. If someone thinks they can sneak into *this* system and not get spotted, they have a surprise coming."

The Rear Admiral paused and glanced over at Jean.

"Councilor Villeneuve," she said formally, "we appear to have a security breach in the Sol System."

He smiled thinly.

"I noticed, Admiral," he said quietly. "There is a high likelihood that I'm expecting them...but we know that the Taljzi have stealth fields of their own. Carry on."

Gabrielli was clearly taken aback by Jean's expecting a stealth-fielded ship, but she nodded firmly in response to his orders.

"I'll make certain Commodore Jardine knows to talk before shooting," she replied. "If they're likely to be friendly, that is."

"I think we'd all prefer that, Rear Admiral," Jean agreed. *No one* would be happy if the Militia accidentally killed Ki!Tana and Coraniss. On the other hand, he really didn't want a Taljzi scout ship in Sol—not while the Grand Fleet was orbiting near Venus without upgrades!

"COUNCILOR, Commodore Jardine is requesting a private channel."

Jean looked up from his communicator, the scroll-like pocket computer currently wide open to allow him to work through the functionally infinite paperwork of a planetary Councilor, to see one of Orbit One's many junior officers standing next to him politely.

"Do you have a secured space available?" he asked calmly.

"Yes, Councilor. If you'll follow me?"

Jean followed the young woman into a small office space attached to the command center. The officer closed the door behind him, leaving Jean to take a moment to double check the security of the room.

His communicator might *look* identical to the ones used by the Duchy of Terra Militia, but it had a few extra pieces. His bodyguards would be furious if he took a secured call without double checking the room!

That took only a few extra seconds, seconds in which his bodyguard commander sent him a message noting that they were now securing the physical access to the room.

The message was surprisingly lacking in passive-aggressive commentary over the fact that the Councilor hadn't told his escorts he was moving. Jean was apparently wearing down his bodyguards.

It had only taken two decades, he supposed.

He tapped a command on the console in the room and opened the com channel Jardine had sent him.

The room in the video feed that answered him, however, was definitely not aboard any ship of Jean's Militia. Mesharom vessels went in for a stark shade of white, where the Militia left many interior spaces as bare metal. The smooth plasticized metal of the room was a clear sign that he was looking at the Mesharom scout ship Ki!Tana had taken out.

The feed was a split screen, with Ki!Tana's squid-like form in one half and Coraniss's massive fuzzy bulk in the other. The Mesharom resembled nothing so much as a three-meter-long orange-and-blue caterpillar.

They'd learned to be better with others during their accidental exile among humanity, but Coraniss was still a Mesharom. They almost certainly had their own half of the ship that Ki!Tana wouldn't enter without permission.

"I was told I was connecting to Commodore Jardine," he said. "*Bonjour*, Ki!Tana, Interpreter Coraniss. It's good to see you."

"The good Commodore agreed to help us keep this under wraps,"

Ki!Tana told him. "It's possible that the Kanzi are watching your communications. Almost certainly, in fact."

Jean straightened, facing the camera head-on as the humor drained from him.

"You found them."

"Two starkillers, ten super-battleships, thirty escorts," Coraniss reeled off. "Logically, the second starkiller is a redundancy. Your system is well defended, by Arm Power standards."

Jean hadn't really *disbelieved* what his Duchess had sent him, but it was a large gap from knowing that the Kanzi might be deploying starkillers against the Imperium to hearing the Mesharom tell him that the Kanzi had brought *two* weapons of mass destruction.

"Mutually assured destruction," he said quietly. "The theory that if they can destroy us, we won't attack them. But we weren't going to *anyway.*"

"Clearly, the Kanzi do not believe this," Coraniss told him. "They did not detect us. We have attached the exact coordinates of their staging zone to this transmission. I am not familiar with the terms of the treaty negotiated between your imperiums, but in the Core, this would be an act of war."

"It is here, too," Jean replied. "A war we can't afford to fight, not until we understand the Taljzi's plan."

"I am not permitted to get more involved than I have," the Mesharom said. "My actions will likely be questioned once the Frontier Fleet lead elements arrive, but I owed your people this much."

"Your intervention is appreciated, Interpreter-Lieutenant Coraniss," he told them. "Neither the Duchy nor the A!Tol Imperium will forget this."

"I suggest you deal with this as quietly as you can," Ki!Tana said. "I will accompany you, if you wish, but I would strongly recommend that you do *not* involve Imperial forces."

"We already have a plan," Jean admitted. "Tan!Shallegh is not enthused with it, but he understands. If you can transfer to

Commodore Jardine's flagship, Third Squadron will be commencing an FTL exercise shortly."

He couldn't leave Earth uncovered, even with the Grand Fleet present. Second Squadron was at Asimov with Vice Admiral Rolfson. Fourth Squadron was in Centauri with Vice Admiral Amandine. That left First and Third Squadron, and First was the more powerful formation. If they moved, they'd draw attention.

Third Squadron might only have eight *Duchess of Terra*–class super-battleships, but Vice Admiral Van der Merwe also had eight *Manticore*-class battleships—and he'd match *Manticore*s against even Kanzi super-battleships any day.

CHAPTER TWENTY-NINE

VICE ADMIRAL PATIENCE VAN DER MERWE WAS A TALL WOMAN from the slums of Johannesburg, with dark brown skin and powerfully-built broad shoulders. Her flagship, *Nelson Mandela*, had been the last *Duchess of Terra*–class ship ever built in the Sol System.

That meant the ship had a thousand places where minor defects identified in the earlier *Duchess*-class ships—and the *Majesty*-class ships they'd been based on—had been fixed in construction. *Nelson Mandela* was a smoothly functioning war machine, if one lacking in the massed hyperfold weapons her newer sisters mounted.

"Welcome aboard, Councilor," Van der Merwe told Jean as he was escorted onto her flag bridge. "We are already underway for our...unscheduled exercise."

"*Bien, bien*," Jean said. "We're rendezvousing with Commodore Jardine?"

"Fifteen minutes before we enter hyperspace, yes," the Admiral confirmed. "Would you care to tell me what this is about, sir?"

"You don't have to call me sir anymore, Patience," Jean told her. "I'm not an Admiral anymore."

"You're not only *an* Admiral to the Militia, sir; you are *the* Admiral," she told him. "We don't have many unscheduled exercises, I have to say. They might be useful to think about in the future. It would help, if nothing else, disguise when we're using one as a cover for something."

Jean smiled.

"Once we're in hyperspace, Admiral," he told her gently. "I have reason to mistrust our information security in Sol."

"That's...a dire statement, sir," Van der Merwe noted. "I didn't think we were overly concerned about Taljzi intelligence operations."

"And that, Vice Admiral Van der Merwe, is why this will remain an unscheduled hyperspatial deployment exercise until our portal closes behind us," he said. "Is that going to be a problem?"

Technically, he had no authority to give Van der Merwe direct orders. He could call Kurzman-Wellesley and get her boss to give her the orders for him—the Militia's *new* Admiral wouldn't hesitate, after all—but she could argue with him.

She chuckled instead.

"That won't be a problem at all, Councilor. The Militia knows who we trust, if nothing else."

He nodded his thanks and stepped up to her shoulder, studying the readiness reports on her ships.

"What have we got for FTL weapons?" he asked quietly.

"The *Manticore*s have six dual-portal hyperspace missiles mounted on their hulls apiece. The *Duchess*es have twelve. Two of our cruisers are *Thunderstorm*-Ds, so they have a battery of single-portal weapons apiece. The other fourteen cruisers are at least refitted with hyperfold cannons, and everything has hyperfold coms."

Sixteen battleships, sixteen cruisers, sixteen destroyers. Jardine had four more ships, but they were *Thunderstorm*-Cs like most of Van der Merwe's cruisers. Older ships, with hyperfold cannon but no hyperspace missiles.

"What are we facing, sir?" she asked after a moment. "I'm guessing not Taljzi, so..."

"Once we're in hyper," he repeated. If the Kanzi had managed to infiltrate a starkiller deployment formation this close to Sol, there was almost certainly someone in Sol with the ability to warn them.

The Kanzi weren't supposed to have hyperfold communicators, but there were enough of them floating around in Sol to at least send a message, even if the starkiller's escorts couldn't reply to it.

Someone was going to pay for this. More immediately, however, Jean Villeneuve intended to blow two starkillers to dust bunnies.

"I SEE slavers are as good as ever at keeping their word," Van der Merwe said bitterly as Jean briefed her.

Ki!Tana loomed in the background of the briefing room, the alien having come aboard as soon as they'd entered hyperspace.

"At least according to Duchess Bond, the High Priestess has no idea what her commanders are getting up to," Jean admitted. "I'm not certain I buy that! *Starkillers* deployed without her authority?"

He shook his head.

"I don't know what kind of government the Theocracy really runs with, but I doubt it's so free of her grip as to allow that."

"It depends on how clever they were," Ki!Tana pointed out. "And the Theocracy Navy Command are past masters at doing what they wish regardless of what the 'Divine Chosen' might order. Unless it's dragged in front of Karal in public, they can do a great many things in the dark."

"And that is what Her Grace wants to do," Jean said with a sigh. "She wants us to engage this Kanzi force. Destroy or capture the starkillers. Drive off or capture the warships. We need proof that she can deliver to the High Priestess to show that her warlords have broken her word for her."

"Politics," Van der Merwe hissed. "The politics of slavetakers and monsters. I'm not entirely sure why we care."

"Because we need their fleets," he told her. "We need their ships. We need their knowledge of the Taljzi. I'm no happier about this than you are, Admiral, but the thought of having Kanzi super-battleships on our side when the Taljzi come warms a lot of hearts."

"I will take what prisoners I must," she told him. "But if they have brought starkillers to the borders of our star system, then my mission is clear: none of them escape, Councilor Villeneuve. We must wipe them out."

"Every ship we destroy today is one that can't be sent against the Taljzi," Jean warned, but he wasn't arguing. Not really. "But you're right. A message needs to be sent: either the Kanzi will keep the High Priestess's word or this whole negotiation *de merde* has been a waste of our time."

THE SCREENS and holograms on *Nelson Mandela*'s flag bridge flashed brilliantly as the Third Squadron of the Duchy of Terra Militia punched through a hole into real space.

Their prey was already reacting. The information that Ki!Tana had provided was, as Jean had expected, entirely correct.

Ten super-battleships formed a rough sphere around two destroyer-sized vessels. Twenty cruisers and ten destroyers screened the capital ships.

The Kanzi couldn't have been expecting an attack, not if they were planning on waiting there for months or even years for the order to strike. Jean had been on the other side of the situation before, commanding the United Earth Space Force when the A!Tol had arrived.

If the Kanzi crews had been his, he'd have been pleased. The formation was adjusting to face them within moments, escorts flowing around the capital ships in well-trained synchronicity to put themselves in front of Van der Merwe's ships.

"All ships, target your hyper missiles on the starkillers," Van der Merwe ordered. "Wait for my command. We'll show them the respect the treaty requires, even if they've broken it."

She paused.

"If they try to run, destroy the starkillers."

She glanced at Jean, but he gave her a "go ahead" gesture. They were both equally positioned to summon the Kanzi to surrender, but this was her squadron. She was still the active duty officer, too.

"Kanzi vessels," Van der Merwe snapped into her recorder. "Your presence here is a violation of *every* treaty between your Theocracy and the Imperium. The presence of starkillers this close to *any* system, let alone a Duchy of the Imperium, is an act of war.

"You will surrender your ships and crew for internment until such time as we negotiate your return with the High Priestess...or you will be destroyed."

She smiled thinly at the recorder.

"And may I remind you, you damn fools, that everything I see is already transmitted to Sol. Within a day, your High Priestess will know how you have betrayed her word."

The message winged its way across space as the Terran force closed.

"Vampire!" someone snapped. "We have missile launches across the board; the Kanzi are engaging."

"That's a response of a kind, isn't it?" Van der Merwe said. "All ships: destroy the starkillers. Deploy Bucklers and continue closing.

"We want them in hyperfold cannon range."

Jean wasn't sure what the Kanzi had been expecting from the Terran fleet, but he doubted it was the tsunami of hyperspace missiles that descended on the starkillers. The same firepower would have almost certainly taken down one of the super-battleships guarding the weapons, but the starkillers weren't warships.

They were automated systems, remote-controlled from a nearby vessel. Without any offensive weapons beyond their primary system, they still had powerful shields—and these were apparently a new system, refitted with antimissile lasers.

Even hyperspace missiles made their final approach in normal space, but there was no way the two massive weapons could stand against the dozens of missiles emerging around them. The starkillers came apart in brilliant flashes of light.

"Please tell me we got scans of them," Van der Merwe said grimly, watching as the enemy salvos crashed towards them. Bucklers and hyperfold cannon were already taking their explosive harvest of the missiles.

"We did," her operations officer confirmed. "Confirmed IDs, both were Class Two Starkillers."

"Fuckers," the Vice Admiral swore. "All right, people, we've got these bastards outgunned. If they're not willing to lay down their arms, let's do it for them."

CHAPTER THIRTY

DESPITE THE EVIDENCE CAWL AND HIS COMPATRIOTS HAD GIVEN her, Annette had only half-believed that the Kanzi fleet command would be so far gone. The data she'd received from the Duchy told her a different story.

An entire *fleet* had been positioned two days flight from her system. A fleet with not one but two weapons designed to kill an entire star system. Despite all of the pretty language and gorgeous ceremony the Kanzi had shown her, they'd been preparing to stab her in the back the entire time.

"I should have known better than to trust slavers," she said aloud.

"Did you?" Maria Robin-Antionette asked quietly, her aide standing at the side of the office Annette was viewing the data in. "Did we ever really *trust* them?"

"We have to trust them at least enough for this goddamn negotiation to have been worth the time," Annette said. "If we can't trust the High Priestess and the Theocracy to honor their agreements with us, then we should never have come. We should have taken the risk that the Taljzi weren't going to show up and hit the Kanzi with the full

Gold Dragon arsenal before they had a chance to build counter-measures."

It had been an option. It hadn't been Empress A!Shall's first choice, but Annette was sure that if she'd added her voice to those who said they should crush the Kanzi and *then* turn their attention on the Taljzi, the plan might have carried the day.

Annette sighed.

"But the Empress doesn't want to see more people die than have to, and I agree with her," she admitted. "This at least got most of our people out of Kanzi slavery. But...if the High Priestess has no control over her military, this entire exercise has been a waste."

"Cawl seemed to think you could make a change with proof," Robin-Antionette pointed out. "Was he wrong?"

"I don't know," Annette confessed. "I don't know the politics here. I don't know the people here. All I know is that all the pretty lights and pretty lies are covering up a goddamn *slave state*. We keep brushing over that, but the people we're trying to negotiate with are fucking *evil*, Maria."

The room was silent.

"I know," her aide finally replied. "But are you willing to write off any chance of peace?"

"No." Annette studied the scans on her screen again and shook her head. "But we just killed a hundred thousand people, Maria. A *hundred thousand* Kanzi spacers—after the damn war between us was supposed to be over."

"They chose that," Robin-Antionette pointed out. "What you have to choose is what happens next. You can ask the Empress. We have a link."

It would take about twelve hours each way unless Annette used the Kanzi starcom, but given that A!Shall was almost three hundred light-years away, that timeframe was a miracle. She couldn't use the starcom for this, either. She didn't trust the Kanzi not to record her conversations there.

"Can you..." She paused thoughtfully as she studied her aide.

"Can you get a flight organized to get me back aboard *Tornado*? Then get invitations out for Rejalla and Cawl, maybe a couple of his daughters too, for dinner aboard her?"

"Someone might ask why we're doing it aboard our ship instead of down here," Robin-Antionette pointed out.

"Down here, I'm using a borrowed Kanzi chef," Annette replied. "On *Tornado*, we have our own people. And we owe Fleet Master Cawl a dinner at the least, don't you agree?"

"I'll make it happen," Maria Robin-Antionette confirmed with a grin. "I doubt I can manage to pull it off without suspicion, but I know I can make sure people stop asking questions."

"That's all we need."

GETTING BACK aboard *Tornado* was surprisingly easy, and Annette didn't even conceal her sigh of relief as she was greeted by saluting Ducal Guards as she came aboard. She hadn't even realized how much being surrounded by Kanzi troops all day was starting to grate on her.

"It's good to see you, your grace," Captain Mamutse told her. The big man shook her hand briskly and gestured for his people to search the shuttle.

"Let's make sure our smurf friends didn't sneak anything aboard while we're waiting for your guests," he told her. "I have to admit, sitting in orbit above a Kanzi world has been more nerve-wracking than I thought."

"You have super-battleships for guard dogs," Annette pointed out. "Their presence has been reassuring for me on the surface as well."

"And the entire Kanzi home fleet is sitting within missile range of us," Mamutse replied. "I'll be ecstatic when we get to go home." He paused. "I don't suppose you coming back aboard means we get to go home?"

"Probably not," she admitted. "We came here with a job to do, Captain, and even if the Kanzi are dragging their feet on it, we need to keep trying until we *know*, one way or another."

"That's what I figured, your grace," he conceded. He paused and checked his communicator quickly. "Our shuttle has picked up Ambassador Rejalla. They'll be back aboard in ten minutes. Fleet Master Cawl's shuttle is on the surface, picking up his daughters. Last ETA we had from them was twenty minutes.

"Can I get you a coffee while we wait?"

"Please," she told him. "We brought some down with us, but the Kanzi have *no* idea how to make a good cup!"

CAWL AND HIS daughters came without any escort at all, to Annette's surprise. That lack definitely seemed to make her Guards feel better as they welcome the Kanzi Fleet Master aboard *Tornado*, but Annette had been willing to order them to behave.

Instead, the four Kanzi were alone as she greeted them.

"Welcome aboard *Tornado*, Fleet Master Cawl," Annette said. "Priestess Cawlstar, Miz Cawldana, Guard Keeper Cawlan."

There was, presumably, some logic to the suffixes added to each daughter's last name. Annette probably even had it somewhere in the cultural files she had access to. Family name conventions, however, hadn't made her priority list at any point.

"It's always a pleasure to walk the decks of a legend," Cawl told her. "Few ships have stories like *Tornado*'s."

"She's seen a lot," Annette agreed. "I still sometimes miss commanding her."

"All who have commanded a starship and given it up for greater tasks feel the same," Cawl said. "This is your show, Duchess. Where do we go from here?"

Annette smiled.

"Ambassador Rejalla is double-checking with *Tornado*'s chef to make sure the food will meet your needs," she told him. "But if you'll follow Captain Mamutse, he'll show you to the dining room."

Tornado had long ago become the personal transport of the Duchess of Terra. Among the many things they'd installed that Annette questioned the usefulness of, the cruiser had a formal dining room.

Mamutse was keeping half an eye on their guests as he led them deeper into his ship, but that was fine by Annette. She was prepared to extend Cawl an informal personal alliance. That didn't mean she was really willing to *trust* him.

She just trusted him more than any other Kanzi she'd met so far.

———

"I'M IMPRESSED," Cawlstar noted later, the priestess leaning back in her chair with a satisfied smirk that crossed species boundaries. "Your chef has done a spectacular job with the riven conduck."

Annette didn't even pretend to understand the name of the dish, but it was apparently what *Tornado*'s senior stewards had put together to feed their Kanzi guests. She supposed that having access to the markets of the Kanzi homeworld couldn't have hurt.

"Excellent as the food has been, none of us believe for a moment that the dinner we are having with the Imperial ambassador and plenipotentiary representative is entirely social," Cawlan noted, Cawl's youngest daughter throwing a warning glance at her father. "What is this about, Duchess Bond?"

Annette was enjoying her fifth cup of coffee since coming aboard *Tornado* and could tell that having *decent* coffee was easing her mood.

The whole situation didn't allow for much easing, though.

"You were right," she told Cawl. "Our scouts located a starkiller deployment squadron positioned to strike at Sol."

The Fleet Master closed his eyes.

"I'd seen the evidence. Heard the rumors. But break my fangs if I hadn't hoped I was wrong."

"What happened?" Cawlan demanded, the other military officer in the room looking suddenly strained.

"My Militia challenged them. They opened fire without communicating," Annette said simply. "They were destroyed."

The dining room was silent and she could almost *see* the meal turning to ash in her guests' mouths.

"How many?" Cawl finally asked.

"A full super-battleship squadron with escorts," Annette told him. "We took prisoners and my people are searching for survivors, but..."

"Space battles do not lend to wounded," the Fleet Master finished for her. "The damn fools just murdered a hundred thousand of our people."

"The *fools* did not," Cawlan snapped. "The *Imperium—*"

"Defended their territory against a violation of the treaties our High Priestess signed," Cawl cut her off. His eyes were closed in grief. "Put the blame on the fur that owns it, daughter. Duchess Bond's people did their duty, the same as I would have in their place.

"Those ships, those crews, should never have been there."

The room was silent.

"You realize," Rejalla finally said into the quiet, "that this is an act of war that breaks the treaties we have most recently negotiated. The Imperium now...cannot trust the word of the Kanzi Theocracy. If we can't trust you to honor as simple a treaty as peace and nonaggression, how could we expect to regard you as allies?"

"They broke the word of the High Priestess, the Divine Chosen," Cawl said harshly. "There will be consequences for that, Ambassador Rejalla. Reesi Karal cannot afford for her will to be blatantly defied.

"Tradition, honor and her *power* demand that she make this right," he continued. "You must present your evidence to her—and you must do so *publicly*, before her entire court.

"Her honor has been tainted. Her word has been broken. Her

word defines our law, our nation. If her word is broken, our laws fail. This must be made publicly clear."

"That sounds damn dangerous," Annette pointed out. "I don't even have a way to get an audience, but I can't imagine that rubbing her failures in her face is a *safe* action."

"It's not," Cawl agreed. "As a Companion of the Divine Chosen, I can get you the audience. As a representative of the A!Tol Imperium, there is only so much she can do to vent her anger at you. So, she will unleash it on those who betrayed her."

"And what happens then? For the alliance?" Rejalla demanded.

Cawl sighed and glanced over at his eldest daughter. "Asiri? You're most familiar with the politics in the government."

"The factions that are pushing against the alliance cannot associate themselves with the betrayal of the Divine Chosen's word," Cawlstar said slowly. "We will have a short period where they will not have the claws to challenge the negotiations.

"There will be no better time to present your counteroffer to the demands that everyone knows you can't meet," the Priestess told Annette. "I don't know what you can offer, Duchess Bond, but once you have challenged her honor with the claws of one hand, you must extend the other with claws sheathed."

Annette took a moment to process the metaphor back to "offer the carrot after the stick."

"It's not our place to tell you what you can offer," Cawl said. "But you will never have a better chance to get a fair offer through our politics and factions."

The Fleet Master carefully rose, leaning on the table and then on his cane.

"I must start quickly if I am to organize an audience for you within a reasonable time. I will attempt tomorrow, but the court has its own games."

"Thank you," Annette told them. "I'm glad to know there are some reasonable souls among the Kanzi."

"There are many," Cawl replied. "But it is hard to see the flaws in the system that makes you powerful and privileged. Some of our people truly enjoy and abuse the structure we have built. Many simply don't know any better.

"It falls to those of us who *see* to guide the rest towards a better place," he said grimly. "It is rarely a pleasant course, Duchess Bond... it is merely the one God calls us to."

CHAPTER THIRTY-ONE

"The court of the Divine Chosen recognizes Her Companion, Fleet Master Shairon Cawl!"

"It's time," Cawl murmured, gesturing for Annette to follow him as he walked into the court of the High Priestess of the Kanzi Theocracy. The old Kanzi was back in the shining white leather uniform he'd worn for his previous appearance, with the white cane in his hand and the golden stone chain wrapped around his neck.

Annette, for her part, wore a stiffly cut black suit. It was among the most formal garments she owned, though she doubted the Kanzi were sufficiently familiar with human style to realize that.

The two of them entered the court alone. Neither had brought guards, though Annette knew that two of her Ducal Guards were with Rejalla in the audience.

It wouldn't make a difference if Reesi Karal decided to go mad and order them executed on the floor of the court. That was within the High Priestess's power.

"Fleet Master Cawl," Karal's voice echoed out as they reached the designated point and Cawl knelt before his mistress's throne. "I was told that you desired an audience. I did not expect to see the Imperial representative with you."

"Divine Chosen, Duchess Bond has brought me news of the most dire stripe," Cawl declared loudly. "We—*you*—have been betrayed by our own."

The quiet murmur of conversation in the audience suddenly cut to silence.

"It is my duty, as a Guardian of the Church, as your Companion, as a Fleet Master of the Kanzi, to bring Duchess Bond before you that she can tell you what she told me."

Karal was silent for a dangerous few seconds.

"Speak, Duchess Bond," she finally said.

Annette took a very careful, very precise step across the line no supplicant was supposed to cross. She heard Cawl inhale in shock behind her as she intentionally broke the protocol.

"You pledged to the A!Tol Imperium peace and nonaggression," Annette reminded the High Priestess. "Your word and name were signed to a treaty that *we* have honored...and you have broken."

"I have ordered no such thing!"

"What you have ordered is irrelevant," Annette replied. She was carrying a projector in her left hand and she activated it. The image of the starkiller strike force appeared above her, a hologram as high as three humans or four Kanzi.

"A standard patrol around Sol discovered this fleet, waiting for the order to strike," she continued. "Starkillers, positioned inside Imperial space with a Kanzi fleet escort. Their presence alone is a gross violation of the treaty you signed, High Priestess—and when challenged by my Militia, they opened fire."

The hologram continued to play through the battle as Annette spoke.

"Missiles and blood have been exchanged, High Priestess Karal, in a battle *your* people started after violating Imperial space. I can only assume that other, similar forces have infiltrated near to other worlds of the A!Tol Imperium.

"As you have offered peace with one hand, you have prepared to destroy us with another! The Imperium will not be so easily fooled!"

The hologram finished and Annette met Karal's gaze. The High Priestess seemed to have been honestly shocked into silence, but she finally rose from her chair and stepped to the edge of the dais.

She wasn't going to step down onto the floor of the court, not with an alien present, but even that was a concession toward informality and a symbolic gesture toward honesty.

"Duchess Bond, you will provide us with all copies of all the sensor information," Karal said flatly. "I have no basis nor reason to disbelieve you. It is not the nature of the Imperium to lie, and yet..."

Some hidden gesture caused Karal's robes to flare out around her, making the tiny blue-furred woman look significantly larger for a few seconds.

"If this is true, *our* honor has been tainted. We cannot let this defiance stand. You have my word, the word of the Divine Chosen, that we will learn the truth and the guilty will be punished.

"You have the word of the Divine Chosen that we did not order this!"

Annette let Karal's words echo to silence in the immense chamber without flinching, and then gently shook her head at the High Priestess.

"It doesn't matter," she told the Kanzi. "Who ordered this *does not matter*. The sword of the Theocracy was bent to the throat of the Imperium even while we argued for peace and alliance. If we cannot trust you with even the basics of peace, how would we trust you at our side with our deadliest weapons?"

There was flexibility in Kanzi protocol. To a point, at least. There was symbolism to everything Karal did that wasn't sitting passively in her throne.

The protocol had no symbolism for the High Priestess stepping down from the dais when an alien was on the court floor. This was not expected to happen. It was not the place of the Divine Chosen to dirty herself so.

Reesi Karal did it anyway. She stepped to the floor and gestured for Annette to come closer.

"All I can pledge is the word of the Chosen of God," Karal said softly. "This was not ordered. It will not be permitted. Those involved will be punished. The alliance between our great empires *will* be concluded."

From this close, Annette was surprised to realize that she could read Karal's features even more clearly than she'd expected. The degree to which human and Kanzi body language was similar was odd at best, but it was more than that.

She could see the bags under Karal's eyes, and where careful makeup had been applied to her fur to help cover the Priestess's exhaustion.

"This is the will of my Empress," Annette told Karal, her tone equally soft. The court's acoustics meant everyone could hear them, even if they whispered. "But it falls to me to judge if you can be trusted.

"Find the hands that set this breach of our treaties into motion. See them punished so that this never happens again, and I will extend some grace," she continued. "Understand that we will *never* provide the Theocracy with hyperspace missiles. If you *prove* that this alliance can be trusted, that we can stand shoulder to shoulder with the Kanzi without fearing a knife in our back, then we will provide hyperfold communication and weapons technology.

"But the Imperium's trust has been betrayed. You must *earn* our faith, High Priestess Karal...or this whole endeavor is *over*."

Annette gave the leader of the Kanzi an abbreviated stiff bow and, without waiting for permission, turned and stalked out of the Court.

She was well aware of how badly she'd just ignored Kanzi court protocol. Every single breach had been intentional and planned.

She wondered if, from the perspective of the Kanzi, that was better or worse than if she'd just been ignorant.

CHAPTER THIRTY-TWO

"HYPERSPACE EMERGENCE IN FIVE MINUTES. ALL HANDS TO battle stations. All hands to battle stations. This is not a drill."

The recorded voice began to repeat its message, but it was quiet on *Bellerophon*'s bridge. They were hearing the muted echo from the hallways—and the bridge crew had been at battle stations for ten minutes.

Most of them, Morgan reflected, had already been there even before that. As was par for the course on this trip, they knew almost nothing about the system they were about to enter. Scans from the Sedetch's system had told them that PG-Three was a trinary system with a red giant primary and two yellow dwarf stars keeping it company.

That was all they knew. No one had entered or left the system via hyperspace during the twelve-hour window they'd been watching the system, but that didn't mean much. Even the most populated star systems didn't have hyperspace traffic coming through every minute or even every day.

The absence of traffic during their approach to the system was more telling of a lack of commerce, if not necessarily a lack of habitation.

It seemed unlikely that a trinary system would have a habitable planet, but it had seemed unlikely that the system they'd found the Precursor starcom in would have a habitable planet. Morgan wasn't making assumptions anymore.

"All weapons and defenses are green," she reported as the clock ticked down. "Bucklers are ready to deploy; Sword turrets are online. All hands are at battle stations. *Bellerophon* is ready for combat, sir."

"*Chancellor Merkel* opening the primary portal, sir," Hume reported. "We're first through."

"Carry on, Commander."

The ship shivered as she passed into normal space and Morgan started running her scans. As she'd expected for a trinary system, there wasn't much in terms of planets. A few charred cinders in tight orbits around the various stars. A mess of debris and rocks that could be generously termed an asteroid belt but wasn't really that organized. Four gas giants.

Wait.

"I have interface-drive signatures!" she snapped. "Multiple signatures, numbers unclear."

"Unclear, Commander?" Vong asked.

"There's too many too close together," Morgan said as she dug deeper into her scanners. "Concentrated around the second gas giant. It's in a steady orbit around the primary, basically in lockstep with the second—"

Her scans finished processing.

"What in the name of God is that?" she half-whispered.

She flipped the object onto the main hologram even as she cursed, focusing her scanners on it as *Bellerophon* drifted closer to it.

"It's an orbital ring of some kind," she explained after a moment. "Scans are making it two kilometers thick, just over a hundred wide and orbiting at a radius of forty thousand kilometers."

The scale of the object failed to make sense. A ring that

surrounded an entire, admittedly small, gas giant? Fifty *million* cubic kilometers of space? What the hell *was* it?

"I don't know if anyone cares at the moment," Hume said slowly from navigation. "But my program says that the constellations from that ring would match one of the last two locations in the Taljzi frescos."

"I think we've found at least one of their core systems," Vong agreed. "Commander Casimir? I'm guessing that's some kind of residential and industrial station. Estimates on what I'm looking at?"

"We don't even have programs for this," Morgan replied. "Running some numbers; give me a moment."

The rest of the flotilla was emerging behind them and Morgan could only be glad that they were a good five light-minutes from the strange structure.

"Emissions match Taljzi across the board. I've got multiple civilian and military ships, but there's too many too close together to get a breakdown." She shook her head. "I'm estimating at least a thousand signatures, but that's including the civilians."

"I'll believe that the Taljzi have transport ships," the Captain said grimly. "I'm not sure I believe they have *civilian* ships. What about the ring itself? Population, industrial capacity, that kind of thing?"

Her numbers finished running and Morgan inhaled sharply.

"From heat and energy signatures, my best guess is that the station is home to at *least* twenty billion people," she said quietly. "That's assuming an industrial capacity equal to the entire Sol System."

And no unknown Precursor tech to handle heat, either. They didn't know enough about the Taljzi technology base to really make judgments like that. The ring station was entirely outside their experience.

"It looks like the gas giant was...bigger at one point," she finally said. "There are hundreds of cloudscoops descending from the ring. I'd say they've been feeding the asteroid belt into the smelters for decades—possibly centuries—while draining the planet for fuel."

"The whole place looks like a giant industrial complex," Vong concluded. "Somehow, I can't see the Taljzi settling here when they were running. They wanted a homeworld, not a factory."

"I *think* the ring is Precursor-built," Morgan noted. "That might have been enough for them. Except..."

She checked Hume's analysis of the constellations and sighed again.

"This was the fifth set of constellations in the frescos, not the last one. There's another system they've settled, but this one is definitely worth our attention."

"Have we been detected yet?" Vong asked.

"I don't know. I haven't spotted a response."

The Captain nodded.

"We'll relay your conclusions to the Flag," he ordered. "I think we need a closer look, but that's Rear Admiral Sun's decision."

THEY TRIED TO BE STEALTHY. None of their ships had stealth fields, and without that technology the Imperium had never learned, hiding in space was almost impossible.

"I'm picking up new interface-drive signatures," Morgan reported twenty minutes later, as the fleet tried to drift towards the ring. "*Big* signatures."

She was still resolving them and stared at her screens in silence as the reality began to sink in.

"Commander?" Vong asked. "Commander Casimir!"

"Sorry, sir." She swallowed. "I'm estimating in excess of two hundred super-battleships have left docking cradles in the last ten minutes. I'm relatively sure I'm looking at an equal number of battle-ships and the same again in escorts. At least eight hundred warships, half of them capital ships."

"There were at least a hundred capital ships already deployed," she continued. "Five hundred battleships and super-battleships, sir."

More ships were showing up on her screens, too. They had been in dock for some reason, presumably refits or refueling or *something*... but now they swarmed out at the scouting flotilla.

"Overkill much?" Ruskin murmured, the junior officer managing to force some semblance of humor. "How badly do they need to outnumber us? You'd think a hundred to one would be enough."

"Orders from the Flag, sir," Antonova reported, her voice very quiet. "The flotilla is going to make a high-speed pass of the ring at two light-minutes, making sure to stay outside established Taljzi missile range.

"We are *not* to engage. This is a scouting pass."

"They're going to fire *something* at us," Vong said calmly. "Commander Casimir? Get our Bucklers in space.

"The Admiral is right. We need more data...but let's make damn sure we don't lose anybody getting it."

"We're going to need *everybody* shortly," Morgan murmured, watching as the immense space station continued to spew out warships. "Current estimate is seven hundred capital ships and rising. What hornet's nest did we stumble into?"

"Unless I miss my guess, Commander, we just stumbled into the Taljzi's main refit and construction yards," Vong told her. "A location that will be very useful at some point in the future—so long as we live to tell everyone about it."

———

THE CLOSER THEY GOT, the worse the numbers looked. There were four capital ships in the scout flotilla, two *Duchess of Terra*-class super-battleships and two *Bellerophon*-class battleships. The escorts weren't quite meaningless, but if it came to a fight, the cruisers wouldn't change anything.

Of course, neither would the capital ships.

"Well, the ring seems to have finally stopped disgorging capital ships, at least," Morgan said quietly. "I make it four hundred and sixty super-battleships and six hundred battleships. Escorts are a mix, but it's looking at just over two thousand ships."

"Three thousand warships all told," Vong said grimly. "Three times the size of the Grand Fleet."

"Yes, sir." She shivered. "They're vectoring after us, sir."

"I know." He shook his head. "So does Admiral Sun. Commander Hume, how are we doing?"

"We're not going to get as close to the ring as the Admiral wanted, sir," Hume reported. "Not if we want to keep the two-light-minute range open."

At least the Terrans had tachyon scanners. Morgan knew what the Taljzi were doing in real time, but they didn't think the Taljzi did. Everything the hostiles saw was two minutes out of date, but the Terrans were acting with live data.

It was the only thing that was going to let them get any information.

"Keep an escape course programmed in," Vong ordered. "They aren't that much faster than us, but I don't trust these bastards not to have surprises up their sleeves for us."

Morgan studied the enemy fleet for a few more seconds and then looked up at her captain.

"I think we've learned all we're going to, sir," she said quietly. "That ring is a nightmare. A single industrial platform to rival an entire rich star system. I'm picking up over three thousand docking stations for ships up to super-battleship size, plus at least *five hundred* construction slips."

And those numbers told Morgan something else. Something terrifying. She shook her head as she said it aloud.

"This wasn't built as a shipyard, sir," she said quietly. "All of that capacity is added on, built by the Taljzi later. I don't know what the damn thing was *built* to be, but being a habitat was an entirely secondary purpose, and being a construction yard wasn't even on the plans.

"It was draining an entire gas giant for power...and I don't think we'll ever know what it was meant to do with that!"

That power supply and the sheer scale of the platform meant it had made a fantastic shipyard and habitat. She suspected the Taljzi didn't know what its original purpose was any more than she did, but they hadn't passed up the opportunity to make use of it.

"Do you think this is their cloning facility?" Vong asked.

"No," Morgan said instantly. "The gas giant is the wrong makeup. Lots of hydrogen, helium, similar things that can be used for power...but not much in terms of carbon or organic molecules. They'd need a source of raw material for that, and a habitable world would give them a more accessible supply."

"So, this definitely isn't their home system, then," the captain said with a sigh. "At least it gives a starting point when we come back."

Morgan shivered at the thought. How could you even attack something like that? Boarding it would be the equivalent of urban warfare...across an entire planetary surface. Several of them, stacked on top of each other.

Coming back was going to be hell, but she didn't see an alternative. Even now, the Taljzi weren't being talkative.

"Orders from the Flag," Antonova reported quietly. "We are to—"

"Vampire!" Ruskin snapped. "Multiple missile launches. *Holy shit!*"

THE TERRAN FLEET was still well outside of the Taljzi's known missile range, but Morgan was grimly certain that the blue-furred bastards weren't wasting ammunition.

"There's not enough missiles," she noted after a moment of studying the incoming fire.

"There seem to be plenty of damn missiles out there!" her subordinate pointed out in a panicked tone.

"Three thousand warships," Morgan replied, perhaps more harshly than required. "But I'm only reading twenty or thirty thousand missiles. Only the capital ships fired, and nowhere their full arsenal."

"I see it," Vong replied. "Commander Hume? Get us out of here, please."

"On it."

"Flag says they're out of range, bluffing," Antonova reported. "We're ordered to evade, but threat priority is not high."

"Casimir? Your take?"

Morgan exhaled. She could see the Flag's logic. They were easily twenty light-seconds—six million kilometers—outside of the Taljzi's known range, but they were also only barely far enough away to make it into hyperspace if they didn't run. Now.

"Sir, they *know* how we beat the Return," she said urgently. "They'll have built a countermeasure—and the easiest countermeasure is a *big* missile with a lot more endurance. One that, say, even their capital ships could only launch thirty of at a time."

The bridge was very quiet for a few seconds.

"Commander Hume," Vong said slowly, studying the real-time display of the incoming missiles. "Maximum-velocity evasion; open a hyper portal as soon as you can.

"Commander Antonova, get me a channel to the Admiral. We need to get the hell out of this star system!"

CHAPTER THIRTY-THREE

"WE'RE CLEAR," HUME REPORTED IN A SHAKY TONE.

"Buckler platforms will self-destruct in ninety seconds," Morgan added, watching the hyperspace portal close behind them. None of the missiles had reached the flotilla, but they hadn't had time to retrieve the defensive platforms.

"Any estimates on what the running time on those things is?" Vong asked.

"Scans show they're almost four times the size of the Taljzi's standard interface missiles," she said quietly, going over the data now that they were safe. "I'd guess they're not even internally launched—they'd be relatively easily mounted on racks on the outer hull."

"Like we do with the D-HSMs," Vong agreed with a sigh. "So, four times the running time?"

"It's not that simple a calculation, thankfully," she told him. "At least twice. Maybe three times. Say...four to five minutes at eighty-five percent of lightspeed. Call it five for safety's sake, so four and a quarter light-minutes of range."

She let that sink in on *Bellerophon*'s silent bridge. Their own hyperspace missiles only had a range of four light-minutes, and even with tachyon scanners, their accuracy sucked at that range. The HSMs biggest vulnerability was their limited terminal attack period.

These super-long-range missiles the Taljzi had rolled out didn't have that problem. They had their entire flight time to keep track of their target, and were coming in fast enough that even the extra warning would help defensive accuracy only so much.

"So, is this a weapon they didn't deploy with the Return, or is it something they've built since?" Vong asked.

"I don't know, sir," Morgan admitted. "The fact that they had so many of their ships in refit slips, though...suggests it was new. They probably had a design on the books for it, but I suspect it went into production after they got the Return's scan data."

The Captain was silent, then glanced over at Antonova.

"Coms, how much of that did we get home?" he asked.

The hyperfold communicator's one big weakness was that it was useless inside hyperspace. Until the flotilla could drop out of hyper, they could receive starcom messages from home...and that was it.

"Everything up until we went through the portal," Antonova confirmed. "The Bucklers with hyperfold coms would have transmitted until they self-destructed. The Imperium will have more data than we will, for a while yet."

Bellerophon and her sisters were a long way from home. It would take hours for their data to reach Earth, the nearest starcom. The starcoms could communicate with them instantly—there was a reason that all four capital ships still carried starcom receivers despite the availability of hyperfold coms—but it would be most of a day before they'd hear anything.

"Flag is ordering everyone to make maximum speed for PC-One," Antonova reported. "We'll refuel and reassess there while we make contact with home."

Morgan surreptitiously checked the fuel status of the fleet and hid a grimace. They had enough hydrogen aboard the flotilla's capital ships to get home. And not much more than that. Even *Bellerophon* and *Rama* needed mass to fuel the matter converters, and every ship needed hydrogen to interact with their antimatter stockpiles and run their fusion plants.

They could fight *a* battle and make it home. Anything more than that, the flotilla would need to refuel.

Her thoughts were interrupted by a flashing alert on her screens, and Morgan swallowed as her heart tried to leap into her mouth.

"We have a hyper portal opening behind us," she said as calmly as she could. "Multiple portals. Computer is still resolving, but they're coming after us."

"I figured," Vong said grimly. "How many of them did they send?"

Morgan was silent for several seconds, watching more and more massive portals tearing through from reality.

"It looks like...all of them, sir."

"WE ARE, thankfully, beyond even what we estimate the range of their new missiles is," Rear Admiral Sun said on a conference a few minutes later. "If they wanted to send their destroyers ahead, those ships do have a speed advantage over us. None of their other ships do.

"A stern chase is a long chase, and they don't have enough of an edge to catch us." He sighed. "Unless we detour somewhere to refuel. Then they will be able to force at least a running battle. I'm relatively certain we can break free at that point, but it won't buy us any more time.

"I also don't want to lead *three thousand warships* back to Earth, people. I'm open to suggestions."

The conference of the flotilla's senior officers was silent. Every eye, including Morgan's, was drawn to the red splotch on their anomaly scanners.

There was no way to break down the fleet pursuing them in detail with the notoriously unclear hyperspace scanners. They could identify the distance to the pursuing fleet, but that was it.

"So long as we're in hyperspace, we can't evade them," Morgan pointed out. "Where else do we run? Kanzi space?"

"The thought is tempting," Sun admitted. "But they're no more capable of standing off this fleet than we are. The massed fleet of the A!Tol Imperium would match them. Barely. How they still have three thousand ships after the losses the Return took..."

"Because their entire economy, their entire *society*, has been structured around coming back and kicking the Kanzi into the next universe," Captain Vong said harshly. "We're not even the damn target; we just happened to be on the board, and their religious imperatives won't let them walk by."

"Sooner or later, we'd have intervened anyway," Sun pointed out. "We may not like the Kanzi much, but I don't think the Empress would have stood by and watched their slave races being exterminated."

"What do we do?" *Rama*'s Captain asked.

"We run," the Rear Admiral told them. "We can't even begin to fight what's chasing us, so we run. PC-One for now, and we hope to get enough time to refuel.

"Hopefully, Command has enough information from our hyperfold transmissions that they can pass on orders. Someone has to have a better idea of what to do about this than we do!"

No one answered.

For her part, Morgan kept staring at the red splotch of hyperspace anomalies. The Taljzi were five hyperspace light-minutes behind them. Depending on the density of hyperspace where they were right now, that was between a light-day and a couple of light-months of real space.

They weren't gaining on the Terran flotilla. They weren't losing, either. They were simply there, inexorably following Morgan at half the speed of light.

Even if they got out of this, she could already tell what was going to be featuring in her nightmares for a while now.

CHAPTER THIRTY-FOUR

THE CONFERENCE ROOM AT THE TOP OF WUXING TOWER WAS silent as the people present stared at the projected hologram. Currently, it was showing the final moments of one of *Chancellor Merkel*'s Buckler anti-missile drones.

"From the vectors and energy levels shown, they almost certainly pursued your task force into hyperspace," Tan!Shallegh finally said into the silence. His skin was a swirling maelstrom of gray, black and purple. Exhaustion. Fear. Sadness.

Jean's skin didn't change colors, but he understood where the A!Tol Fleet Lord was coming from.

"Can we stop them?" he finally asked. "If they come here, can we stop them?"

"The Ducal Militia can't," Admiral Kurzman-Wellesley said. "If we recall Admiral Rolfson from Asimov and Admiral Amandine from Centauri, we can concentrate our full force. But sixty-four capital ships—seventy-four, if we collect the other scattered deployments and Admiral Sun's flotilla—cannot stand against a *thousand*."

"It is not and will never be the sole task of your Militia to defend this system," Tan!Shallegh said sharply. "The Grand Fleet is here.

We aren't going anywhere. This is an Imperial System and the Imperial Navy will defend it.

"I will send reports and requests for reinforcements to the other Fleet Lords. We will concentrate as much force as we can here. The refits must be accelerated."

"There's only so much accelerating we can do," Elon Casimir told them. "I have faith in the ability of my people to produce miracles, but we're already refitting sixty capital ships at once. We're *gutting* their energy weapons and missile magazines. We can only do that so quickly."

"Then we need to make damn sure that you're done with the current group before the Taljzi arrive," Jean snapped, feeling so very tired and old. "We must prepare to defend our homeworld once more."

Twice before, he had commanded hopeless defenses of Sol. Once against the A!Tol, which he'd lost, and once against the Kanzi, where they'd managed to hold until the Imperium relieved them.

"There is another option we *have* to consider," General Wellesley-Kurzman reminded them, his voice very soft...and cold. As if he were freezing his own heart to allow him to even say the words, even his British upper lip failing at this task.

"We don't know that this fleet is beginning their new offensive," he continued. "It is entirely possible they are just engaging in a degree of overkill against Sun's flotilla... In which case we need to consider sacrificing the flotilla."

Wellesley-Kurzman's words hung in the air like knives.

"My *daughter* is on that fleet," Casimir shouted. "We can't just write them off."

"I know Morgan as well as anyone else in this room," James Wellesley-Kurzman said flatly. "And there are thirty thousand more people in that flotilla, and they matter just as much to those who love them.

"But there are eleven *billion* people in this star system. We owe it to them to make certain we choose the best path, regardless of our personal feelings."

"*Ça suffit!*" Jean bellowed, rising to his feet. "We will not write off thirty thousand spacers on the *possibility* that the enemy will not pursue further. If they have sent out three thousand ships, they are not merely chasing Admiral Sun. They are launching their second Return."

"Then they must be brought here," Tan!Shallegh told them. "I will gather every ship, every weapon I can. We will form a shield of steel and fire over your world, and we shall drive the Taljzi back."

"They have superior technology and weapons," the General pointed out. "And no intention of landing troops. If they blast your fleet, they will bombard Earth and destroy the people we are sworn to defend."

"Then we must be ready, James," Jean said gently. "Do you really have it in you to order Admiral Sun's fleet to their deaths?"

The commander of the Ducal Guard chuckled mirthlessly as he shook his head.

"No," he admitted. "No, I don't. I don't have it in me to blithely surrender, not unless this entire argument went against me. But someone had to say it, didn't they?"

"I'm not sure I agree with that logic, General," Jean replied. "But we are decided, then?"

The people in the room weren't really qualified to speak for the Duchy of Terra, let alone the A!Tol Imperium. The three military men and the Ducal Consort could decide the choices of the Terran Militia, though...and Tan!Shallegh was the Empress's nephew, as humans counted things.

If they chose to bring the enemy to Sol, to put the Duchy's Militia and the Imperium's Navy between the Taljzi and humanity...no one would argue.

"We have no good choices," Elon Casimir half-whispered. "We have spent two decades building a fleet to shield our world. Now we have no choice but to prove that we can."

"Three-to-one odds," Tan!Shallegh said, surprisingly calmly. "We know they now have an equally ranged weapon to our hyperspace missiles, but it is far from equally *capable*.

"And this system has significant fortifications, and we established hyperspace-missile-armed stations and mines when we faced the first Return. This is a battle we can win."

Jean chuckled softly.

"I'm not sure I have your optimism, Fleet Lord. But I can tell you one thing: this is Sol. We will not yield until we are broken."

"I would remind you, old friend, that I—of all people—know that," the being who'd forced Earth's surrender said slowly. "I have faith in your people. I have faith in my Grand Fleet. I have faith that the Imperium will reinforce us, and I have faith, above all else, that we will not fail."

Jean nodded.

"It's decided, then," he said firmly. "Admiral Kurzman-Welles-ley? Pass the orders to your subordinates. Your Vice Admirals are to bring their fleets here to Sol.

"And Rear Admiral Sun is to retreat here. If the enemy will follow him, then he will lead them into the face of every ship and missile we can muster. If the Taljzi will come to Sol, then they will face us all."

JEAN SAT in his office in silence, staring at a screen that happily informed him he had a secured encrypted link to the starcom in orbit. He could transmit to Rear Admiral Sun, but Sun wouldn't be able to respond.

Kurzman-Wellesley was busy having live and near-live conversations with his Vice Admirals. Once those four officers were in Sol with their ships, they'd form the core of the defense. In many ways, those conversations were more important than the one Jean had to have.

Sighing, he turned on his camera and began to record.

"This message is for Rear Admiral Octavius Sun from Councilor Jean Villeneuve. Priority Alpha Alpha One."

He paused, giving whichever poor bastard received this message a chance to pause it and deliver it to the Admiral. His orders weren't exactly classified, but he'd prefer that Sun chose the distribution rather than it being carried by the rumor mill.

"Octavius, this is Jean Villeneuve," he greeted the other officer. "We've received all of your data from PG-Three. By the time you receive this, I imagine you'll already be aware that the Taljzi fleet was leaving the system in pursuit of your force."

He shook his head.

"I'm forced to presume that they were almost ready to launch as it was and you didn't accelerate things much," he admitted. "They're chasing you, but I doubt they'd have sent their entire fleet after you unless they intended to follow through.

"The Imperium is now under Code Tsunami."

The A!Tol were an amphibious race that favored coasts and islands for their settlement. The phrase that translated literally as *tsunami* had a lot of connotations the word didn't have in English.

The translation was *correct*...but sometimes Jean felt that *Apocalypse* would fit better.

"Your orders are to lure the Taljzi to Sol," Jean told Sun. "We will concentrate every ship, every Imperial Navy detachment, every weapon we can here. The Grand Fleet is already here. There is nowhere else short of the Imperium's Core Worlds that can stand against the Taljzi as well as we can.

"I can do the math, Octavius." The numbers and calculations were on the screen next to him, in fact. "You're fourteen to sixteen days from Sol, depending on the vagaries of hyperspace. Even Duchess Bond is at least eighteen days from home. It will be *twenty-two* days before the refits on the first tranche of Grand Fleet capital ships are done.

"Your *orders* are to return to Sol." Jean paused and considered his next words very carefully. "But the math says that we need at least an extra week. I don't know if you can steal that for us. I don't know if it's even possible.

"All I can tell you is what we need. Beyond that, I trust in the skill and courage of yourself and the officers and spacers under your command."

Jean was silent for several seconds.

"Bring them home, Octavius," he told the man on the tip of the spear. "We'll be waiting for you."

CHAPTER THIRTY-FIVE

THE MESSAGE MADE ANNETTE'S BLOOD RUN COLD.

She couldn't argue with the logic of the decision her military commanders and Tan!Shallegh had made. Sol was the best-protected system they could reasonably lead the Taljzi to, and if the genocidal bastards were willing to be led around by Sun's flotilla, that was the only course they could follow.

She stared blankly at the wall of the office the Kanzi had lent her and was torn. Concluding the alliance she was here to put together could, at least in theory, help turn the tide of the battle to come...but she wasn't convinced that was going to happen in anything resembling a reasonable time frame.

When push came to shove, she was the *Duchess of Terra*. There was only one place for her to be while her planet was under attack.

"Maria," she called her aide in. The blonde woman stepped into the office a moment later, carrying a coffee cup and looking like she'd just woken up.

"Did you get copied on any of the messages I just got?"

Robin-Antionette shook her head.

"There might be something summarizing for me, but I hadn't got to it yet," she admitted. "What's going on?"

"The end of the fucking world," Annette summed up. "There's a fleet of three thousand warships chasing Rear Admiral Sun, and his orders are to lure them to Sol to face off with the Grand Fleet."

The coffee cup hit the floor as Annette's aide stared at her in horror.

"Shit."

Both women had children and partners on Earth. Annette could at least be certain that her daughters—at least the twins, her paired heirs—would be evacuated from the Sol System in the face of that level of threat.

The Robin-Antionette children would *probably* be evacuated with them, but it wasn't as certain a thing.

"What do we do?" Robin-Antionette finally asked, seeming only barely aware of the shattered cup at her feet.

"The only thing we can do and be true to our oaths and ourselves," Annette told her. "Start packing and organize a shuttle. We leave as soon as Mamutse can get a bird down to pick us up. Fleet Lord !Olarski's super-battleships are needed...and I have only one place if the Duchy is under attack."

"Of course," her aide responded. "Someone should tell Rejalla."

"You get the shuttle sorted. I'll talk to the Ambassador," the Duchess promised. "Let's get moving. I can't stay on this planet long enough to change anything now, so let's wash its dirt from our feet and go home."

"YOU'RE LEAVING," Rejalla said the instant the channel opened. "I got an update from the Navy side, your grace," she continued before Annette could speak. "Your place is on Terra."

Annette chuckled, an almost-mirthless sound despite her amusement.

"It's good to know I'm predictable," she replied.

"You're an Imperial Duchess," the Anbrai told her. "You wouldn't be one if you were the type to stay here while your world was in danger. I can finish the negotiations once the Church recovers from your kneecapping the other day."

"There's no more flexibility," Annette warned. "You know that. What I offered is the best they're going to get."

"What I'm hearing says they know that. Karal is just waiting for her people to validate your evidence so she can announce her acceptance of your terms right after announcing a slew of executions."

The Anbrai shivered her immense shoulders.

"I think she figures that might bring the sun to the mountain? Certainly, the kind of demonstration of power that level of treason is going to lead to will make people unwilling to argue."

Annette grimaced.

"I don't feel overly bad for the people who decided to send starkillers to my homeworld, but that's still a disturbing image."

"Agreed. You'll get your alliance, Duchess. If we're lucky, in time to get ships to Sol to turn the tide of this battle."

"I can only hope. But for now, I have to go," Annette said.

"You do," Rejalla confirmed. "I'll have my people get on making sure your shuttle is clear. No obstacles, no delays. You have my word."

"Thank you. We're far enough away as it is, and I can't help but feel that eight super-battleships may make the difference in what's to come."

The Anbrai winced.

"Not on their own, from what I hear, but every detachment we can get to Sol is one more stone on our side of the mountain. Good luck, your grace."

"Thank you, Ambassador."

ANNETTE WAS TOSSING the assorted paraphernalia that had ended up scattered around the front sitting area of their suite into a suitcase when the front door slid open without warning.

The two Guards in the room had been helping her pack, but they went for their weapons as a trio of Kanzi marched into the room unannounced. Annette recognized the uniforms of the three soldiers and gestured her people to relax.

They wore commando power armor under what would have been called cloth of gold on Earth. Two of them carried stunners at the ready, but the third was carrying a scanner box.

All three had plasma carbines slung from their shoulders, an unspoken threat if Annette's Guards caused trouble.

"Stand down," she ordered aloud. "What is the meaning of this?" she demanded of the Mahalzi solders.

The Mahalzi were the "Sons of God." Kanzi special forces, used as infiltrators, elite commandos...and the bodyguards of the Divine Chosen.

They didn't answer her, but the one with the scanner said a single word.

"Clear."

Two more Mahalzi entered the room, armed similarly to the first three.

"Your weapons," they told Annette's Ducal Guards.

"Not a—"

"Give them up," Annette snapped. She knew her people. She also knew that the stunners her people officially carried were only going to get them in trouble—and the plasma pistols the guards had concealed in sensor-proof boxes would get them killed. They weren't *carrying* those, at least, and her people weren't stupid.

There was a long moment of silence, and the Guards handed over their stunners. Other Mahalzi checked the doors into the other rooms of the suite.

It was suddenly *very* clear that Annette and her people didn't actually own these rooms, something the Kanzi had so far been quite careful not to drive home. There was only one reason Annette could think of for this level of intrusion and security, but that made no sense.

Another pair of Mahalzi entered the room. These two were flanking a small Kanzi woman wearing a white robe.

Annette could see more Mahalzi blocking off the corridor outside as they sealed the door behind Reesi Karal. She very carefully put aside the suitcase she'd been packing and sat down on the couch as the leader of the Kanzi Theocracy walked slowly across the suite.

"We need to talk, Duchess Bond."

"I didn't think speaking with the Divine Chosen like this was allowed," Annette said quietly.

"It isn't." Karal looked at her Mahalzi guards. "Everything is secure?"

"Jammers are up, power is disabled. The only recorders in here are in our armor."

"Turn them off," the High Priestess ordered.

"Your Divi—"

"Turn. Them. Off." Karal bit off each word. "No record of this conversation will exist; am I clear?"

"As the rising sun, Your Divinity."

The Mahalzi obeyed and drifted toward the outside of the room. Annette's Guards followed them, leaving the two women alone in the center of the suite.

Whatever this was about, Annette was expecting the next few minutes to be *very* interesting.

CHAPTER THIRTY-SIX

KARAL STOOD FOR A FEW MOMENTS, UNTIL SHE CLEARLY realized that even sitting, Annette was as tall as she was standing. With a concealed sigh, the unquestioned dictator of a hundred star systems took her own seat and met Annette's gaze.

"I have been briefed on what your scouting flotilla found," she told Annette quietly. "From the state of your suite and the shuttle trip you have arranged, I presume you are returning to Terra?"

"Immediately," Annette confirmed. "These negotiations have dragged on long enough. You know the Imperium's position. You can finish it with Rejalla."

"There is no need," Karal replied. "Announcements and investigations and so forth can wait, but we know the reality. Your terms are acceptable and I will announce as such as soon as my Inquisition has completed their task."

"Their task?" the human questioned.

"Identifying everyone behind the betrayal you discovered," Karal said flatly. "They will die clean deaths, but for what they have done, they will die."

The blue-furred woman shook her head.

"My inclination is to be less than clean," she admitted. "But I know that would offend your Imperium, and you are the wounded clan in this matter. Your opinions matter, in this at least."

Annette was silent, waiting to see what more Karal had to say.

"The High Priestess was first and foremost the mediator between the Clans," Karal reminded her. "In time, the Clans ceased to be the core of our society and the Great Church replaced them. They have never recovered from nor accepted this."

Which, Annette reflected, was always convenient for the Theocracy government. The Clans did enough raiding, slaving and murder without sanction that it covered up a lot of sanctioned operations.

"The time of their freedom is rapidly coming to a close," the High Priestess said. "You must understand this, and relay it to your Empress. I *understand* that the Kanzi cannot continue as they have."

That was...one hell of an admission from the woman charged with protecting Kanzi society.

"That could mean a lot of things, High Priestess," Annette said slowly.

"Of the Core Powers, only the Wendira do not see our slavery as a mortal crime," Karal told her. "Our closest neighbor sees it as a justification for war—and my own Fleet Masters are prepared to embrace atrocities and war to protect it.

"My duty, my sworn oath, is to preserve the Kanzi," the Priestess said, her voice calm. "First and above all else. Then I am sworn to protect the lesser children...only then am I tasked to preserve the Great Church."

She smiled thinly.

"The structure of our society and our slavery-based economy isn't mentioned anywhere in my oaths."

"You're a reformer," Annette suggested very, very carefully.

"Hardly. I am a realist," Karal said. "My predecessor saw that we had to change and began this course. I will continue on it. Give me thirty years, Duchess Bond, and 'slavery' in the Kanzi Theocracy will be mere form. Give me sixty, and it will be replaced by tiers of citizenry."

A caste-based society, with separate but at least theoretically equal citizens, Annette guessed. That had its own problems—as Earth had seen over the years—but it was better than outright slavery, she supposed.

"That's a long damn time for the people already in chains," she pointed out.

"If I move faster, I destroy our people," the High Priestess told her. "I am not a reformer, as you label it. They serve a quite specific sect of our church. As High Priestess, I must be *above* those divisions, those arguments.

"My priestesses can argue words and meanings. I must guide the Kanzi into the future—and we do not have a future if we continue to antagonize every race around us."

"Why are you telling me this?" Annette asked.

"Because I need your Imperium to give me that time," Karal said harshly. "To understand that I can't change everything by the next turning of the world. I need your Empress to understand that we are changing, that we are moving towards where she wants us."

"I can do that," Annette replied. "I can't promise A!Shall will believe it—or that the Imperium can make policy based on that."

"All I truly ask is that you honor the nonaggression pact we made," Karal replied. "Give me thirty years of peace, and we won't need to go to war."

"You're assuming the Taljzi will give us that long."

Karal's expression could charitably have been called a smile. Maybe. It showed a *lot* of teeth.

"That is *officially* why I am here," she told Annette. "The details and valleys of the treaty may not be sorted out, but I know what I want and your Empress wants. I see no reason to wait for the ink and signatures to honor our shared intention."

That was...promising.

"What are you offering?"

"I need you and Fleet Lord !Olarski to accompany Fleet Master Cawl when he leaves in about nine hours," Karal told her. "He will proceed from here to a mustering point where we have gathered our equivalent to your Grand Fleet, at which point he will take command of said assemblage.

"We do not have hyperspace missiles or similar grand technological secrets, Duchess Bond," the High Priestess said grimly. "But we have some surprises of our own—and we have three hundred capital ships available to commit to the defense of Sol.

"If you'll take them."

SURPRISE AND GRATITUDE, with a healthy leavening of fear for her family and her world, kept Annette going until they were aboard the shuttle.

The interface-drive craft shot away from the massive mesa that housed the Golden Palace, and she shook her head as she studied the heart of the Kanzi civilization. She'd come here expecting a bunch of unapologetic slaving madmen.

What she'd got...she wasn't quite sure. A planet full of people, with their own idiosyncrasies, laws and culture. Parts of that were offensive to her—she would *never* be okay with slavery—but she'd been surprised to discover just how active and alive that debate was among even the Kanzi.

She wasn't sure if the galaxy would give Reesi Karal her thirty years—or if removing the substance without changing the labels would even prove possible. The history of her own United States warned of the difficulties there.

But at least the leadership of the Theocracy was *trying*.

And even if they were slaving, evil bastards, they were apparently sending a battle fleet to help protect Earth.

"Duchess Bond," Robin-Antionette interrupted her thoughts. "I have Fleet Master Cawl calling for you."

"Link him to my seat and drop the privacy screen," Annette instructed. The screen slid down around her a moment later, a one-way mirror that blocked sound and sight for everyone outside it.

It wasn't perfect security, but it was as good as she was going to get on a shuttle in flight.

"Fleet Master," she greeted the old smurf on her screen.

Cawl bowed.

"Duchess Bond. I just received my orders, from the hands of the Divine Chosen herself. I suspect you're in much the same state as I am."

"In a shuttle, hoping my homeworld doesn't get annihilated before I get home?" Annette asked.

A flash of discomfort crossed Cawl's face, and he bowed his head in acknowledgement.

"The shuttle part, at least," he admitted. "If I could borrow the fleets from here as well as the Shadowed Armada, I'd have over four hundred capital ships to help you with. But we will never expose Arjzi."

"Anymore than we would send the fleets from A!To," Annette conceded. "I understand. What is this 'Shadowed Armada,' Fleet Master?"

"The fleet we were spending a *lot* of effort making certain the Imperium didn't know about," he told her with a chuckle. "But different times bring different winds. The Shadowed Armada is a reserve fleet that has received every technological update and advance we have. They are the only fully upgraded capital ships in the Theocracy."

"So, they have compressed-matter armor and antimissile defenses," the Duchess of Terra concluded. "We saw those on your lighter ships fighting the Taljzi before."

"And we have a fleet of capital ships with them, yes," Cawl agreed. "There are a few other surprises, but I have only recently been briefed on them myself. I never expected to command one of our Great Armadas, Duchess. Such is reserved for the most trusted Fleet Masters, at the direct command of the High Priestess."

"If it's that big an honor, will we have a problem with the current commander?" Annette asked. That was a situation she couldn't get involved in...and one that could cause real trouble.

"No. *She* was involved in the deployment of the starkillers," the Fleet Master said coldly. "An Inquisitor with Mahalzi support will arrive thirty hours before us. There will be no one to argue my assumption of command."

He sighed.

"There won't be time to invite you over to my flagship for dinner before we get underway," he continued, changing the subject entirely. "I would love to repay your hospitality, but the winds of time wait for no one.

"We'll transmit our course and destination to your *Tornado* and escorts as soon as I'm aboard *Chosen of the Rising Sun*. We will speak again later, Duchess Bond."

Annette nodded and the call closed.

Cawl would be assuming command of a fleet that had just had their commanding officer publicly executed. That was going to go *swimmingly*, she was sure.

They couldn't afford delays. Even if she went straight to Sol from Arjzi, she might not arrive in time. With the detour...all she could do was hope that the Grand Fleet held.

And that this "Shadowed Armada" was enough to carry the day.

CHAPTER THIRTY-SEVEN

THE CONFERENCE WAS VERY QUIET AS REAR ADMIRAL SUN LAID out their orders. It wasn't as massive a group as it could have been, and Morgan found herself feeling very out of place.

The capital ships' Captains, XOs and tactical officers were joined by the Captains of the escorts and the squadron commanders. It wasn't a tiny meeting, but it was small enough to feel entirely dwarfed by the threat they were facing.

"We need to buy Sol eight days," Sun concluded as he summarized Councilor Villeneuve's orders. "Even if we were to attempt to engage the enemy head-on, I don't think we'd manage to make them take eight days to kill us."

"More like eight *minutes*."

Morgan wasn't entirely sure who had spoken, beyond that it wasn't someone aboard *Bellerophon*.

"Unfortunately, that's functionally true," Sun allowed. "This pursuit so far has given us some interesting intelligence on our enemy, though."

Morgan nodded. After forty-eight hours, the Taljzi capital ships had started falling behind. They might be able to sustain the same pace as the Terran flotilla for a while, but they clearly didn't have the strategic endurance of the tried and tested Imperial designs the Ducal Militia used.

Of course, they could do that because they'd left a vanguard of two hundred or so cruisers that were easily capable of keeping up with the Terrans. Capable, in fact, of forcing the Terran flotilla to balance sprint mode versus regular speed.

"How long can we sustain our current pace?" Sun asked.

"Long enough to get back to Sol," Vong said. "I'm not sure if we can pull an extra eight days out of our engines, though. We're pushing it, especially on the older ships."

"We don't have a choice. We could bloody the hell out of their vanguard, but I don't think we could take them," the Rear Admiral admitted. "Even if we could, it would take time. Time in which the *rest* of that monster fleet would be catching up."

"We can't assume that they'll follow us if we detour and try to play matador, either," Commodore Hillary Huber said. The commander of the destroyer contingent somehow managed to look less tired than everyone else. Her ships could sustain this speed forever—but on the other hand, if even half a dozen cruisers caught up to the destroyers, they were dead.

"We need to give them a reason to follow us," Morgan said, very carefully. "We need to piss them off. Give them a bloody nose so they don't think as logically as they should.

"If they don't know we're in live communication with home whenever we're out of hyperspace, they might think they have all the time in the world," she continued. "Chasing down the mosquito that bit them might seem worth it then."

The conference was silent.

"She's right," Rear Admiral Sun told the others. "We *can* give the vanguard a bloody nose. We need to make them think they can catch us—and to be fair, if we're going to try and drag this out for an extra eight days, we need fuel."

Every ship in the flotilla could get home. Even fight a battle along the way, most likely.

But to run around in deep hyperspace for an extra week would run them down past fumes.

"I don't think PC-One is our best option," Vong pointed out. "They know that system better than we do. There's definitely gas giants we can refuel at there, but they know which ones. There's no real games we can play to buy us time. PC-One is their home ground."

"The places that we know better than them are in the Imperium, though," Sun replied. "That's risky. We don't have a lot of wiggle room there."

"That's not really true," Commander Tanzi pointed out, *Bellerophon*'s executive officer looking thoughtful. "The Imperium hasn't scouted this far out, true, but we've scouted pretty far beyond our borders.

"We may not know the systems at the edge of our scouting sphere as well as we would the ones near Sol or deeper into the Imperium, but we know them better than these bastards do. There's got to be at least a handful that will have enough gas giants that we can deke out the Taljzi vanguard and refuel."

Morgan wasn't the only officer running the data search as Tanzi was speaking. Her old boss, Commander Masters—now the executive officer aboard *Rama*—got the answers first, though.

"There are four systems on the edge of our sphere of known space with three or more gas giants," he said, transmitting the data into the conference channel. "This one"—a star flashed gold—"has *five*, plus three stars."

"A trinary," Sun said slowly. "That will make their lives hell to find us."

"Especially since the third star is a brown dwarf," Masters said. "A relatively *cool* brown dwarf. There's no way they'd guess it from a distant scan, but the scouting survey suggests that we should be able to refuel from CDX-25-C."

"From a star?" Vong asked carefully.

"Technically, a sub-stellar object," Huber pointed out. "On the cooler end in this case." The destroyer commodore shook her head. "Not sure the escorts could do it, but the capital ships should be able to."

"And since the bastards won't expect that, we can fuel up before they catch up to us," Vong concluded. "Then we can punch them in the nose and run at a vector away from home. Best case, they follow us and we can drag this out for the time we need."

He sighed.

"Worst case, Sol is no worse off than if we *don't* try this. And we'll get an extra scanner run of a system that it sounds like we might try and exploit in future, too."

The admiral looked around the video conference.

"Anyone have any suggestions or adjustments?" he asked. "If not, pass the word to your navigators. We're changing course away from PC-One towards CDX-25. We'll want to make at least a quick drop out of hyperspace to send reports back home, but that'll need to stay as brief as possible.

"Plan for twenty-four hours from now and make sure everyone knows there will be a mail call." Vong looked tired. "If we're going to try and bloody the Taljzi's nose, this may be the last time a lot of our people get to write home."

THE ONLY REASON Morgan's quarters weren't even quieter than the conference room had been at times was because she was playing music. The quadrilingual crooning echoing through her room— Japanese, English, Cantonese and Korean—had been the popular music of her teen years in Hong Kong.

She honestly wasn't sure if the songs were better or worse for being able to understand all four languages. Certainly, her stepmother had always enjoyed the music, despite being a quintessential American in many ways.

Without a translator earbud, Annette Bond didn't speak Korean at all, and her Japanese and Cantonese were atrocious. Certainly not good enough to follow the twisting multilingual lyrics of Hong Kong pop of the late twenty-third century.

Her parents were on her mind as she stared at her communicator. She'd tossed it onto the table in her quarters and was trying to somehow muster up the words to leave a message for her parents. To say something—*anything*—to the Duchess and the Ducal Consort.

Or, hell, to Annette Bond and Elon Casimir. Neither point of view was being particularly helpful right now.

Her door chimed and she sighed.

"Come in."

Victoria Antonova stepped through the door, an officers'-mess takeout bag in each hand as she smiled at Morgan.

"Chief Langley told me you hadn't been by the mess to eat," she told her lover. "Figured I'd correct that."

She put the two bags on the table, next to the communicator, and grinned.

"And since I *may* have signed off on the Chief Steward getting an extra data allotment on tomorrow's mail call so he can send a video-mail to both his daughter and his ex-wife, well, *voilà*."

Victoria opened one of the bags to reveal two bottles of red wine.

"The food's about what you expect from the mess," she confessed, "but Langley picked the wine himself. I know nothing."

Morgan laughed.

"I know a bit more than that about wine," she told Victoria as she examined the labels. "And this is better than I would expect to find on a warship." She rose to kiss Victoria. "Just where did the data allotment you bribed him with come from, Victoria? We're only going to be in n-space so long."

"It's mine," Victoria admitted in a suddenly quiet voice. "Realized I had nobody back home I cared enough to send a note to. There's a letter on file for my da. It's all he'll need."

Morgan wrapped her arms around Victoria.

"So, you're here," she murmured.

"Better here than anywhere else." The coms officer shook her head. "Don't get me wrong; Da will miss me, but I don't have anything new to say to him. Whereas *you*, well, I have so much I haven't had a chance to say yet."

"I feel like I should say *something* to my parents," Morgan said. "For God's sake, they had to have both signed off on asking us to buy more time." She shook her own head, leaning against Victoria's shoulder.

"I *understand* that, but I know they have to be feeling like shit," she continued. "I think I have to say something."

"That's fair." Victoria kissed Morgan's hair. "But is that for them...or for you? Don't you think they know?"

Morgan chuckled.

"They know," she admitted. "I love them both, but I didn't pick up the iron spine and occasionally callous devotion to duty from nowhere."

"Then let them know you understand and that you'll make it home," Victoria replied. "It's what they need to hear, I suspect. And once you're done that, well, I did bribe some apparently quite nice wine out of the mess!"

CHAPTER THIRTY-EIGHT

JEAN VILLENEUVE WENT OVER THE DATA REAR ADMIRAL SUN had sent them again, hoping for some key or answer he hadn't spotted the first eleven times.

He couldn't disagree with Sun's plan. The enemy's inability to keep up with the scouting flotilla for extended periods gave them an opportunity.

Of course, the scouting flotilla was still outmassed over three to one by the cruisers and destroyers of the Taljzi vanguard. Cruisers shouldn't fight battleships at any odds, but at that ratio Jean might have risked it himself.

Patrick Kurzman-Wellesley didn't even bother to knock before walking into Jean's office. The broad-shouldered Admiral helped himself to a cup of coffee while the Councilor continued to review the data, and then dropped heavily into the chair across from him.

"I wish I could argue with Sun," Kurzman-Wellesley said finally.

"As do I," Jean agreed. "But he's right. This is the only way for him to buy the time we need. I just don't like what the cost looks like it's going to be." He raised a hand, studying it as it trembled, and wondering when that had started.

"Which means I have a damn important question for you, *mon ami*. What can we do with that week if Sun manages to buy it?"

Kurzman sighed.

"Well, geography helps us," he said. "It'll bring Mars in closer alignment with Earth, buy us a bit less volume to cover."

While there were stations scattered across the Solar System, Mars's gravity well had ended up anchoring a lot of industry and colonization. The Duchy had access to enough habitable planets in the zone that treaty and tradition had deeded to humanity to make terraforming the planet unnecessary...but it was happening anyway.

Slowly, to be sure, but it was happening, and that meant that Mars was the second largest concentration of people in the system.

"That helps," Jean conceded. "What about DragonWorks?"

The secret laboratory station and attached shipyards were suspended inside Jupiter. Jupiter was...not conveniently aligned with Earth and Mars right now.

"Jean, we're going to have to write off everything outside the asteroid belt," Kurzman-Wellesley said flatly. "We simply don't have the ships, the maneuverability, or the firepower to shield that kind of volume.

"DragonWorks will have to go dark. They're buried deep enough that they're basically immune to weapons fire from outside the planet, but the Taljzi are just as capable of diving into gas giants as we are."

The Admiral shook his head.

"The best defense DragonWorks has is us keeping the Taljzi busy."

"I don't suppose they have any miracles we can churn out in an extra week?"

"I don't know about miracles, but it looks like they'll have four *Bellerophon*-Bs ready to go if Sun buys us that much time. They won't have undergone trials or anything of the sort, but they'll be complete and they'll have weapons."

"Crews?" Jean asked.

"We'll be poaching them from anywhere we can get them," Kurzman admitted. "They'll be scratch-built, lose some effectiveness...but each of those ships gave up their dual-portal missiles to double the original class's single-portal launchers. They'll be a rude surprise."

"The problem is that I'm certain the Taljzi are going to have surprises of their own," Jean pointed out. "We need to be ready for that."

"A thousand ships." The Admiral sighed. "Well, twelve hundred or so, including all of ours. I can barely comprehend that fleet, Councilor, let alone the horde coming at us."

"The first tranche of Grand Fleet refits will be complete if Sun buys us enough time, correct?"

"We need eight days from him. If he gets us that, we'll be as ready as we're going to be."

"What about reinforcements?" Jean asked.

"You'll need to talk to Tan!Shallegh," Kurzman admitted. "My understanding is that we'll have at least a couple more capital ship squadrons, but we're looking at over a thousand capital ships alone coming our way."

"I know." Jean looked back at Sun's data. "We need to consider evacuating."

His subordinate was silent for a long time.

"I know," he finally conceded. "That's outside my authority. Outside yours, too. You'll need to take that to the Council."

"How many *can* we evacuate?" Jean said.

"A lot of people are already evacuating themselves," Kurzman-Wellesley pointed out. "If we rent enough ships, we can probably move...fifty million? Maybe a hundred, given twenty days?"

Out of eleven billion people.

"I'll talk to the Council. We need to do what we can, even if it won't be enough."

"We need to get the Heirs out," the Admiral replied. "I'm surprised we haven't yet."

Leah and Carol Bond were the fifteen-year-old twin daughters of Annette Bond and Elon Casimir. Megan and Alexis, the younger daughters, weren't considered the primary Heirs, but Jean knew they also needed to be moved to safety.

He sighed.

"Because Leah and Carol are their mother's daughters," Jean said. "And they're arguing against it. They feel someone from the family has to be here if we're facing this."

"Their father is still here. Their mother's on her way back. We need to secure the succession."

"I'll talk to them, too," Jean agreed. "They do understand. They just don't want to abandon their people. We'll get them on a ship, I promise."

"Along with as many other people as we can," Kurzman agreed.

JEAN UNDERSTOOD ONLY one of the four languages being bellowed from the speaker in the corner of the living room of the penthouse apartment. He'd much preferred the softer crooning of the previous decade's Hong Kong pop, but the twins were big fans of the current iteration.

The English was entirely innocent, but what limited Cantonese the Admiral did know suggested that that portion of the lyrics, at least, was a string of curses.

At his age, however, he figured hating pop music was just part of the job description.

All four of the Bond girls were sitting in the living room waiting for him. Alexis, at all of eight years old, looked confused. The older girls all looked impatient.

And stubborn. They definitely looked stubborn.

"Uncle Jean," Leah Bond greeted him. The elder of the twins, Leah was the designated Heir of the Duchy of Terra, the young woman who would assume Annette's role if something happened to the Duchess.

"Leah. Carol. Megan. Alexis." Jean listed off all of their names as he took a seat. The song playing hit a particularly screamy chunk of Japanese, and he paused as he recognized a phrase he'd heard most often from Fleet Lord Harriet Tanaka.

The first human officer in the Imperial Navy had a foul mouth when she didn't think anyone around her could understand what she was saying.

"I... Did she just suggest what I think she suggested?" he said, looking at the speaker.

Carol flushed and turned the radio off.

"Probably," she admitted. "Na Hua Lam does like disturbing the people who understand all four languages."

"Which you do." Jean glanced around the four girls in the room. Alexis gave him a perfectly innocent eight-year-old smile and he sighed. "All of you do."

Even with translator earbuds covering most of their language needs, Hong Kong's higher-tier schools had insisted on providing their students with a working knowledge of the most common languages in the city for centuries. They'd seen no reason to change that now, so all of the girls spoke at *least* four languages.

"We're not leaving, Uncle Jean," Leah said suddenly. "We can't. All of Earth looks to Mom's family. If we run, people will panic."

"If *Annette* ran, people would panic," Jean corrected gently. "If Elon ran, people would panic. If we evacuate four *children*? I think everyone will understand."

"And if we get evacuated and no one else does?" Carol asked. "That's just...wrong, Uncle Jean. We can't leave and let everyone else take risks we won't."

"You and Leah are both in the Council meeting in two hours," Jean pointed out. "That's when I'm going to try and convince the Ducal Council to sign off on a mass evacuation. It won't be just you."

"What about our friends?" Megan asked. "The Robin-

Antionettes? Our school? Do we just evacuate the rich and important?"

Jean had probably had as much to do with raising the girls as anyone else other than their parents and nannies. Their questions made him *proud*, but they were definitely making his life harder.

"It will be a random lottery for tickets on the evacuation ships," he said quietly. "A few strategically important people will be guaranteed seats, but the vast majority will be via lottery."

"Then put us in the lottery," Leah told him. "If our names come up, we'll evacuate with the rest, but we shouldn't get special treatment."

"Leah...you *should*," he said flatly. "You *have to*. You even more than your sisters. We have to secure the succession. I can put the rest of the girls in the lottery, but I need to evacuate *you*. I won't leave them behind if I do."

"So, what, you're going to have Uncle James stun us and load us onto a transport with Ducal Guards?" Leah demanded.

"If I must," he admitted. "We need you to be safe, girls. Your mother needs you to be safe...but so do the people of your Duchy. You don't get to have a choice here. This is the downside of your duties and your privileges."

The eldest Bond girl glared at him, but he met her gaze levelly.

"I could use you tonight," he told her. "I don't know if I can get the Council to sign off on a mass evacuation, but you two could help swing the vote. I need you to help me get the evacuation underway... and I need you four on the first ship out.

"Duty calls, my ladies. We don't always get a choice in what it wants."

The four exchanged glances. Alexis looked much less confused— and much more scared. The twins were definitely the drivers here, but Megan had her own opinions.

"Okay," Leah finally said after half a minute of the silent communication of sisters. "Carol and I will come with you to the Council meeting. Megan, Alexis—can you start packing? Get help if you need it."

"Thank you," Jean said quietly.

"How badly am I going to hate the word *duty* by the time I'm Mom's age?" Leah asked bluntly.

"Worse than you can imagine," he admitted.

"WE CAN'T EVACUATE billions of people!"

Her Royal Highness Dr. An Sirkit, Princess of Thailand and Councilor for Health Affairs, sounded more tired than anything else.

Jean could sympathize. If anyone on the Council *wasn't* exhausted right now, they probably weren't doing their jobs.

"No, we can't," he agreed. "Estimates I'm getting range from three to five million evacuated per day, assuming we're running them all to Kimar and then bringing the ships right back here."

"That's a lot of people by any scale except how many people there are on Earth." Li Chin Zhao didn't just sound tired. He looked ill. His bulk was beginning to fold on itself in a way that Jean didn't like.

"It's better to get as many people as we can to safety than to risk everyone," Leah Bond pointed out, the Heir sitting across from Jean at the table.

He was carefully not noticing that Leah had put on new makeup since their earlier meeting, covering up the red eyes from crying. That realization made him feel like an ass, but he needed her safe.

He'd put up with upsetting her to achieve that.

"That's also talking about shutting our civilian shipping down entirely," Karl Lebrand noted. The old American was still a titan of industry, his fingers in a dozen pies. Casimir's Nova Industries had a dominant position in military construction, but Lebrand's Excelsior Group held an equivalent share in civilian shipping.

"We have to consider priorities," Elon Casimir said slowly.

"What's the point in making money if we can't keep our people safe?"

"What does the Duchess think?" Pierre Larue asked. Once a member of the Governing Council of the United Earth Space Force, he'd been a member of the Council from the beginning.

Even now, there hadn't been a lot of turnover on the Council. Jean knew every face around him and their biases and problems.

"She's not in communication," Carol Bond pointed out. "And we all know what she'd say. She'd want us to evacuate as many people as we could."

"We don't need civilians to defend this system," Leah continued, picking up from her sister. "We need the yards running. We need the fortifications online, and we need the Grand Fleet and Ducal Militia ready to protect us.

"But the more people we get to safety, the better. Councilor Villeneuve, what are the chances that we can hold?"

Trust one of the Heirs to ask the question Jean didn't want to answer.

"As things currently stand?" he said quietly, looking around the room. He owed this room his honesty.

"One in ten at best," he admitted. "If Rear Admiral Sun buys us the time to finish the refits and get the first *Bellerophon*-Bs out, *and* Duchess Bond makes it here with the Kanzi, one in five. Maybe one in four.

"We are utterly outgunned. Large portions of the defending fleet are badly outclassed. Our best-case scenario is that we inflict a pyrrhic victory on the bastards, leaving them too exhausted and shattered to continue on."

He swallowed hard.

"However, unlike the A!Tol when they came here—or even the Kanzi when they tried to take us away from the Imperium—the Taljzi aren't here to conquer."

He let that sink in for a few seconds.

"If we lose this battle, the Taljzi will level Earth. Anyone we don't evacuate will die. We owe it to our citizens, to our people, to our Imperium...to our *species* to make sure as many people get away as possible."

"We have to launch the evacuation," Leah Bond told them all. She met her father's gaze across the table, and Elon Casimir bowed his head in acknowledgement.

Jean concealed an approving nod as the young Heir made the decision for them all.

There would be a vote. There would be more discussion...but the Duchess's Heir had made the decision, and Jean now knew that everyone was going to fall in line.

CHAPTER THIRTY-NINE

THE SCOUTING FLOTILLA TORE INTO REAL SPACE AT OVER HALF the speed of light. There was no slowing down or carefully calculated speeds this time. Three capital ships and their escorts arrived in CDX-25 without slowing, their course selected to make it appear that they were heading for the largest—and farthest from CDX-25-C—gas giant.

Instead, the fleet intentionally emerged several seconds late. They arrived in the trinary system almost six light-hours from their faked destination, *far* closer to the stars than was wise.

Morgan winced against nausea and tried to blink away the suddenly sparkling lights in her eyes. The lights remained, but the nausea faded as she focused on her console.

"Estimate enemy real-space emergence in forty-eight minutes," she reported. "We won't know if we fooled them until then."

"That's the risk," Vong agreed. "Commander Hume, ETA to C?"

"Just over five minutes," the navigator replied. "Engineering reports they are preparing for the fuel dive."

Bellerophon, like any other capital ship, carried the gear for skimming hydrogen from the atmosphere of a gas giant. It was a safe and reliable process.

It would also take the flotilla just over a day to fully refill their tanks. In the best possible case, Morgan estimated that they were going to have ten hours.

So, instead, the entire flotilla was going to dive *into* the outer corona of a brown dwarf. They also had the gear for that type of refueling and it was much faster.

It was also a lot less safe. The capital ships were almost certainly going to be fine. The escorts...should be. Morgan didn't like attaching thousands of lives to "should be fine," but what choice did they have?

"Keep your eyes peeled, Commander Casimir," Vong ordered. "I need to know the moment the vanguard leaves hyperspace. We don't know for sure what makes it up, and I want a breakdown as soon as you can give it to me."

"Yes, sir."

They were pretty sure the vanguard was all cruisers and destroyers. What wasn't going to help was that they knew Taljzi destroyers and battleships had stealth fields. They hadn't been deployed yet in this pursuit, but the smurfs had used them to deadly effect in their First Return.

Once the vanguard entered CDX-25, Morgan and the other tactical officers would be able to get a solid ID on their enemy. If they were fast enough, they'd catch any stealthed ships that came through, so they'd at least know to look for *something*.

Emergence would also be the first time they'd know whether they'd fooled the enemy—and whether they had ten hours to refuel before they engaged the Taljzi or minutes.

The next forty-odd minutes were going to be *very* long.

"COMMANDER CASIMIR, can you take a look at this?" Antonova asked softly. "I'm picking up a strange signal. I'm wondering if you can sort it out?"

"Can do." Morgan tapped a command, linking her system into the coms and studying the signal. Sometimes, the ship's algorithms assigned things as communications that really should come to the tactical system.

A moment later, she shook her head.

"Definitely coms," she admitted, mentally taking back her assumption that the algorithm had screwed up. "Encrypted signal. It's...familiar, though."

"Yeah, I thought the same and was wondering if you recognized it," the coms officer said. "It's not in our databanks."

Morgan looked at the irritatingly familiar signal for a few seconds, then grabbed her communicator.

"That's because it's not something the Duchy officially encountered," she replied. She brought up a program that Ki!Tana had installed on her personal communicator a long time ago, and nodded as it processed.

"It's the Tortuga recognition signal," Morgan announced. "The Laian Exiles are here. If I'm tracking this right, CDX-25-B4."

She shook her head and then looked back at Captain Vong.

"The Taljzi are going to fly right past them. If we're picking up the ghost of the signal, the Taljzi can track it—and they don't seem inclined to let anyone live around them."

"I'm not overly inclined to worry about pirates and slavers, Commander," Vong noted drily.

"The Exiles haven't been pirates since, well..." Morgan sighed. "Since the Duchess blew three-quarters of the pirates that home-based there to ash. They're not our enemies, and we have their cousins back home.

"I don't know if Vice Admiral Tidikat is in contact with his old friends, but I doubt he'd be happy if we accidentally got them wiped out."

"Plus, don't we kind of owe them?" Antonova suggested. "They did help us out when we first collided with the galaxy."

By buying Annette Bond's prizes and stolen goods, Morgan knew, but that money had helped the Duchy get to where it was today.

"We can't protect them," Vong pointed out. "Any more than we can stop these bastards ourselves."

"But we can warn them," Morgan said. "I have codes they'll recognize. We can tell them to hide—if they cut the recognition signal and dive deep before the Taljzi arrive, they should be safe."

There was a long silence on the bridge, then Captain Vong sighed.

"Give the codes to Commander Antonova," he ordered. "Tell them what's coming. I may not like what A!Ko!La!Ma! stands for, but..."

A!Ko!La!Ma! was the A!Tol name for the mobile space station humanity had nicknamed Tortuga, a pirate and smuggler haven where Annette Bond had homebased *Tornado* while acting as a privateer against the A!Tol. It was run by the Laian Exiles, the losers of an ancient civil war, and a number of those exiles had immigrated to Earth when Bond had invited them.

"I'm not going to stand by and let the Taljzi murder anyone," Vong continued after a moment. "Regardless of whether we owe them."

"NINETY SECONDS TO ATMOSPHERIC ENTRANCE," Commander Hume reported. "Permission to be terrified, sir?"

"Granted," Captain Vong said with a chuckle. "Has anyone *ever* done this?"

"On a gas giant, yeah," Hume confirmed. "On a *brown dwarf*? I don't think so."

"Well, I guess we get to set new records." Vong glanced at the timer, then back at Morgan.

"Any word from our carapaced friends?" he asked.

"Their recognition signal is gone," Morgan reported. "I don't think we're going to get more data from them than that. We were too far to pick up Tortuga in the first place."

Vong grunted.

"I guess that explains the smugglers we ran into on our way out," he noted. "They must have been headed here."

"Guess that's our good deed for the month," Antonova said. "I'll let you know if I hear anything from them."

"If I were them, I'd be sitting in my comfortably heavily armored space station, buried inside a gas giant and watching us through long-range probes," Morgan replied. "And wondering if humans were *born* crazy or if it's just the ones around Duchess Bond."

Vong chuckled again.

"I've met your stepmother *and* Rear Admiral Sun," he pointed out. "Trust me. Octavius Sun was perfectly sane before he met the Duchess. I can't say the same for Commander Masters, though. He seemed sane enough, but this crazy idea was his."

"Well, I'll let you know if it works in forty-five seconds," Hume reported. "How are our shields, Casimir?"

Morgan checked her systems.

"Shields are recording increased heat levels, nothing worrisome, though. We're good to keep going."

"That's good, given that we haven't even entered the dwarf yet," the navigator replied. "*Watch* those numbers, Casimir. If I need to break us off, I have to know *immediately*."

Morgan bit down on a harsh rejoinder. Kumari Hume was flying a battleship *into a star*. She deserved some leeway.

BELLEROPHON'S SHIELDS weren't as advanced as many of her other systems. There was no real difference, qualitatively, between the shields of *Chancellor Merkel* and the two smaller ships. The *Bellerophon*-class ships had more power to fuel the defensive system, but the technology was almost identical.

Right now, Morgan was wishing that they've stolen new shield tech from *somebody* around when they were stealing the microbots that reinforced the battleship's hull, her tachyon scanners or her matter-converter power plants.

CDX-25-C wasn't large enough to fuse hydrogen, which meant that the fuel the flotilla needed was present. It *was*, however, large enough to be fusing deuterium and lithium. It was cold enough that they could enter the dwarf...and hot enough that Morgan's shields were starting to strain.

"Orders from the Flag: escorts are to close up to reinforce each other's shields," Antonova reported.

"How are we doing, Casimir?" Vong asked.

"We're okay," she admitted. "I'm getting enough interference that I'm having problems reading the data from our hyperfold probes. Forty minutes to estimated Taljzi emergence."

"How long do we need to sustain this to refuel?" the Captain asked grimly.

"Escorts will be fully fueled in four hours. We'll be ready in six. *Chancellor Merkel* would need twelve to be fully ready to go," Hume reported.

"We're not getting that much time," Morgan said. "Not unless the Taljzi are even more scared of this stunt than we are."

"I wouldn't be surprised," Vong admitted. "This is hell. We'll need to send the escorts out as soon as they're fueled. They'll be vulnerable, if nothing else."

And that was assuming that the smaller ships *survived* that long. Morgan had the shield data from the rest of the flotilla feeding to her screens, and the destroyers were *not* doing great.

"When do we pull the escorts out?" she asked.

"That's up to Admiral Sun and their skippers," Vong replied. "Keep your eyes on our shields and on the Taljzi. We need to know when they get here and *where* they arrive."

"I know, sir," she said quietly. "Our eyes are open. I'm just worried about whether we'll still be here when they get here."

"We will be," the Captain said flatly. "I'm more concerned about what they're going to do when they realized we're *inside* the brown dwarf."

CHAPTER FORTY

THE TALJZI CLEARLY HADN'T BEEN ENTIRELY FOOLED. THEY emerged on the closer side of the gas giant that *Bellerophon* and her sisters had tried to look like they'd been aiming for, almost a light-hour closer to the Terran flotilla than they'd been expecting.

"Enemy has entered real space," Morgan announced. "Two hundred and twenty hulls, still scanning for breakdown. Current distance, four point seven light hours."

She grimaced.

"Enemy appears to have detected us. They are moving in our direction, current velocity point six five lightspeed. ETA, seven hours fifteen minutes."

Bellerophon's bridge was very quiet.

"Well, we never expected to get *Chancellor Merkel* fully fueled anyway," Vong said aloud. "How long until HSM range?"

"Assuming we don't maneuver to evade them, we'll range on them in about seven hours," Morgan reported. "I don't know the range on their new long-range missiles, but I doubt they've got the shielding to make it into the brown dwarf."

For the same reason, even their dual-portal hyperspace missiles were useless. Their *escorts* were being strained by fueling up inside the half-ignited star. Any missile or probe they fired was going to get vaporized before it reached the surface.

Morgan sighed as a new report reached her screen.

"Fifty ships just disappeared," she told the bridge crew. "Stealth fields. I got a decent-enough scan to make sure none of them are battleships, but that means we've got the closest to final numbers we're going to get."

"How bad, Commander?"

"One hundred and fifty cruisers, averaging one point five megatons. Seventy destroyers, averaging five hundred thousand tons. I'm guessing they kept most of their destroyers back with the main fleet."

"I thought all of their destroyers had stealth fields," Vong asked.

"So did I, but fifty just went into stealth and twenty didn't," Morgan confirmed. "I'll task one of my teams to keep an eye on those twenty. If they're different than what we're used to, we need that data."

"And our invisible friends?"

"I don't think they're any faster than the rest of the escorts, but we've got post-processing analysis underway," she said. "My guess is that they're with the rest of the fleet and just using their stealth screens to frustrate our targeting."

"What about the Laians?" Antonova asked.

"As dark as dark can be," Morgan said. "I can't pick them up, and I know which gas giant they're hiding in. They're almost certainly safe from the Taljzi."

"Lucky them," Hume muttered. "When do I get to haul my ship *out* of the burning cinder, sir?"

"When doing so lets us shoot the bastards with hyperfold guns," Captain Vong said grimly. "It's time to kick the Taljzi in the nose, but given that they have us outmassed four or five to one, let's see if we can set the range to *our* preference."

MORGAN WAS ALMOST USED to the seemingly eternal drag of time before battle. This time seemed even worse than normal, however. They were continually watching their shields and fuel status, making certain that they were surviving the hell that they'd immersed themselves in.

"Admiral Sun is ordering the escorts to exit the brown dwarf on the opposite side from the Taljzi," Antonova reported. "The destroyers' shields are being pressed to the limit; they *need* to get out and recharge."

"They should be fully fueled by now anyway," Morgan noted. "Are we maneuvering with them?"

"Any orders?" Vong asked.

"He wants us to rotate underneath them. We and *Rama* are to pull up to join them once our tanks are full."

"Hume?"

"Another eighty minutes," the navigator reported.

"Take us after the escorts. Casimir, keep an eye on our blue friends. Moving around down here is going to be *very* obvious."

"Yes, sir," she confirmed. The entire battleship shivered as *Bellerophon* moved through the upper levels of the brown dwarf's atmosphere. Her shield status reports were well into the yellow, but they were fine so far.

They wouldn't be if anyone could shoot at them, but hiding in the not-quite-star helped with that.

"The Taljzi will reach us about an hour after we're fueled," she noted. "I...I don't know what they're going to do at that point. They certainly can't fire missiles at us until we leave the dwarf."

"I'd come in after us, use their godawful disruptors at point-blank range," Vong said. "They'll bleed for it, but they have the ships to spare. That said, it won't matter. We'll sortie out before they get that close, to protect the escorts if nothing else."

"And they know we can't stay down here forever," Morgan conceded. "They can just wait us out."

"Speaking of, how long until their main force arrives?"

"Another eighteen hours."

"We want to be on our way by then," Vong said quietly. "We can bloody the nose of two hundred cruisers and destroyers. We can't even scratch the paint of a thousand capital ships."

"ORDERS FROM THE FLAG." Antonova's voice echoed through the long-standing silence on *Bellerophon*'s bridge. "All ships are to engage with hyperspace missiles. Capital ships are to hold until enemy has reached ten light-seconds, then sortie and engage with hyperfold cannons."

"The escorts are going to come under fire pretty quickly," Morgan said as she dialed in her HSM launchers. "Even with the brown dwarf shielding them, they can only deal with so many missiles."

"So, keep the bastards busy," Vong ordered. "You have your target, Commander?"

"Yes, sir."

The "lucky" cruisers that Rear Admiral Sun's staff had flagged for the first salvo were each flagged for a *Bellerophon* or eight *Thunderstorm*-Ds.

They could only hit four ships at a time, but previous experience suggested that forty-eight hyperspace missiles was enough to take down Taljzi escorts.

"Fire when ready," *Bellerophon*'s Captain said calmly.

There was no sign that *Bellerophon*'s most powerful weapons had spoken other than the status change on Morgan's screen. Inside her hull, eight hyperspace portals had opened. Six missiles had been launched into each before they closed.

Even *Bellerophon*'s scanners couldn't track the weapons in flight. Seeing into hyperspace was difficult at the best of times. That was part of the HSMs' advantage.

Almost two hundred missiles appeared in the middle of the

SHIELD OF TERRA   265

Taljzi vanguard, diving toward their designated targets with suicidal determination.

Some of the missiles emerged inside their targets. There was no saving those ships. Two of the Taljzi cruisers vanished as the missiles appeared.

The other two were almost instantly wrapped in a lattice of lasers and other energy weapons. The missiles had a terminal flight time of under a second—and inside that second, every one of the Terran missiles died.

Their targets were haloed in the fire of antimatter annihilation, but they'd avoided the direct hits that would have collapsed their defenses. Morgan gritted her teeth at the further evidence of the Taljzi's upgrades, but her target had been one of the unlucky ones.

She moved to the next cruiser on her list and opened fire in sequence with the rest of the flotilla.

"Direct hits are starting to look like the reliable way to kill them," Vong said grimly from behind her. "Any chance of improving our odds?"

"Not really," she admitted. "We have real time on where they are right now, but the missiles still have up to a ten-second flight time in hyperspace where we can't update their course."

The second salvo died uselessly amidst the Taljzi fleet. Without direct hits, the antimissile defenses ripped apart the weapons before they could hit.

"We're hurting them," Morgan pointed out. "Even close-range antimatter explosions are doing a number on their shields—but we'd be better off hitting them with regular point-eight missiles at this point."

A third salvo flashed into hyperspace, but new orders were already coming down from Rear Admiral Sun. Morgan nodded as she read them.

"We're concentrating the flotilla's fire on a single target. Slaving our launchers to *Rama*—Commander Masters has the shot."

Rama's XO was *Bellerophon*'s former tactical officer. He and

Morgan were probably the two most experienced officers in the Imperium with the new hyperspace missiles, and he was senior.

"Let's see what happens," she murmured as a cruiser died in the third salvo and the entire flotilla's long-range weapons fired as one for the fourth.

"Ten minutes to hyperfold-cannon range," Vong observed. "I was rather hoping there were going to be a lot fewer of them left when we pulled that stunt out of our hat."

Morgan shook her head.

"We get what we get at this point. We're in regular-missile range in less than five minutes."

THE MASSED HYPERSPACE launchers seemed to do the trick. Morgan watched Masters's salvos carefully, making sure she followed what he was doing.

What worked, after all, would need to be duplicated.

There was no attempt to concentrate the hyperspace missiles this time. Demonstrably, the Taljzi's anti-missile defenses were capable of handling every HSM the Terrans could deploy. They needed direct hits.

Masters was trawling for those by spreading the missiles out, blanketing the zone where he expected their target to be when the missiles arrived. It only took one missile emerging inside a cruiser's shields to wreck the target.

The Taljzi ships had compressed-matter armor, but the cruisers didn't have enough to stand off the antimatter explosions. Their capital ships, Morgan knew, would be a different story.

The First Return hadn't had active antimissile defenses. They definitely hadn't had systems capable of shooting down hyperspace missiles during their terminal attack—a trick that Morgan wasn't entirely certain her defensive software and systems could handle.

In the handful of months since the First Return had been wiped out, the Taljzi had clearly refitted a large portion of their fleet to counteract the weapon systems the Imperium had used against them.

Refits and upgrades or not, however, each of the massed salvos from the two *Bellerophon*s and their lesser sisters wrecked a cruiser. A dozen cruisers were smashed to wreckage before the Taljzi vanguard drew into the range of their regular interface-drive missiles.

They'd just been counting on over four times that many kills by this point.

"Taljzi are firing on the escorts," Morgan reported grimly as her scanners lit up with red icons. "Two minutes to impact."

"Any orders from the Flag?" Vong asked.

"Capital ships are to move out and support the escorts," Antonova confirmed a moment later. "Once we've rendezvoused with the cruisers and destroyers, we're to swing around and make a maximum-velocity pass of the Taljzi force at two million kilometers."

Morgan nodded to herself. They could hit the Taljzi with everything in their arsenal at that range—though passing at maximum velocity meant they'd be in range for only a handful of shots from each of their short-ranged systems.

It also meant they'd avoid the terrifyingly deadly disruptors the Taljzi used at short range and hopefully manage to do more damage than they took.

"Casimir?" Vong said.

"Already setting it up," she confirmed. "Missiles are still slaved to *Rama*, and I'll release the D-HSMs to Commander Masters once we're clear of the dwarf."

The dual-portal missiles were *much* bigger than the single-portal versions and no more effective. Between the two *Bellerophon*s, though, that was an extra fifty missiles to reinforce one of the salvos with.

Morgan could only hope it would be enough. There might only be cruisers and destroyers in the vanguard facing them, but there were a *lot* of missiles out there already.

CHAPTER FORTY-ONE

For a moment, the tide of missiles swarming down on the tiny handful of Terran escorts seemed unstoppable. Then, finally, the three capital ships hiding in the brown dwarf came into play.

Chancellor Merkel led the way, blazing out of CDX-25-C at her full point six five *c* sprint speed. The *Duchess of Terra*–class ships couldn't sustain that speed for very long, but it was enough to put the massive super-battleship between her escorts and the incoming fire.

Buckler drones spewed from the sides of the immense warship, lasers coming to life as soon as the defensive platforms were clear of *Merkel*'s shields.

Bellerophon and *Rama* were moments behind her, their own drones and turrets coming to life in a suddenly blossoming forest of laser beams.

The cruisers and destroyers had their own Bucklers out, and the incoming missiles hadn't been targeted on the capital ships. Their maneuver forced the Taljzi fire to run the gauntlet of the battleships' defenses before they even reached the escorts.

It was enough for the first salvo. Only a handful of missiles struck home, easily shrugged aside by the escorts' shields. The second salvo was better, the Taljzi managing to adjust some of their programs in-flight, but the shields were still enough.

By the third salvo, the Taljzi had finally retargeted on the capital ships. The escorts weren't quite in position yet, which left *Bellerophon* and her sisters taking the massed fire of almost a hundred and forty warships.

They were outnumbered fifty to one...but they were capital ships.

There was no way they could stop every missile, but they could stop a *lot* of them. Thousands of missiles descended on the three star-ships. Thousands died—and dozens made it through regardless.

"Shields are holding," Morgan reported. "Escorts are forming up; they won't get as clean a shot at us again."

"Holding" was the most positive spin she could put on it. *Bellerophon*'s shields were intact. They could probably even have taken a couple more salvos like that...but they couldn't have taken five more.

And if the Taljzi cruisers had anything like the magazine capacity of their Kanzi kin, they had a lot more than five salvos left.

"Get us in formation, link our defenses, return fire," Captain Vong ordered calmly. "We'll make our charge when the Flag gives the word. Until then, hammer them with what we've got."

Morgan's first salvos of interface-drive missiles were launching before he'd even finished saying "return fire."

———

THE ESCORTS SHOT FORWARD at point six *c* and never slowed. As they reached the capital ships, *Bellerophon* and the other big ships matched that speed.

The Taljzi were already heading toward them at point six *c,* and the range started evaporating in seconds. Two light-minutes of range would disappear in barely more than three minutes at that velocity, even if the interface drives didn't suffer from time dilation.

Morgan used those two minutes to set up her firing pass. They'd get one shot from the plasma lance and two apiece from the proton beams and hyperfold cannons.

"Contact in ninety seconds," her senior NCO murmured. "I've got the plasma lance dialed in. You're sure you want the proton beams focused on one target?"

"We know the Taljzi have antiproton curtains," Morgan pointed out. "We need to overload them. Even keeping all of our beams on one target, I'm not sure we'll manage it."

Missiles continued to hammer both sides, and Morgan winced as a flashing icon on her screen informed her that one of the *Thunderstorm*-Ds had lost shields. The cruiser's heavy compressed-matter armor held for long enough to get the shield back up, but damage icons encased the ship on her displays.

The next warning icon marked a destroyer that wasn't that lucky. Her armor wasn't enough to withstand the fire that came through once her shields fell. A second destroyer joined her.

They still had all of the cruisers when they hit hyperfold cannon range, however, and Morgan hit the button that launched her firing pattern.

The entire battleship shivered as the plasma lance that ran her entire length spoke. Near-*c* packets of plasma flashed along *Bellerophon*'s spine and followed a magnetic channel that lashed out and caught the nearest cruiser.

The channel only held for four seconds. It was more than long enough to gut the cruiser from end to end.

Her proton beams were as ineffectual as she'd feared. Even a few more seconds might have been enough to overwhelm her target's defensive curtains, but she didn't have those seconds. The ship she'd targeted with her proton beams survived.

None of the ships she targeted with her hyperfold beams were as lucky. Explosive bursts of energy targeted and deployed in real time were *much* easier to get inside the targets' shields.

Bellerophon wasn't the only ship firing, but Morgan's ship obliterated seven Taljzi cruisers during the firing pass. *Rama* claimed the same, and *Chancellor Merkel* destroyed six ships herself.

Between the three capital ships and twenty-six surviving escorts, they wrecked over thirty Taljzi cruisers in exchange for three cruisers of their own.

"Shields are in rough shape, but we're still here," she reported as they broke clear of the Taljzi fleet. "They focused on the battleships and the cruisers. We're clear of energy range; it's down to just missiles now."

They'd *hammered* the Taljzi vanguard by now. The smurfs had started with a hundred and fifty cruisers and had lost over a third of them. The destroyers hadn't even been targeted by the Terran strikes, but most of the ones with the cruisers were gone, too.

Morgan realized they'd forgotten about the stealthed destroyers too late to warn anyone else.

The Terran flotilla's sensors finally punched through the stealth screens at a million kilometers. Fifty destroyers hung directly in their path, velocities already swinging around to match the fleeing scouts.

"Retarget, *hit them!*" Morgan snapped. It took her a moment to realize that Captain Vong had said the same thing, her fingers already flying over her console.

Bellerophon's guns woke half a second before anyone else's, hyperfold cannons hammering the destroyers with unavoidable and deadly fire.

The destroyers slid into the half-million-kilometer range of their disruptors a moment later and all hell broke loose.

A quarter of the Taljzi ships were already gone, and the hyperfold cannons of the Terran fleet ripped through the remainder like a hot knife through butter. The destroyers didn't have the shields or armor to withstand the point-blank firepower of three capital ships.

What they had was a weapon that almost ignored the shields and armor of those same capital ships. Chunks of the Terran ships' hulls exploded under fire from the Taljzi's disruptors, sending ship after ship lurching out of position.

Bellerophon was lucky. Kumari Hume reacted when Morgan started shooting, spiraling the ship out of the space where the Taljzi were expecting her. They lost armor and sensors but nothing significant.

Chancellor Merkel wasn't so lucky. An entire arch of the super-battleship's flowing, elegant design disappeared into a fireball that sent the starship reeling. Chunks of her core hull disappeared and dozens of her weapons went offline—but the super-battleship was still there when the last Taljzi destroyer died.

Rama wasn't. Half of the *Thunderstorm*-Ds died with the battle-ship, and Commodore Huber's destroyers expended themselves trying to save the bigger ships.

"*Chancellor Merkel* has lost her hyper portal projectors!" Antonova reported. "Flag is ordering us to open a portal as soon as we can and get the fleet out." Morgan's blonde girlfriend swallowed hard and looked over at Captain Vong.

"If *Merkel* can't make the portal, we're to leave her behind," she said quietly. "Rear Admiral Sun says that order is nondiscretionary."

"Fuck that garbage," Vong snarled. Morgan wasn't sure she'd ever heard the Captain swear before, and certainly not *that* fiercely.

"Commander Hume, I want a portal and I want it *now*."

The entire battleship shivered as a missile slipped through a gap in their shields. Morgan got the energy field restabilized a moment later and their armor handled the hit, but it was a warning sign of how bad things were getting.

"On it!" Hume barked. "Fair warning, this is going to *suck*."

Reality tore open in front of the battleship, and *Bellerophon* shivered again under the strain. Half of Morgan's weapons systems went offline as power conduits overloaded or just failed.

Hitting the portal felt like they'd flown into a brick wall. Only the automatic safety restraints kept Morgan from being flung from her chair as they smashed their way into hyperspace.

"Hold the portal," Vong snapped. "Hold it until *everyone* is through."

Chancellor Merkel was the last ship through, two seconds later, followed by a swarm of missiles that slipped through before Hume cut the emitters. They'd left the Bucklers behind, which left them stopping the last salvo with just their onboard turrets.

Morgan desperately tried to shore up her shields, but the battleship's power-management system had been strained to the breaking point by the hyper portal.

Bellerophon's shields failed.

CHAPTER FORTY-TWO

"DAMAGE REPORT."

Vong's voice sounded strained, which Morgan could only sympathize with. Her restraints had dug into her shoulders and left bruises. She doubted she was the only one—the restraints were an automated emergency measure, which meant they weren't designed to be comfortable.

She wasn't entirely certain she'd remained conscious through the entire sequence of hits. There were red warning icons across her displays, and she groaned as she reviewed them.

"Someone please have good news," she said aloud. "Because I think I'm the bad news gal right now."

"Anyone?" Vong asked, a bit of dry humor edging through the strain.

"We still have an interface drive," Hume replied. "We're underway with the rest of the battle group at point five five c. I wouldn't want to take us any faster than that, not without a lot of surveys by Engineering, at least."

"That'll do. Do we have hyper emitters?"

There was a long silence.

"No," Hume admitted. "We're missing about half of the emitters; we can't open a portal on our own."

"Casimir?"

She sighed.

"I hope we enjoyed our hyperspace missiles, skipper," she told him. "Because we don't have any anymore. Or missiles in general, for that matter." She ran down the icons on her screen and shook her head.

"I have twelve hyperfold cannons and six proton beams," she concluded. "That's it. Lance might be repairable, but I'm waiting on reports. We've still got half of our Sword turrets and our shields are back up to full, but we are basically toothless."

"Engineering is reporting that we've lost one of the mass converters, at least temporarily," the engineering liaison officer reported. "Fusion cores are still online and Converter Two is still operational."

"So, we can fly but we can't fight," Vong summarized. "All right. Antonova—get me the Admiral."

A few seconds later, Octavius Sun appeared on the screen. The Admiral looked in roughly the same shape as *Bellerophon*'s bridge crew, with a visible tear in his uniform where his emergency straps had cut through it.

"Captain Vong. Your status?" Sun asked.

"Our offensive weapons are shot," the Captain replied. "We have shields and drives and some defensive turrets, but we're down a converter, so I'd hesitate to even try and energize the beam weapons we have left."

"That's better than I expected," Sun admitted. "*Chancellor Merkel* has about half her missile armament but is otherwise in about the same shape. Portal projectors?"

"We've got about half left. We can't open a portal ourselves."

"Same as *Merkel*," the Admiral agreed. "We're still trickling in reports from what's left of the escorts, but it doesn't look good."

Morgan hadn't looked at the escorts. Doing so now, she inhaled sharply and shivered.

Commodore Hillary Huber wasn't going to be escorting anyone else to safety. None of the destroyers had made it out, which meant the Terran Commodore had died with her command.

Somehow, she didn't think that the Taljzi were going to take prisoners.

Out of thirty destroyers and cruisers and four capital ships, the entire scouting flotilla was down to six cruisers and two capital ships.

Their plan to bloody the Taljzi vanguard had *not* gone as planned.

"WE CAN'T PLAY MATADOR ANYMORE," Vong said bluntly on the senior officers' call an hour later. "We can only risk point five five *c* until the vanguard leaves CDX-25, then we need to push back up to point six at least."

"The main fleet is heading our way still as well," Morgan reminded everyone else. She was trying not to think too much about *Rama* and Commander Masters. She and her old boss had clashed initially, but they'd grown into good friends.

Now he was dead.

"They're also running at point five five *c* for the moment and are at least a few days behind," she continued. "There's a chance the vanguard will rendezvous with them and reassess their plans. We got hurt today, but they got bloody *massacred*. We killed almost a hundred and fifty warships, well over half the strength of their vanguard."

"And a minor piece of good news is that it looks like we successfully covered for the Laians," Vong pointed out. "That wasn't really a priority, but the Duchy owes them enough for that to be worth it on its own."

"It would be more worth it if they could convince their cousins to lend us a few dozen war-dreadnoughts," Commander Tanzi said grimly. "A couple billion tons of Republic heavy warships would make me feel a *lot* more comfortable."

"About the only way the Exiles could get the Republic to send warships would be to say 'Here we are, come get us,'" Sun replied. "They'll almost certainly find a way to pay us back, but I wouldn't expect it to be that direct."

He shook his head.

"Nothing in this flotilla is combat-capable and we don't have a way to communicate with home," he admitted grimly. "Running is all we can do...and we're battered enough that, sooner or later, they're going to catch us."

"So, we run," Vong replied. "That was the plan in the first place. Run and see if they follow."

"In their place, I'd follow," the Rear Admiral agreed. "Get the navigators together. We'll want to grab at least one current, see if we can get ourselves further away from these bastards. I'd like to think we have better charts of this area, but it's not guaranteed.

"*Chancellor Merkel* isn't up for pushing for an extra eight days, though," he said grimly. "We'll see how much we can buy Terra, but short of intentionally sacrificing our ships, we have a hard limit on how long we can run—and that won't let us lead the bastards straight to Sol."

A lot of people had died to get this far. Morgan wasn't sure how much more death it was going to take to bait the Imperium's trap.

She was selfish enough to hope it wouldn't require hers.

"WELL, SOMEONE IS FOLLOWING US," Morgan observed quietly as the survivors of the Taljzi vanguard split. "Looks like ten ships are coming after us to keep a link. The rest are heading towards the main fleet."

"That gives us some time," Vong acknowledged. "Thank God. How far behind us is the main fleet?"

"Hard to say at this point," she admitted. "Distance in hyperspace is garbage, but I'd say a light-day or so. If we stopped in space, it would take them two days to catch up."

Bellerophon and her compatriots were running for a hyper current that would actually take them away from Sol as it bought them distance from their pursuers. The course Morgan had seen would bring them almost directly home from the other end of the current, arriving there in just over five days.

If they kept the Taljzi two days behind them, well, that would buy the time they needed.

"Four hours to the hyper current," Hume reported. "Think they'll be able to follow us?"

"It looks like," Morgan confirmed. "We've got about thirty-six light hours' range for the anomaly scanners in hyperspace, so I'm guessing they have at least twenty-four."

That distance translated into at least several light-months and usually at least one or two light-years in real space.

"New orders from the Flag," Antonova reported. "We're to accelerate up to point six *c* along our current course. To quote that Admiral, 'Let's at least make them think we're *trying* to get away.'"

"Make it happen, Commander Hume," Vong ordered. The Captain looked around the bridge. "Then let's stand down the ship to status B. Hume, you're on duty with me. Antonova, Casimir. Get the hell off my bridge and go sleep."

None of the bridge crew had left for more than a bathroom break for over twenty-four hours now, and Morgan nodded gratefully to the Captain as she rose. Checking her own systems, she sent a note to her Chiefs to do the same thing.

There wasn't much for her department to *do*. The safety systems meant she hadn't lost as many people as she could have, but they didn't have guns to run anymore.

MORGAN WAS tired enough that she made it all the way to the door to her quarters before she realized Antonova was walking with her. Leaning against the wall, she gave the blonde woman an apologetic look.

"Sorry, Victoria," she said. "I'm...shattered."

"Me too," Victoria said. "I wasn't planning on trying to seduce you, if that's what you're thinking."

Morgan chuckled and opened the door to her quarters. They both stepped inside and she wrapped Victoria in her arms as soon as the door was closed.

She didn't even kiss her lover. They just stood there for a minute, holding each other.

"My people are fine," Victoria told her, finally kissing her hair. "Coms wasn't even hit particularly hard."

"Mine are not," Morgan whispered. "And...Commander Masters. *Fuck.*"

She collapsed against Victoria, the taller woman holding her tightly.

"I can't do this on duty," she continued.

"We're not on duty," the other officer told her. "Come with me."

Morgan didn't even have the energy to argue as Victoria led her into the bathroom, gently removing both of their uniforms as she turned on the water.

Despite everything, they still had hot water, and Victoria pulled them both into the shower. It was a cramped space, not really designed for two people, but the point wasn't really to get *clean* right now.

The hot water was mostly just to hide the tears neither of them could show.

CHAPTER FORTY-THREE

Victoria ended up sleeping in Morgan's quarters. It was probably a violation of etiquette, though not of the Articles, but Morgan suspected that Captain Vong knew perfectly well what was going on.

She doubted he'd dismissed the two women together by accident, at least.

Exhausted as they were, it still took them longer than she'd expected to fall asleep. She wasn't sure she'd have been able to sleep at all without the other woman holding her.

It felt like she'd barely managed to finally get her eyes closed when she was thrown from the bed by a violent impact...and left floating suspended in the air in darkness.

"Victoria?" she asked.

"I'm here," the other officer replied. "Lights?"

"Computer!" Morgan barked. "Lights!" Voice commands weren't her usual preference for controlling the lighting in her room, but without gravity, she wasn't going to find her communicator or reach the light control panel.

The lights didn't come on for a moment. When they did, they

were much dimmer than she'd expected, a mode she took a second to recognize as an emergency power-saving.

The lack of gravity and dim lighting did fascinating things to Victoria Antonova's naked body, she noted distantly as she scanned the room for her clothes.

"Gravity's gone," Victoria said, stating the obvious. "Lights in emergency mode. This section of the ship is running on batteries."

Artificial gravity was the single most power-intensive secondary system on a warship. Morgan, like the rest of the Militia, had undergone zero-g training.

Five years before.

"Give me a moment." She managed to get herself to a wall, then kicked off for her clothes. It wasn't a comfortable landing, but it got her where she needed to be.

The pile of clothes went mostly ignored for the first minute as she extracted both of their communicators. She carefully threw Victoria's to her, then checked her own.

"This is Commander Casimir, checking in," she said crisply. "Bridge?"

"This is the bridge," an unfamiliar voice replied. "CPO Sujay Janvier. Captain Vong is injured. Commander Tanzi is assuming command as soon as she can get to secondary control. What's your status?"

"I'm uninjured but in my quarters with no gravity," Morgan replied. "What's *Bellerophon*'s status?"

"I don't know," the CPO admitted. "All power is down. Engineering is scrabbling to find the problem, but we've lost external communications and scanners."

"I'll be there ASAP," Morgan promised. "Get my Chiefs on looking into the sensors. I'll have my communicator if Tanzi needs to get ahold of me, understood?"

"Yes, sir." Janvier paused. "Vong was the only officer on the bridge," he admitted. "I can keep things together up here, but I'm not qualified to fly the ship!"

"I am, if need be," Morgan told her. "I'll be there, Chief. Keep a lid on it."

She looked over at Victoria, who was finishing her version of the same conversation with one of her own Chiefs.

"Catch," she told her lover, tossing the other woman's clothes across the room. "Thank God for uniforms that double as emergency gear!"

BY THE TIME they made it to the bridge, the lights in the corridors were at least up to normal levels of dim, the emergency-lighting mode switching out.

The battleship was still lacking gravity, though, and getting from Morgan's quarters to the bridge had proven a bruising and frustrating experience.

"Sirs!" Chief Janvier greeted them as they drifted into the space with a salute. "Commander Tanzi is in secondary control and has assumed command."

Morgan gave the Chief a nod and levered herself into her seat.

"Commander," she greeted the XO as she linked in to the main video channel. "Commander Antonova and I are on the bridge now. What *happened*?"

Commander Batari Made was *Bellerophon*'s chief engineer, and the Indonesian woman looked shattered.

"*Kami kacau*. We fucked up," she said bluntly. "Too many conduits were running just below the red line, too many systems had been pushed to the edge, and this is still a new ship. First in her class.

"We blew the interface drive when we entered the hyperspace current," Made concluded. "We don't have engines. The last matter converter is gone, too, but we're getting the fusion and antimatter cores rebooted. Given that we can't get the drive online, we'll have enough power for everything left."

'Everything left.'

"Shields?" Morgan asked.

"Shields, guns, gravity," the engineer confirmed. "We can't dodge and we can't run, but we can sure as *kotoran* fight." She paused. "With what we have left, anyway."

Morgan's console wasn't showing her *much*. A lot of their scanners were down, but she had *some* anomaly systems still live. Enough to show that the rest of the flotilla had stopped around them.

"What's going on with our coms?" Antonova asked, all business now.

"Lack of power," Made admitted. "Once we get another fusion core online, you should have short-range transceivers. We won't have the power for hyperfold coms for a while, but...well, we'd need to be outside hyperspace to use that, anyway."

"And we couldn't make a hyper portal even before this," Tanzi said with a sigh. "All right. Made—I want you to get power back and then give me a survey on the engines. Let me know when you have an estimate on the repair."

"I have it already," Made replied. "There's no repairing the drives. Not outside a shipyard—and there's no way in hell we're getting her to a shipyard. She's gone, sir. It's only a question of what we do now."

The call was silent for several seconds.

"Then get me a survey on the guns," Tanzi said grimly. "I need to know if we have *anything* that can be used in hyperspace that's repairable."

"Sir?"

"There isn't enough space on the rest of the flotilla to evacuate our entire crew, people," the XO told the battleship's senior officers very, very quietly. "Some of us are going to have to stay behind—and since the Taljzi don't take prisoners, I think we're going to shove whatever guns we can pull together down their furry blue throats!"

"SO, THAT'S THAT," Morgan's Chief told her. "We can get the lance and half the proton beams, and if we cannibalize everything, it looks like we can pull together half a dozen missile launchers."

"Thanks," she said. "Send the update over to Commander Tanzi," she ordered.

"Yes, sir."

She shook her head as her subordinate walked away in the freshly restored gravity, looking at the console in front of her. Twenty-four proton beams, a plasma lance and six missile launchers. It was a pale shadow of *Bellerophon*'s armament, but it would be enough to sell their lives dearly if they could sucker the Taljzi in close enough.

"We've got a confirmed count for how many people the rest of the squadron can squeeze aboard," Antonova reported. "There'll be... about four hundred we can't move."

"I have to stay," Tanzi said instantly. "Vong's unconscious, so he goes over on the first shuttle."

The Captain had been standing when the gravity had failed, and smashed his head. He'd *probably* live, but they were being careful with the head wound.

"Most of the people we need will be mine," Morgan said. "We basically only need engineers and gunners. The weapons we have left will need about a hundred people and, well, a hand up here. I'll stay."

"Are you sure, Commander?" Tanzi asked.

"It's my job, sir." Morgan avoided Antonova's eyes on the screen. She didn't want to die—but she'd be *damned* if she'd leave her people to die without her. "I suggest we have Engineering and my people draw lots for who stays and send everyone else over immediately."

Five hundred techs, engineers and gunners could get everything they could possibly fix online before the Taljzi arrived. Morgan was quite sure of her and Tanzi's ability to come up with a scheme to lure the smurfs into lance range—and she knew from vivid experience that *Bellerophon*'s plasma lance could gut even a Taljzi super-battleship.

That her suggestion would see Victoria Antonova sent to safety also definitely registered in her mind.

"That makes the most sense to me," Tanzi admitted. "All right, people. If you're not Engineering or Tactical, get your shit together. First shuttle leaves in ten minutes. Last one in an hour—and we should have everyone ready and off the ship by then; am I clear?"

The command channel closed and Morgan stared at her displays in silence for several seconds, waiting for what she knew had to be coming.

"You don't have to volunteer to get yourself killed to protect me, you know," Victoria said softly behind her.

"Every second we buy is a better chance that you and the others make it home safely," Morgan told her. "And I was telling the truth, too. This is my place. If someone is going to man this girl's guns on the ride into hell, it's my damn job to stay with my people."

"And convince the XO to make sure I get kicked off, huh?"

"That's not my job," Morgan admitted. "That's just a nice bonus."

"For who, exactly?" Victoria demanded.

"Me. My job says I'm here. Yours doesn't—and if I do mine right, I buy *you* time. I get *you* to safety."

"And I don't get a say in this?"

"We don't need a coms officer," Morgan said bluntly. "We do need a tactical officer. If you were to stay, it would be a waste of life. I *have* to stay."

"No. You don't."

Morgan sighed and turned her chair to look at Victoria. The two CPOs backing up the tactical console were maintaining an admirable pretense of deafness.

"I do," she said quietly. "We both know it. We can argue over this and have this be the last conversation we ever have, or you can accept it and go knowing that I love you."

They were both silent for several seconds, and then Victoria

Antonova calmly broke the Articles to thoroughly kiss her girlfriend on the bridge of a warship.

"Damn you, Morgan Casimir," she told her. Morgan thought there were tears in Victoria's eyes...but it was hard to tell through the tears in her own eyes.

"Go, Victoria," Morgan said. "Keep everyone else safe. I'll buy you the time."

"I know," the Russian woman told her. "I know you will. I love you, too."

They embraced for what both of them knew would be the last time, and Morgan wasted several precious seconds watching Victoria walk out of the bridge.

Then she blinked away the tears, swallowed her fear and got back to work.

CHAPTER FORTY-FOUR

THE BRIDGE FELT LIKE A GHOST TOWN AS *CHANCELLOR MERKEL* and the remaining cruisers blasted away from *Bellerophon*. Morgan and Commander Tanzi were the only ones left in a space designed to play host to almost fifty officers and technicians.

"I take it Antonova gave you an earful," Tanzi said into the silence after a few minutes.

"Yes, sir," Morgan confirmed with a cautious glance at the acting captain.

Tanzi laughed.

"Casimir, knowing who is sleeping with who is part of the XO's job," she pointed out. "So is knowing when not to poke at a situation. She should be safe enough aboard *Merkel*."

"She will," Morgan agreed. "Assuming we do our job. Any ideas for making us more obvious to the Taljzi?"

"Engineering is going to keep trying to trigger the interface drive every few minutes," Tanzi told her. "It won't *work*, but it'll keep us flashing up on their anomaly scanners. That'll help lure them to us. What are we going to do when they get here?"

"My people think they can break free the Bucklers," Morgan

replied. "We'll have most of our normal missile defense; see if we can use that to lure them all the way in."

She shook her head.

"Honestly, the only thing I'm hoping for is to get a super-battleship into plasma-lance range," she admitted. "I'm eighty percent sure we can kill one of the bastards if we range on them, so all we need is for them to get close enough."

"I wish we could set it up so they were looking for us in the wrong place," Tanzi said thoughtfully. "I feel like we should be able to do something with the portal emitters. Exotic matter is expensive enough, after all."

Between the portals in the HSM batteries and the ship's main hyperdrive, they had a *lot* of broken emitters.

"That's an engineering question, sir," Morgan admitted, her eyes back on the anomaly scanner. "I mean, we still have most of a day. If we can manage something clever, I'm on board. I'm counting on one shot. Everything after that is a bonus."

Tanzi chuckled.

"Everything after that is more dead smurfs, and after everything we've seen on this trip, I can't argue with that."

"WE CAN'T TURN the emitters into portal mines or something similarly miraculous," Made told the other two officers. The three of them were the only commissioned officers left—none of them had drawn the short straw. They'd all volunteered.

"But we might be able to use them to fake the repeated start-up attempts we're doing right now," she said slowly. "It wouldn't look quite right, but it would pulse up on their anomaly scanners."

"If we can get them aiming even a few thousand kilometers in the wrong direction, that could buy us a second shot with the lance," Morgan told her. "A second lance shot means a second dead super-battleship. If I get long enough with the proton beams, I might screw somebody up with those as well."

"We're doing everything we can," Made told her. "I'll talk to some of the Chiefs I have left; we should be able to rig up some kind of decoys. Hyperspace being hyperspace, we might manage to make it so they can't target us until they're in the visibility bubble."

One light-second was as far as regular sensors could see in hyperspace. Beyond that, everything was running on anomaly scanners. Usually, Morgan wouldn't even try to fire her plasma lances or proton beams at something outside the visibility bubble, but today she'd try anyway.

"I wouldn't mind buying us a few fractions of a second after that, but I'll take what I can get," she told the engineer. "Every quarter-second is another pulse from the proton beams. Every second or so is another lance target."

"We've done what we can to the hardware on the guns we have left," Made told her. "Strip down the software limiters, and they're going to regret you touching them." She shrugged expressively. "It's not like we're firing more than two or three times, right?"

That was a new thought—and Made was right. Some of the limitations on her weapons were hardware, but a lot weren't. A lot of her software was coded around needing the weapons to last the expected lifetime of the ship.

If that lifetime was measured in seconds, well, blowing out the focusing crystals of a proton beam or overloading the plasma lances' magnetic conduits suddenly didn't look that important, did it?

"I'll talk to *my* Chiefs," she said with a smile. "Let's make these bastards regret ever poking at *Bellerophon*."

None of them were going to get to go home. They knew that now. But Morgan would be *damned* if she'd go down without spitting in the Taljzi's eye along the way.

"WELL, it looks like our furry friends are feeling paranoid," Morgan noted.

The Taljzi force that had reached them was another forward detachment, a hundred ships strong. They were still a full light-minute away in hyperspace, but they were launching missiles.

A lot of missiles. The new vanguard was apparently *not* all cruisers.

"I'm guessing ten battleships, ninety cruisers," she continued. "I'm feeding our anomaly scanner data to the Bucklers. We'll see how many we can clean up."

She looked at the number of missiles the Taljzi had launched and shook her head.

"I'm pretty sure we're going to lose some of Commander Made's decoys."

"That's what we build them for," Tanzi said calmly. "Will we make it?"

"Seventy-thirty," Morgan replied. "How lucky are you feeling?"

"Dumb question," the acting captain of the doomed warship told her. "I wouldn't be buying lottery tickets today."

"Well, if we live through this, we should probably consider it."

That got a surprised laugh from the acting captain, and enough amusement to tide the two women over as the missiles came screaming toward *Bellerophon* at eighty percent of the speed of light.

"For what we are about to receive, may the Lord make us truly thankful," Tanzi murmured. "One way or another, Commander Casimir, this has been a hoot. Let's see how it all shakes ou—"

"What the fuck?" Morgan said as Tanzi trailed off, both of them staring at the anomaly scanner. "Is that a *new* hyperspace current?!"

It wasn't a very long one. It started maybe a dozen light-hours away, but it compressed that entire distance into a single hyperspace light-minute.

Hyperspace currents didn't form like that. Morgan had never even *heard* of hyperspace doing anything *like* that...and then the stealth fields dropped.

Twelve brand-new hyperspatial anomaly signatures now hung between the crippled battleship and the Taljzi vanguard. The incoming missile fire simply...vanished—and a tsunami of *new* missiles appeared, heading toward the Taljzi ships with their mother-ships in hot pursuit.

"What the *fuck*?" Tanzi said, echoing Morgan's comment. "The current is disappearing. *Nobody* can just...*create* a current like that."

Morgan was studying the signatures and she slowly shook her head.

"I'd forgotten," she admitted. "Mom—Duchess Bond—said she'd seen it done once. By a Mesharom Frontier Fleet detachment."

Twelve ships collided with a hundred, and all the Terrans could do was watch as two full squadrons of the Mesharom Frontier Fleet demonstrated to the Taljzi why the galaxy was terrified of the big caterpillars.

Destructive as the battlecruisers were, though, a ship died as they closed. Then another. The Mesharom were smashing the Taljzi, but they were losing ships...and so far as Morgan knew, they shouldn't have been.

"They've got the same problem we do in hyperspace," Tanzi said slowly as the battle unfolded. "Hyperfold guns and hyperspace missiles only work in real space."

As she spoke, however, the Mesharom's missiles cut through the Taljzi's defenses like they weren't even there. Laser systems that had successfully wiped out entire salvos of Imperial hyperspace missiles in their terminal attack sprints barely even decimated the tightly spaced salvos of point eight five *c* interface-drive missiles.

"I *want* their missiles' computers," Morgan concluded. "They've got to be ignoring the Taljzi's jammers completely."

Taljzi ships were dying. A *lot* of them—but their missiles were just as fast, if not as smart. Like *Bellerophon*, the Mesharom ships relied on tachyon scanners and hyperfold cannon to augment their missile defenses.

In hyperspace, none of that worked. A battlecruiser died. Then another. And *another*—and both fleets were still on a suicide charge, the Taljzi desperately aiming to get their disruptors into range.

Then, suddenly, there were only five icons left. All Mesharom. In a single moment, three Mesharom battlecruisers, six Taljzi battleships and thirty Taljzi cruisers vanished.

"Okay," Tanzi said slowly. "You might want their missile computers. I want whatever the hell *that* was."

"You can ask," Morgan suggested, watching the surviving Mesharom battlecruisers turn back toward them. "But I'd suggest we prioritize that *below* getting a ride home."

CHAPTER FORTY-FIVE

THE IMAGE OF A GIANT RED-AND-BLACK CATERPILLAR ON THE viewscreen wasn't something that Morgan would normally associate with a feeling of complete and utter relief. Today, however, the sight of a Mesharom Interpreter meant that they'd *survived*.

"I am Interpreter-Captain Shexbetai of the Mesharom Frontier Fleet vessel *Shivering Dawn*," the Mesharom introduced themself. "I am the senior Interpreter of Squadron Commander Istival's Task Force."

"I am Commander Tanzi, Acting Captain of the Duchy of Terra ship *Bellerophon*. We appreciate your timely intervention, Interpreter-Captain," Tanzi told the Mesharom. "We were not expecting to survive engaging the Taljzi vanguard." She paused. "I regret the losses you suffered saving us, Captain."

"The defeat of these fools is a necessity for the survival of the galaxy," Shexbetai said calmly. "Our losses were in pursuit of that goal. Rescuing your vessel was certainly intended, but do not feel responsible."

Tanzi bowed her head.

"*Bellerophon* does not currently have functioning engines," she said carefully. "Would it be possible for you to transport our remaining crew to Sol?"

"Yes." Shexbetai's answer was simple enough. "Do you have shuttles left?"

"We do," the acting captain confirmed. "Enough to transport everyone."

"Approach *Shivering Dawn*," the Interpreter ordered. "We will take you aboard my ship." They paused. "Do not expect to meet with any of my people. We will adjust the ship to make you a private space. It will be comfortable enough."

"Interpreter-Captain, an hour ago, we all *knew* we were going to die," Tanzi told the Mesharom. "You could provide us with a cold metal floor and we'd be happy right now."

Even Morgan had no ability to read Mesharom body language, but she thought the giant caterpillar looked rather pleased with themself in response to that comment.

"That would be a failing on the part of the Mesharom Frontier Fleet," they noted. "We can do better than that.

"We do need to get moving, Commander Tanzi. Our force cannot fight the entire Taljzi fleet."

There was a long pause.

"Of course, we are simply Interpreter-Shepherd Adamase's scouting force. I think the Taljzi will find more than one surprise waiting for them in your home system."

The video cut out and Morgan, the only other person on the bridge, met Tanzi's gaze.

"It seems like we get to live, sir," Morgan suggested.

"Pass the word to your people," the acting Captain ordered. "If there's anything they can't stand to leave behind, have them pack it. One bag per person; let's not impose *too* much on our rescuers."

"What about *Bellerophon* herself?"

Tanzi sighed.

"You, Made and I will be the last ones off," she said slowly.

"Without Captain Vong, it will take all three of our overrides to initiate the scuttling procedure."

"With the damage we've taken, I'm not sure the standard scuttling process will even work," Morgan warned.

The Duchy of Terra didn't rig their ships with intentional self-destructs, but there were definitely ways to convert power conduits and fusion cores into massive explosives that would gut the ship.

"Then we and Made will come up with a different answer," Tanzi said grimly. "We still have the power cores, though, so I think the regular self-destruct should function well enough."

* * *

EACH OF THE shuttles left aboard *Bellerophon* could carry fifty people. More than that, really, for the short hop over to *Shivering Dawn*, but they had ten of them.

Nine of them had already left as the three officers gathered at the console in the flight control center.

"Everyone is aboard Shuttle H and waiting for you," the engineering NCO acting as chief of the deck told them. "Flight pattern is locked in; I'm not even needed up here anymore."

"Then go get on the shuttle," Commander Tanzi ordered. "No point in having anyone hanging around unnecessarily. We might screw up the timers and blow the ship up with us aboard."

The Petty Officer didn't wait for the order to be repeated, disappearing out the door as Made worked away at the console.

"A lot of our scuttling protocol really does call for using the power conduits as local charges," Made noted. "I'm rigging up the lance to overload to replace a lot of that, but the main blast is still going to be the fusion cores."

"Will that be enough?" Morgan asked. *Bellerophon*'s hull was armored with an average of five centimeters of compressed-matter armor, coming in at nearly a ton per square centimeter.

"With the lance overload, it should gut the ship quite handily," the engineer confirmed. "I'm reprogramming our microbots to do nasty things first, though. They'll dismantle the entire support structure of the CM armor and start tearing apart anything they can reach."

Morgan shivered.

One of the techs the Imperium had developed based on scans of Mesharom warships and analysis of the Precursor wreck in Alpha Centauri had been the active microbots that supported their warship hulls. Not quite nanotech, the tiny robots were extraordinarily capable and normally acted as an automatically repairing substructure beneath the compressed-matter plating.

"They can do that?" she asked.

"That's one of the things I need your overrides for," Made admitted. "It's almost hard-coded into the microbots that they only touch the standard feedstock for them to build more of themselves. I can change that, but the software to do so is locked behind a pile of security for a reason.

"Same with overloading the lance and the cores," she continued. "If you can plug in your codes, Commanders."

Tanzi typed in her authentication code on one console and Morgan followed suit on the other. Made typed in her own and then activated her programs.

Nothing visibly happened, but Made studied her screen and then grunted in satisfaction.

"*Bellerophon*'s armor is now disintegrating and the overloads are starting," she told the other two women. "*Kita kacau, ayo pergi.*"

Morgan didn't speak Indonesian and it wasn't loaded into her translator earbud, but she could guess the meaning of that from context.

Let's go.

And, well, some decorative additions.

CHAPTER FORTY-SIX

"Councilor, we have a message from Rear Admiral Sun," Jean Villeneuve's aide informed him through the door. "There's more to the data packet, but the wrapper says that no one is to access the data packet until you, Admiral Kurzman-Wellesley, the Duchess or Consort Casimir have seen his cover message."

That...didn't sound good.

"Shouldn't Sun be in hyperspace?" Jean asked. The last reports out of the CDX-25 System hadn't been pretty, but they had at least told him that much.

"It looks like he dropped a relay drone out of hyperspace to transmit," his aide told him. "Everything else is locked behind that wrapper."

"Make sure the message reaches everyone on that list," Jean ordered. "The Duchess is on *Tornado*, but !Olarski has starcom receivers on her ships. She can relay to Bond."

"Of course, Councilor," the aide replied, bobbing his head. "Should I engage your privacy protocols?"

"Yes, thank you, Colin," Jean agreed. "I'll let you know once I've finished."

Both he and Colin Barrow were clearly guessing that the message was bad news.

The door closed behind his aide and Jean sat back down at his desk. For a few moments, he simply stared at the furniture in his office.

He hadn't chosen any of it himself. Bond had hired one of the best workspace designers on the planet to take on the Councilor's offices in Wuxing Tower, and she'd done incredible work. Jean had intended to have it remade to the naval standard he was used to when he moved in, but it had taken less than a week for the smooth corners and neutral woods to grow on him.

With a sigh, he touched a raised bit of "wood" on his desk. A screen unfolded out of the desk, bringing up a desktop with the ancient envelope icon of a waiting message blinking in one corner.

The desktop quickly replaced itself with the image of Rear Admiral Octavius Sun, sitting in his office aboard *Chancellor Merkel*. The room looked the worse for wear, with splotches on the walls where models or paintings had fallen down and not yet been replaced.

"This message is for Duchess Annette Bond and Consort Elon Casimir," Sun said, his tone soft. "I am copying Admiral Kurzman-Wellesley and Councilor Jean Villeneuve so that they can make sure the *rest* of what we're transmitting gets to where it needs to go, but this part is a personal message."

Jean realized he was clenching his fists.

"There is no easy way to say this: *Bellerophon* and four hundred and eighty-three of her crew, are now MIA, presumed destroyed. One of the three officers to remain behind and con her into her final battle was Commander Morgan Casimir."

"*Merde.*"

The single word didn't encompass Jean's feelings. He'd known Morgan since she was the tiny daughter of the United Earth Space Force's primary shipbuilder. He'd seen her grow from a child to a woman, one of the finer officers to serve in the Militia he'd created.

"We overstressed *Bellerophon*'s systems. She was a new ship and we may have missed something." Sun shook his head. "It's hard to be sure. She took a lot of damage—none of my remaining ships are undamaged—and then her gravitational-hyperspatial interface momentum engine failed when we attempted to enter a hyperspace current to gain distance on our pursuers."

The recording was silent for several seconds.

"With our losses, we didn't have enough life support to evacuate all of *Bellerophon*'s crew. Since the crew that remained behind had to be able to fight her, most of those personnel were from the Tactical Department. Commander Casimir...refused to allow her people to go into battle without her.

"The expectation was that *Bellerophon* would lure the Taljzi vanguard into an engagement and attempt to destroy hostile capital ships with her plasma lance.

"There was no likelihood of survival."

Jean had to pause the recording and force himself to unclench his fists. Morgan Casimir might be the most personal of the losses from this disaster, but if the flotilla had been in rough enough shape that they couldn't evacuate *Bellerophon*'s crew, he'd lost thousands of his people.

He restarted the message, understanding the weary exhaustion in Sun's eyes.

"Duchess Bond. Consort Casimir. It was not my task to protect Commander Casimir above any other. She did her duty. It does fall to me to inform you of her fate." Sun sighed. "*Chancellor Merkel* is the only remaining capital ship of my command. Half of my cruisers are gone and I've lost all of my destroyers.

"I have failed to preserve the lives of the officers and crew under my command. We are now en route to Sol. Our ETA from the receipt of this message should be five to six days, depending on the vagaries of hyperspace.

"The Taljzi will be at least a day behind us. It is unlikely they will be more than two. I can only hope that the blood we have spent to get this far has bought enough time."

Sun was looking down at his hands instead of the camera now, and he exhaled slowly.

"My people and ships don't have another holding action in them. Frankly, neither do I."

THE DATA PACKET under the wrapper was much what Jean expected. He forced himself to go through it, to distract himself from the fact that he'd just learned over ten thousand of his people had died.

The fact that the first item in the packet was a list of the lost ships and known dead personnel didn't help.

Twelve thousand, four hundred and eighty-seven officers and crew confirmed missing, presumed dead. It would have been worse, but both *Jean Chrétien* and *Bellerophon* had seen significant portions of their crews evacuated.

It turned out that privacy protocols and dedicated aides were no match for the Ducal Consort of Terra. The door to Jean's office flung open without preamble and Elon Casimir stormed past Colin Barrow, ignoring the younger man.

"Well?" Casimir demanded, standing in front of Jean's desk.

"You saw the same message I did," Jean said simply. "You know everything I do."

"*You* let her go on that damn mission," the Consort snapped. "*You* convinced me that she'd be safe enough in our damn Militia to let her sign up!"

"Do you really think you could have stopped her?" Jean asked. "Do you really think *Annette* would have let you? She was your daughter, Elon Casimir—but she was Annette's daughter, too.

"She made her choice. No one made her stay. Rank hath its privileges, Elon, and she *chose* to stay with her people."

"She *died*, Jean," Casimir shouted. "My daughter is *dead*."

"Yes."

Jean let the single word hang in the air as he looked at his old friend.

"Yes, Elon, she died." He blinked away tears as he looked down at his desk. "And twelve thousand other people died with her. Not all of them made a choice, other than to put on the uniform.

"An entire Taljzi battle fleet, equal to the combined forces of our entire Imperium, is heading our way. If we survive, it will be at the cost of thousands more officers like Morgan. Officers who chose to put on the uniform and put themselves in the face of the enemy.

"I can't change that," Jean told Casimir. "I can't save those men and women—and I couldn't save Morgan. If you and Annette want my resignation for that, you can have it. I'm too old for this damn war."

There was a long, long silence in Jean Villeneuve's office, and then Elon Casimir collapsed bonelessly into a chair.

"Dear God, I think we all are," he murmured. "But I never...I never expected to outlive any of my daughters, Jean."

"I know. That's why we evacuated the younger girls...but Morgan was an adult. She made her own choice. Like I did, a long time ago."

He shook his head.

"The A!Tol at least wanted us to surrender. The Taljzi just want us to die."

"We won't let that happen," Casimir said fiercely. "*Morgan* wouldn't have let that happen."

"COUNCILOR? CONSORT?" Barrow stuck his head through the door somewhat hesitantly. "I have Admiral Kurzman-Wellesley calling for you."

The aide had to come in, Jean realized, because the privacy protocols that stopped him receiving calls were still active.

"For both of us?" he asked.

"Yes, Councilor. It seemed urgent."

The Admiral would have been the other one getting the message from Sun, so Jean guessed that made sense. He sighed.

"Connect him through."

The broad-shouldered image of the Militia's senior Admiral materialized above Jean's desk, eyeing both of them carefully.

"We've all had better days," he said bluntly. "You two sober?"

"So far," Casimir admitted. "I'm barely out of the 'accusing Jean' part of grief so far."

"Good. I need you both aboard *Vindication* as soon as you can get here. We had another unexpected hyper portal, and this time, I wasn't expecting Ki!Tana with a scout ship."

"Anyone we IDed?" Jean demanded.

"Not yet." Kurzman-Wellesley shook his head. "But I'm guessing we have visitors. I'm *hoping* they're friendly, but Tan!Shallegh and I are scrambling two squadrons of *Vindication*s to meet them."

Unless it was the entire Taljzi fleet—and what they knew about Taljzi stealth fields suggested they didn't work in hyperspace—thirty-two *Vindication*-class super-battleships could probably deal with it.

"You want us to speak for Earth," Jean concluded.

"Yeah," Kurzman-Wellesley agreed. "And if it turns out to be nothing, well, I have some damn good brandy up here, so we can all get drunk toasting Morgan's memory together."

CHAPTER FORTY-SEVEN

"My people and ships don't have another holding action in them. Frankly, neither do I."

Annette Bond stared at the frozen recording for a long time. She could guess what the data in Sun's packet contained, and she knew that !Olarski and Cawl would both need it, to one degree or another, but she wasn't processing that well yet.

She'd been there the night Morgan had been born. That also meant she'd been there the night Leanne Casimir, Morgan's mother, had died.

Even in the twenty-second century, some women still died in childbirth. Even now, with every advantage of Imperial medicine, it happened. Even before the Annexation, it had been rare enough to be almost unheard-of, but it happened.

Leanne Casimir had been one of the unlucky ones. The wrong artery had torn and she'd bled out despite the doctors' best efforts. Her husband had been one of Earth's wealthiest men. She'd had the best equipment and the best people.

She'd still died, and left behind a squalling baby and a stunned and broken husband. Annette Bond had been Elon Casimir's personal pilot then, in the aftermath of her involuntary retirement from the UESF.

And now that little girl was gone. She'd followed in her stepmother's footsteps, and like her mother, she'd been one of the unlucky ones.

Someone was going to have to tell the rest of the girls, but neither of their parents was with them. Jess Robin-Antionette had been evacuated with them, and they knew the bodyguards and nannies who surrounded them, but they *should* have had their parents for this.

The mother and the woman were torn by grief, but the Duchess and the military commander were looking at other aspects of it.

Eight days. They had at most eight days until the Taljzi reached Sol.

Blinking away her tears, Annette brought up her access to *Tornado*'s scanners. Twenty-eight super-battleships escorted the cruiser—an eight-ship echelon of the A!Tol Imperial Navy and two ten-ship squadrons of the Kanzi Theocratic Navy.

Another hundred or so escorts were spread out around those. They were still at least a day from their destination, and from the conversations Annette had had, even Cawl wasn't entirely sure how many ships would be waiting for them there.

It was entirely possible that the Shadowed Armada had torn itself apart when the Inquisition had attempted to arrest its commanders. Officers with starfleets at their command rarely went quietly, regardless of their race or guilt.

If her math was right, it was *another* seven days from the Shadowed Armada's anchorage to Sol. There shouldn't have been a Kanzi fleet—especially not a *major* one—anywhere near that close, and the irony of wishing they hadn't been so far away wasn't lost on Annette.

There was nothing she could do to make ships move faster, however, and she closed the sensor feed in favor of a set of files stored on her communicator.

A minor advantage of being the ruler of a world was that you didn't need to be a shutterbug to have albums upon albums of high-quality pictures and video of your children.

Deep in hyperspace, she couldn't even attempt to comfort her husband. All she could do was look at images of Morgan as a teenager and a young officer and let the tears come.

CHAPTER FORTY-EIGHT

Super-battleships never went anywhere on their own, and this was no less true when thirty-six of them were moving at once.

Each of the capital-ship squadrons in Jean's Militia had an attached cruiser squadron and destroyer squadron. There were more escorts in the Militia than that, but those squadrons were never supposed to be detached from their capital ships.

They'd picked up that ratio from the Imperial Navy, which meant that Tan!Shallegh's flagship and her accompanying squadron had similar escorts.

Deploying thirty-six capital ships meant over a hundred warships were blazing out from Earth toward the ghosts.

"Computer analysis confirms what we expected," Tidikat said. The Laian looked like a giant scarab beetle standing on its hind legs. His shell was heavy carapace and his head looked almost squished, but Jean was used to Laians by now.

Especially to Tidikat, who had led the Exiles who had settled on Earth. Tidikat's mate, the shipbuilder Orentel, was one of the top techs at DragonWorks. Their monogamous relationship was apparently unusual by Laian standards but didn't even raise eyebrows among humans.

"Stealthed ships?" Jean asked.

"It appears that we are looking at three of them," the Laian replied. "None large. We're trying to break down their course with a greater degree of accuracy, but all we have ascertained is that they split up after entering the system."

Jean grunted.

"If they're Taljzi, that's new tech," he noted. "If it's the Mesharom, you'd think they'd say hel—"

"*Unexpected portal!*"

Every eye on *Vindication*'s flag bridge was suddenly riveted to the main holographic display, where the icon of an opening hyperspace portal hung in the middle of the room.

"Emergence point is ten point six million kilometers away," the tech reported, her voice calming after her initial shocked announcement. "Estimated portal size...seven hundred kilometers?!"

"That's a fleet," Jean said slowly. "Have we detected anything coming through?"

"No, sir," the tech admitted after a moment, her voice small. "We haven't detected any ships."

The portal cut off in mid-admission and Jean stared at the display.

"Take the formation to battle stations, Vice Admiral Tidikat," he said calmly. Technically, he was a civilian now and couldn't give anyone orders. In practice, well...First Squadron went to battle stations.

They hadn't been much short of them in the first place. An unknown presence in the Solar System? The Militia wouldn't trust it. It didn't matter *who* it was—and they'd have been paranoid in peace, let alone now that they were effectively at war.

"Run the processing cycles," Jean continued. "If they haven't IDed themselves in about a minute, stand by for saturation antimatter bombardment."

He *wanted* to think it was the Mesharom, but this kind of stunt was going to get someone killed if they didn't behave *right now*.

THERE WAS fifteen seconds left on Jean's deadline when the Mesharom finally decided to behave.

First, the three scout ships they'd sent into the system ahead of their fleet dropped their stealth fields, flanking the defenders on all sides. It would have been more threatening if Jean and his people didn't know Mesharom scout ships didn't carry any weapons at all.

After that, the rest of the Mesharom Frontier Fleet detachment started decloaking. One squadron at a time, each group of six eight-million-ton battlecruisers appearing after each other.

"How many?" he asked in a forcefully bored tone. He'd be damned if he was going to show any fear or concern for the overdramatic caterpillars.

"Sixty," Tidikat told him. "Ten squadrons."

The big beetle shook his arms in the equivalent to a human shrug.

"My understanding was that Shepherd Adamase was bringing twelve squadrons?" he asked.

"Are they still hiding ships?" Jean said, directing the question to the sensor techs.

"It doesn't look like it. Sixty battlecruisers, eight scout ships," one of them replied.

"Incoming transmission," a com tech reported. "Standard Mesharom request for minimum persons present."

Jean managed not to roll his eyes.

"Elon, Patrick?" he addressed the Consort and his senior Admiral. "Let's go chat with the fuzzy bastard."

"Use my office," Tidikat told them, gesturing to a door off the bridge. "The breakout room should serve your needs."

"I helped design the *Vindication*s," Jean pointed out with a chuckle. "Unless you did something unexpected with the very first one, it most definitely will serve."

THE THREE OF them took seats in the small meeting room attached to the office, and the connection linked through the screen that covered the entire wall.

Even with the screen of that size, Jean knew that Adamase was being scaled down to fit on it. The Interpreter-Shepherd was almost four meters tall if fully extended, an immense furred alien that resembled a caterpillar or millipede.

Adamase was dark green, without the patterns than Jean had seen on other representatives of the species. He didn't know what that meant for them, but he did know what the Mesharom's *rank* meant.

Interpreter-Shepherd Adamase was responsible for a region of space that covered most of an arm of the Milky Way. The A!Tol Imperium, the Kanzi Theocracy and at least a dozen other smaller powers still too large to be absorbed fell into their area of responsibility.

Adamase commanded the Mesharom Frontier Fleet in that area. They were responsible for enforcing the Kovius Treaty that guaranteed certain rights to sentient races and a list of other treaties the Core Powers made all of the Arm Powers sign off on.

They were also, as humanity had learned the hard way, tasked with making sure that technology belonging to the Precursor race that had once conquered them stayed lost.

Jean wasn't sure *why*—he knew Annette Bond knew more but had been sworn to silence—but he knew that part of Adamase's job was to make sure no one ever used Precursor technology on a massive scale.

Given that it appeared the Taljzi were using a Precursor cloning facility to mass-produce their soldiers and spacers, it seemed the Frontier Fleet Shepherd's predecessor might have failed at that task.

"Councilor Jean Villeneuve. Consort Elon Casimir. Admiral Patrick Kurzman-Wellesley." Adamase intoned each of their names in greeting.

"It seems that you have managed to poke the steam vent quite thoroughly. My scouting elements report a rather impressive armada heading this way."

"Unless you know where the Precursor facility they are using is, we needed to find their home systems," Jean replied. "Though we weren't expecting this."

"We do not," the Mesharom confirmed. "Someone would have had to search the area, yes. And clearly, this fleet was already prepared to attack. What is your plan?"

"We are concentrating as much of our forces as we can in the Sol System," Kurzman-Wellesley told Adamase. "What's left of Rear Admiral Sun's force will fall back here, hopefully drawing the entire Taljzi fleet onto Sol's defenses rather than striking our more-vulnerable colonies."

"Against this enemy, even Sol is vulnerable," Adamase observed. "My last reports suggest that you are being successful in luring the Taljzi in this direction, however, so I will hold my core fleet here to assist in the defense."

"We can only thank you," Jean said. "The assistance of the Mesharom Frontier Fleet is immeasurable."

"Wait, you have up-to-date reports?" Kurzman asked. "How?"

"We have ways to cross the hyperspatial boundary for communications," Adamase told him simply. "And my scouting elements moved to track your scouting flotilla."

"You know what happened to *Bellerophon*, then?" the Admiral said quietly.

"Not yet," the Mesharom admitted. "My last report was that my scouting flotilla commander had decided to ambush the Taljzi vanguard and see if they could retrieve your battleship. I do not know how that ended."

Jean inhaled as if struck. If a Mesharom squadron had been in the area, *Bellerophon* might have been spared.

"Shepherd Adamase," Elon Casimir said, the Consort speaking for the first time in this call. "My *daughter* is aboard *Bellerophon*. If you could let us know what you learn of their fate, we would be greatly appreciative."

"You have nothing to give us but your gratitude," Adamase warned him. "For today, that will suffice. I will pass on whatever we learn.

"Otherwise, my fleet will take up positions in your asteroid belt. Our stealth fields will allow for some interesting surprises for the Taljzi. We will remain in contact."

The channel cut off and Jean sighed. Even Mesharom Interpreters could get curt and abrupt. Strange species.

"Morgan may be alive," Casimir said slowly.

"She *might* be," Jean cautioned. "Even if the Mesharom intervened, that wouldn't guarantee *Bellerophon*'s survival. We..." He sighed, swallowing hard. "We need to assume the worst until we get news, Elon."

"Maybe you do," Casimir replied harshly. "But we're talking about my daughter. *I* need to cling to any hope I can."

THEY RECONVENED SHORTLY AFTERWARD in Kurzman-Wellesley's office aboard the super-battleship. In an actual combat action, the Admiral would command from aboard the battle station Orbit One, which was why *Vindication* was a "shared" flagship.

The Admiral extracted a bottle of brandy from the cupboard in his office, then pulled a beer from the fridge for himself.

"Brandy would be against your brand, would it, Admiral?" Jean asked with a forced attempt at humor.

"Just not feeling it tonight," Kurzman admitted, opening his beer and taking a slug. "Been a roller coaster of a day."

"That it has," Jean agreed.

The Admiral looked over at Casimir.

"We've got seven days, give or take. Is it enough?" he asked.

The Consort sighed and drained a glass of expensive brandy in a single swallow. He coughed and shook his head.

"It should be," Casimir said. "We'll have the first tranche of the Grand Fleet's super-battleships refitted and the *Bellerophon*-Bs should be online as well. It's not as much as I'd like, but it's sixty-four super-battleships with S-HSM launchers and four brand-new battle-ships that will make most people's super-battleships hesitate."

"Rolfson will be here before them as well," Kurzman-Wellesley confirmed. "That's another two *Bellerophon*s, plus the rest of our super-battleships. That gets us to sixty-six Militia capital ships, at least."

"And the Grand Fleet." Jean shook his head. "We won't hear from Annette for another day or so, but what I'm hearing is that the Kanzi are at least eight days out. I don't think they're going to make it for the opening numbers."

"We're only outnumbered three to one," Kurzman said. "We've faced worse."

"That was when we had hyperspace missiles and they didn't have anything resembling a counter," the Councilor pointed out. "Now they have these long-range sublight missiles and have implemented anti-missile defenses capable of shooting down hyperspace missiles.

"Our advantages got negated pretty damn quickly, which is terri-fying all on its own. If they can refit three thousand ships in a few months, we may be seriously screwed in the long run."

"We don't know enough about this damn cloning process of theirs," Casimir said grimly. "If it's as close to an infinite supply of personnel as it seems like...I don't know if we can make up the deficit."

"There has to be a limit," Jean replied. "From what I understand, you can't produce an adult with preloaded memories. You produce a baby with no memories. Accelerated growth only does so much."

"That's *our* tech," the Consort reminded him. "These bastards are playing with Precursor technology, and we don't even begin to understand the limits of that."

"I know," Jean said with a sigh.

Their fears were interrupted by a signal on all three of their communicators. Jean opened his up and saw a text message, a relayed note from Interpreter-Shepherd Adamase.

Scout flotilla reported in. Taljzi vanguard destroyed. Bellerophon *irretrievable but remaining crew evacuated.*

Morgan Casimir confirmed among rescued crew. My scouts will be in Sol in two days.

Jean stared at the text for long seconds, then swallowed his own brandy in one gulp.

"Thank god for antisocial caterpillars," he said aloud. "If we have a chance in this damn war, it's because they decided to get involved."

Elon Casimir didn't respond. The Ducal Consort was slumped in his chair, staring at his communicator in silence as he blinked away tears.

CHAPTER FORTY-NINE

"We have no secondary confirmation yet," Elon's recorded image said. "On the other hand, after everything we've gone through with them, I'm hardly inclined to start mistrusting Adamase.

"If they tell me their people evacuated Morgan, I trust them. My little girl—*our* girl—is okay, Annette."

Annette knew her husband well enough to tell that he'd been crying. He looked shattered—and relieved.

Which was fair, since that was about how she felt. She wouldn't even be able to respond to him for at least another two hours, with *Tornado* still in hyperspace.

Elon had at least had their friends to support him. She wasn't alone—the Duchess of Terra was never truly *alone*—but Maria Robin-Antionette was the only friend she had aboard the cruiser.

It had been a long time since she'd had to face this kind of blow without her husband and friends at her side, which made the truth an immense relief.

"Are you all right, ma'am?" her aide asked gently. "That sounds... pretty positive."

"It is," Annette agreed, wiping away the tears she was only

willing to let a tiny handful of people see. "It sounds like Morgan is fine. For now, at least."

She shivered.

"Because there's no way she *isn't* going right back aboard a warship for the defense of Sol," Annette admitted, as calmly as she could. "Even if I thought we could stop her, I wouldn't. She put on the uniform, the same as I did so many years ago."

"She'll be fine, Annette," Robin-Antionette told her.

Annette sighed.

"She'll be a soldier, Maria. One of millions currently gathering to protect our home system. She won't be 'fine.' She'll be in the line of fire, on one of the warships placed between the Taljzi and our citizens."

"And she wouldn't be anywhere else," Annette's aide pointed out. "Neither would you."

"Neither would Leanne," Annette replied. "She gets it from both of her mothers."

And it wasn't like anyone had even *tried* to convince Elon Casimir to evacuate alongside their daughters. He might not be a soldier, might not be a spacer tasked with leading people into battle, but Annette's husband wasn't going to abandon Earth in the face of the enemy.

"So, what now?" Robin-Antionette asked.

"We back up Cawl as best as we can while keeping his furry blue feet to the fire," Annette said firmly. "Even if this 'Shadowed Armada' started moving the moment we arrived, we'll get to Sol a day after the Taljzi are expected.

"The sooner he kicks his people into motion, the better. The Mesharom aren't going to turn this around on their own."

"Weren't they sending bigger ships, too?" the aide asked.

"War-spheres, apparently, yeah," Annette confirmed. "They're still four months away. The centermost of the Core Powers is a *very* long way away, it turns out. I don't even know how many of the things they're sending or even what they look like."

She shook her head.

"All I really know is that anyone who *does* know anything about them starts getting really nervous when they hear the Mesharom are sending real warships."

ANNETTE HAD RETURNED to *Tornado*'s mostly empty flag bridge by the time they emerged from hyperspace. She spent the last few minutes before their arrival looking up the system the Kanzi had chosen to anchor their Shadowed Armada on.

It was, just barely, outside of the forty-light-year zone around Sol that the Kovius Treaty deeded to humanity. Even if it hadn't been, the system had almost nothing to recommend it. It was a binary pair of red dwarf stars, too cold to even begin to have useful worlds. A single paltry gas giant orbited both stars in a not-quite-figure-eight.

Any rocky worlds had been turned to debris long before, leaving the system with that gas giant as the only point of interest. The *only* thing the system could ever have been used for was as a refueling station, and there were better systems for that—systems with extractable resources and even habitable planets—relatively close by.

But the system was close to a hyperspace current that wrapped around the Coreward border of the Theocracy and could get them to Sol in seven days. The Kanzi had likely been setting the place up as a secret anchorage even before humanity came onto the local scene.

The holotank at the center of the flag bridge flickered as they crossed through the hyperspace portal, and Annette swallowed a shocked curse as the image of the star system updated.

Intellectually, she'd been warned that the Shadowed Armada was on the same scale as the Grand Fleet. It was an entirely different feeling, she realized, to see a fleet of a thousand warships poised a week's flight from her home.

The Armada's anchorage was a mess of tanks and cloudscoops,

massive fusion-powered facilities churning out the antimatter that fueled capital ships.

Around it hung the Armada they were there to collect. Ten squadrons of super-battleships and fifteen of battleships. Two hundred and fifty capital ships and what looked like eight hundred cruisers and destroyers.

She sighed.

"That is one hell of a fleet to discover was being quietly pointed at your own throat," she said aloud. "If only we could have got them to *Asimov*, too."

The same geometry that made the system a convenient anchorage to threaten most of the A!Tol Imperium meant that the Shadowed Armada wouldn't have been able to reinforce against the First Return.

They were, thankfully, in position to move against the *Second*. Assuming, of course, that the smurfs actually followed orders and fell into line behind Fleet Master Cawl.

There was no starcom there, and the Kanzi didn't have hyperfold communications yet. There was no way to know how the Inquisitor that High Priestess Karal had sent ahead of them had fared.

At least the entire Armada was still there. There hadn't been the kind of mass mutiny that would have left the fleet incapable of combat.

A year earlier, Annette would have *preferred* that kind of internal conflict among the Kanzi. Now, much as they still set her teeth on edge, she needed them.

And right now, she needed them to get to Sol in time.

THEIR CONVOY of Imperial and Kanzi ships met the main formation of the Shadowed Armada without anyone shooting at each other, which Annette took for a good sign.

With a thousand ships in play, they were scattered in a rough circle around the gas giant. They certainly weren't assembled into anything resembling a travel formation...which Annette took for a bad sign.

"Shuttle leaving Fleet Master Cawl's flagship, heading towards one of the super-battleships that was already here," the young Lieutenant running her-bare bones flag bridge staff reported. "Codes suggest the Fleet Master is aboard."

Annette opened a channel to the bridge.

"Captain Mamutse?"

"Your grace?" the Captain replied instantly.

"I'm feeling paranoid. Is Cawl's shuttle inside our missile defense net?"

"As it happens, I flagged it as a priority defense target as soon as it launched," Mamutse told her. "Something about this whole situation is twinging my paranoia as well. If someone tries to take a potshot at the Fleet Master, they'll have to get through our defenses and his flagship's."

"Good." Annette looked at the fragile-seeming icon. If something happened to Cawl now, this whole alliance was going to come down in crashing flames.

"The pilot seems to be feeling the same way," Mamutse noted. "They're moving dangerously fast for this kind of environment."

With this much paranoia on display, it would almost have been a relief if Cawl's shuttle *had* come under fire. Instead, it made its way to its destination without any interruption at all, and Annette released a breath she didn't know she'd been holding.

"Let's keep our eyes peeled," she suggested to Mamutse. "It wasn't that long ago this entire fleet was being aimed at Sol. I can't imagine they're any happier to have a full echelon of Imperial super-battleships hanging around than we are to be here."

Mamutse snorted.

"I'll be happy to have this fleet in Sol when the Taljzi arrive, but them being this close pisses me off," he told her. "I'm guessing you noticed they're not set up to go anywhere, though?"

"Yeah," she admitted. "I noticed that, too."

"WAIT, THAT'S STRANGE."

"Lieutenant Coburn?" Annette asked.

"We just have a whole *bunch* of shuttles launching," he reported. "About thirty or forty from Cawl's escort, but dozens more from various ships in the Armada. That's...weird."

"Get me Fleet Lord !Olarski," Annette told him. "If something is going on, we need to be ready."

"Wait—I have an incoming communication for you from one of the super-battleships."

"One of Cawl's?" she asked.

"No. Not one of the ones he arrived with or the one he boarded an hour ago," Coburn said.

"Put it through," Annette ordered, curious now.

The image that appeared in the holotank was a new one to her. It was definitely a Kanzi, but they wore stylized black leather armor that encased them from shoulder to toe. They'd covered their head with a hood and wore a mask of the same black leather as the rest of their armor as they faced the camera.

"Duchess Dan!Annette Bond," the strange Kanzi greeted her. "I am the Divine Chosen's Inquisitor. The situation aboard the Shadowed Armada is...complex at the moment.

"It was my duty to deal with the problems here before you and Fleet Master Cawl arrived. Fleet Master Estel is dead, but he had far more allies woven through the fabric of his Armada than even my worst shadows had anticipated.

"With Fleet Master Cawl's able assistance, I expect to have the situation resolved in the next seventeen hours," the Inquisitor continued. Seventeen hours was a Kanarj day.

"Every minute we delay risks lives and ships," Annette said coldly. "I was told that this Armada would be reliable."

"And we were wrong," the Inquisitor replied. "We underestimated the corruption. It is rare for an Inquisitor to fail, and the responsibility is mine and mine alone, but we knew the Armada was led by traitors.

"I can only promise, by Her Divine Chosen's honor, that this will be resolved soon. But I cannot make it already be over." They bowed their masked head. "I must ask, however, that you do not attempt to intervene.

"If A!Tol troops were to interfere, it would confirm the worst shades and claims of our rebels. This is an internal matter, Duchess Bond. It will be resolved."

"And if I were to insist on hearing that from Fleet Master Cawl himself?" she replied. "I don't know you, Inquisitor. You aren't even showing me your face."

"An Inquisitor has no face. No name. We are the shadow of the Divine Chosen, nothing more. Fleet Master Cawl is..." The Inquisitor paused, then nodded sharply.

"Fleet Master Cawl was betrayed when he boarded what was to be his new flagship," the Inquisitor admitted. "He was seized by traitor forces, an action that triggered an armed counter-mutiny.

"Fighting rages throughout *Chosen Sword*, but Fleet Master Cawl is currently a prisoner. We *will* retrieve him and he *will* take command of this Armada," the Inquisitor said grimly. "But your involvement would only make matters worse.

"I ask for your faith, your grace...and your patience. I know we are owed neither, but I have no choice."

"You have twelve hours," Annette said coldly. "In twelve hours, Imperial Marines will storm *Chosen Sword* to retrieve Fleet Master Cawl. Are we understood?"

She *saw* the Inquisitor wince through the black leather armor.

"You are understood," they conceded.

CHAPTER FIFTY

DESPITE THE WARNINGS, THE TRIP ABOARD THE MESHAROM battlecruiser was surprisingly comfortable. Where the A!Tol Imperium and the Duchy of Terra used active microbots only to support the outer hull, the entire interior of a Mesharom vessel was made of the machines.

That allowed them to create a pocket of the ship that was perfectly tailored to human sensibilities in terms of gravity and temperature, with individual quarters for everyone. Even the beds appeared to have been made out of the microbots, but they were surprisingly comfortable.

The "guests" didn't see any of their hosts for the entire voyage, but there was a collection of segmented, worm-like robots to take care of their needs. The only food was bland Universal Protein, but it was hardly the first time most of *Bellerophon*'s crew had been reduced to eating the artificial substance on its own.

It was the fourth day, according to Morgan's communicator, when the robots sought out the officers.

"Commander Casimir, please follow this unit," the robot that had found Morgan instructed. "A final briefing awaits."

If they were already close enough to Sol for a final briefing, the ships were even faster than Morgan suspected. The ability of the Mesharom ships to manipulate hyperspace made them *much* more capable of covering long distances than Arm Powers—or even other Core Powers, from what she knew.

In any case, though, there was no point in being rude to their hosts. She followed the robotic worm and realized that Made and Tanzi were also being led to the meeting.

A new door opened in the wall as they approached, and they were silently guided deeper into the battlecruiser. Morgan wasn't really surprised when they were led into the presence of Interpreter-Captain Shexbetai, except in that the Mesharom normally didn't like to deal with multiple aliens at once.

"Commanders," Shexbetai greeted them. "We will be entering the Sol system in just over one of your hours. Once we reach orbit of Earth, you will be provided access to your shuttlecraft. You will be capable of making it home from there, one presumes."

"I believe we can manage that, yes," Tanzi said with a smile. "Your hospitality and assistance are appreciated, Interpreter-Captain. Your kindness won't be forgotten."

"Your people owe the Mesharom much already," the Interpreter pointed out. "But we share an enemy in these Taljzi fools. Certainly, we lack the ability to project enough power this far out from the Core to deal with them ourselves."

"I don't want to speak for my government, but I doubt we will turn aside any aid you can offer," Morgan told the Mesharom.

"Your government has already said as much, Commander; do not worry," Shexbetai replied. "Interpreter-Shepherd Adamase awaits us with the main body of our fleet. Too many Frontier Fleet officers have died to these fools. They will learn."

There was no real threat to Shexbetai's translated tone, but Morgan shivered anyway. The Mesharom were not known for being anything less than...*thorough* once angered.

Their anger would likely be to the A!Tol Imperium's benefit, but it was still a dangerous thing to be around.

"We will need to coordinate our people to make sure that we're all ready to go," Commander Tanzi said. "Is there anything you need from us, Interpreter-Captain?"

"No," Shexbetai told them. "Just...please get your people off my ship. We are allies of a sort today, but I won't pretend my crew is enjoying your presence."

"IS anyone surprised we're being routed directly to Wuxing Tower?" Morgan's pilot said dryly. "I didn't think we'd even flagged ground control that you were aboard, sir, but everyone else is going to Orbit One."

Morgan sighed.

"I really wish they wouldn't do shit like that," she admitted. "It's not like there aren't fifty other people on this shuttle whose families would love to see them."

"True enough," the pilot agreed. "But I can't begrudge it, not really. We all know we're back in space in twenty-four hours. I hope as many of us as possible get to see our families, but we swore an oath."

"We did," Morgan confirmed. "And I'll be in space with you, whatever ship they put me on."

"Oorah, sir," the pilot replied. "Wuxing Tower in sixty seconds."

Hong Kong was beneath them now and she looked over her hometown with relief. She hadn't expected to come home when she'd decided to stay on *Bellerophon*. Instead, all of her people had survived.

Thanks to the Mesharom. That wasn't a debt she'd forget anytime soon.

She realized there was a crowd on the roof of Wuxing Tower as they approached. A thin line of Ducal Guards kept them back from the landing pad, but it definitely wasn't just her father.

As they got closer, she realized it wasn't even media, and she grinned as what her father had done sunk home.

"I see my father has learned some lessons from my mother over the years," she murmured to the pilot as they swung in for a landing. "See anyone you know?"

"Trying not to, sir," the pilot told her. "I can't fly with tears in my eyes."

The shuttle settled down on the hard concrete and the pilot finally looked out into the crowd and smiled—as he started to cry.

"That's my wife," he half-whispered. "And my little girl."

"Come on, Chief," Morgan told him. "Let's get everybody out to meet their families. We only have so much time, so let's take advantage of it!"

MORGAN'S FATHER held on to her for at least a minute in silence as the crowd around them swarmed the people she'd brought home.

"How did you pull this off?" she demanded. "Some of these people should have been on the other side of the planet!"

"There was no way I *wasn't* going to see you," Elon Casimir told her. "So, Zhao and I pulled some strings and made sure everyone's family was on call. We probably didn't get everybody lined up perfectly, but I think we got at least ninety percent of people's families ready to meet them.

"The ones we missed are already being shipped around. Everyone from *Bellerophon* is going to get thirty-six hours."

"And then?" Morgan asked.

"That's up to Jean. He and Zhao are working on it as we speak."

Morgan looked around.

"I was half-expecting both of them," she admitted.

"Jean is buried," her father told her. "And Zhao..." He sighed. "Zhao's here, but he wasn't up for coming upstairs and facing the crowd. He's not doing well."

Morgan winced. "Is he waiting?"

"He's working, but he'd be sad if you didn't come see him," Elon Casimir said. "I don't know how much longer we'll have him for, my dear. The man needs to retire.

"Before the job kills him."

"I don't think he has retirement in him, Dad," Morgan replied. "Let's go. I owe him a hug at least. The twins?"

"Your sisters have all been evacuated to Kimar. They're waiting on a transport there to move them deeper into Imperial Space."

"How deep are we talking?" Morgan asked.

"A!To," her dad confessed. "The Empress herself will take them in, until this situation with the Taljzi is dealt with. No one is safe this close to them. We're evacuating ten million people a day, and it's not enough."

"No." Morgan sighed. "So, we fight."

"So, we fight," Elon Casimir confirmed. "I've done everything I can to make sure you have the swords to stand against this enemy. I just don't know if I've done enough."

"If you haven't, no one could have," she told her father. "Come on."

IT HAD PROBABLY BEEN six months since Morgan had seen Li Chin Zhao, and the Duchy's Treasurer had gone visibly downhill since then. His skin had gained a looseness she'd never seen before, and he didn't rise when she entered the room.

"Morgan. It's good to see you," he said in a hoarse voice. "Jean will be here in a few. They're still sorting assignments for *Bellerophon*'s crew."

"It's good to see you, too, Uncle Li," Morgan said gently, taking a seat across from him. "Are you doing okay?"

"No," he said with a chuckle. His eyes were still bright and focused on her. "My body is falling apart around me, child. Been doing so for a long time, but it's catching up with me of late. The timing could be better."

"There's always going to be a crisis of some kind," she told him. "If your assistants aren't ready to step up, you're not half the leader I think you are."

He laughed, then choked and sighed. He glanced over at her father.

"Your father said the same," he admitted. "This crisis, though...it's something different. Something new and terrifying. I'm not leaving until it's over. I'll talk to your mother once the battle's done, I promise."

"You'd better," Morgan said fiercely. "You've given the Duchy twenty years. How much more can we ask?"

"A lot," Zhao told her. "A lot. And I'd give it if I could, but you're not wrong. I don't know how much longer I have. I'd rather spend it working, frankly. What other legacy does a man like me have?"

She turned a pointed eye on the wall of his office, a collection of images of construction projects, space stations and ships Zhao's office and skill had helped fund over the last two decades.

"Looks like you've got a few," she said.

"The entire Militia, for one," Jean Villeneuve said from the door. "Are you going to listen to her, Li? Or is James going to have to drag you from this office by force?"

"I'd *break* if you tried that," Zhao pointed out dryly. "The point is made, people. It was already made." He shook his head and winced. "Does the Commander get her orders directly from the Councilor for the Militia this time?"

Villeneuve chuckled.

"She already got the thirty-six-hour stand-down," he pointed out. "After that, you're reporting aboard *Jaki*, one of the new *Bellerophon*-Bs."

"I didn't think any of them were scheduled to be ready," Morgan said. The *Bellerophon*-Bs should still be months from completion.

"Four of them will be...in thirty-six hours," Jean said with a chuckle. "You'll be *Jaki*'s XO. Tanzi will be in command."

Executive officer. Morgan shook her head slowly.

"I don't know if I'm ready for that, Uncle Jean," she admitted carefully. She wouldn't have said that in a more formal setting, but while she might be sitting in a room with the key members of her planet's government, she was also sitting in a room full of family friends.

"Neither is anyone else I can steal to be senior officers on the new ships," Jean told her. "You've fought the Taljzi. That puts you ahead of many—and I'm already poaching the remotely qualified XOs to command the damn things.

"*Chancellor Merkel* is due back in four to five days. We expect the Taljzi a day or so behind her. We'll finish the refits on the first four Grand Fleet squadrons after Rear Admiral Sun arrives and before the Taljzi.

"But that's all we get, Morgan," the Councilor said quietly. "We're picking up another four capital-ship squadrons from the Imperial Navy, and that's it. About fourteen hundred ships to stand against three thousand."

"What about the Mesharom?" she asked.

"They'll punch above their weight, but those battlecruisers are smaller than our battleships," her father pointed out. "The Kanzi are at least seven days away. We're still waiting for word from Annette; she should have reached their Shadowed Armada by now.

"What we have is all we can count on. We have to hold the Solar System with it. Which means that, as much as I want to wrap you in cotton and put you behind a billion fortifications, humanity needs you on a warship."

"I wouldn't *let* you hide me," Morgan said fiercely. "There's nowhere else I'd be but in the line of battle."

Her father bowed his head.

"I know," he admitted. "You are your mother's daughter. *Both* of your mothers."

CHAPTER FIFTY-ONE

JEAN WATCHED THE FORMATIONS TAKE SHAPE ACROSS HIS SOLAR system. He'd never in his life expected to see a fleet like this in his home. Fourteen hundred warships, two hundred of them his.

The United Earth Space Force he'd risen through the ranks of had commanded two hundred warships at its peak. Those two hundred fusion-torch warships had required a total crew of three hundred thousand officers and enlisted.

The current Duchy of Terra Militia, with their seventy-two capital ships and a hundred and forty-four escorts were crewed by just over half a million sentients. The vast majority of them were humans, but there were other races present aboard his ships as well. Mostly Laians from the Exile enclave, but there were others as well.

Eleven hundred and twenty warships of the A!Tol Imperial Navy had been gathered to protect his system. Seventy squadrons, twenty-five of capital ships and forty-five of cruisers and destroyers, were now spread around his system.

Fleet Lord Harriet Tanaka, the highest-ranked human officer in the Imperial Navy, was acting as Tan!Shallegh's second-in-command.

Where the A!Tol war leader commanded the forces directly above Earth, Tanaka had five squadrons of super-battleships emplaced around the Raging Waters of Friendship Yards.

The complex had grown vastly over the two decades, funded by both the Duchy and the Indiri financing cartels that had underwritten the original project. It was the third largest shipbuilding complex in the Imperium now.

Of course, the Indiri home system held the second, fourth, sixth and eighth largest complexes, making that system the second largest source of Imperial warships. Financing Sol's expansion hadn't hurt the Indiri in the end.

All of the Duchy's squadrons were concentrated around Earth, reinforced by another fifteen squadrons of Imperial capital ships. Tan!Shallegh led that force, containing his other five squadrons of super-battleships.

The remaining five squadrons of battleships were split between the asteroid belt, supporting the eleven six-ship squadrons of Mesharom battlecruisers, and Jupiter. The Imperium stood guard over DragonWorks for now.

Even as Jean was going over the data, the last work was being done on the *Bellerophon*-Bs. They were light-years from what would normally be called complete, but with *three thousand ships* about to descend on his star system, what choice did he have?

Fourteen hundred warships. The most powerful fleet Jean had ever seen with his own eyes...and he couldn't believe they would win. In his darkest moments, Jean Villeneuve knew that humanity's *real* hope lay in the continuous stream of transports evacuating civilians.

They were up to twelve million people a day. It was a mind-boggling number, but they still hadn't evacuated even *one* percent of the Sol System's populace.

If Jean Villeneuve failed, ten billion people were going to die... and he couldn't see any way to succeed.

FOUR VICE ADMIRALS, one Admiral and one tired Councilor gathered in Orbit One's secure conference room, and Jean Villeneuve looked over his subordinates.

Patrick Kurzman-Wellesley knew everything Jean did. He looked as solid as ever, but Jean knew him well enough to know he was afraid.

Tidikat was unreadable. Even for a Laian, he was good at hiding his emotions. Almost two decades of practice meant that Jean could usually read the big beetles, but Tidikat was perfectly controlled today.

Vice Admiral Patience Van der Merwe didn't have the advantage of being an alien but was almost as unreadable for that. Jean knew the South African Admiral had been briefed when she'd made it back from Alpha Centauri with her squadron, but if she was as scared as she should be, she didn't show it.

Vice Admiral Cole Amandine was the youngest of the Duchy's senior flag officers and clearly hadn't learned Van der Merwe's forced impassiveness. He looked grimly determined...but terrified.

Harold Rolfson had been the last to arrive, the massively bearded Icelandic officer who'd held Asimov against the Taljzi *trying* to appear as boisterous as ever.

Like Kurzman-Wellesley, Jean knew Harold Rolfson too well to be fooled.

"I don't believe I need to explain the situation to you five," he told them. "We are going to be outnumbered two to one. Based off the data from their encounters with Rear Admiral Sun's fleet, we've lost most of our advantages over them as well.

"Consort Casimir's people are working on refining our targeting algorithms to give them less time to shoot down the HSMs, but the terminal approach is an inherent weakness of the system."

"They had no active missile defense at Asimov," Rolfson pointed out. "They went from *nothing* to a system superior to our own in months. That's...frankly terrifying.

"We smashed the First Return, but they had no counter for hypermissiles or hyperfold cannons. They still don't have much of a counter for the latter, but we'll lose a *lot* of people closing to ten light-seconds through their missiles."

"And at that range, we are vulnerable to them getting their disruptors into range," Tidikat noted precisely. "We have more advantages than we are considering. This is our home ground."

Jean made a throwaway gesture.

"We have the fortifications, the constellations and several shoals of preplaced dual-portal hyperspace missiles," he agreed. "All told, they're worth maybe another squadron or two of capital ships.

"We didn't build Sol's defenses to stand off three thousand warships." He shook his head. "Even A!To's defenses couldn't stand off this fleet. That's why we lured them here."

"Seems like we could have made better plans than that," Van der Merwe noted. "There are other places we could have fought them."

"Where?" Rolfson snapped. "Asimov? Centauri? Kendricks? How many tens of millions of lives are you prepared to trade for *time*, Admiral? We couldn't have stopped them anywhere else, either."

"If we fail to stop them here, those colonies are just as dead," she pointed out. "I don't see what we've gained in fighting them here."

"Those fortifications," Jean told her. "And Sol is better positioned for the hyperspace currents than most of our colonies. Our Kanzi reinforcements couldn't make it anywhere else in time."

"I can't believe we're relying on the smurfs to save us," Amandine said. "We've been fighting them or preparing to fight them since we knew what the galaxy actually looked like."

"They don't want to get mass-murdered any more than we do," Rolfson replied dryly. "We're all better off if we fight together. If they get here in time. Do we have a timeline on that?"

"No." Jean shook his head. "The last I heard, which is about a day out of date now, is that the Shadowed Armada was dealing with a mutiny and the Duchess was waiting to see how that shook out."

"And this is why I don't want to trust the smurfs," Rolfson said with a sigh. "We need them. They need us. But fuck if they don't seem to realize any part of that!"

"It's in Annette Bond's hands," Jean replied. "If anyone can handle it..."

CHAPTER FIFTY-TWO

Datastreams flickered across the hologram on *Tornado*'s flag bridge, Captain Mamutse's techs and analysts doing their best to identify the shifting balance of power in the Shadowed Armada.

The Imperial ships had pulled back. !Olarski hadn't gone so far as to deploy Buckler drones to protect the squadron, but Annette was tempted to order it.

So far, however, it looked like the Inquisitor was carrying the day. No one was going so far as to engage the weapons on their warships, but fighting had to be raging on half the capital ships in the fleet.

At least the warships were intact.

"Fleet Lord?" she asked !Olarski as the A!Tol appeared in her hologram. "Are your Marines ready?"

"I'm not even certain where to send them, but yes," the officer replied. "Is sending our troops in really the best idea, Dan!Annette Bond?"

"I don't have a damn clue," she admitted. "As to where to send them, stand by to board *Chosen Sword*. I care about retrieving Fleet

Master Cawl. The rest of the damn smurfs can go hang, but that man promised me a fleet."

The A!Tol snapped her beak in a harsh chuckle.

"My Marines are ready to go retrieve him on your order," she said. "How much is left on your deadline?"

"Minutes," Annette told her. "We don't have time for this bullshit."

"Your grace, incoming call."

"That will be the Inquisitor," Annette said to !Olarski. "We'll speak soon."

The techs once again connected the masked Kanzi to her flag bridge, and she looked at the Inquisitor levelly.

"Twelve hours, I said," she noted. "It looks to me like active fighting is continuing across your fleet, Inquisitor. I'm about to order Fleet Master Cawl retrieved by Imperial Marines. I'm not seeing any reason not to."

The Inquisitor bowed their head.

"I cannot permit that," they told her. "I'd hoped to resolve this relatively quietly, but your deadline leaves me no choice."

"What do you mean?" Annette demanded.

"Your grace!"

The exclamation from her techs drew her attention back to the main holographic display. For the first time since they'd arrived, the massive proton-beam batteries of the Kanzi warships had come to life. An entire squadron of super-battleships disappeared as their sisters turned their weapons on them.

"More shuttles launching; *Chosen Sword* is now flanked and being targeted by two more super-battleships."

"Those ships were in mutineers' hands, Duchess Bond, but they had officers and crew aboard who were still resisting," the Inquisitor said, their voice sad. "My point, I think, has been made. I will have Fleet Master Cawl in contact with you momentarily.

"Please do not do anything...rash before then."

The channel cut and Annette looked at the icons that had been a hundred and sixty million tons of warships and probably seventy or eighty thousand sentient beings.

"We needed them to move," !Olarski said very quietly. "I don't know if we were prepared to pay this price...but we needed them."

IT WAS another twenty minutes before Cawl finally opened a communications channel to Annette. The old Kanzi was missing his cane, leaning bodily against a table of some sort as he leveled a tired gaze on the camera.

"The mutiny is over, Duchess Bond," he told her. "I doubt you are any happier with the shadows of its ending than I am, but I cannot argue with the Inquisitor's choice."

"Are you all right?" she asked. Cawl wasn't necessarily a friend, but she was at least somewhat concerned for him.

"I'll live. Mostly just feeling like a foolish old man right now," he admitted. "If I'd simply taken command from my own ship, I don't know if any of this would have happened."

"Or perhaps you would have had an outright space battle on your hands," Annette pointed out. "We can't know. Are you in command now?"

"Close enough," he said. "I'm still establishing what subordinates I have left that aren't traitors. I'm sorry, your grace. It will take some time before the Shadowed Armada is ready to move."

She winced.

"My people," she whispered.

"I know. I will move stars and mountains and worlds to get the Armada in motion, Duchess Bond, but a third of my senior officers were traitors and I'm not sure I even have half of the others left," he told her.

"I will reorganize my command structure and we will be underway as quickly as possible, but stars move the Kanzi, not the other way around."

"I don't know how much time we have," she warned him.

"I know."

The call was silent for several seconds.

"I will do all I can," he promised. "We *will* make it to your people in time. If it can be done, it will be. My High Priestess gave her word.

"*I* gave my word."

CHAPTER FIFTY-THREE

"WELCOME ABOARD *JAKI*, SIR," THE OFFICER WAITING FOR Morgan told her with a sharp salute. He was a Lieutenant Commander, maybe a year younger than she, with skin that managed to be a shade *darker* than the Duchy of Terra Militia's black uniform.

"I'm Lieutenant Commander Kaikara Bale," he introduced himself. "*Jaki*'s tactical officer." He smiled brightly. "I suspect I feel as underqualified for that role as the rest of *Jaki*'s officers, but for my sins, I am the senior officer aboard."

Morgan returned the salute and stepped across the vague line demarcating the difference between DragonWorks Station and *Jaki*.

"And now you are," Bale concluded. "Until Captain Tanzi reports aboard. I'll admit, my understanding was that the two of you would arrive together."

"We were on different shuttles, LC," Morgan told the man doing her old job. "And I know DragonWorks better than she does." She returned his brilliant smile. "I lived here for a year when I was younger."

There'd been an assassination attempt on the Duchess's family and, well, the stepdaughter had been easily shuffled to safely. DragonWorks was as safe as Sol got, the station still embedded well within Jupiter.

"What's *Jaki*'s status?" she asked as she fell in beside Bale. "We may as well wait for Captain Tanzi. Her shuttle docked barely five minutes after mine."

The tactical officer snorted gently.

"Jaki was one of the legendary ancestor-twins of Uganda," he noted. "That Jaki is, presumably, long dead. This *Jaki* probably envies him."

Morgan winced. "That bad?"

"Ehhhh." It was a long, drawn-out sound as the tactical officer shook his head. "It could be worse, but we haven't had trials. Haven't had tests. We haven't even had our *Captain* aboard yet, let alone our entire crew.

"Everything *looks* like it's hanging together, but we have pre-deployment trials for a reason, sir. We're taking her right out of the construction slip and into battle. I can't say I love the idea, but…"

"But we don't have a choice," Morgan said pointedly. "So, how are we doing?"

"Last of our HSMs should be aboard by midnight," Bale said crisply. "We don't have any duals, so at least we're not dealing with the big guys. Antimatter-tank fueling is scheduled for oh six hundred hours tomorrow. Consumables and crew will be coming aboard until about eighteen hundred hours tomorrow."

"And if my math is right, we shouldn't be taking her into battle until two days *after* that at the earliest," Morgan replied. Twenty-four hours before that, she might even finally get to see Victoria Antonova again.

The other woman might even one day forgive her for choosing to remain behind. Morgan wasn't taking bets, though. It wouldn't be consistent with her luck…and it would be far more than she deserved.

"That sounds like we have plenty of time," Captain Anja Tanzi told the two junior officers as she entered the boarding bay herself. "How much of the crew do we have aboard so far?"

Bale looked a little terrified, but he swallowed and faced his superiors as steadily as he could.

"We're up to about thirteen hundred as of last count," he reported. "Each of you was on a transport that was supposed to be bringing another five hundred. My understanding is that we'll get another five hundred tomorrow, with the consumables, and we are to pick up our last fifteen hundred crew in Earth orbit once we're fueled and ready to deploy."

"I'm glad *someone* knows what's going on there," Tanzi told him. "All I'd received so far was assurances that I would *have* a crew." She shook her head. "It should say everything that we have a *battleship* that is the Captain's first command and the XO's first XO slot. And, I believe, the tactical officer's first TO slot, correct?"

"Yes, sir," Bale confessed.

"We're fortunate enough that Commander Made will be joining us as chief engineer tomorrow," Tanzi noted. "Apparently, the powers that be decided to keep *Bellerophon*'s idiots together."

"I'm guessing Admiral Kurzman-Wellesley decided we should get another chance to die together," Morgan replied.

Bale glanced from one woman to the other and audibly swallowed.

"Please tell me there's a joke there I'm missing, sirs."

Morgan chuckled.

"No, LC," Tanzi told him. "Just the gallows humor of people who *knew* they were going to die already this week. Once you've been through that, well, everything else seems easy."

"THEY FIXED the access issue for Charlie-Six," Morgan noted as she went over the schematics for the *Bellerophon*-B with the Captain. "Commander Masters and I flagged that early on, but I never expected to see it fixed."

The rearmost battery of hyperfold cannons had ended up sufficiently removed from *Bellerophon*'s rapid-transit system to make it almost impossible for the crew to reach it in time.

On *Jaki*, however, a new transit tube split off from the main system along the arch that mounted Charlie-Six.

The thought of Commander Masters, however, caused Morgan to wince. They'd started off on the wrong foot, but he'd been a good officer and a solid mentor.

And he'd been well on his way to being a good friend, before he'd died with *Rama*.

"I thought the problem there was the power conduits?" Tanzi asked. "I saw the report and Engineering's analysis of it."

The three-dimensional schematic zoomed in.

"Oh. That would explain it," the Captain said. "They added a third matter converter and restructured the entire power distribution system since the D-HSMs were gone."

"Replaced the antimatter cores with it, looks like," Morgan agreed. "We kept the fusion secondaries, but we don't carry any antimatter except the warheads for the HSMs now."

"She's a hell of a ship," Tanzi concluded. "Feel up to this, XO?"

Morgan snorted.

"Do you, skipper?" she asked.

"Hell, no. But we don't have a choice, so we make it happen. Concerns?"

"That entire new power distribution grid," Morgan admitted. "The power grid was what killed *Bellerophon* in the end. I mean, the fact that we kept tearing her apart and rebuilding her can't have helped, but it was the grid that went in the end."

"And since we're the first *Bellerophon*-Bs commissioned, there's been barely any full-scale testing," Tanzi agreed. "I'll put a bug in Made's ear. He'll watch it."

"Otherwise, crew," the newly fledged executive officer continued. "We're roughly sixty percent crewed right now and we're moving to Earth in four hours. The reports I'm seeing right now? The Militia doesn't *have* our last fifteen hundred crew. Or the same number for the other Bs.

"Even Jean Villeneuve can't conjure six *thousand* trained personnel out of thin air."

"What do you think the answer is going to be?" Tanzi asked.

Morgan thought about it. From the way the Captain phrased it, *Tanzi* had guessed the answer. But that was a lot of people...as many, in fact, as had served aboard *Jean Chrétien*.

"How many extra hands does Rear Admiral Sun have stuffed aboard his ships?" she asked aloud. "Most of *Bellerophon*'s crew. Most of *Jean Chrétien*'s crew. Not so many, sadly, from *Rama*."

"The last number I saw before we left the group behind was about seventy-two hundred rescuees," Tanzi told her. "So, I don't think we'll get the rest of our crew when we get into Earth orbit—but we will get them before the Taljzi get here."

"That's going to be rough," Morgan admitted. "We don't have enough time to integrate the crew we already have. Adding over a third of the crew at the last minute?"

"They're all trained Militia personnel. It could be worse."

"Could be, yeah. Could be a lot better, too."

"If we can't take the joke, we shouldn't have signed up," Tanzi said. "We'll make do, Commander."

"That we will, sir." Morgan sighed. "That we will."

CHAPTER FIFTY-FOUR

MORGAN HADN'T REALIZED JUST HOW BEAT-UP *CHANCELLOR Merkel* was until she saw the super-battleship carefully lurch into Earth orbit, surrounded by her near-identical but undamaged sisters.

With eighteen other *Duchess of Terra*–class super-battleships around her, it was much clearer how badly the warship had been damaged during their desperate flight back to Sol.

In many ways, the surviving cruisers had been luckier. That was mostly because the cruisers that *hadn't* been lucky hadn't made it.

Morgan found herself saluting the other survivors of the scout flotilla on the holographic display in *Jaki*'s Secondary Control. They'd made it home. There'd been moments she hadn't thought *any* of them were going to make it, but they all had.

"Bale, do we have an update from Command on the Taljzi?" she asked the tactical officer.

Bale currently had the watch on the bridge, while Morgan held down the backup command center. Technically, that put the junior officer in command of the battleship.

In practice, it was a measure to make him feel more comfortable while Captain Tanzi was off duty. Morgan was comfortable in her ability to stand a watch without problems, at least, even if she was still intimidated by the pile of work that came with her new role.

Jaki's only barely completed status didn't help with the new XO's workload.

"Rear Admiral Sun reported their lead elements were about sixteen light-hours behind him," Bale told her. "That would put them about twenty-four hours out now, except that the main element was trailing quite a bit behind.

"Analysis is suggesting forty-eight to sixty hours."

"Thanks."

Morgan looked at her status reports one more time and saw a new message pop up.

Pulling it up, she saw it was one of the two things she was waiting for. The message was a confirmation from HerCom—the Militia's Human Resources Command—that *Jaki* would be getting her crew allotment.

The attachments were huge. A list of sixteen hundred and thirty-two names, with their appended records, took up a lot of space.

It took Morgan all of two seconds to confirm that Victoria Antonova wasn't on the list. They were getting the communications officer from *Squall*, a Lieutenant Commander Manas Abbes.

That was potentially a good thing, she supposed. As executive officer, she couldn't be romantically involved with any of *Jaki*'s crew. She was going to miss the other woman, though.

Even if she *was* expecting Antonova's next communication to be pithy at best.

In the absence of any message from her lover, however, Morgan set herself to work. She'd be responsible for meeting the officers, but right now she needed to divvy up those sixteen hundred–plus names between her junior officers and senior NCOs. Everybody would need to be met by somebody, and they really had *less* than two days to get everybody aboard and settled.

Her personal hopes and complications could be dealt with later.

MORGAN HAD JUST FINISHED CARVING up the list and sending it off to the various subordinates when Captain Tanzi walked into Secondary Control, looking like Magical Mr. Mistoffelees had swallowed the canary.

"Well, XO, I've got bad news for you and good news for you," Tanzi told her, leaning against the central command chair and grinning down at Morgan.

"Sir?"

"The bad news is that Commander Victoria Antonova specifically requested she be assigned to a different ship than you," her Captain told her.

"Oh." Morgan had half-expected that. It was still a bit of a punch to the gut.

"The good news is that we'll need your countersignature on her Form SMD-36-A7," Tanzi continued. "Since the form of said request was a notification of long-term relationship, requiring postings without a chain-of-command conflict."

Tanzi handed Morgan her communicator and the younger officer stared at a form she'd never actually studied before.

The Duchy of Terra Militia had a sensible standard on fraternization: don't let it happen up or down the chain of command. The tactical officer dating the coms officer was fine. The *executive* officer dating, well, anybody, was not.

To help meet that standard, they asked that members of the Militia register long-term relationships. It also allowed for certain benefits and perks—for example, the right to communicate while on secured postings.

Morgan double-checked the date stamp on the form. Victoria had submitted it about an hour before arriving in Sol, which meant she'd known Morgan had survived *Bellerophon*'s intended final stand.

She tapped the command to digitally sign the document, then looked up at her Captain.

"Thank you, sir," she told Tanzi.

"Want some advice, Commander?" the older woman asked. "I don't date girls, but I'm guessing some rules are much the same."

"Sure."

"You're swamped. She's swamped. But you've had prep time and she's been thrown directly onto a new ship without much warning. Take the time to make a call, or at least record a message. You're not going to see each other until this is over—and it could easily be the last chance you have to talk."

Morgan swallowed.

Intentions and desires were a frail shield against the tidal wave sweeping toward Sol. Her Captain was right.

INTENTIONS AND DESIRES were *also* a frail shield against the responsibilities involved in being executive officer of a capital ship with a crew of just under forty-five hundred souls.

It was over two hours later, an hour after she was officially off duty, before Morgan had everything in sufficient order that she could take time for herself. She should probably have used the time to sleep, but she could spare a few minutes.

She *needed* to take those few minutes.

An advantage to everyone being in orbit of Earth was that there was no need to use hyperfold communicators or relay through a starcom or anything of the sort. *Jaki* directly hailed *Guan Yu* and Morgan was able to place her call directly to Victoria's communicator.

She was expecting to leave a recording, but instead the communicator picked up instantly.

"Sorry, Chief," she heard Victoria say. "This is important. Can our chat wait?"

"That your girl?" a gruff male voice replied. "Hell, yeah, this can wait. You've been off shift for four hours, boss!"

"Get out, Chief," Victoria ordered, laughing. A moment later, a video channel opened and the blonde officer appeared above the desk in Morgan's office.

Victoria was in a similar if smaller office, equally plain and unadorned. Neither of them had brought much from *Bellerophon,* and there'd been no time to assemble their usual paraphernalia.

"Morgan. Thank you. I...wasn't sure when I'd find the time."

"Neither was I," Morgan admitted. "Just figured I owed it to you to be the one to make it."

"You did," Victoria told her. "Only one of us went off to try and get herself *killed,* after all."

"That wasn't the point. That was just...the side effect."

"Important side effect, don't you think?" Victoria demanded. "You got lucky. Impossibly lucky. I almost lost you."

"I know." Morgan searched for words for several moments, then shook her head and settled on the simplest.

"I'm sorry. I can't even promise it won't happen again," she admitted, "but I'm sorry. This is my life—our life."

"I know." Victoria was silent, and the two of them just looked at each other for a minute.

"I know," she finally repeated. "I'm not going to say I'm not angry —I'm pissed—but I do understand. I put on the uniform, same as you. Soldiers and spacers have dealt with this forever, so I guess we keep dealing with it."

"If you want," Morgan said quietly. "*I* want to, but...even I have to admit that signing up for a last stand is pretty egregious."

Victoria stared at her for several seconds and then started laughing.

"*Egregious* is one word for it, I suppose," she conceded. "You're nuts, Morgan Casimir. But that's what I was getting into, and I knew it. So, yeah, I'll keep dealing with it if you do. We're both going to be in the middle of the fight that's coming."

"We'll make it through," Morgan promised. "I don't know how, but I know my mom is working on it. And if I have faith in *anyone*, it's in my mother."

"You and the rest of planet Earth, my dear," Victoria admitted. "You and the rest of planet Earth."

CHAPTER FIFTY-FIVE

"They're late."

Admiral Patrick Kurzman-Wellesley's voice echoed across the virtual conference, and Jean Villeneuve shook his head.

"*Oui, mais je ne m'en plains pas,*" he noted. The only person on the call who wouldn't understand at least that much French was Tan!Shallegh—and the A!Tol didn't even speak English on his own.

"I am concerned about what the delay may entail," that worthy noted.

There was no question who was in command of Sol's defenses today. Jean and Kurzman-Wellesley—and General Wellesley-Kurzman, for that matter—were on the call as a courtesy more than anything else.

Each of Tan!Shallegh's three subordinate Fleet Lords commanded more firepower than the entire Duchy of Terra Militia. One of those Fleet Lords was human, at least, but Jean wasn't familiar with the Rekiki Fleet Lord Okan or the Frole Fleet Lord Iphibit.

It was quite the eclectic collection of beings, he had to admit. An A!Tol in command, a giant squid that seemed to belong in Jean's worst nightmares. Three subordinate Fleet Lords: one human, one crocodilian centaur and one being that could pass for Earth's mythological Grays.

Interpreter-Shepherd Adamase was on the call mostly by virtue of being the only Interpreter in the Mesharom fleet who was prepared to be on even a virtual call with that many aliens. They were not, as Jean understood, actually in command of the Frontier Fleet detachment.

Adamase's authority was political. They'd been promoted from Frontier Fleet to a bureaucratic position that gave them authority *over* Frontier Fleet while no longer being part of it.

Their role in this meeting, in fact, had many similarities to Jean's own.

"If the Taljzi are waiting for something, we may yet learn to regret their delay," Tan!Shallegh continued. "Between Rear Admiral Sun and Interpreter-Commodore Installai, they took heavy losses."

"Those losses are minimal in comparison to their main strength," Harriet Tanaka pointed out. The Japanese Fleet Lord was the only person on the call who'd faced the Taljzi in battle. "All told, they lost, what, three hundred or so ships? Almost entirely escorts? A tenth of their numbers and *maybe* a twentieth of their firepower.

"We're still utterly outgunned. And scattered across the system, at that."

"No system as heavily populated as Sol is easily defended," Tan!Shallegh replied. "What would you suggest, Fleet Lord?"

"We need to consolidate our defenses," Tanaka said. "Ninety-eight percent of Sol's population lives inside the asteroid belt. With the transport we're currently using to evacuate Earth, we can move that entire population to Mars or Earth in a day."

"At the price of not evacuating ten million people from the system," Jean said. He wasn't arguing. He could see Tanaka's point. There were roughly two hundred million people scattered across the outer system—mostly in the Jupiter planetary system.

"We can guarantee safety for ten million at the price of nearly guaranteeing the deaths of two hundred million," the Japanese officer said. "We should have evacuated the outer system a week ago."

Jean winced. *That* decision had arguably been his, but he hadn't even thought of that point.

"What about DragonWorks?" he asked.

"The entire complex is inside Jupiter," Tanaka replied. "Sink it another thousand kilometers and they'll never see it."

The Councilor sighed.

"I had not considered reducing our potential exposure like that," he admitted. "Fleet Lord Tanaka is right. We have the time and we can save lives by moving people inside the Belt."

It might not save those people. But Harriet Tanaka was right—*not* moving them would almost certainly condemn them.

But trying to save them once the Taljzi arrived could easily cost enough ships to condemn Earth.

———

"IT IS...A LESS-THAN-OPTIMAL SITUATION," James Wellesley-Kurzman said very carefully twelve hours later. "We have the transports to move them, but we're talking about the kind of people who packed up everything and moved to the back end of nowhere...or whose parents did.

"None of these settlements are more than sixty years old. A lot of them postdate the Annexation, and I'd say about a quarter of them at least are out there to avoid A!Tol or Ducal attention."

"I know that," Jean said patiently. The Englishman on the other end of the com wouldn't be filling him in on background detail if it wasn't necessary.

"Hell, let's throw in that something like thirty thousand of them were kidnapped by an A!Tol rogue faction before we even knew the Imperium existed," he said. "We still need to get them to safety."

"Most of the folks around Jupiter were basically waiting for the call," Wellesley told him. "I didn't think I was going to be able to move two hundred million people, but we actually had half of them moved in ten hours."

"And the other half?"

"The other half is scattered in colonies of twenty to thirty thousand at most, and they are *not* being helpful," the General admitted. "The ones that go dark to avoid us are probably safe from the Taljzi, too, so long as they keep their heads down."

"And the rest?"

"The rest are either scattered to high heaven or actively avoiding us *without* being stealthy about it," Wellesley said grimly. "We're chasing them in assault shuttles, trying to take control of their systems so we can get them rescued. I'm not even sure what level of force to *use*."

"Hence you're talking to me." Jean nodded.

"Exactly."

"To misquote a famous and rightfully disrespected countryman of mine: stun them all and let God sort them out," the Councilor said flatly. "You have wide dispersal stunners on the assault shuttles. The A!Tol used the same things to disable entire Army Corps when they landed.

"Unless the settlements have unusual levels of shielding, you should be able to disable the entire populace. Stun them, board the platforms, haul them in-system. Borrow destroyers from the Militia for support."

Jean shook his head.

"Hell, I don't think we even need the transports for the space-based colonies. Asteroid and moon colonies, sure, but just move the entire damn station for the spaceborne ones."

"That's a violation of their rights," Wellesley-Kurzman pointed out. "That's why I haven't given that order."

"We're under attack, General," Jean said. "The Council has already declared a state of emergency. Under *that* authority, I can give that order—and I am, James. Better angry and with a stun hangover than vaporized by the Taljzi."

"Understood, sir," the General said crisply. "We'll get them to safety. No matter what."

THE TRAIL of icons making their way across Jean's display was disturbing. There had been hundreds of small settlements out beyond the Belt, and James Wellesley-Kurzman had taken his orders to heart.

After they'd stunned and seized the first dozen settlements, people had begun to realize that the Ducal Guard was entirely serious in their intent to get everyone to safety, regardless of what the "brave pioneers" residing in Sol's outer system might want.

They were cooperating now, but even so, Jean knew that at least a third of the icons moving through the asteroid Belt were full of unconscious people being checked over by Guard and Imperial Marine medics.

Those medics were stretched thin. No one had expected to have to deal with hundreds of thousands of stunned civilians.

The alternative, however, was to condemn them to death, and Jean didn't have it in him. Despite what he'd told James Wellesley, he knew that the state of emergency wasn't going to cover this. Some of the settlements had gone dark before the search teams had made it out to them.

They'd learn soon enough if that was sufficient to keep them safe. Jean wasn't prepared to take that bet.

He'd exceeded his authority. He knew that, even if he could trust that Wellesley hadn't. Even if Wellesley had known, they'd both understood what Jean was doing.

Earth needed those tens of millions of stubborn, brave *idiots* who'd been determined to make their own lives. They needed them as a safety valve, as a counterculture, as the child prepared to say when the Emperor was naked.

Humanity would never survive, never thrive, without their dissidents. Even if they didn't need them for that, the spacers were some of Earth's best and brightest.

They needed them more than they needed one more soldier-turned-politician. When they came clamoring for Jean's career, he'd give it to them. To protect both the Guards he'd sent into the fray and the Duchess he'd sworn to serve.

A ringing alert interrupted his thoughts, and Jean Villeneuve sighed as he saw the red lights splashing across the outer system.

The Taljzi were almost twenty-four hours later than even their most optimistic projections.

It didn't matter.

Duchess Bond and the Kanzi were still days away. No additional Imperial reinforcements were anywhere near them now.

Red icons continued to pour onto his screen, the computer rapidly giving up on trying to identify individual ships even on the screen that covered his office wall.

He tapped a command, opening an emergency channel that would reach every member of Bond's Ducal Council, wherever they were, whatever they were doing.

"The Taljzi are here," he said simply. "It's begun."

CHAPTER FIFTY-SIX

"BATTLE STATIONS, BATTLE STATIONS. ALL HANDS TO BATTLE stations. This is not a drill. Battle stations, battle stations."

Morgan's new office was maybe fifty steps from her battle station in Secondary Control. At a run, she could make it in seconds.

Running, of course, was a bad example to set for the crew. Instead, she took a deep breath and made sure her uniform with its integrated emergency systems was on and sealed. A moment glancing over her office screens told her what she needed to know immediately, and then she *calmly* set off down the corridor.

Stepping into the "big chair," she brought up the repeater screens. She could mimic anything her secondary crew down here were looking at—and was automatically mirroring Captain Tanzi's screens on the main bridge.

She took a glance around Secondary Control and linked to the bridge.

"Secondary Control is online," she reported. "Linked into the command sensor networks for Formation Alpha."

With most of the population beyond the Belt evacuated, they'd managed to reduce the defense to three formations.

Formation Alpha hung in orbit of Earth. The entire Ducal Militia, backed up by Tan!Shallegh's own detachment.

Formation Bravo orbited with the Raging Waters of Friendship Yards. It was the most powerful of the Imperial formations, and an entirely Imperial formation under Fleet Lord Harriet Tanaka.

Formation Charlie was hidden in the Belt, primarily anchored on Interpreter-Shepherd Adamase's Mesharom battlecruisers.

Between them, those formations totaled almost fifteen hundred warships, the single most powerful force Imperial history recorded as ever being mustered in this corner of the galaxy.

They were outnumbered over two to one by the force showing up on the main holographic display in Secondary Control.

"Do we have a final number yet, skipper?" Morgan asked Tanzi very quietly.

"No. Looks like they were waiting for reinforcements."

What Morgan was seeing was bad enough.

The Taljzi had picked up an extra hundred or so super-battleships somewhere and a few more battleships as well. Five hundred and fifty super-battleships formed the core of the incoming fleet, and seven hundred battleships flanked them.

There were over two thousand escorts, but they almost didn't matter. Not in the face of twelve hundred and fifty capital ships.

"Any orders from the Fleet Lord?" Morgan asked.

"Hold position for now; let them come to us," Tanzi replied.

"We can only hold the ship at battle stations for so long."

"I know that. So does Tan!Shallegh. We'll stand down to Status Bravo if they wait long enough, but somehow I'm not expecting that."

Morgan chuckled. There was no humor in it.

"So, we fight."

"We knew that from the beginning."

Morgan nodded, studying the data. New icons flickered for a moment and she shivered as she realized what they were.

"I'm registering missile strikes," Bale reported from the bridge. "I don't know what they're shooting at...but I'm guessing the settlements that went dark."

More icons flashed across her screen. Each represented somewhere between five and thirty thousand dead civilians who hadn't listened to the warnings and hadn't been found by the Guard.

"Any sign that they've detected DragonWorks?" she asked.

"No," Bale replied. "They're launching at everything they see. Some of what's blowing up has already been abandoned... It's not as bad as it looks."

"It's still pretty bad," Morgan said. "But they aren't shooting at the research base?"

"You demonstrated before that gas giants make a pretty solid shield," Bale pointed out. "It looked like Tortuga made it out safely, after all."

"That was the hope," she agreed. "But I have friends on Dragon-Works. I can't say the same about Tortuga."

She'd lost enough friends in the last few weeks, and she'd almost certainly lose more before the day was done. It was good to know at least *some* were safe.

If the station managed to successfully hide, DragonWorks might be all that was left of Sol in a few days.

───────────

THE FOLLOWING MINUTES PASSED EXCRUCIATINGLY. With over three thousand warships in the outer system, there was no way the defenders could sortie. That meant all that they could do was watch as the Taljzi forces spread out.

And spread out. And spread out.

By the end of the first hour, there were cruiser squadrons positioned around Jupiter and each of its Trojan asteroid clusters. More destroyers and cruisers were strung out like beads along the gas giant's orbit.

They weren't close to each other. What they were, however, was close enough that nothing could make it in or out of Sol without being intercepted by at least a Taljzi destroyer and probably several cruisers.

Along the way, they identified and destroyed dozens, if not hundreds, of spaceborne habitats. Many, as Bale had noted, were empty.

Many were not.

There might have been some habitats or asteroid colonies that had managed to successfully go dark and disappear, avoiding the Taljzi's scanners, but Morgan couldn't see them if they were there.

Her best guess was that at least two million people died within three hours of the Taljzi's arrival.

"What are they *doing*?" Bale asked.

"It's a siege, LC," Morgan told him. "They've cut off any attempt for us to retreat or bring in supplies without launching a major attack. They can move their main force"—still over fifteen hundred warships strong, mostly capital ships—"to intercept any attempted breakout, and their escorts can take down any freighters."

"They know that we can just keep producing everything on Earth, right?"

"Oh, they know," Morgan agreed. "They'll get to that. It's interesting, though."

"How so, Commander?" Tanzi asked, the Captain interjecting into the conversation. "I can see their logic."

"It's a cautious logic, sir," Morgan pointed out. "Before, the First Return seemed willing to accept any and all losses. They destroyed their own ships, took insane casualties and kept coming.

"These guys seem *much* more concerned about making sure they can control their losses."

She shook her head.

"It isn't going to save them losses, not when they run into a Mesharom-organized meat grinder on their way in, but it's something to watch for."

"Can we use it?" Tanzi asked.

"That's as much on Tan!Shallegh as anything else," Morgan admitted. "But I think so. If they're unwilling to take losses, we can make them flinch. If we can make them flinch, we can buy time."

"And if we can buy time, the Kanzi can get here," *Jaki*'s Captain concluded.

MORGAN WAS ABOUT to suggest that they stand the crew down from battle stations when the status icons around the main Taljzi fleet shifted.

"Bogey Force One is moving towards the inner system," Bale reported. "Course appears to be directly for Earth. ETA one point five hours."

That was assuming that the fleet didn't slow down to pass through the asteroid belt. That was a fair assumption, really. Unlike the accretion disk of the black hole DLK-5539, Sol's asteroid belt didn't come anywhere near the media depiction of an asteroid belt.

Of course, the fact that the Mesharom fleet was concealed inside the Belt would make a sprint to Earth a bad idea for the Taljzi. Morgan wasn't sure it was going to be a bad-enough idea to change the fate of the human homeworld, but it might buy them time.

New data flowed across her screens as orders came down from Tan!Shallegh.

"Lieutenant Commander Bale, prepare our HSM launchers, if you please," Tanzi ordered. "We are to synchronize hypermissiles with all of Formation Alpha and stand by for orders from the Flag."

Morgan glanced over the notes. The Mesharom and the rest of Formation Charlie were to hold fire, allowing the Taljzi to enter the inner system unchallenged. Formation Bravo was to remain in position around the Yards.

There was too much flexibility to the course of a fleet under interface drive. It took six seconds to completely change vector at half the speed of light. The Taljzi could easily decide to go for the shipyards at any moment short of the final clash.

"Expect them to begin deploying their long-range missiles as they pass Mars's orbit," Morgan told Bale. "Our Bucklers are live and watching for fire, but human intervention can be everything."

"I'm on it, sir."

They'd range on the Taljzi a few minutes before that, but their accuracy would suck. And...wait.

"Lagos, can you double-check our coms?" she ordered their coms officer. "I'm getting interference on the tachyon-scanner feed from the drones watching the Taljzi fleet."

Imperial tachyon scanners still only had a light-minute of range. With the enemy still forty-plus light-minutes away, they were relying on hyperfold-equipped drones to give them live information. She was getting data from those sensors, but large chunks of the Taljzi fleet were started to get lost in a new interference pattern.

"It's not the com channel," Lieutenant Commander Jimena Lagos replied. "That's in the original data."

Morgan tapped commands, diving deeper in and looking in as much detail as she could.

"Fuckers."

"Commander?" Tanzi demanded.

"I don't know how, but they're jamming the tachyon scanners," Morgan said grimly. "It's a localized field around their ships, so we aren't getting proper targeting data at all. We already can't update the targeting while the missiles are in hyperspace, now we don't even have solid data to start."

Her channel to the bridge was silent for several seconds.

"Pass it up the chain, Commander," Tanzi ordered. "The Fleet Lord is going to have to consider that."

They'd already learned that the Taljzi could shoot down their hyperspace missiles in their second-or-less terminal sprint. They needed direct hits...and if the Taljzi could jam their only faster-than-light sensor, the odds of getting those hits had just gone way down.

CHAPTER FIFTY-SEVEN

JEAN STOOD ON *VINDICATION*'S FLAG BRIDGE AND FOLLOWED THE reports being fed up the chain of command. He had a moment of pride on realizing that Morgan Casimir had been the first to put the pieces together, but it was quickly swallowed by the realization of just how screwed they were.

With two developments, the Taljzi had completely negated the Imperium's advantage in combat. Since the Imperium's hyperspace missiles were based on the Mesharom weapon, he was grimly certain the Mesharom version wouldn't be much more effective than the Imperium's.

"We'll want to change the fire weighting," Tan!Shallegh said calmly on the virtual conference of Formation Alpha's commanders. Jean probably shouldn't have been on that conference. On the other hand, he *definitely* shouldn't have been aboard one of Earth's battleships.

Even Kurzman-Wellesley had been relegated to Orbit One. Jean was watching over Tidikat's shoulder—or would have been, if the two-meter-tall beetle had anything that remotely resembling such a body part.

"We were assuming we needed direct hits, but the lethality of a twenty-gigaton direct hit counterbalances some of that requirement," the A!Tol continued. "As the enemy decreases our hit probabilities, the use of saturation hyperspace bombardments becomes more and more necessary."

Saturation wasn't a word that belonged in description of space combat.

"Our previous estimation was that it would take approximately three hundred missiles to guarantee an interior hit and three interior hits to guarantee the destruction of an enemy capital ship.

"We'll start by doubling those numbers."

Jean swallowed hard and checked his communicator to make sure he was right. That was basically every S-HSM launcher in Formation Alpha sent at a single target expecting a single kill.

Formation Bravo didn't even *have* enough S-HSMs to pull off what Tan!Shallegh was suggesting, though Fleet Lord Tanaka had most of the stockpile of D-HSMs, which she could use to stiffen the numbers.

No one was quite sure how many HSM launchers the Mesharom had, but Jean suspected that Formation Charlie could manage an equivalent effectiveness if not necessarily as many missiles.

"We don't have the munitions to sustain that for long," Fleet Lord Okan said grimly. The second-ranked Imperial officer in Formation Alpha and the formation's accepted third-in-command was tapping his talons together as he studied his data. "I don't think we even have a hundred HSMs per launcher."

"Then we will use them all," Tan!Shallegh replied. "There are manufactories in Terran orbit that can produce more. Every minute we buy ourselves is a chance for more reinforcements to arrive. If I can expend HSMs to destroy capital ships at minimal risk to our fleets, then I will do so.

"These are dark waters. I will see our people through to the other side of them."

"HSM range in fifteen minutes," someone reported.

"They have a slight range advantage but our long-range weapons are better," the A!Tol Fleet Lord continued. "We will hold off on committing Formations Bravo or Charlie until we have a better feel for our enemy."

"And if they keep coming for Earth?" Kurzman-Wellesley asked.

"Then Formation Alpha will be the reef to Bravo and Charlie's incoming tide," Tan!Shallegh replied. "We may die. We may fail Earth...but the Taljzi will pay for riding these waves. This is Imperial territory.

"We will not yield."

⸻

"THERE ARE days I am sorry that we answered Annette Bond's invitation to join her," Tidikat said quietly to Jean. "They are few. Your people have been good to us."

"But when we're staring death in the face, I can't imagine it's easy to think this was the best plan," Jean replied.

"No," the Laian agreed. "I find myself sympathizing with my ancestors, though."

Jean glanced over at the scarab beetle–like alien.

"Oh?"

"They fought a war for everything they believed was right and just," Tidikat noted. "They served the Ascendant Kings. Now, I don't even know who failed whom. But there are no more Ascendant Kings and we are exiled, barred from ever returning home."

"And you sympathize with them?"

"They would not yield. Neither will I," the alien told him. "We know these Taljzi would ignore my people. We aren't 'false images of God' in their minds. Neither are the A!Tol or the Rekiki or half a dozen of the other races gathered out here."

That thought had never even occurred to Jean. He'd grown so used to thinking of the Taljzi as a monolithic force of destruction that he'd forgotten there was a *point* to their mass murder. The non-bipedal races in the Imperial Fleet weren't anathema to the Taljzi.

Of course, *humanity* was...and so the Fleet was there.

"Thank you," Jean said quietly.

"You gave my partner and me a home," the Laian replied. "My people, my children. We lived on the surface of a world for the first time in generations. No, Admiral Villeneuve, I do not regret our choice.

"Nor this war. Let the eggless fools come. We will defend our world, our shared nest, against any tide, any storm."

"Together," Jean replied.

"Orders from the Flag!" A tech turned to look back at Tidikat. "Targeting priorities for the hyperspace missiles."

"Tan!Shallegh has the shot," Tidikat replied. "We fire on his command."

IT WAS impossible to make out the individual icons on the holographic display, and Jean didn't even try. They were only projections, anyway, since even the ships launching the hyperspace missiles couldn't reliably track them once they entered hyperspace.

Every eye on *Vindication*'s flag bridge was focused on the result when they emerged. For a few seconds, antimatter explosions lit up the sky, building on each other until it was closer to a single massive explosion than thousands of individual ones.

"Target eliminated," a sensor tech reported. "Internal hits, as expected. Everything that arrived outside the target's shields was destroyed."

That wasn't *quite* as impressive as it sounded, given that there were almost as many Taljzi warships in the force currently passing Mars's orbit as the Imperium had fired missiles.

But there was one fewer super-battleship now, and a second salvo blasted into hyperspace as Jean watched.

Another capital ship died and a third salvo blasted into space.

"It appears we're wasting firepower," Tan!Shallegh finally said, the A!Tol's words transmitted to every flag officer. "Spread the bombardment for the next salvo. See if we can catch two ships at a time."

The third salvo hadn't been trying for that, but it looked like they'd clipped one of the battleships in the process of destroying a super-battleship.

Three super-battleships down should have been a major contribution to any battle. Instead, over five hundred of the immense twenty-million-ton starships remained.

"Enemy long-range missiles launched. ETA three minutes."

"Anyone got an estimate on how many of those things there are?" Jean asked quietly as a wave of red icons appeared on the display.

"Computer is suggesting..." The tech swallowed, double checking his numbers. "Computer is suggesting twenty thousand...plus or minus ten percent."

A two-thousand-missile error. On the other hand, that was a *lot* fewer missiles than twelve hundred capital ships and a thousand escorts should have been able to launch.

"These long-range weapons of theirs must be huge," Tidikat stated Jean's thought aloud. "How much of their regular firepower did they give up for them?"

"I'm going to guess not enough to make a difference, but enough that they're going to regret it," Jean said firmly. "No change to their course?"

"None. They're heading straight for Earth," Tidikat replied. "They seem to be rather single-minded about this."

"They have the biggest hammer for a thousand light-years in any direction. I'm not surprised we look like a nail," Jean said. "We need Formation Bravo."

"Tanaka has deployment discretion," Tidikat reminded him quietly. "I have faith in her judgment."

"So do I," Jean agreed. "But there's also twenty thousand missiles out there that feel like they're aimed right at my head."

THE A!TOL Imperium might not have access to whatever insanely efficient tracking and targeting tool the Taljzi were using for their missile defense, but they *did* have access to tachyon scanners and hyperfold cannon. The scanners might be jammed around the Taljzi ships, but the invaders' missiles were a long way from that interference.

A perimeter of Buckler drones hung half a million kilometers away from the main fleet, their own tachyon scanners reaching out into space to track the incoming missile salvos in real time. The missiles entered the range of the Buckler's near-instantaneous energy weapons and started to die.

The older Buckler drones that still made up half of the formation didn't have hyperfold cannon. They were still being fed live data on exactly where incoming missiles were as they fired, and their lasers were lightspeed weapons.

A second shell of drones hung at a quarter million kilometers from the fleet, and a third was wrapped around the fleet itself. Every ship in Formation Alpha had a full complement of Sword turrets as well as tachyon scanners, hyperfold cannon, and full access to the data from the drone shells.

Twenty thousand missiles crashed down on that defensive shield like raindrops on a campfire. Unlike the hyperspace missiles, interface-drive weapons didn't carry warheads. They didn't need them, not when impact collapsed the interface-drive field and released all of the pent-up kinetic energy of a weapon traveling at point eight five *c*.

The death of an interface-drive missile was a silent thing, just a *pop* of collapsing drive fields and vaporizing metal. It took an impact with a larger object for an interface drive to release its theoretical kinetic energy.

There was no immense explosion as antimatter warheads built on each other like the one around the Taljzi fleet.

The incoming fire just vanished.

There was another salvo behind it. And another one behind that one. Every salvo of long-range missiles was smaller than the one before it, though, as super-battleships continued to die under the pounding of Formation Alpha's HSMs.

"We'll be in their standard missile range in forty seconds. Ours ten after that," someone reported, and Jean nodded grimly.

The long-range weapons had to have taken up a massive portion of the Taljzi's capacity, but there were still over two thousand warships heading their way. The conventional firepower of that fleet would dwarf anything they could deploy.

"Flag is issuing targeting orders," Tidikat told Jean. "Continuing to focus fire on designated pairs of super-battleships." The Laian clicked his mandibles with a worried note. "If we keep this up, we might kill fifty or so of them before they wipe us out."

"More than that," Jean replied. "Plus, unless Tanaka has lost her edge since Asimov, they're about to learn why trying to bull through everything is a bad idea. Even when you *do* have the biggest hammer."

THE COMPUTERS GAVE up trying to count the incoming fire. The number that was being attached to the red blob on the display had a thirty percent error in it...and was well over a hundred thousand.

"Stand by to return fire," Tidikat ordered, his translated voice calm. It wasn't like his crew could tell the difference between whether the Laian was calm or had just ordered his translator to keep a calm tone.

Jean was suddenly jealous of the opportunity to do the latter.

"Range," someone reported. "Missiles away."

Their computer had a better track on their own missiles, but the numbers were still eye-glazing for Jean. This entire engagement was entirely outside of any scale he was used to. Outside of any scale *anyone* was used to.

That was probably a good chunk of why the Taljzi weren't being clever...and why being clever on the defenders' part might come back to bite Earth.

"Hold on! Incoming hyperspace missile fire!"

Jean didn't catch who had spoken—but he saw the result as Formation Bravo finally engaged. Unable to target the Taljzi fleet without spending thousands of missiles to kill a single ship, Fleet Lord Tanaka had chosen to target something the enemy *couldn't* shield with their jammers.

Formation Bravo's hyperspace missiles emerged in the middle of the missile salvo, twenty-gigaton antimatter warheads wiping dozens of regular missiles out of existence at a time. Over half of the Taljzi salvo vanished in a massive ball of fire.

And unlike Formation Alpha, Harriet Tanaka wasn't anchored to Earth. Her fleet swept toward the Taljzi at half the speed of light, cutting through the gap in missile range before they could react.

"Orders from the Flag! Formation to advance to hyperfold cannon range!"

The Taljzi fleet recoiled from Formation Bravo's charge and the attendant missiles—and then Formation Alpha charged as well. The Return went from having the situation entirely in hand, ready to drown the defenders in an incomprehensible deluge of missiles, to being pinned by two fleets out for blood.

They still had the edge in numbers, but they clearly hadn't been expecting Tanaka to intervene quite so aggressively.

For a few seconds, the Taljzi formation rippled as they reorganized under fire. They were still firing, and there was only so much the defenders could do to stop the incoming missiles.

Icons flashed red on Jean's display and he swallowed, knowing that every red icon meant hundreds or thousands of lives lost. But for every Imperial ship that disappeared, two Taljzi icons disappeared.

Those were losses the Taljzi could *take*. They'd done it before... but this time, they chose not to.

"Taljzi breaking off at point six five *c*."

"Let them go," Tan!Shallegh ordered instantly. "Harass them with HSM fire until they're out of our range. The Mesharom will take a chunk out of them, make sure they fall back to the outer system, but we'll let them go."

The A!Tol's skin was the dark green of grim determination.

"Time is our ally today, not theirs."

CHAPTER FIFTY-EIGHT

THE TALJZI COULDN'T HAVE WALKED MORE PERFECTLY INTO THE ambush if Morgan had been setting their course herself.

Jaki's new XO could tell that the smurfs hadn't been planning on entering the Belt again. Their headlong flight at a sprint speed the Imperium hadn't known they possessed had slowed as they cleared the range of the defenders' hyperspace missiles.

While they didn't need to head directly toward their destination, it was certainly easiest, and the Taljzi force had been heading to a rendezvous point between Mars's orbit and the Belt. Well outside of range of the forces around Earth but in position to launch a new assault on any of the three targets available.

Unfortunately for them, the Mesharom Frontier Fleet Squadrons had spent the entire time the Taljzi had been fighting the Imperials moving through the Belt with their stealth fields active. The asteroid belt wasn't enough to hide fleets normally...but it was enough to allow the stealthed ships to get closer than they normally would.

And the Taljzi had positioned themselves barely half a light-minute away from the Belt. Close enough that the Mesharom were in regular-missile range as well as hyperspace-missile range.

They had to drop the stealth fields to fire, but the Taljzi didn't have tachyon scanners. The first warning they had of humanity's Core Power allies was the complete destruction of thirty super-battleships.

Their tachyon jammers had been focused toward Earth, not the asteroid belt. A hundred thousand Taljzi paid for that mistake as the Mesharom fire washed over them.

The regular missiles, traveling at the point eight five c the Imperium hadn't yet duplicated, were mere seconds behind the hyperspace weapons—*fractions* of a second behind the light announcing their arrival.

The very defenses that had shredded the Imperial's HSMs, however, turned out to be equally effective against regular missiles. Even surprised and with missiles coming from an unknown vector, Bogey Force Alpha managed to destroy most of the incoming missiles.

Most. These were *Mesharom* missiles and even the massed defenses of thousands of warships weren't enough to blunt their terrifying efficiency.

More capital ships died as the Mesharom lashed the Taljzi with everything they could bring to bear. The smurfs returned fire desperately, but they also ran for it. They turned vertical relative to the ecliptic plane and fled from the Mesharom at their full speed.

The whole mess was over in roughly three minutes, but by then, the Taljzi Return was clearly headed for the outer system and relative safety.

Over two hundred super-battleships and battleships didn't make it out with them.

Morgan shook her head in stunned awe at the casualty figures. It hadn't been a bloodless victory by any means—a dozen Mesharom battlecruisers had died in the ambush and the Imperials had lost twenty super-battleships of their own.

So far, the four squadrons of upgraded *Vindication*s in the Grand Fleet were still intact. So were the warships of the Ducal Militia, though Morgan knew that was pure fluke. Except for the *Bellerophon*s, they were no better defended than the Imperial Fleet.

Even the *Bellerophon*s just had better armor. Almost all of the defenders had hyperfold cannons, Sword turrets, Buckler drones and tachyon scanners. Only the microbot reinforcement layer under their armor made the new ships any more survivable.

"Orders from the Flag!" Lagos reported. "All forces are to converge at RV-Juliet-Six," he announced aloud as he reviewed the orders.

"That makes sense," Morgan replied as she brought up the location of J-6. It was a ballistic orbit, halfway between Earth and Mars. Far enough out that they could intercept any strike toward Mars. Close enough in that they could protect Earth and the shipyards.

"We have the interior position. We can intercept them now that we have them dialed in." It had been the lack of information that had forced their split formation before. Now they didn't need it.

"What about their stealth ships?" Bale asked from the bridge. "If they sneak past us and hit the Yards..."

"The Mesharom are *much* better at picking up stealth ships than we are," Morgan pointed out. "Even their scanners aren't perfect at it, but we'll have plenty of warning if they start splitting out stealthed battleships.

"And the Yards, like Earth and Mars, have significant defensive constellations. If they want to throw stealthed destroyers at them..." Morgan shook her head with an only partially forced chuckle.

"Let them. It'll save the fleet some ammunition," she concluded.

CONCENTRATED TOGETHER at the rendezvous point, it was hard not to feel that the Grand Fleet was the most powerful force in existence. The solid ranks of everything from Terran-built super-battleships to Mesharom battlecruisers to the distinctive lines of A!Tol-designed cruisers filled the sky around *Jaki*.

Sitting near the center of all that metal and power, it was easy for Morgan to feel confident—until she looked at what her scanners were showing her of the outer system.

The Taljzi were maintaining the siege. They'd brought so many ships that deploying just over a *thousand* of them to make sure no civilians or minor forces made it in or out was something they could do.

Even having lost over two hundred capital ships, they still had a thousand of them. Another thousand escorts, even having used a thousand cruisers and destroyers to establish the siege.

It was mind-boggling.

It was also, it seemed, a massive-enough investment that even the Taljzi were cautious about losing it.

"They could have taken us," Tanzi said quietly on their private channel. "If they'd stuck in with the Grand Fleet, the Mesharom would have had to give up their stealth to try and save our asses. Outnumbered two to one, I don't think we'd have been able to keep them out of disruptor range."

"The Mesharom would have made them regret that," Morgan pointed out. "Everything I'm seeing suggests that their close-in energy weapons are a close sibling to the Taljzi's disruptors."

"We would have made them regret closing with us no matter what," her Captain replied. "But we'd have died. To the last ship—I don't doubt that every Imperial and Mesharom Captain out here would have held as hard as the Militia—but we'd have died and they'd have won.

"Why didn't they?"

"Because they wouldn't have had anything left," Morgan said as she looked over the enemy's losses. "A close-range engagement, where we had full use of hyperfold cannons and the Mesharom brought their disruptors into play? We'd have gutted them. They'd have been lucky to have *any* capital ships left."

"Would the fleet you saw at Asimov have done it?" Tanzi asked, and Morgan paused.

"I think so," she admitted. "They were entirely too willing to lose ships and people in the blink of an eye. Even the fights we had with this fleet getting here, they were always willing to expend ships. Why now?"

"I think this might be all they have left," the Captain said slowly. "Or, at least, such a large contingent that even the *time* cost of replacing the ships and crews starts to become a factor. I don't care how infinite their resources are; they're not growing ships—or *people* —from nothing."

"Replacement time has to still be a factor," Morgan agreed slowly. "So, they can afford to lose a few hundred ships here or there, but when dealing with *thousands,* they still have to be careful."

"And I don't think they have any better idea what they're doing with fleets of this size than we do," Tanzi noted with a chuckle.

CHAPTER FIFTY-NINE

THE TALJZI GAVE THEM SIXTEEN HOURS OF PEACE WHILE THEY decided what they were going to do next. After six hours, most of the fleet stood down to Status Bravo. Morgan was sent to sleep while Tanzi held the deck on her own.

The Captain was asleep when the Taljzi finally made their move. Morgan was watching everything she could from *Jaki*'s bridge when the icons started lighting off with new movement tags.

"What have we got, Bale?" she demanded.

"Taljzi are moving towards the Belt. They're taking it slow, only ten percent of lightspeed."

"Sir, we have an incoming broadband transmission from the Taljzi," Lagos reported. "Looks like every ship in the fleet is getting it."

"Play it," Morgan ordered.

There was nothing distinctive between a Taljzi and a Kanzi in terms of their physical appearance. The female Kanzi on the screen was familiar to Morgan, though. She had paler fur than most, with scars burnt into her face and breasts above the black leather kilt and harness that was all she wore.

She looked, in fact, *absolutely* identical to the Taljzi who had commanded the First Return.

"I am the Return of the Mind of God," she intoned. Notes on the screen informed Morgan that she was speaking an archaic dialect of the main Kanzi language. The only reason *Jaki* even had files for that dialect was that the Taljzi had used it once before.

"I bring the judgment of the Mind of God upon the false children of this world. His will declares that all who profane the holy image of the divine shall die.

"But there are warriors and innocents here who are not false images," she continued. "Those who are touched with the spark of mind but do not profane the divine are not our enemy. We will permit the war fleet of the A!Tol to leave this place."

She smiled, baring teeth that had been filed to sharp points.

"We have no such mercy for the traitors to the Ancients. False children and false servants will die alike.

"We bring you the divine will of the Mind of God. Kneel and you will die quickly. Challenge His will and you will die painfully."

The recording froze and the bridge crew of the human warship stared at the screen in silence.

"Wake the Captain up," Morgan ordered. "Keep us at Status Bravo for now; wait for orders from the Flag to bring us to battle stations."

"Sir," Lagos paused. "Do you think..."

"That the Imperium will betray us at this point?" Morgan laughed. "No. We've come this far with the squids and the rest. We'll stand together.

"To the end. Regardless of what the Taljzi may think."

"THANK YOU, XO," Captain Tanzi said after she'd relieved Morgan. "Guesses as to what we're going to see?"

"They're going to make at least one attempt to go around us, probably to hit Earth, but realize they can't," Morgan guessed. "Then they may pull back to reconsider again. Either way, they'll come straight for us pretty quickly and run into Interpreter-Shepherd Adamase's surprise."

"What happens if they detect the surprise?" Tanzi asked. "Or, hell, just keeping swinging wide to try and hit Mars or the Yards?"

Morgan shrugged.

"Then the Mesharom wasted a lot of ammunition and we fight a straight-up battle," she said. "I don't know Tan!Shallegh's mind, but I'd guess we're going to put ourselves between the Taljzi and the populated planets with as many Bucklers as we have in space. Play spiky turtle."

"He's known for being more aggressive than that," Tanzi pointed out. "A head-on assault, attempting to get into hyperfold range and stay out of disruptor range, seems more his style."

"Context, sir," Morgan reminded her Captain. "That would probably inflict the most damage on the Taljzi, but we'd get wiped out. He won't risk that until the Kanzi get here. Right now, we're playing for time. So, spiky turtle."

"Makes sense," Tanzi agreed. "Either way, it's almost five minutes before they get near the Belt at their current pace. Get to Secondary Control."

"Already on it," the blonde XO said with a crisp salute.

Jaki was over a kilometer and a half long, and Secondary Control was six hundred meters from the bridge. Only the rapid-transit tubes made getting there in under five minutes reasonable, and the system delivered Morgan to her battle station with almost two minutes to spare.

"Commander, excellent timing," the Lieutenant acting as her backup coms officer told her. "Tan!Shallegh is responding to the Taljzi—he's copying the entire fleet!"

"Play it," she ordered.

She'd met Tan!Shallegh in person, which meant she could tell that the Fleet Lord was pulling every camera trick available to a holographic projection out of the book. They were making him larger, more imposing, a looming shadowy figure looking down at the Taljzi receiving his message.

"I am Fleet Lord Tan!Shallegh of the A!Tol Imperium," he said fiercely. "I am tasked by both my Empress and the people of the world below to secure their peace and liberty against all threats."

There was an odd tone to his words. They sounded familiar to Morgan, like she'd heard much of it before.

"You command that I and my fellows who are not 'profanities' by your strange rules flee before you. You say we will be safe.

"I have heard these words, or those like them, before. From enemy and ally alike. Rarely are they true. Those of my brothers and sisters who have believed them have presided over the deaths of millions.

"I speak for the Empress A!Shall," he said flatly. "I speak for the Houses of the Imperium, for twenty-nine races and half a trillion souls, and I tell you this:

"This world is ours. We will not kneel. Leave or be driven from this place."

Morgan finally recognized the words. Not all of it was identical, but Tan!Shallegh clearly remembered the speech the Governing Council had given when he'd arrived to annex Earth.

It was somehow right that he threw those same words in the teeth of the Taljzi.

"Anyone expect them to run?" she asked softly as the transmission faded.

"No," Tanzi said bluntly from the bridge. Seconds ticked away. "And there's their answer."

The entire Taljzi fleet had just come up to full speed, lunging toward the defenders at half the speed of light.

Right on the course the Mesharom had projected twenty-four hours earlier...

THE TALJZI, as the Militia had discovered in DLK-5539, had specialized munitions for minelaying. They used a short-ranged missile with a heavy antimatter warhead.

The Imperium and the Mesharom didn't have anything of the sort. What the Mesharom had, however, was a tachyon-scanner-equipped AI platform that could activate missiles left cold in space. The tachyon scanners couldn't localize individual Taljzi ships through the jamming fields, but they could definitely see the Taljzi *fleet*.

Morgan wasn't sure how many weapons the platform could control, but the Mesharom had deployed a hundred of them scattered throughout the zone they'd anticipated the Taljzi attacking through.

These weren't hyperspace missiles...but there were also thousands of them. Tens of thousands. Only about half were Mesharom weapons, but that probably made it worse for the Taljzi. Missiles lit off from amidst the asteroids, traveling at speeds varying from point five to point seven five *c*.

Even linked into the targeting platforms, Morgan had no idea how many missiles were being fired off. The entire Taljzi formation disappeared under a blizzard of small green icons, and while they'd clearly been prepared for an attack, they hadn't expected something of this scale.

"Orders from the Flag," Lagos reported. "We are to advance and engage with hyperspace missiles."

Morgan nodded as Tanzi acknowledged the orders and *Jaki's* engines came to life.

"It doesn't look like we're actually doing that much damage," she said quietly. "Took out a bunch of escorts, but we're only damaging capital ships. No kills there."

"Sixty seconds to HSM range," Bale reported.

"Try and flag damaged capital ships," Morgan told him. "I imagine we'll get targeting instructions from the Flag, but if we don't, let's focus on ships that have taken a beating."

Tanzi gave her a crisp nod, the Captain focused on coordinating their course with the thousand-plus ships around them.

"And there's the last of our preplaced missiles," Bale announced. "Gods. How many *was* that?"

"I don't know," Morgan admitted. "The Mesharom set it up; I wasn't paying close attention. Somewhere around two hundred thousand?"

The tactical officer shook his head on her screen.

"We took out about a hundred and fifty cruisers and destroyers. Maybe two or three battleships. Lot of damaged ships across the entire fleet, but nothing material against that scale."

"It wasn't meant to really damage them," Morgan told him. "Captain?"

"It's supposed to make them blink," Tanzi agreed. "HSM range in ten seconds. Do we have orders from the Flag?"

"Coming in now," Bale reported. "Stand by."

Ten seconds seemed to stretch for at least a few minutes, but then new green icons sparkled across Morgan's display. A saturation bombardment from the massed fleet; her displays showed they were targeting four super-battleships that looked damaged.

None of the four ships survived...and it seemed the Taljzi had had enough. The entire fleet flipped in space, dodging backward before the third salvo could launch.

The second took its own toll, but the enemy once again broke free of the defenders and fled back beyond the Belt.

This time, the defenders were completely untouched.

CHAPTER SIXTY

A HOLOGRAPHIC DISPLAY OF THE SOL SYSTEM OCCUPIED THE BIG projector at the heart of *Tornado*'s flag bridge. Red icons splotched the outer system, and a single large group of green icons marked the position of the Grand Fleet inside the Belt.

The defenders had done a spectacular job of bloodying the Return's nose. The newfound loss-sensitivity of their alien foe was helping, but that wouldn't have been enough if Tan!Shallegh and the rest of the Grand Fleet's commanders hadn't been *inflicting* those losses.

The numbers Annette Bond was getting from the starcom were still terrifying. The Return had lost about fifteen percent of its hulls and almost twenty percent of its tonnage.

Their super-battleships had been the focus of the defenders' fire all along, and over two hundred of the big ships were history now. All told, the Return had gone from twelve hundred and fifty capital ships to just under a thousand.

The escort losses had been lighter since the Grand Fleet had focused on the heavier units. They were down to a *mere* seventeen hundred–plus cruisers and destroyers.

The Grand Fleet had paid dearly for those victories, but their losses paled in comparison to the damage they'd inflicted. They'd bought Earth time, but Annette could run the math on the numbers they were sending her by starcom.

The Imperium and Militia had expended two-thirds of their hyperspace missiles and a third of their interface-drive missiles. It was hard to assess the Mesharom's expenditures, but the Core Power ships didn't have access to ready resupply.

The Taljzi had, probably unknowingly, blockaded the Sol System's main HSM production facility away from the planet and the defenders. The facilities attached to DragonWorks could churn out five thousand hyperspace missiles a day now, but those missiles were useless to a defending fleet over thirty light-minutes away.

"Duchess Bond," a now-familiar voice greeted her as a channel opened from *Chosen Sword*. Cawl inclined his head to her. "I presume you have reviewed the most recent download from your people?"

"It doesn't look good," she admitted. "Your Armada is better upgraded than I'd feared, but without hyperfold cannons or hyperspace missiles, you're range-limited compared to the forces we'll face."

The eight *Vindication*s escorting *Tornado* had hyperfold cannons but not hyperspace missiles. The Taljzi had a significant range advantage over the fleet Annette was leading to relieve her home.

"My fleet at least has antimissile defenses and compressed-matter armor," Cawl pointed out. "Better than those you originally sold the Imperium, Duchess Bond. I am not overly concerned by the Taljzi's range advantage."

The old Kanzi shook his head.

"I would be far more concerned about your people's hyperspace missiles. I am glad to see those turned on my enemies instead of my own ships."

Annette sighed.

"I don't see any good options for deploying your fleet," she admitted. "None that don't risk brutal losses."

"There are only two options, and both have risks," Cawl countered. "We can attempt to evade the Taljzi and rendezvous with your Grand Fleet, at which point we hope that assaulting the system becomes too intimidating for the Taljzi and they will either leave or try and besiege us.

"In the latter case, I presume your Imperium has more ships coming?"

"Nothing like the Grand Fleet," she said. "Every HSM-equipped ship in the Imperium is in Sol."

That wouldn't be true forever. It wouldn't even be true for long—every ship under construction in the massive yards in the Indiri and A!Tol home systems had been paused for long enough to reconfigure the designs for the modern systems. It would be three months still before *any* yard in the Imperium produced a new warship.

At that point, however, they would be producing a stream of warships with every advance DragonWorks had put together. It would be an entirely new Imperial Fleet, one that could overwhelm anything short of the Core Powers—and would be able to match most of them.

They would only have so many ships of those classes for years yet, though, which meant that much of the struggle against the Taljzi would be fought by ships with hyperfold cannons at best.

There were, so far as Annette understood, another ten squadrons of capital ships heading toward Sol in various formations. A hundred and sixty fast battleships, battleships and super-battleships, plus their escorts.

More would come, but that was all that was likely to arrive in the near future. They might be enough to make a difference. They might not.

"And if we don't think we're going to get enough reinforcements?" she finally asked Cawl.

"Then our second choice may be the best," he told her. "What my people would call a strike for God's will. We emerge from hyper-space outside the enemy fleet, as close as we can manage, and attack them immediately.

"This presumes that the Grand Fleet will sortie as soon as they detect us," Cawl continued. "We attempt to trap the Taljzi between ourselves and Tan!Shallegh. If we are lucky, we may be able to destroy or break their fleet, forcing the remnants to surrender or flee."

A "strike for God's will." Annette chuckled.

"We'd call that a 'Hail Mary,'" she told him. "Or going for broke. That's a very all-or-nothing plan, Fleet Lord."

"Yes," he confirmed. "It has vastly greater risk than attempting to join the Grand Fleet. I believe it may also be our best chance for a positive resolution...and it is definitely our only chance for an imme-diate resolution."

"Even victory would see your fleet shattered," Annette said.

"Even combining our forces with your Grand Fleet, we don't match their numbers and we remain significantly outmassed and outgunned," he pointed out. "There is no strategy that will not see both our fleets take major losses. The Taljzi may be concerned about losing this fleet, but they will still not retreat without a fight.

"We *must* defeat them. Must crush them if we are to have the time to be ready for a counterstrike."

"It's a little soon to be thinking about a counterstrike, isn't it?" Annette replied. "With three thousand warships in my star system."

"Every action leads into the next," Cawl told her. "We must consider what we plan for the future even as we plan for the now. We need to save your system, but we also need to crush this fleet to buy ourselves time."

"Three thousand warships," Annette echoed. "You know that if we hammer directly into them, we could lose everything?"

"Yes."

Cawl's word hung on the call for a long moment.

"My hope is that in the worst-case scenario, we damage them sufficiently that they are unable—or at least, unwilling—to engage your system's defenses. But I do not see a better solution, Duchess Bond.

"A direct strike is our only hope for victory. We risk everything... but if we do not, I fear we will *lose* everything."

Annette looked back at the three-dimensional image of Earth and Sol. Even with the evacuation, there were over nine billion people in her system. Her oath was to protect them.

"It's your Armada, Fleet Master Cawl," she conceded. "I couldn't override you if I wanted to." She sighed. "And I don't want to. I want to see my people safe."

"Then to the heart of the enemy it is."

Annette chuckled.

"'From hell's heart I stab at thee,'" she quoted. "Let's take these bastards down, Fleet Master."

CHAPTER SIXTY-ONE

"It looks like they're preparing for another attack," Kurzman-Wellesley warned Jean over the com. "I'm surprised they gave us as much as they did."

"*Oui et non*," Jean replied. "They could have come in at any point in the last thirty-six hours, but they've spent that time filling the asteroid belt with probes. They know we don't have any more ambushes left, they know we've evacuated the Belt settlements and they know where all of our ships are.

"They've made certain we have no tricks left. We don't have much left to do."

"So, they come straight at us, but this time, they know where everything is." The English Admiral sighed. "The odds don't look good, Jean."

"The odds look terrible, old friend," the Councilor replied. "I'm surprised we've pushed things out this far. They're going to regret this, but I can't see a way out. Not anymore."

The channel was silent for a long time.

"And nobody we can send to run off to save us this time," Patrick Kurzman-Wellesley, who had been the original executive officer of

Tornado when she'd gone into exile, noted sadly. "They've still got the system sewn up tight. Any single ship or freighter we try to send out will get blown to pieces."

"And any major fleet movement they'll see in time to intercept us. They're not enough faster than us to hit anywhere in the inner system without us intercepting, but I don't think we can get anybody out."

"I'm glad we got Bond's kids out," the Admiral said after a few more moments of silence. "Wish we could have got more people out with them, but at least the Heirs will survive."

"You and I won't be so lucky," Jean said quietly.

"No. But it's a fair cop, I suppose. We made our choices a long time ago, didn't we?"

Jean cut his response off as he noted the icons on his screen.

"Here they come," he said instead. "Point five *c* towards the Belt. I make the course directly for Earth."

"They *do* realize we're building missiles at the yards, right?" Kurzman-Wellesley asked.

"If they take Earth, nothing else matters. We'll bleed them. They're going to regret ever tangling with Sol, but..."

"Hold that thought," Kurzman-Wellesley snapped. Something on his screen was going off that Jean didn't have on his. Then he turned his gaze from his displays back to Jean and gave the Councilor for the Militia the biggest grin Jean had ever seen on him.

"That was the system hyperspatial anomaly scanners," he told Jean. "We just had a *massive* signature show up, inbound *fast*. A thousand signatures and some change."

"Taljzi reinforcements?" Jean asked. That wouldn't fit with Kurzman-Wellesley's grin, though. That grin spoke to *hope*.

"Close, but not to their benefit," the Englishman told him. "They're coming in from Kanzi space. It looks like Her Grace hasn't lost a scrap of her luck or her timing. My estimate is that they'll drop out of hyperspace just as the bastards hit the Belt."

And while the Belt might not be as dense as media like to portray it, it was dense enough that no one was escaping into a hyper portal in the middle of it.

"Make sure Tan!Shallegh knows," Jean ordered. "If Bond is bringing a hammer, then it's up to us to provide an anvil."

"ALL SHIPS of the Grand Fleet, this is Fleet Lord Tan!Shallegh."

Like everyone else, Jean's attention was drawn to the image of the A!Tol that appeared on the displays around him.

"The Taljzi appear to be making their final move. Their entire fleet is now heading for Earth at half the speed of light."

The Fleet Lord let that sink in.

"The Grand Fleet does not have the ships to stop them. We have the courage and will, but we lack the firepower. They know this and their plan is predicated on it.

"What the Taljzi *do not know* is that Duchess Bond is on her way. The mistress and guardian of the world behind us is less than a twentieth-cycle away with over a thousand warships.

"It falls to us to lure the Taljzi in and *hold*. We must pin them down in the asteroid belt and provide the reef on which Dan!Annette Bond's wave will *break them*."

The alien's dark eyes held the camera for a few long moments, and Jean suspected every being in the fleet felt that Tan!Shallegh was looking directly at them.

"The lives of ten billion innocents ride on us. We shall not fail. The Grand Fleet will move in five minutes."

Vindication's flag bridge was silent, then Jean looked at Tidikat.

"Are we ready?" he asked softly.

"As we can be," the Laian replied. "When the Duchess returns, we will not be found wanting."

Jean nodded grimly, studying the screens.

"Yet I will try the last," he murmured, the words of an ancient English playwright rolling gently off his tongue. "Before my world I throw our warlike shield. Lay on, Macduff, and damned be him that first cries 'Hold, enough!'"

Tidikat looked at him oddly, then chittered his mandibles.

"I will note that Macbeth *lost* that battle," the alien reminded him. "But yes. Here at the end, we are the last shield of Terra—and we will not yield."

———

TAN!SHALLEGH'S five-minute time mark had a very specific purpose, and Jean smiled grimly as he saw it take shape.

The defending fleet wasn't rushing. They were moving out to meet the incoming Taljzi at a calm point five *c*, both fleets moving at well under their maximum speed. The light-minutes disappeared as minutes ticked by.

Jean tapped commands on his display, adding a series of concentric spheres around each fleet. The defenders didn't have very many hyper missiles left—unless the Mesharom were holding back, which he couldn't rule out—but they were still the longest-ranged weapons on the board.

When they slid into HSM range, the Imperial fleet turned. Now, instead of lunging headlong toward the Taljzi, they were moving at ninety degrees. Their speed cut in half as they drew a new course that was arcing inside the asteroid belt.

And they opened fire. Green trails marked the swarms of hyperspace missiles as the Grand Fleet unleashed on their enemy.

There was no holding back this time. Another display on Jean's screens showed how many of the FTL weapons the fleet had left, and the number was dropping precipitously. At maximum rate of fire, the Imperial component of the Grand Fleet would run out of hyperspace missiles in just over two minutes.

They managed to stay out of Taljzi range for that time, too. By the time they ran out of FTL missiles, the Taljzi had lost dozens more capital ships.

This time, however, there was clearly going to be no retreat. They increased their speed, cutting through the asteroid belt toward the Grand Fleet as the HSM bombardment halted.

Their own long-range missiles opened fire, and Jean watched for the order that would commit the Grand Fleet to the final action.

Without HSMs, they had to close to regular missile range. Once they'd done that, the battle would only end when one side retreated... and Jean wasn't expecting anyone to retreat this time.

"Order from the Flag is 'Execute,'" a communications officer said quietly.

"Pass it on," Tidikat ordered.

The Grand Fleet's course changed once more. Instead of cutting away from the Taljzi, they now turned to charge into their teeth. There was no controlled half-of-lightspeed approach this time. Now the entire force flung themselves on the Taljzi at over sixty percent of the speed of light.

As they charged, the Mesharom demonstrated that they *did* still have HSMs left. Their weapons tore into the Taljzi fleet, buying critical moments of distraction that allowed the Grand Fleet to close.

They didn't close without a cost. Ships died as the Taljzi's long-range missiles struck home, but the loss ratio was still heavily in the Grand Fleet's favor when they reached regular missile range.

Jean's computer screens gave up trying to count missiles the moment the Return launched. The Grand Fleet's fire only added to the confusion. There were almost as many *warships* in the battle-space as there'd been missiles in most of the engagements he'd seen in his career.

"Taljzi are maneuvering; they are attempting to evade close action for now," Tidikat said grimly. "They appear more concerned by our hyperfold cannons than they are enamored of their disruptors."

"They have twice our missile launchers," Jean replied. "I'd want to play at this range too."

"We are pushing them back towards the edge of the Belt, but also towards the no-portal zone around Jupiter," the Laian Vice Admiral told him.

"All of this is being relayed to Bond," Jean noted, watching as two of Tidikat's super-battleships came apart under the pounding. Ten thousand of his Militia crew were gone in a moment, and those were only the losses he could see.

"She'll hit where she needs to. She can see everything."

From the way the missile swarms were reaching out for each other, Jean wasn't sure they'd be there to greet her.

"However this ends, Vice Admiral, I will never regret that Annette Bond invited your people to come here," Jean said quietly. "It has been an honor and a pleasure."

CHAPTER SIXTY-TWO

WITH EVERY HYPERSPACE MISSILE FROM HER MAGAZINES SPENT, *Jaki* had nothing more to contribute to the battle than any other battleship in the Grand Fleet.

Less, in fact, Morgan realized. They'd given up a good chunk of the missile armament another eleven-million-ton battleship might have had for their HSM launchers. They had enough missiles to play, but they weren't going to be changing the tide of this battle today.

Much as she very much wanted to.

The Taljzi were managing to hold the Grand Fleet at missile range. Their speed advantage wasn't enough to keep the Grand Fleet out of their own range, but it was enough to keep them outside of hyperfold-cannon range.

"Your mother can get here anytime," Captain Tanzi told Morgan as three of the Imperial cruisers providing close escort to *Jaki* came apart under a bombardment that had probably been aimed at the battleship.

"You have as much ability to tell her that as I do," Morgan pointed out. Her fingers were flying across her console as she responded to her captain, linking the Buckler drones that the cruisers had been controlling into her own network—pulling them into place to fill the gaps their motherships had left.

She managed it in time, and the drones eviscerated the next salvo heading their way.

"We can't keep this up for much longer," Tanzi said. "We've lost a tenth of the Fleet already!"

As they spoke, Morgan felt the entire battleship lurch under her feet as a missile made it through everything—including the *shields*—to hit the hull.

"Made, where are my shields?" the Captain demanded.

"Localized failure; it's back up," the engineer replied. "Armor held. No major damage."

"They're targeting the capital ships, same as we are," Morgan told Tanzi. "We're getting hammered, but the Duchess can only get here so quickly."

"Sirs!" Bale's voice interjected, breaking in a way Morgan would only have expected from a much younger man. "*Vindication!*"

Morgan followed the tactical officer's warning and focused her screens on the Ducal flagship.

Vindication was the first of her class, an immense warship almost rivaling the Taljzi super-battleships in size. She didn't have hyperspace missiles, but she had Buckler drones, Sword turrets, compressed-matter armor, hyperfold cannons, tachyon scanners...

The only warships in the Imperial Navy more powerful were her sixty-four sisters that the Grand Fleet had put through a refit to have hyperspace missile launchers installed.

And *Vindication*'s luck had run out. She writhed in the fire as the Taljzi missile swarm moved across the defending formation. The Militia's First Squadron was now the main target, and thousands of missiles poured in on the super-battleships.

The Grand Fleet couldn't save any individual ship. Their hope was to save *enough* ships that Bond could carry the day when she arrived...but they couldn't protect a specific ship.

Vindication vanished with the rest of her squadron, sixteen of the most powerful warships Earth had ever built obliterated in under a minute. The Taljzi missile swarm sought out new targets, as if they hadn't just torn the heart out of the Militia.

"Is there any chance the Councilor made it out?" Tanzi asked.

"No," Morgan said flatly, before Bale could even double-check his readings. She'd already been watching. "There were escape pods...but the Taljzi shot them all down."

It probably hadn't been intentional, but for that alone, Morgan Casimir wanted to kill them all.

SPACE BATTLES DIDN'T REALLY TURN on determination. A loss of morale could turn the tide, as ships broke formation and fled, but the furious determination that filled the Duchy of Terra Militia didn't have much opportunity to show through the mostly automated systems that loaded their missiles.

Morgan could feel the new tone on her bridge, however, and could see it in the "body language" of the ships around her. She watched as, ever so slowly, ship after ship slowly began to slide into the lower tiers of their sprint modes.

Those demanded more power than was usually deployed in battle, but the Grand Fleet wasn't going to be launching any mass pursuits. A slow, almost-Brownian motion edged the range down as the Grand Fleet moved slightly faster toward their enemies.

"Orders from the Flag," Lagos reported. "All ships are to stand by for maximum sprint on the Fleet Lord's order. All capital ships are to engage at point six five and attempt to close to hyperfold-cannon range."

Morgan concealed a smirk. The A!Tol Imperial Navy, it seemed, taught the same first rule of being an officer that the Duchy of Terra Militia did: never give an order you know won't be obeyed.

Tan!Shallegh knew he couldn't order his fleet to stop trying to close the range. But he *could* make sure they did in a coordinated mass, as part of a strategy.

"Are we ready, Casimir?" Tanzi asked.

Morgan glanced over her status reports.

"We're out of HSMs and all of our Bucklers are deployed," she noted. "The drones can move with us, our missile magazines are at fifty percent, the capacitors for the plasma lance are fully charged. We are as ready for a close engagement as we can be."

"Good. Because we're going to ram this battleship down those bastards' throats," the Captain said fiercely. "I'm not planning on leaving *anything* for your mother."

Morgan chuckled, but she understood completely.

"Look at the timing, sir," she said quietly. "Five imperial marks says that Tan!Shallegh gives the order when the tachyon scanners detect the Kanzi."

The Taljzi, after all, didn't *have* tachyon scanners. The only advantage the Grand Fleet retained over their enemies was real-time sensor data. With an entire second fleet about to drop on the enemy, that might well be enough.

"Sucker bet," Tanzi said. "Damn, I guess we are leaving the smurfs some targets. Got an estimate?"

Morgan looked at the last scan data again.

"It's hyperspace, skipper," she said, as calmly as she could as another salvo of Taljzi missiles slammed home against *Jaki*'s shields. "Even this close, there's minutes of variability, especially—"

Her sensors exploded with light as a massive hyper portal tore open in the Sol System and Morgan swallowed.

"Especially if they push how close they open their portal," she concluded, watching in awe as the Shadowed Armada of the Kanzi Theocracy plunged into Sol space—*inside* missile range of the Taljzi fleet.

"ATTACK."

Morgan doubted that Fleet Lord Tan!Shallegh had ever given a more unnecessary order in his life. The entire Grand Fleet took the arrival of the Kanzi fleet as the signal for the charge they'd been preparing and *lunged* forward.

For a minute, they closed at a "mere" ten percent of lightspeed, the Taljzi maintaining the fifty-five percent of light that had kept them outside weapons range before. The smurfs weren't denying the closer engagement, but they weren't encouraging it, either.

Then the first missiles from the Shadowed Armada arrived. The Kanzi, Morgan realized, had upgraded their missiles.

Both the Imperium and the Theocracy had been using a point seven five *c* weapon when they'd last fought, in the skies of this very star system. The Imperium had developed a point eight *c* weapon, bringing them nearly into line with the Core Powers.

The Kanzi had developed a point eight *five* missile. Eighty-five percent of lightspeed was the theoretical maximum speed of the interface drive, and it wasn't a sustainable speed. The drive field only had a life expectancy of about eighty seconds.

More than enough to cross the sixty-five light-seconds between the Kanzi and their cloned cousins. The missiles came screaming out of the night, and the lack of tachyon scanners meant the Taljzi had less than ten seconds' warning that the Theocracy ships had even arrived.

Missiles tore their way through the Taljzi fleet from an angle they weren't expecting. Ten seconds was enough to retask defenses...but not enough to do it *well*.

Caught between two fires, dozens of Taljzi ships died. Morgan's scanners told her the grim truth, though: the Taljzi *still* outnumbered and outgunned the combined fleets.

"They're bringing in the siege detachments," Bale reported. "We've got a *lot* of cruisers and destroyers heading our way."

"They only matter in the hundreds," Morgan replied. "Watch the damn main fleet! They're turning."

The Taljzi had seen exactly what Morgan had seen and made their decision. They could probably have kept both fleets in missile range with a bit of effort, but that would force them to split their missile defenses.

They'd still win, but it would be a risky fight.

Instead, they were changing course and coming right at the Grand Fleet.

CHAPTER SIXTY-THREE

"Damn."

Annette's curse hung in the air of *Tornado*'s deathly silent flag bridge.

Captain Mamutse had informed the Duchess of Terra where his ship belonged in no uncertain terms. There wasn't a single flag officer in either the Imperial Echelon guarding her or the Theocracy Armada she'd been lent that was going to let her be anywhere near the fighting.

Tornado was at the rear of the Kanzi formation, close enough to watch everything and even contribute missiles but far enough away that the entire Shadowed Armada would probably be obliterated before she came under fire.

The Taljzi commander was smarter than she'd hoped for. The degree to which they'd tried to keep the Grand Fleet at missile range had given her hope that they'd *keep* trying to stay at missile range. At that distance, being caught between two fleets would have seriously disadvantaged them.

Instead, they were attempting to defeat Sol's defenders in detail.

Worse, unless she missed her reading, they were now focusing their fire on the Mesharom Frontier Fleet warships.

Those were the only ships with weapons that matched their disruptors. Both sides had missiles, and the defenders had hyperfold cannons and plasma lances, but the disruptors were far deadlier inside their limited range.

"Any chance we can get into energy-weapon range before they get into disruptor range of the Grand Fleet?" she asked quietly.

"No."

Mamutse didn't attempt to soften it. The Captain knew perfectly well that Annette could do the math herself—or she'd have been opening a channel to Fleet Master Cawl and Fleet Lord !Olarski to demand they charge into suicide range.

The Kanzi *didn't* have plasma lances, hyperfold cannons or disruptors. Cawl had been cagey on just what the Shadowed Armada was carrying for energy weapons, but Annette's people's scans suggested that they were next-generation proton beams.

Probably equal to anything even the Core Powers deployed for that system, but that was because the Core Powers had developed entirely superior systems.

"Time to disruptor range?" she asked quietly.

"They're heading towards each other at full speed," Mamutse told her. "A minute. Not much more."

Missiles continued to hail down on the Taljzi, and so far, the Shadowed Armada was untouched. The Return was continuing to focus all of their fire on the Grand Fleet.

Annette didn't like what she was seeing. Even if they somehow made it through this, the Grand Fleet was done as a fighting force. The remaining ships would take weeks to years of repairs—even the Mesharom ships, and the Imperium *couldn't* fix the Mesharom ships.

"There's got to be something we can do," she whispered. "My *daughter* is in that fleet."

Mamutse grunted.

"Brother. Sister. Uncle. Couple of in-laws, too," he reeled off, his voice equally soft. "My kid isn't old enough yet, but I've enough family over there."

She nodded concession to his gentle point.

"We're doing everything we can," he told her. "The Kanzi missiles are better than I dared hope. They're taking a toll."

And even as Annette watched the fleet bear down on her daughter and the rest of her homeworld's defenders, a thousand escorts swarmed their way. Those ships didn't have the weight to change the balance, but they'd help—

"What the *hell* was that?" someone demanded.

The largest concentration of Taljzi cruisers, almost a hundred ships strong, had just disappeared. Where a moment before they'd been rushing to reinforce their main fleet, now there was a giant storm of tachyon static.

And when it cleared, Annette could make out the distinct signature of a massive hyper portal. Someone had used the portal *itself* as a weapon, ripping dozens of the cruisers in half with a single strike.

The fate of the rest wasn't really in question, however, as Annette Bond stared at the icons that had *emerged* from said portal.

During the Centauri Incident, a single war-dreadnought of the Laian Republic had visited Sol. They'd later fought the Militia at Alpha Centauri, and the Republic had come away from the Incident with a grudging respect for the Imperium and humanity.

That informal nonaggression pact had allowed the Laians to gain the upper hand over their own enemies, and her intelligence suggested they'd been keeping a wary eye on the Taljzi.

She still had never expected to see *ten* Laian war-dreadnoughts in the Sol System. Two *billion* tons of Core Power super-warships now loomed just outside the asteroid belt—and if there was any question as to their intent, they immediately cut their course for the Taljzi Return.

They couldn't get there in time to change what was going to happen to the Grand Fleet, but Annette was already running the numbers. The Taljzi couldn't press a disruptor-range engagement with Tan!Shallegh's force *and* evade the Republic fleet.

"I don't know what they're doing here," Mamutse said aloud. "But I take back every mean thing I ever said about the Laians."

The Taljzi must have seen them just as they crossed into hyper-fold-cannon and plasma-lance range. They'd done everything within their power to avoid that range so far, and the Grand Fleet was demonstrating why as they tore entire squadrons to pieces—but the Return didn't press the attack into disruptor range.

Instead, they turned again. Drives pushed up to point *seven* light-speed, the fastest Annette had ever seen a starship move, as the Taljzi Return ran the numbers and realized they couldn't win.

They could destroy the Grand Fleet, but with the capital-ship component of a Republic battle fleet in the system, they couldn't win.

They couldn't even *survive* if they courted that engagement—and even the Taljzi were unwilling to risk this fleet.

"Get me a channel to Tan!Shallegh," Annette ordered as the truth struck home. "He is *not* to pursue. I don't care what strings I have to pull!"

The A!Tol appeared on her screen.

"Dan!Annette Bond," he greeted her. "It seems we have more friends than we thought. We'll finish this, I promise."

"No, you won't," she cut him off. "I'll call A!Shall if I have to, Tan!Shallegh. *Do not pursue.* Let them run."

"That is outside your authority to order," the Fleet Lord said dangerously.

"Don't be a damned fool, Tan!Shallegh. The Laian Republic doesn't send war-dreadnoughts without escorts. You can be grateful for the arrival of ten war-dreadnoughts...but they should be accompanied by *hundreds* of attack cruisers."

Tan!Shallegh paused, his skin flashing colors in confusion.

"It's a bluff. *Whose?*"

"I don't know, Fleet Lord, but I know your fleet can't win this battle," she said gently. "Let them go. Let them run. We'll have our chance at them soon enough."

NOTHING except for the absence of the usual escorts supported Annette's theory initially. The war-dreadnoughts swept majestically toward the Taljzi fleet, and the Taljzi ran. They ran fast enough that the Laians could never bring them to range, though not fast enough that the Grand Fleet and the Shadowed Armada didn't batter them with missiles every step of the way.

By the time they fled into hyperspace, the handful of surviving super-battleships were crippled wrecks being towed by the barely two hundred surviving battleships. Even with the units that had been spread out around Sol, only fifteen hundred ships escaped Sol.

It was a crushing victory by any measure. That it had been bought with the complete destruction of half the Grand Fleet and the reduction of the other half to barely combat-capable wrecks made it a painful victory, but it was still a crushing one.

The Laians waited a full ten minutes after the Taljzi portal had closed before slowing to a gentle halt and dropping the illusion that Annette had anticipated.

Instead of ten war-dreadnoughts, ten attack cruisers hung just outside the asteroid belt. Attack cruisers painted a familiar red color.

"Incoming transmission," one of Annette's people reported. "It's a radio signal, but we've IDed a nearby hyperfold relay. You'll have live coms."

"Put it on," Annette ordered.

The Laian that appeared on her screen was even more immense than she remembered him. He wore a simple bandolier made entirely of gold, and it was clear that at some point in the past, his bulk had *broken* his carapace.

For a lesser Laian, that would have meant death, but the leader of

Tortuga had apparently warranted truly incredible care. His carapace had been repaired, reinforced with cybernetic weaves.

Weaves that were, of course, washed in gold.

"I am High Captain Ridotak of the Crew of Tortuga," he said simply. "I wish to speak to Duchess Annette Bond."

"Greetings, High Captain," Annette told him. She knew enough Laian body language to pick up Ridotak's surprise at the speed of her reply. "There's a communicator relay near you. It can't pretend to be a war-dreadnought, but it's useful in its own way."

"So it is," Ridotak agreed. "You know, I presume, that your daughter warned us of the arrival of the Taljzi in our system?"

"It was mentioned," Annette said carefully.

"She did. They may have been mere words, but they saved us—and many would not have bothered," the old Laian said. "So, we owed a debt to queen and hatchling alike, and I saw a way to pay it back."

"Your ships fooled everything we had," she told him. "I don't think even the Mesharom saw through you."

"It is a useful trick. It seems it may be the last useful trick left in our arsenal, but it is useful nonetheless." He bowed, stiffly. "Our debt is paid, Duchess Bond. All debts, from all time, I think.

"Pass my greetings to Ki!Tana. Somehow, I'm sure she's in the middle of this somewhere!"

"Thank you, High Captain," Annette told him. "This will not be forgotten."

"Please, forget, forget," he replied with a mandible-chattering chuckle. "Think of our reputation if people realize we do even occasional good deeds!"

CHAPTER SIXTY-FOUR

JAKI WAS ONE OF THE LUCKY ONES. SHE WAS, BY ANY reasonable standard, combat-capable.

Morgan wasn't sure they were actually capable of, say, entering hyperspace. They certainly didn't have any missiles left of *any* type, their defensive drones were history, and a third of their Sword turrets had actually been blasted *off* the outer hull.

But she was intact, she could maneuver—even if Morgan was quite certain Commander Made would happily murder anyone who suggested taking her into sprint mode—and she could defend herself.

That put her in the top ten percent of the surviving warships of the Grand Fleet...and left her tasked as a tug for her less fortunate sisters.

"Status report, Commander Casimir?" Captain Tanzi asked as she walked into the bridge.

"*Corralled Dreams* is in a stable orbit one point five light-seconds from the Raging Waters Yard," Morgan reported. "Shuttle transfers of her crew are already underway."

The Rekiki-crewed super-battleship had been one of the ships refitted with hyperspace missile launchers before the battle. That gave her priority with the repair crews.

"Good. You're relieved," Tanzi told her. "Pack your things; you need be on a shuttle in an hour."

Morgan was quite sure she was outright gaping at her commanding officer.

"Sir?"

"Your presence has been formally requested for multiple state funerals," Tanzi said gently. "Villeneuve wasn't the only unofficial uncle you lost, Commander. Your stepmother sent a message with the details, but you're needed in Hong Kong."

"That doesn't feel right, sir," Morgan admitted. "I'm not the only one who lost people."

"No, but the people you lost are getting state funerals, so tradition says you get to be there," Tanzi told her. "I can't break free every member of my crew who lost someone, Casimir, but if I've got the hammers to break you free, I'm going to do it.

"Shuttle. One hour. Nondiscretionary. Am I clear?"

"Yes, sir."

MORGAN DIDN'T HAVE a chance to play her mother's message until she was aboard the shuttle. She was also, thankfully for her conscience, far from the only person being shuttled back to Earth for funerals and compassionate leave.

It was being restricted to spouses and direct siblings for the moment. Morgan knew that had to be breaking Kurzman-Wellesley's heart, but the Militia *needed* their remaining ships crewed and ready.

They couldn't trust that the Taljzi might not turn around to check if they'd been fooled, after all.

Settling into her seat, she closed the privacy shield and opened the message. A tiny holographic icon of Duchess Bond appeared above her lap.

"Morgan." The Duchess paused, seemingly unsure how to begin. "You're officially being recalled for Jean Villeneuve's funeral," she finally said. "I'm going to miss him. We all are, but that's only the beginning."

Morgan's stepmother shook her head.

"There are at least twenty people who died who'd deserve state funerals if they'd passed in the normal state of affairs, but I can't even tell who's *dead* yet in space," she admitted. "It seems wrong to be holding state funerals when some people aren't even sure if their loved ones are dead or not yet.

"But that's government for you, I suppose. Jean will be buried with full honors. So will Tidikat. And so..."

Annette Bond sighed and bowed her head.

"And so will Li Chin Zhao," she said finally. "He went into a seizure during the final minutes of the battle. There was...nothing anyone could do."

The message was silent as Morgan struggled with her own emotions.

"If anyone had earned a quiet, easy death, it was Zhao. That, it seems, is not what fate had in store for him."

Morgan had seen her "Uncle Li" go through his seizures. She couldn't imagine the one that had killed him had been any gentler about it than his usual ones.

"You'll be here for all three of those funerals. Partly because *you* knew them all, and partly to stand in for your sisters. We haven't decided if it's safe to bring them home yet."

Her stepmother rubbed her face in her hands.

"If this is victory, why does it taste like ashes?" she asked rhetorically. "It's selfish of me, I know, but I'm looking forward to seeing you. I need to know you're safe, my dear. With my own eyes, not just the sterile notes of forms and email.

"Your father and I will meet your shuttle."

SOMEHOW, they'd managed to keep the fact that the Duchess and Ducal Consort were in the military spaceport at the edge of Hong Kong quiet. Morgan found herself wrapped in her father's embrace before anyone could even say a word.

"I'm okay," she told him. "A lot of people aren't."

Masters had never come home from the scouting expedition. Villeneuve was gone, vaporized with *Vindication*. A dozen more names that Morgan had known *well* were gone, too.

There would be no one on Earth who hadn't lost someone after this. It had taken Morgan hours to work up the courage to make sure that Antonova was alive. *Achilles* had been beaten into a wreck, the *Bellerophon*-class battleship literally broken in two by the end...but Morgan's girlfriend was alive.

She felt guilty about that, too.

"We know," Annette told her, leaning into the embrace with her husband and stepdaughter. "There's a car waiting to take us home. The funerals start tomorrow."

The Duchess shook her head. "We don't have bodies for most of them, after all."

Morgan struggled against tears but managed to make it over to the car without having to blink away more than a handful.

She was wondering why there were *two* aircars sitting next to the three combat planes that would provide overwatch for the Duchess's flight.

"Rank has its privileges," Annette murmured in her ear. "And in this case, well, Commander Antonova was already on Earth and unassigned. It was easy enough to arrange without pulling strings at all."

The blonde com officer stepped out of the second aircar as Morgan approached, a silly smile on her face.

"I didn't believe it when your mom called," she admitted as she embraced Morgan. "If nothing else, I'd have expected her to delegate that."

Morgan chuckled into Victoria's hair.

"Then you don't know my mother...yet," she told the other woman. "We're going to have to fix that, I think."

They were going to have time. That was what the sacrifices of the last few weeks had bought. They and billions of others were going to have time.

It wasn't much. It just had to be enough.

CHAPTER SIXTY-FIVE

FOUR STATE FUNERALS IN FIVE DAYS WAS HEART-WRENCHING and brutal. There was no other way to put it. That all four had been for officers and politicians that Morgan Casimir had known since she was five years old certainly didn't help.

There would be more. She'd be standing in the twins' lieu for those. She didn't know them as well, so they wouldn't be quite as brutal.

The aftermath of Zhao's funeral was the harshest, and she stood there amidst the wake like a black-clad banshee, screaming "you too are mortal" at people trying to engage in the light-hearted joviality Li Chin Zhao would have insisted on.

Zhao had no children. To Morgan's knowledge, he'd never even had a lover in his life. His focus had been first China and then the Duchy. That hadn't stopped him from being an amazing "Uncle Li" to Morgan and her half-sisters.

It was a wake. A celebration of life. All Morgan wanted to do was sit in the corner and drown her sorrows.

"Funerals suck," a Japanese-accented voice said next to her.

Morgan looked up to realize that Fleet Lord Harriet Tanaka had snuck up on her, and tried to snap to attention.

"At ease, Casimir," Tanaka told her. "We're here as representatives of our services. We're not on duty."

"Yes, sir," Morgan said crisply.

Tanaka chuckled and shook her head.

"You remind me of my son some days," she said. "He's so far managed to avoid getting dragged into the middle of *every* battle of a new war, though."

"It wasn't the plan," Morgan replied.

"It wasn't anyone's plan." Tanaka sighed. "This is about Li Chin Zhao tonight, his life. Not the future. But if you can spare me some time tomorrow, Commander Casimir, I'd appreciate it."

"You're a Fleet Lord of the Imperium, sir," Morgan pointed out.

"And you're scheduled to pay homage to a lot of incredible people this week," the older woman told her. "And you are your mother's daughter. While you are on duty, you remain merely a Militia Commander, but in this environment, well." Tanaka shrugged. "*Lady* Casimir is probably a more appropriate title."

Morgan shivered.

"I've spent my life trying to avoid that particular anvil," she pointed out.

"I know. But the duty of your family calls regardless," Tanaka told her, pointing towards a drifting cluster of senior auditors. "Tell Camber I say hello."

Morgan hadn't recognized Amanda Camber—Director-at-Large of the Terran Development Corporation and one of Li Chin Zhao's personal hatchetwomen—until Tanaka pointed her out.

She was about to thank the flag officer, and then she realized the other woman had disappeared.

With a sigh, she pasted a smile on her face and went to meet the woman most likely to be replacing Li Chin Zhao on her stepmother's Council.

FLEET LORD HARRIET TANAKA had borrowed one of the "hotel" offices in Wuxing Tower, spaces set aside for visiting bureaucrats and officers of the Duchy and the Imperium alike. It was a spartan space, though nowhere in Wuxing Tower was allowed to go *entirely* undecorated.

Morgan noted subtle murals along the walls of the room, but her main attention was drawn to the massive hologram of a ship hanging above the desk. Tanaka was studying it and gestured Morgan wordlessly to a seat.

"Coffee, Commander?" she asked. "Tea? Water?"

"Coffee would be good. Black, please."

"You grew up here in Hong Kong, and yet you are *such* an American soldier," Tanaka told her—but she produced an already-prepared cup of coffee.

As Morgan wrapped her hands around the cup, Tanaka pointed to the ship.

"Familiar?"

Morgan studied the design.

"In some ways," she said slowly. "I can see the bones of a *Bellerophon* in there, but she's much bigger."

"Nine point three megatons bigger than the B," Tanaka confirmed. "Just over twenty million tons, the largest warship ever commissioned by the A!Tol Imperium."

The tiny Japanese woman hummed to herself as she studied the ship.

"A week ago, she was planned to commission into the Duchy of Terra Militia as *Galileo*," the Fleet Lord continued. "None of that is true anymore."

"She's being delivered to the Imperial Navy," Morgan presumed.

"Exactly. There are four of these ships at DragonWorks. All have now been purchased by the Navy. The Duchy of Terra Militia is going to be understrength for a while now, I'm afraid, as the Navy is going to be coopting most of the construction of the Yards here in Sol —and everywhere else."

That didn't sound great for Victoria Antonova's chances of getting back onto a warship, though Morgan already had a slot she didn't expect to lose.

"She's going to commission as *Jean Villeneuve*," Harriet Tanaka said quietly. "We've got about three months to sort out her crew, but it's already been decided she's going to be a mixed-race ship. Jean wouldn't have had it any other way."

Morgan wasn't sure why she was being given this briefing, but one didn't rush flag officers.

"We've already picked her captain: an A!Tol, some relation to the Empress that I won't pretend to make sense of: Tan!Stalla. I'd *like* to get her XO picked out ASAP, let the two officers get used to each other as they pull a crew together.

"As it happens, Commander Casimir, I have a blank check for recruiting personnel from the Duchy of Terra Militia right now," Tanaka continued. "Normally, you'd lose at least a rank switching over, but that wouldn't happen this time."

She shrugged.

"It wouldn't happen anyway in your case. You're the single most experienced officer we have with regards to the HSMs and the Taljzi. *Jean Villeneuve* will carry ninety-six hyperspace missile launchers... and she and her sister will be leading the fight against the Taljzi."

"What are you saying, sir?" Morgan asked carefully, wanting to be *very* sure of what she was hearing.

"The Duchy of Terra Militia will no longer be asked to carry this fight, Commander. Indeed, it will not be *permitted* to. It is the task of the Imperial Navy to defend these stars, to strike against enemies that attack the Imperium.

"*Jean Villeneuve* and her sisters will be at the forefront of that mission...and I want you to take a transfer to the Imperial Navy to act as her executive officer."

The Japanese woman smiled.

"Is that clear enough for you, Commander Casimir? What do you say?"

Morgan swallowed and studied the warship, but a thought struck her before she could answer.

"I'm inclined to accept your offer, Fleet Lord," she admitted. "But I need to at least *talk* to my girlfriend first."

"I wouldn't have it any other way, Commander. Responsibility flows in many directions, after all."

Morgan grinned. Even Annette Bond's daughter, it seemed, could learn *some* lessons.

JOIN THE MAILING LIST

Love Glynn Stewart's books? Join the mailing list at

GLYNNSTEWART.COM/MAILING-LIST/

to know as soon as new books are released, special announcements, and a chance to win free paperbacks.

ABOUT THE AUTHOR

Glynn Stewart is the author of *Starship's Mage*, a bestselling science fiction and fantasy series where faster-than-light travel is possible–but only because of magic. His other works include science fiction series *Duchy of Terra, Castle Federation* and *Vigilante,* as well as the urban fantasy series *ONSET* and *Changeling Blood*.

Writing managed to liberate Glynn from a bleak future as an accountant. With his personality and hope for a high-tech future intact, he lives in Kitchener, Ontario with his wife, their cats, and an unstoppable writing habit.

VISIT GLYNNSTEWART.COM FOR NEW
RELEASE UPDATES

facebook.com/glynnstewartauthor

OTHER BOOKS
BY GLYNN STEWART

For release announcements join the
mailing list or visit **GlynnStewart.com**

STARSHIP'S MAGE
Starship's Mage
Hand of Mars
Voice of Mars
Alien Arcana
Judgment of Mars
UnArcana Stars
Sword of Mars
Mountain of Mars
The Service of Mars
A Darker Magic (upcoming)

Starship's Mage: Red Falcon
Interstellar Mage
Mage-Provocateur
Agents of Mars

Pulsar Race: A Starship's Mage Universe Novella

DUCHY OF TERRA
The Terran Privateer
Duchess of Terra
Terra and Imperium
Darkness Beyond
Shield of Terra
Imperium Defiant
Relics of Eternity
Shadows of the Fall
Eyes of Tomorrow (upcoming)

VIGILANTE
(WITH TERRY MIXON)
Heart of Vengeance
Oath of Vengeance

Bound By Stars: A Vigilante Series
(With Terry Mixon)
Bound By Law
Bound by Honor
Bound by Blood

TEER AND KARD
Wardtown
Blood Ward (upcoming)

CHANGELING BLOOD
Changeling's Fealty
Hunter's Oath
Noble's Honor
Fae, Flames & Fedoras: A Changeling Blood Novella

ONSET
ONSET: To Serve and Protect
ONSET: My Enemy's Enemy
ONSET: Blood of the Innocent
ONSET: Stay of Execution
Murder by Magic: An ONSET Novella

FANTASY STAND ALONE NOVELS
Children of Prophecy
City in the Sky

Printed in Great Britain
by Amazon

59554077R00260